The Secret of the Night

The Secret of the Night

Gaston Leroux

MINT
EDITIONS

MINT EDITIONS

The Secret of the Night was first published in 1914.

This edition published by Mint Editions 2021.

ISBN 9781513137216 |
E-ISBN 9781513287942

Published by Mint Editions®

 MINT
EDITIONS

minteditionbooks.com

Publishing Director: Jennifer Newens
Design & Production: Rachel Lopez Metzger
Project Manager: Micaela Clark

Contents

I

Gayety and Dynamite

Barinia, the young stranger has arrived."

"Where is he?"

"Oh, he is waiting at the lodge."

"I told you to show him to Natacha's sitting-room. Didn't you understand me, Ermolai?"

"Pardon, Barinia, but the young stranger, when I asked to search him, as you directed, flatly refused to let me."

"Did you explain to him that everybody is searched before being allowed to enter, that it is the order, and that even my mother herself has submitted to it?"

"I told him all that, Barinia; and I told him about madame your mother."

"What did he say to that?"

"That he was not madame your mother. He acted angry."

"Well, let him come in without being searched."

"The Chief of Police won't like it."

"Do as I say."

Ermolai bowed and returned to the garden. The "barinia" left the veranda, where she had come for this conversation with the old servant of General Trebassof, her husband, and returned to the dining-room in the datcha des Iles, where the gay Councilor Ivan Petrovitch was regaling his amused associates with his latest exploit at Cubat's resort. They were a noisy company, and certainly the quietest among them was not the general, who nursed on a sofa the leg which still held him captive after the recent attack, that to his old coachman and his two piebald horses had proved fatal. The story of the always-amiable Ivan Petrovitch (a lively, little, elderly man with his head bald as an egg) was about the evening before. After having, as he said, "recure la bouche" for these gentlemen spoke French like their own language and used it among themselves to keep their servants from understanding—after having wet his whistle with a large glass of sparkling rosy French wine, he cried:

"You would have laughed,
Feodor Feodorovitch. We had sung songs on

the Barque (note 1) and then the Bohemians left with their music and we went out onto the river-bank to stretch our legs and cool our faces in the freshness of the dawn, when a company of Cossacks of the Guard came along. I knew the officer in command and invited him to come along with us and drink the Emperor's health at Cubat's place. That officer, Feodor Feodorovitch, is a man who knows vintages and boasts that he has never swallowed a glass of anything so common as Crimean wine. When I named champagne he cried, 'Vive l'Empereur!' A true patriot. So we started, merry as school-children. The entire company followed, then all the diners playing little whistles, and all the servants besides, single file. At Cubat's I hated to leave the companion-officers of my friend

---

1. The "Barque" is a restaurant on a boat, among the isles, near the Gulf of Finland, on a bank of the Neva.

at the door, so I invited them in, too. They accepted, naturally. But the subalterns were thirsty as well. I understand discipline. You know, Feodor Feodorovitch, that I am a stickler for discipline. Just because one is gay of a spring morning, discipline should not be forgotten. I invited the officers to drink in a private room, and sent the subalterns into the main hall of the restaurant. Then the soldiers were thirsty, too, and I had drinks served to them out in the courtyard. Then, my word, there was a perplexing business, for now the horses whinnied. The brave horses, Feodor Feodorovitch, who also wished to drink the health of the Emperor. I was bothered about the discipline. Hall, court, all were full. And I could not put the horses in private rooms. Well, I made them carry out champagne in pails and then came the perplexing business I had tried so hard to avoid, a grand mixture of boots and horse-shoes that was certainly the liveliest thing I have ever seen in my life. But the horses were the most joyous, and danced as if a torch was held under their nostrils, and all of them, my word! were ready to throw their riders because the men were not of the same mind with them as to the route to follow! From our window we laughed fit to kill at such a mixture of sprawling boots and dancing hoofs. But the troopers finally got all their horses to barracks, with patience, for the Emperor's cavalry are the best riders in the world, Feodor Feodorovitch. And we certainly had a great laugh!—Your health, Matrena Petrovna."

These last graceful words were addressed to Madame Trebassof, who shrugged her shoulders at the undesired gallantry of the gay Councilor. She did not join in the conversation, excepting to calm the general, who wished to send the whole regiment to the guard-house, men and horses. And while the roisterers laughed over the adventure she said to her husband in the advisory voice of the helpful wife:

"Feodor, you must not attach importance to what that old fool Ivan tells you. He is the most imaginative man in the capital when he has had champagne."

"Ivan, you certainly have not had horses served with champagne in pails," the old boaster, Athanase Georgevitch, protested jealously. He was an advocate, well-known for his table-feats, who claimed the hardest drinking reputation of any man in the capital, and he regretted not to have invented that tale.

"On my word! And the best brands! I had won four thousand roubles. I left the little fete with fifteen kopecks."

Matrena Petrovna was listening to Ermolai, the faithful country servant who wore

always, even here in the city, his habit
of fresh nankeen, his black leather belt,
his large blue pantaloons and his boots
glistening like ice, his country costume in
his master's city home. Madame Matrena
rose, after lightly stroking the hair of her
step-daughter Natacha, whose eyes followed
her to the door, indifferent apparently to the
tender manifestations of her father's orderly,
the soldier-poet, Boris Mourazoff, who had
written beautiful verses on the death of the
Moscow students, after having shot them, in
the way of duty, on their barricades.

Ermolai conducted his mistress to the
drawing-room and pointed across to a door
that he had left open, which led to the
sitting-room before Natacha's chamber.

"He is there," said Ermolai in a low voice.

Ermolai need have said nothing, for that
matter, since Madame Matrena was aware

of a stranger's presence in the sitting-room by the extraordinary attitude of an individual in a maroon frock-coat bordered with false astrakhan, such as is on the coats of all the Russian police agents and makes the secret agents recognizable at first glance. This policeman was on his knees in the drawing-room watching what passed in the next room through the narrow space of light in the hinge-way of the door. In this manner, or some other, all persons who wished to approach General Trebassof were kept under observation without their knowing it, after having been first searched at the lodge, a measure adopted since the latest attack.

Madame Matrena touched the policeman's shoulder with that heroic hand which had saved her husband's life and which still bore traces of the terrible explosion in the last attack, when she had seized the infernal machine intended for the general with her bare hand. The policeman rose and silently left the room, reached the veranda and lounged there on a sofa, pretending to be asleep, but in reality watching the garden paths.

Matrena Petrovna took his place at the hinge-vent. This was her rule; she always took the final glance at everything and everybody. She roved at all hours of the day and night round about the general, like a watch-dog, ready to bite, to throw itself before the danger, to receive the blows, to perish for its master. This had commenced at Moscow after the terrible repression, the massacre of revolutionaries under the walls of Presnia, when the surviving Nihilists left behind them a placard condemning the victorious General Trebassof to death. Matrena Petrovna lived only for the general. She had vowed that she would not survive him. So she had double reason to guard him.

But she had lost all confidence even within the walls of her own home.

Things had happened even there that defied her caution, her instinct, her love. She had not spoken of these things save to the Chief of Police, Koupriane, who had reported them to the Emperor. And here now was the man whom the Emperor had sent, as the supreme resource, this young stranger— Joseph Rouletabille, reporter.

"But he is a mere boy!" she exclaimed, without at all understanding the matter, this youthful figure, with soft, rounded cheeks, eyes clear and, at first view, extraordinarily naive, the eyes of an infant. True, at the moment Rouletabille's expression hardly suggested any superhuman profundity of thought, for, left in view of a table, spread with hors-d'oeuvres, the young man appeared solely occupied in digging out with a spoon all the caviare that remained in the jars.

Matrena noted the rosy freshness of his cheeks, the absence of down on his lip and not a hint of beard, the thick hair, with the curl over the forehead. Ah, that forehead—the forehead was curious, with great over-hanging cranial lumps which moved above the deep arcade of the eye-sockets while the mouth was busy—well, one would have said that Rouletabille had not eaten for a week. He was demolishing a great slice of Volgan sturgeon, contemplating at the same time with immense interest a salad of creamed cucumbers, when Matrena Petrovna appeared.

He wished to excuse himself at once and spoke with his mouth full.

"I beg your pardon, madame, but the Czar forgot to invite me to breakfast."

Madame Matrena smiled and gave him a hearty handshake as she urged him to be seated.

"You have seen His Majesty?"

"I come from him, madame. It is to Madame Trebassof that I have the honor of speaking?"

"Yes. And you are Monsieur—?"

"Joseph Rouletabille, madame. I do not add, 'At your service—because I do not know about that yet. That is what I said just now to His Majesty."

"Then?" asked Madame Matrena, rather amused by the tone the conversation had taken and the slightly flurried air of Rouletabille.

"Why, then, I am a reporter, you see. That is what I said at once to my editor in Paris, 'I am not going to take part in revolutionary affairs that do not concern my country,' to which my editor replied, 'You do not have to take part. You must go to Russia to make an inquiry into the present status of the different parties. You will commence by interviewing the Emperor.' I said, 'Well, then, here goes,' and took the train."

"And you have interviewed the Emperor?"

"Oh, yes, that has not been difficult. I expected to arrive direct at St. Petersburg, but at Krasnoie-Coelo the train stopped and the grand-marshal of the court came to me and asked me to follow him. It was very flattering. Twenty minutes later I was before His Majesty. He awaited me! I understood at once that this was obviously for something out of the ordinary."

"And what did he say to you?"

"He is a man of genuine majesty. He reassured me at once when I explained my scruples to him. He said there was no occasion for me to take part in the politics of the matter, but to save his most faithful servant, who was on the point of becoming the victim of the strangest family drama ever conceived."

Madame Matrena, white as a sheet, rose to her feet.

"Ah," she said simply.

But Rouletabille, whom nothing escaped, saw her hand tremble on the back of the chair.

He went on, not appearing to have noticed her emotion:

"His Majesty added these exact words: 'It is I who ask it of you; I and Madame Trebassof. Go, monsieur, she awaits you.'"

He ceased and waited for Madame Trebassof to speak.

She made up her mind after brief reflection.

"Have you seen Koupriane?"

"The Chief of Police? Yes. The grand-marshal accompanied me back to the station at Krasnoie-Coelo, and the Chief of Police accompanied me to St. Petersburg station. One could not have been better received."

"Monsieur Rouletabille," said Matrena, who visibly strove to regain her self-control, "I am not of Koupriane's opinion and I am not"—here she lowered her trembling voice—"of the opinion His Majesty holds. It is better for me to tell you at once, so that

22

you may not regret intervening in an affair where there are—where there are—risks— terrible risks to run. No, this is not a family drama. The family is small, very small: the general, his daughter Natacha (by his former marriage), and myself. There could not be a family drama among us three. It is simply about my husband, monsieur, who did his duty as a soldier in defending the throne of his sovereign, my husband whom they mean to assassinate! There is nothing else, no other situation, my dear little guest."

To hide her distress she started to carve a slice of jellied veal and carrot.

"You have not eaten, you are hungry. It is dreadful, my dear young man. See, you must dine with us, and then—you will say adieu. Yes, you will leave me all alone. I will undertake to save him all alone. Certainly, I will undertake it."

A tear fell on the slice she was cutting. Rouletabille, who felt the brave woman's emotion affecting him also, braced himself to keep from showing it.

"I am able to help you a little all the same," he said. "Monsieur Koupriane has told me that there is a deep mystery. It is my vocation to get to the bottom of mysteries."

"I know what Koupriane thinks," she said, shaking her head. "But if I could bring myself to think that for a single day I would rather be dead."

The good Matrena Petrovna lifted her beautiful eyes to Rouletabille, brimming with the tears she held back.

She added quickly:

24

"But eat now, my dear guest; eat. My dear child, you must forget what Koupriane has said to you, when you are back in France."

"I promise you that, madame."

"It is the Emperor who has caused you this long journey. For me, I did not wish it. Has he, indeed, so much confidence in you?" she asked naively, gazing at him fixedly through her tears.

"Madame, I was just about to tell you. I have been active in some important matters that have been reported to him, and then sometimes your Emperor is allowed to see the papers. He has heard talk, too (for everybody talked of them, madame), about the Mystery of the Yellow Room and the Perfume of the Lady in Black."

Here Rouletabille watched Madame Trebassof and was much mortified at the undoubted ignorance that showed in her frank face of either the yellow room or the black perfume.

"My young friend," said she, in a voice more and more hesitant, "you must excuse me, but it is a long time since I have had good eyes for reading."

Tears, at last, ran down her cheeks.

Rouletabille could not restrain himself any further. He saw in one flash all this heroic woman had suffered in her combat day by day with the death which hovered. He took her little fat hands, whose fingers were overloaded with rings, tremulously into his own:

"Madame, do not weep. They wish to kill your husband. Well then, we will be two at least to defend him, I swear to you."

"Even against the Nihilists!"

"Aye, madame, against all the world. I have eaten all your caviare. I am your guest. I am your friend."

As he said this he was so excited, so sincere and so droll that Madame Trebassof could not help smiling through her tears. She made him sit down beside her.

"The Chief of Police has talked of you a great deal. He came here abruptly after the last attack and a mysterious happening that I will tell you about. He cried, 'Ah, we need Rouletabille to unravel this!' The next day he came here again. He had gone to the Court. There, everybody, it appears, was talking of you. The Emperor wished to know you. That is why steps were taken through the ambassador at Paris."

"Yes, yes. And naturally all the world has learned of it. That makes it so lively. The Nihilists warned me immediately that I would not reach Russia alive. That, finally, was what decided me on coming. I am naturally very contrary."

"And how did you get through the journey?"

"Not badly. I discovered at once in the train a young Slav assigned to kill me, and I reached an understanding with him. He was a charming youth, so it was easily arranged."

Rouletabille was eating away now at strange viands that it would have been difficult for him to name. Matrena Petrovna laid her fat little hand on his arm:

"You speak seriously?"

"Very seriously."

"A small glass of vodka?"

"No alcohol."

Madame Matrena emptied her little glass at a draught.

"And how did you discover him? How did you know him?"

"First, he wore glasses. All Nihilists wear glasses when traveling. And then I had a good clew. A minute before the departure from Paris I had a friend go into the corridor of the sleeping-car, a reporter who would do anything I said without even wanting to know why. I said, 'You call out suddenly and very loud, "Hello, here is Rouletabille."' So he called, 'Hello, here is Rouletabille,' and all those who were in the corridor turned and all those who were already in the compartments came out, excepting the man with the glasses. Then I was sure about him."

Madame Trebassof looked at Rouletabille, who turned as red as the comb of a rooster and was rather embarrassed at his fatuity.

"That deserves a rebuff, I know, madame, but from the moment the Emperor of all the Russias had desired to see me I could not admit that any mere man with glasses had not the curiosity to see what I looked like. It was not natural. As soon as the train was off I sat down by this man and told him who I thought he was. I was right. He removed his glasses and, looking me straight in the eyes, said he was glad to have a little talk with me before anything unfortunate happened. A half-hour later the entente-cordiale was signed. I gave him to understand that I was coming here simply on business as a reporter and that there was always time to check me if I should be indiscreet. At the German frontier he left me to go on, and returned tranquilly to his nitro-glycerine."

"You are a marked man also, my poor boy."

"Oh, they have not got us yet."

Matrena Petrovna coughed. That us overwhelmed her. With what calmness this boy that she had not known an hour proposed to share the dangers of a situation that excited general pity but from which the bravest kept aloof either from prudence or dismay.

"Ah, my friend, a little of this fine smoked Hamburg beef?"

But the young man was already pouring out fresh yellow beer.

"There," said he. "Now, madame, I am listening. Tell me first about the earliest attack."

"Now," said Matrena, "we must go to dinner."

Rouletabille looked at her wide-eyed.

"But, madame, what have I just been doing?"

Madame Matrena smiled. All these strangers were alike. Because they had eaten some hors-d'oeuvres, some zakouskis, they imagined their host would be satisfied. They did not know how to eat.

"We will go to the dining-room. The general is expecting you. They are at table."

"I understand I am supposed to know him."

"Yes, you have met in Paris. It is entirely natural that in passing through St. Petersburg you should make him a visit. You know him very well indeed, so well that he opens his home to you. Ah, yes, my step-daughter also"—she flushed a little—"Natacha believes that her father knows you."

She opened the door of the drawing-room, which they had to cross in order to reach the dining-room.

From his present position Rouletabille could see all the corners of the drawing-room, the veranda, the garden and the entrance lodge at the gate. In the veranda the man in the maroon frock-coat trimmed with false astrakhan seemed still to be asleep on the sofa; in one of the corners of the drawing-room another individual, silent and motionless as a statue, dressed exactly the same, in a maroon frock-coat with false astrakhan, stood with his hands behind his back seemingly struck with general paralysis at the sight of a flaring sunset which illumined as with a torch the golden spires of Saints Peter and Paul. And in the garden and before the lodge three others dressed in maroon roved like souls in pain over the lawn or back and forth at the entrance. Rouletabille motioned to Madame Matrena, stepped back into the sitting-room and closed the door.

"Police?" he asked.

Matrena Petrovna nodded her head and put her finger to her mouth in a naive way, as one would caution a child to silence. Rouletabille smiled.

"How many are there?"

"Ten, relieved every six hours."

"That makes forty unknown men around your house each day."

"Not unknown," she replied. "Police."

"Yet, in spite of them, you have had the affair of the bouquet in the general's chamber."

"No, there were only three then. It is since the affair of the bouquet that there have been ten."

"It hardly matters. It is since these ten that you have had..."

"What?" she demanded anxiously.

"You know well—the flooring."

"Sh-h-h."

She glanced at the door, watching the policeman statuesque before the setting sun.

"No one knows that—not even my husband."

"So M. Koupriane told me. Then it is you who have arranged for these ten police-agents?"

"Certainly."

"Well, we will commence now by sending all these police away."

Matrena Petrovna grasped his hand, astounded.

"Surely you don't think of doing such a thing as that!"

"Yes. We must know where the blow is coming from. You have four different groups of people around here—the police, the domestics, your friends, your family. Get rid of the police first. They must not be permitted to cross your threshold. They have not been able to protect you. You have nothing to regret. And if, after they are gone, something new turns up, we can leave M. Koupriane to conduct the inquiries without his being preoccupied here at the house."

"But you do not know the admirable police of Koupriane. These brave men have given proof of their devotion."

"Madame, if I were face to face with a Nihilist the first thing I would ask myself about him would be, 'Is he one of the police?' The first thing I ask in the presence of an agent of your police is, 'Is he not a Nihilist?'"

"But they will not wish to go."

"Do any of them speak French?"

"Yes, their sergeant, who is out there in the salon."

"Pray call him."

Madame Trebassof walked into the salon and signaled. The man appeared. Rouletabille handed him a paper, which the other read.

"You will gather your men together and quit the villa," ordered Rouletabille. "You will return to the police Headguarters. Say to M. Koupriane that I have commanded this and that I require all police service around the villa to be suspended until further orders."

The man bowed, appeared not to understand, looked at Madame Trebassof and said to the young man:

"At your service."

He went out.

"Wait here a moment," urged Madame Trebassof, who did not know how to take this abrupt action and whose anxiety was really painful to see.

She disappeared after the man of the false astrakhan. A few moments afterwards she returned. She appeared even more agitated.

"I beg your pardon," she murmured, "but I cannot let them go like this. They are much chagrined. They have insisted on knowing where they have failed in their service. I have appeased them with money."

"Yes, and tell me the whole truth, madame. You have directed them not to go far away, but to remain near the villa so as to watch it as closely as possible."

She reddened.

"It is true. But they have gone, nevertheless. They had to obey you. What can that paper be you have shown them?"

Rouletabille drew out again the billet covered with seals and signs and cabalistics that he did not understand. Madame Trebassof translated it aloud: "Order to all officials in surveillance of the Villa Trebassof to obey the bearer absolutely. Signed: Koupriane."

"Is it possible!" murmured Matrena Petrovna. "But Koupriane would never have given you this paper if he had imagined that you would use it to dismiss his agents."

"Evidently. I have not asked him his advice, madame, you may be sure. But I will see him tomorrow and he will understand."

"Meanwhile, who is going to watch over him?" cried she.

Rouletabille took her hands again. He saw her suffering, a prey to anguish almost prostrating. He pitied her. He wished to give her immediate confidence.

"We will," he said.

She saw his young, clear eyes, so deep, so intelligent, the well-formed young head, the willing face, all his young ardency for her, and it reassured her. Rouletabille

40

waited for what she might say. She said nothing. She took him in her arms and embraced him.

II

NATACHA

In the dining-room it was Thaddeus
Tchnichnikoff 's turn to tell hunting stories.
He was the greatest timber-merchant in
Lithuania. He owned immense forests and
he loved Feodor Feodorovitch (note 1) as
a brother, for they had played together all
through their childhood, and once he had
saved him from a bear that was just about
to crush his skull as one might knock off a

---

1. In this story according to Russian habit
General Trebassof is called alternately
by that name or the family name
Feodor Feodorovitch, and Madame Trebassof
by that name or her family name,
Matrena Petrovna.—Translator's Note.

hat. General Trebassof 's father was governor of Courlande at that time, by the grace of God and the Little Father. Thaddeus, who was just thirteen years old, killed the bear with a single stroke of his boar-spear, and just in time. Close ties were knit between the two families by this occurrence, and though Thaddeus was neither noble-born nor a soldier, Feodor considered him his brother and felt toward him as such. Now Thaddeus had become the greatest timber-merchant of the western provinces, with his own forests and also with his massive body, his fat, oily face, his bull-neck and his ample paunch. He quitted everything at once—all his affairs, his family—as soon as he learned of the first attack, to come and remain by the side of his dear comrade Feodor. He had done this after each attack, without forgetting one. He was a faithful friend. But he fretted because they might not go bear-hunting as in their youth. 'Where, he would ask, are there any bears remaining in Courlande, or trees for that matter, what you could call trees, growing since the days of the grand-dukes of Lithuania, giant trees that threw their shade right up to the very edge of the towns? Where were such things nowadays? Thaddeus was very amusing, for it was he, certainly, who had cut them away tranquilly enough and watched them vanish in locomotive smoke. It was what was called Progress. Ah, hunting lost its national character assuredly with tiny new-growth trees which had not had time to grow. And, besides, one nowadays had not time for hunting. All the big game was so far away. Lucky enough if one seized the time to bring down a brace of woodcock early in the morning. At this point in Thaddeus's conversation there was a babble of talk among the convivial gentlemen, for they had all the time in the world at their disposal and could not see why he should be so concerned about snatching a little while at morning or evening, or at midday for that matter. Champagne was flowing like a river when Rouletabille was brought in by Matrena Petrovna. The general, whose eyes had been on the door for some time, cried at once, as though responding to a cue:

"Ah, my dear Rouletabille! I have been looking for you. Our friends wrote me you were coming to St. Petersburg."

Rouletabille hurried over to him and they shook hands like friends who meet after a long separation. The reporter was presented to the company as a close young friend from Paris whom they had enjoyed so much during their latest visit to the City of Light. Everybody inquired for the latest word of Paris as of a dear acquaintance.

"How is everybody at Maxim's?" urged the excellent Athanase Georgevitch.

Thaddeus, too, had been once in Paris and he returned with an enthusiastic liking for the French demoiselles.

"Vos gogottes, monsieur," he said, appearing very amiable and leaning on each word, with a guttural emphasis such as is common in the western provinces, "ah, vos gogottes!"

Matrena Perovna tried to silence him, but Thaddeus insisted on his right to appreciate the fair sex away from home. He had a turgid, sentimental wife, always weeping and cramming her religious notions down his throat.

Of course someone asked Rouletabille what he thought of Russia, but he had no more than opened his mouth to reply than Athanase Georgevitch closed it by interrupting:

"Permettez! Permettez! You others, of the young generation, what do you know of it? You need to have lived a long time and in all its districts to appreciate Russia at its true value. Russia, my young sir, is as yet a closed book to you."

"Naturally," Rouletabille answered, smiling.

"Well, well, here's your health! What I would point out to you first of all is that it is a good buyer of champagne, eh?"—and he gave a huge grin. "But the hardest drinker I ever knew was born on the banks of the Seine. Did you know him, Feodor Feodorovitch? Poor Charles Dufour, who died two years ago at fete of the officers of the Guard. He wagered at the end of the banquet that he could drink a glassful of champagne to the health of each man there. There were sixty when you came to count them. He commenced the round of the table and the affair went splendidly up to the fifty-eighth man. But at the fifty-ninth—think of the misfortune!—the champagne ran out! That poor, that charming, that excellent Charles took up a glass of vin dore which was in the glass of this fifty-ninth, wished him long life, drained the glass at one draught, had just time to murmur, 'Tokay, 1807,' and fell back dead! Ah, he knew the brands, my word! and he proved it to his last breath! Peace to his ashes! They asked what he died of. I knew he died because of the inappropriate blend of flavors. There should be discipline in all things and not promiscuous mixing. One more glass of champagne and he would have been drinking with us this evening. Your health, Matrena Petrovna. Champagne, Feodor Feodorovitch! Vive la France, monsieur! Natacha, my child, you must sing something. Boris will accompany you on the guzla. Your father will enjoy it."

All eyes turned toward Natacha as she rose.

Rouletabille was struck by her serene beauty. That was the first enthralling impression, an impression so strong it astonished him, the perfect serenity, the supreme calm, the tranquil harmony of her noble features. Natacha was twenty. Heavy brown hair circled about er forehead and was looped about her ears, which were half-concealed. Her profile was clear-cut; her mouth was strong and revealed between red, firm lips the even pearliness of her teeth. She was of medium height. In walking she had the free, light step of the highborn maidens who, in primal times, pressed the flowers as they passed without crushing them. But all her true grace seemed to be concentrated in her eyes, which were deep and of a dark blue. The impression she made upon a beholder was very complex. And it would have been difficult to say whether the calm which pervaded every manifestation of her beauty was the result of conscious control or the most perfect ease.

She took down the guzla and handed it to Boris, who struck some plaintive preliminary chords.

"What shall I sing?" she inquired, raising her father's hand from the back of the sofa where he rested and kissing it with filial tenderness.

"Improvise," said the general. "Improvise in French, for the sake of our guest."

"Oh, yes," cried Boris; "improvise as you did the other evening."

He immediately struck a minor chord.

Natacha looked fondly at her father as she sang:

"When the moment comes that parts us at the close of day, when the Angel of Sleep covers you with azure wings;

"Oh, may your eyes rest from so many tears,
and your oppressed heart have calm;
"In each moment that we have together,
Father dear, let our souls feel harmony
sweet and mystical;
"And when your thoughts may have flown
to other worlds, oh, may my image, at least,
nestle within your sleeping eyes."

Natacha's voice was sweet, and the charm of it subtly pervasive. The words as she uttered them seemed to have all the quality of a prayer and there were tears in all eyes, excepting those of Michael Korsakoff, the second orderly, whom Rouletabille appraised as a man with a rough heart not much open to sentiment.

"Feodor Feodorovitch," said this officer, when the young girl's voice had faded away into the blending with the last note of the guzla, "Feodor Feodorovitch is a man and a glorious soldier who is able to sleep in peace, because he has labored for his country and for his Czar."

"Yes, yes. Labored well! A glorious soldier!" repeated Athanase Georgevitch and Ivan Petrovitch. "Well may he sleep peacefully."

"Natacha sang like an angel," said Boris, the first orderly, in a tremulous voice.

"Like an angel, Boris Nikolaievitch. But why did she speak of his heart oppressed? I don't see that General Trebassof has a heart oppressed, for my part." Michael Korsakoff spoke roughly as he drained his glass.

"No, that's so, isn't it?" agreed the others.

"A young girl may wish her father a pleasant sleep, surely!" said Matrena Petrovna, with a certain good sense. "Natacha has affected us all, has she not, Feodor?"

"Yes, she made me weep," declared the general. "But let us have champagne to cheer us up. Our young friend here will think we are chicken-hearted."

"Never think that," said Rouletabille. "Mademoiselle has touched me deeply as well. She is an artist, really a great artist. And a poet."

"He is from Paris; he knows," said the others.

And all drank.

Then they talked about music, with great display of knowledge concerning things operatic. First one, then another went to the piano and ran through some motif that the rest hummed a little first, then shouted in a rousing chorus. Then they drank more, amid a perfect fracas of talk and laughter. Ivan Petrovitch and Athanase Georgevitch walked across and kissed the general. Rouletabille saw all around him great children who amused themselves with unbelievable naivete and who drank in a fashion more unbelievable still. Matrena Petrovna smoked cigarettes of yellow tobacco incessantly, rising almost continually to make a hurried round of the rooms, and after having prompted the servants to greater watchfulness, sat and looked long at Rouletabille, who did not stir, but caught every word, every gesture of each one there. Finally, sighing, she sat down by Feodor and asked how his leg felt. Michael and Natacha, in a corner, were deep in conversation, and Boris watched them with obvious impatience, still strumming the guzla. But the thing that struck Rouletabille's youthful imagination beyond all else was the mild face of the general. He had not imagined the terrible Trebassof with so paternal and sympathetic an expression. The Paris papers had printed redoubtable pictures of him, more or less authentic, but the arts of photography and engraving had cut vigorous, rough features of an official—who knew no pity. Such pictures were in perfect accord with the idea one naturally had of the dominating figure of the government at Moscow, the man who, during eight days— the Red Week—had made so many corpses of students and workmen that the halls of the University and the factories had opened their doors since in vain. The dead would have had to arise for those places to be peopled! Days of terrible battle where in one quarter or another of the city there was naught but massacre or burnings, until Matrena Petrovna and her step-daughter, Natacha (all the papers told of it), had fallen on their knees before the general and begged terms for the last of the revolutionaries, at bay in the Presnia quarter, and had been refused by him. "War is war," had been his answer, with irrefutable logic. "How can you ask mercy for these men who never give it?" Be it said for the young men of the barricades that they never surrendered, and equally be it said for Trebassof that he necessarily shot them. "If I had only myself to consider," the general had said to a Paris journalist, "I could have been gentle as a lamb with these unfortunates, and so I should not now myself be condemned to death. After all, I fail to see what they reproach me with. I have served my master as a brave and loyal subject, no more, and, after the fighting, I have let others ferret out the children that had hidden under their mothers' skirts. Everybody talks of the repression of Moscow, but let us speak, my friend, of the Commune. There was a piece of work I would not have done, to massacre within a court an unresisting crowd of men, women and children. I am a rough and faithful soldier of His Majesty, but I am not a monster, and I have the feelings of a husband and father, my dear monsieur. Tell your readers that, if you care to, and do not surmise further about whether I appear to regret being condemned to death."

Certainly what stupefied Rouletabille now was this staunch figure of the condemned man who appeared so tranquilly to enjoy his life. When the general was not furthering the gayety of his friends he was talking with his wife and daughter, who adored him and continually fondled him, and he seemed perfectly happy. With his enormous grizzly mustache, his ruddy color, his keen, piercing eyes, he looked the typical spoiled father.

The reporter studied all these widely-different types and made his observations while pretending to a ravenous appetite, which served, moreover, to fix him in the good graces of his hosts of the datcha des Iles. But, in reality, he passed the food to an enormous bull-dog under the table, in whose good graces he was also thus firmly planting himself. As Trebassof had prayed his companions to let his young friend satisfy his ravening hunger in peace, they did not concern themselves to entertain him. Then, too, the music served to distract attention from him, and at a moment somewhat later, when Matrena Petrovna turned to speak to the young man, she was frightened at not seeing him. Where had he gone? She went out into the veranda and looked. She did not dare to call. She walked into the grand-salon and saw the reporter just as he came out of the sitting-room.

"Where were you?" she inquired.

"The sitting-room is certainly charming, and decorated exquisitely," complimented Rouletabille. "It seems almost a boudoir."

"It does serve as a boudoir for my step-daughter, whose bedroom opens directly from it; you see the door there. It is simply for the present that the luncheon table is set there, because for some time the police have pre-empted the veranda."

"Is your dog a watch-dog, madame?" asked Rouletabille, caressing the beast, which had followed him.

"Khor is faithful and had guarded us well hitherto."

"He sleeps now, then?"

"Yes. Koupriane has him shut in the lodge to keep him from barking nights. Koupriane fears that if he is out he will devour one of the police who watch in the garden at night. I wanted him to sleep in the house, or by his master's door, or even at the foot of the bed, but Koupriane said, 'No, no; no dog. Don't rely on the dog. Nothing is more dangerous than to rely on the dog. 'Since then he has kept Khor locked up at night. But I do not understand Koupriane's idea."

"Monsieur Koupriane is right," said the reporter. "Dogs are useful only against strangers."

"Oh," gasped the poor woman, dropping her eyes. "Koupriane certainly knows his business; he thinks of everything."

"Come," she added rapidly, as though to hide her disquiet, "do not go out like that without letting me know. They want you in the dining-room."

"I must have you tell me right now about this attempt."

"In the dining-room, in the dining-room. In spite of myself," she said in a low voice, "it is stronger than I am. I am not able to leave the general by himself while he is on the ground-floor."

She drew Rouletabille into the dining-room, where the gentlemen were now telling odd stories of street robberies amid loud laughter. Natacha was still talking with Michael Korsakoff; Boris, whose eyes never quitted them, was as pale as the wax on his guzla, which he rattled violently from time to time. Matrena made Rouletabille sit in a corner of the sofa, near her, and, counting on her fingers like a careful housewife who does not wish to overlook anything in her domestic calculations, she said:

"There have been three attempts; the first two in Moscow. The first happened very simply. The general knew he had been condemned to death. They had delivered to him at the palace in the afternoon the revoluntionary poster which proclaimed his intended fate to the whole city and country. So Feodor, who was just about to ride into the city, dismissed his escort. He ordered horses put to a sleigh. I trembled and asked what he was going to do. He said he was going to drive quietly through all parts of the city, in order to show the Muscovites that a governor appointed according to law by the Little Father and who had in his conscience only the sense that he had done his full duty was not to be intimidated. It was nearly four o'clock, toward the end of a winter day that had been clear and bright, but very cold. I wrapped myself in my furs and took my seat beside him, and he said, 'This is fine, Matrena; this will have a great effect on these imbeciles.' So we started. At first we drove along the Naberjnaia. The sleigh glided like the wind. The general hit the driver a heavy blow in the back, crying, 'Slower, fool; they will think we are afraid,' and so the horses were almost walking when, passing behind the Church of Protection and intercession, we reached the Place Rouge. Until then the few passers-by had looked at us, and as they recognized him, hurried along to keep him in view. At the

Place Rouge there was only a little knot of women kneeling before the Virgin. As soon as these women saw us and recognized the equipage of the Governor, they dispersed like a flock of crows, with frightened cries. Feodor laughed so hard that as we passed under the vault of the Virgin his laugh seemed to shake the stones. I felt reassured, monsieur. Our promenade continued without any remarkable incident. The city was almost deserted. Everything lay prostrated under the awful blow of that battle in the street. Feodor said, 'Ah, they give me a wide berth; they do not know how much I love them," and all through that promenade he said many more charming and delicate things to me.

"As we were talking pleasantly under our furs we came to la Place Koudrinsky, la rue Koudrinsky, to be exact. It was just four o'clock, and a light mist had commenced to mix with the sifting snow, and the houses to right and left were visible only as masses of shadow. We glided over the snow like a boat along the river in foggy calm. Then, suddenly, we heard piercing cries and saw shadows of soldiers rushing around, with movements that looked larger than human through the mist; their short whips looked enormous as they knocked some other shadows that we saw down like logs. The general stopped the sleigh and got out to see what was going on. I got out with him. They were soldiers of the famous Semenowsky regiment, who had two prisoners, a young man and a child. The child was being beaten on the nape of the neck. It writhed on the ground and cried in torment. It couldn't have been more than nine years old. The other, the young man, held himself up and marched along without a single cry as the thongs fell brutally upon him. I was appalled. I did not give my husband time to open his mouth before I called to the subaltern who commanded the detachment, 'You should be ashamed to strike a child and a Christian like that, which cannot defend itself.' The general told him the same thing. Then the subaltern told us that the little child had just killed a lieutenant in the street by firing a revolver, which he showed us, and it was the biggest one I ever have seen, and must have been as heavy for that infant to lift as a small cannon. It was unbelievable.

"'And the other,' demanded the general; 'what has he done?'

"'He is a dangerous student,' replied the subaltern, 'who has delivered himself up as a prisoner because he promised the landlord of the house where he lives that he would do it to keep the house from being battered down with cannon.'

"'But that is right of him. Why do you beat him?'

"'Because he has told us he is a dangerous student.'

"'That is no reason,' Feodor told him. 'He will be shot if he deserves it, and the child also, but I forbid you to beat him. You have not been furnished with these whips in order to beat isolated prisoners, but to charge the crowd when it does not obey the governor's orders. In such a case you are ordered "Charge," and you know what to do. You understand?' Feodor said roughly. 'I am General Trebassof, your governor.'

"Feodor was thoroughly human in saying this. Ah, well, he was badly compensed for it, very badly, I tell you. The student was truly dangerous, because he had no sooner heard my husband say, 'I am General Trebassof, your governor,' than he cried, 'Ah, is it you, Trebassoff ' and drew a revolver from no one knows where and fired straight at the general, almost against his breast. But the general was not hit, happily, nor I either, who was by him and had thrown myself onto the student to disarm him and then was tossed about at the feet of the soldiers in the battle they waged around the student while the revolver was going off. Three soldiers were killed. You can understand that the others were furious. They raised me with many excuses and, all together, set to kicking the student in the loins and striking at him as he lay on the ground. The subaltern struck his face a blow that might have blinded him. Feodor hit the officer in the head with his fist and called, 'Didn't you hear what I said?' The officer fell under the blow and Feodor himself carried him to the sleigh and laid him with the dead men. Then he took charge of the soldiers and led them to the barracks. I followed, as a sort of after-guard. We returned to the palace an hour later. It was quite dark by then, and almost at the entrance to the palace we were shot at by a group of revolutionaries who passed swiftly in two sleighs and disappeared in the darkness so fast that they could not be overtaken. I had a ball in my toque. The general had not been touched this time either, but our furs were ruined by the blood of the dead soldiers which they had forgotten to clean out of the sleigh. That was the first attempt, which meant little enough, after all, because it was fighting in the open. It was some days later that they commenced to try assassination."

At this moment Ermolai brought in four bottles of champagne and Thaddeus struck lightly on the piano.

"Quickly, madame, the second attempt," said Rouletabille, who was aking hasty notes on his cuff, never ceasing, meanwhile, to watch the convivial group and listening with both ears wide open to Matrena.

"The second happened still in Moscow. We had had a jolly dinner because we thought that at last the good old days were back and good citizens could live in peace; and Boris had tried out the guzla singing songs of the Orel country to please me; he is so fine and sympathetic. Natacha had gone somewhere or other. The sleigh was waiting at the door and we went out and got in. Almost instantly there was a fearful noise, and we were thrown out into the snow, both the general and me. There remained no trace of sleigh or coachman; the two horses were disemboweled, two magnificent piebald horses, my dear young monsieur, that the general was so attached to. As to Feodor, he had that serious wound in his right leg; the calf was shattered. I simply had my shoulder a little wrenched, practically nothing. The bomb had been placed under the seat of the unhappy coachman, whose hat alone we found, in a pool of blood. From that attack the general lay two months in

bed. In the second month they arrested
two servants who were caught one night
on the landing leading to the upper floor,
where they had no business, and after that
I sent at once for our old domestics in Orel
to come and serve us. It was discovered
that these detected servants were in touch
with the revolutionaries, so they were
hanged. The Emperor appointed a provisional
governor, and now that the general was
better we decided on a convalescence for
him in the midi of France. We took train
for St. Petersburg, but the journey started
high fever in my husband and reopened
the wound in his calf. The doctors ordered
absolute rest and so we settled here in the
datcha des Iles. Since then, not a day has
passed without the general receiving an
anonymous letter telling him that nothing
can save him from the revenge of the
revolutionaries. He is brave and only smiles
over them, but for me, I know well that
so long as we are in Russia we have not a

moment's security. So I watch him every minute and let no one approach him except his intimate friends and us of the family. I have brought an old gniagnia who watched me grow up, Ermolai, and the Orel servants. In the meantime, two months later, the third attempt suddenly occurred. It is certainly of them all the most frightening, because it is so mysterious, a mystery that has not yet, alas, been solved."

But Athanase Georgevitch had told a "good story" which raised so much hubbub that nothing else could be heard. Feodor Feodorovitch was so amused that he had tears in his eyes. Rouletabille said to himself as Matrena talked, "I never have seen men so gay, and yet they know perfectly they are apt to be blown up all together any moment."

General Trebassof, who had steadily watched Rouletabille, who, for that matter, had been kept in eye by everyone there, said:

"Eh, eh, monsieur le journaliste, you find us very gay?"

"I find you very brave," said Rouletabille quietly.

"How is that?" said Feodor Feodorovitch, smiling.

"You must pardon me for thinking of the things that you seem to have forgotten entirely."

He indicated the general's wounded leg.

"The chances of war! the chances of war!" said the general. "A leg here, an arm there. But, as you see, I am still here. They will end by growing tired and leaving me in peace. Your health, my friend!"

"Your health, general!"

"You understand," continued Feodor Feodorovitch, "there is no occasion to excite ourselves. It is our business to defend the empire at the peril of our lives. We find that quite natural, and there is no occasion to think of it. I have had terrors enough in other directions, not to speak of the terrors of love, that are more ferocious than you can yet imagine. Look at what they did to my poor friend the Chief of the Surete, Boichlikoff. He was commendable certainly. There was a brave man. Of an evening, when his work was over, he always left the bureau of the prefecture and went to join his wife and children in their apartment in the ruelle des Loups. Not a soldier! No guard! The others had every chance. One evening a score of revolutionaries, after having driven away the terrorized servants, mounted to his apartments. He was dining with his family. They knocked and he opened the door. He saw who they were, and tried to speak. They gave him no time. Before his wife and children, mad with terror and on their knees before the revolutionaries, they read him his death-sentence. A fine end that to a dinner!"

As he listened Rouletabille paled and he kept his eyes on the door as if he expected to see it open of itself, giving access to ferocious Nihilists of whom one, with a paper in his hand, would read the sentence of death to Feodor Feodorovitch. Rouletabille's stomach was not yet seasoned to such stories. He almost regretted, momentarily, having taken the terrible responsibility of dismissing the police. After what Koupriane had confided to him of things that had happened in this house, he had not hesitated to risk everything on that audacious decision, but all the same, all the same—these stories of

Nihilists who appear at the end of a meal, death-sentence in hand, they haunted him, they upset him. Certainly it had been a piece of foolhardiness to dismiss the police!

"Well," he asked, conquering his misgivings and resuming, as always, his confidence in himself, "then, what did they do then, after reading the sentence?"

"The Chief of the Surete knew he had no time to spare. He did not ask for it. The revolutionaries ordered him to bid his family farewell. He raised his wife, his children, clasped them, bade them be of good courage, then said he was ready. They took him into the street. They stood him against a wall. His wife and children watched from a window. A volley sounded. They descended to secure the body, pierced with twenty-five bullets."

"That was exactly the number of wounds that were made on the body of little

Jacques Zloriksky," came in the even tones of Natacha.

"Oh, you, you always find an excuse," grumbled the general. "Poor Boichlikoff did his duty, as I did mine.

"Yes, papa, you acted like a soldier. That is what the revolutionaries ought not to forget. But have no fears for us, papa; because if they kill you we will all die with you."

"And gayly too," declared Athanase Georgevitch.

"They should come this evening. We are in form!"

Upon which Athanase filled the glasses again.

"None the less, permit me to say," ventured the timber-merchant, Thaddeus

Tchnitchnikof, timidly, "permit me to say that this Boichlikoff was very imprudent."

"Yes, indeed, very gravely imprudent," agreed Rouletabille. "When a man has had twenty-five good bullets shot into the body of a child, he ought certainly to keep his home well guarded if he wishes to dine in peace."

He stammered a little toward the end of this, because it occurred to him that it was a little inconsistent to express such opinions, seeing what he had done with the guard over the general.

"Ah," cried Athanase Georgevitch, in a stage-struck voice, "Ah, it was not imprudence! It was contempt of death! Yes, it was contempt of death that killed him! Even as the contempt of death keeps us, at this moment, in perfect health. To you, ladies and gentlemen! Do you know anything lovelier, grander, in the world than contempt of death? Gaze on Feodor Feodorovitch and answer me. Superb! My word, superb! To you all! The revolutionaries who are not of the police are of the same mind regarding our heroes. They may curse the tchinownicks who execute the terrible orders given them by those higher up, but those who are not of the police (there are some, I believe)—these surely recognize that men like the Chief of the Surete our dead friend, are brave."

"Certainly," endorsed the general. "Counting all things, they need more heroism for a promenade in a salon than a soldier on a battle-field." "I have met some of these men," continued Athanase in exalted vein.

"I have found in all their homes the same— imprudence, as our young French friend calls it. A few days after the assassination of the Chief of Police in Moscow I was received by his successor in the same place where the assassination had occurred. He did not take the slightest precaution with me, whom he did not know at all, nor with men of the middle class who came to present their petitions, in spite of the fact that it was under precisely identical conditions that his predecessor had been slain. Before I left I looked over to where on the floor there had so recently occurred such agony. They had placed a rug there and on the rug a table, and on that table there was a book. Guess what book. 'Women's Stockings,' by Willy! And—and then—Your health, Matrena Petrovna. What's the odds!"

"You yourselves, my friends," declared the general, "prove your great courage by coming to share the hours that remain of my life with me."

"Not at all, not at all! It is war."

"Yes, it is war."

"Oh, there's no occasion to pat us on the shoulder, Athanase," insisted Thaddeus modestly. "What risk do we run? We are well guarded."

"We are protected by the finger of God," declared Athanase, "because the police—well, I haven't any confidence in the police."

Michael Korsakoff, who had been for a turn in the garden, entered during the remark.

"Be happy, then, Athanase Georgevitch," said he, "for there are now no police around the villa."

"Where are they?" inquired the timber-merchant uneasily.

"An order came from Koupriane to remove them," explained Matrena Petrovna, who exerted herself to appear calm.

"And are they not replaced?" asked Michael.

"No. It is incomprehensible. There must have been some confusion in the orders given." And Matrena reddened, for she loathed a lie and it was in tribulation of spirit that she used this fable under Rouletabille's directions.

"Oh, well, all the better," said the general. "It will give me pleasure to see my home ridded for a while of such people."

Athanase was naturally of the same mind as the general, and when Thaddeus and Ivan Petrovitch and the orderlies offered to pass the night at the villa and take the place of the absent police, Feodor Feodorovitch caught a gesture from Rouletabille which disapproved the idea of this new guard.

"No, no," cried the general emphatically. "You leave at the usual time. I want now to get back into the ordinary run of things, my word! To live as everyone else does. We shall be all right. Koupriane and I have arranged the matter. Koupriane is less sure of his men, after all, than I am of my servants. You understand me. I do not need to explain further. You will go home to bed—and we will all sleep. Those are the orders. Besides, you must remember that the guard-post is only a step from here, at the corner of the road, and we have only to give a signal to bring them all here. But—more secret agents or special police—no, no! Good-night. All of us to bed now!"

They did not insist further. When Feodor had said, "Those are the orders," there was room for nothing more, not even in the way of polite insistence.

But before going to their beds all went into the veranda, where liqueurs were served by the brave Ermolai, as always. Matrena pushed the wheel-chair of the general there, and he kept repeating, "No, no. No more such people. No more police. They only bring trouble."

"Feodor! Feodor!" sighed Matrena, whose anxiety deepened in spite of all she could do, "they watched over your dear life."

"Life is dear to me only because of you, Matrena Petrovna."

"And not at all because of me, papa?" said Natacha.

"Oh, Natacha!"

He took both her hands in his. It was an affecting glimpse of family intimacy.

From time to time, while Ermolai poured the liqueurs, Feodor struck his band on the coverings over his leg.

"It gets better," said he. "It gets better."

Then melancholy showed in his rugged face, and he watched night deepen over the isles, the golden night of St. Petersburg. It was not quite yet the time of year for what they call the golden nights there, the "white nights," nights which never deepen to darkness, but they were already beautiful in their soft clarity, caressed, here by the Gulf of Finland, almost at the same time by the last and the first rays of the sun, by twilight and dawn.

From the height of the veranda one of the most beautiful bits of the isles lay in view, and the hour was so lovely that its charm thrilled these people, of whom several, as Thaddeus, were still close to nature. It was he, first, who called to Natacha:

"Natacha! Natacha! Sing us your 'Soir des Iles.'"

Natacha's voice floated out upon the peace of the islands under the dim arched sky, light and clear as a night rose, and the guzla of Boris accompanied it. Natacha sang:

"This is the night of the Isles—at the north of the world. The sky presses in its stainless arms the bosom of earth, Night kisses the rose that dawn gave to the twilight. And the night air is sweet and fresh from across the shivering gulf, Like the breath of young girls from the world still farther north. Beneath the two lighted horizons, sinking and rising at once, The sun rolls rebounding from the gods at the north of the world. In this moment, beloved, when in the clear shadows of this rose-stained evening I am here alone with you, Respond, respond with a heart less timid to the holy, accustomed cry of 'Good-evening.'"

Ah, how Boris Nikolaievitch and Michael Korsakoff watched her as she sang! Truly, no one ever can guess the anger or the love that broods in a Slavic heart under a soldier's tunic, whether the soldier wisely plays at the guzla, as the correct Boris, or merely lounges, twirling his mustache with his manicured and perfumed fingers, like Michael, the indifferent.

Natacha ceased singing, but all seemed to be listening to her still—the convivial group on the terrace appeared to be held in charmed attention, and the porcelain statuettes of men on the lawn, according to the mode of the Iles, seemed to lift on their short legs the better to hear pass the sighing harmony of Natacha in the rose nights at the north of the world.

Meanwhile Matrena wandered through the house from cellar to attic, watching over her husband like a dog on guard, ready to bite, to throw itself in the way of danger, to receive the blows, to die for its master—and hunting for Rouletabille, who had disappeared again.

III

The Watch

She went out to caution the servants to
a strict watch, armed to the teeth, before
the gate all night long, and she crossed
the deserted garden. Under the veranda
the schwitzar was spreading a mattress for
Ermolai. She asked him if he had seen the
young Frenchman anywhere, and after the
answer, could only say to herself, "Where
is he, then?" Where had Rouletabille gone?
The general, whom she had carried up to
his room on her back, without any help, and
had helped into bed without assistance, was
disturbed by this singular disappearance.
Had someone already carried off "their"
Rouletabille? Their friends were gone and
the orderlies had taken leave without being
able to say where this boy of a journalist had

gone. But it would be foolish to worry about the disappearance of a Journalist, they had said. That kind of man—these journalists—came, went, arrived when one least expected them, and quitted their company—even the highest society—without formality. It was what they called in France "leaving English fashion." However, it appeared it was not meant to be impolite. Perhaps he had gone to telegraph. A journalist had to keep in touch with the telegraph at all hours. Poor Matrena Petrovna roamed the solitary garden in tumult of heart. There was the light in the general's window on the first floor. There were lights in the basement from the kitchens. There was a light on the ground-floor near the sitting-room, from Natacha's chamber window. Ah, the night was hard to bear. And this night the shadows weighed heavier than ever on the valiant breast of Matrena. As she breathed she felt as though she lifted all the weight of the threatening night. She examined everything—

everything. All was shut tight, was perfectly secure, and there was no one within excepting people she was absolutely sure of— but whom, all the same, she did not allow to go anywhere in the house excepting where their work called them. Each in his place. That made things surer. She wished each one could remain fixed like the porcelain statues of men out on the lawn. Even as she thought it, here at her feet, right at her very feet, a shadow of one of the porcelain men moved, stretched itself out, rose to its knees, grasped her skirt and spoke in the voice of Rouletabille. Ah, good! it was Rouletabille. "Himself, dear madame; himself."

"Why is Ermolai in the veranda? Send him back to the kitchens and tell the schwitzar to go to bed. The servants are enough for an ordinary guard outside. Then you go in at once, shut the door, and don't concern yourself about me, dear madame. Good-night."

Rouletabille had resumed, in the shadows, among the other porcelain figures, his pose of a porcelain man.

Matrena Petrovna did as she was told, returned to the house, spoke to the schwitzar, who removed to the lodge with Ermolai, and their mistress closed the outside door. She had closed long before the door of the kitchen stair which allowed the domestics to enter the villa from below. Down there each night the devoted gniagnia and the faithful Ermolai watched in turn.

Within the villa, now closed, there were on the ground-floor only Matrena herself and her step-daughter Natacha, who slept in the chamber off the sitting-room, and, above on the first floor, the general asleep, or who ought to be asleep if he had taken his potion. Matrena remained in the darkness of the drawing-room, her dark-lantern in her hand. All her nights passed thus, gliding from door to door, from chamber to chamber, watching over the watch of the police, not daring to stop her stealthy promenade even to throw herself on the mattress that she had placed across the doorway of her husband's chamber. Did she ever sleep? She herself could hardly say. Who else could, then? A tag of sleep here and there, over the arm of a chair, or leaning against the wall, waked always by some noise that she heard or dreamed, some warning, perhaps, that she alone had heard. And tonight, tonight there is Rouletabille's alert guard to help her, and she feels a little less the aching terror of watchfulness, until there surges back into her mind the recollection that the police are no longer there. Was he right, this young man? Certainly she could not deny that some way she feels more confidence now that the police are gone. She does not have to spend her time watching their shadows in the shadows, searching the darkness, the arm-chairs, the sofas, to rouse them, to appeal in low tones to all they held binding, by their own name and the name of their father, to promise them a bonus that would amount to something if they watched well, to count them in order to know where they all were, and, suddenly, to throw full in their face the ray of light from her little dark-lantern in order to be sure, absolutely sure, that she was face to face with them, one of the police, and not with some other, some other with an infernal machine under his arm. Yes, she surely had less work now that she had no longer to watch the police. And she had less fear!

She thanked the young reporter for that. Where was he? Did he remain in the pose of a porcelain statue all this time out there on the lawn? She peered through the lattice of the veranda shutters and looked anxiously out into the darkened garden. Where could he be? Was that he, down yonder, that crouching black heap with an unlighted pipe in his mouth? No, no. That, she knew well, was the dwarf she genuinely loved, her little domovoi-doukh, the familiar spirit of the house, who watched with her over the general's life and thanks to whom serious injury had not yet befallen Feodor Feodorovitch—one could not regard a mangled leg that seriously. Ordinarily in her own country (she was from the Orel district) one did not care to see the domovoi-doukh appear in flesh and blood. When she was little she was always afraid that she would come upon him around a turn of the path in her father's garden. She always thought of him as no higher than that, seated back on his haunches and smoking his pipe. Then, after she was married, she had suddenly run across him at a turning in the bazaar at Moscow. He was just as she had imagined him, and she had immediately bought him, carried him home herself and placed him, with many precautions, for he was of very delicate porcelain, in the vestibule of the palace. And in leaving Moscow she had been careful not to leave him there. She had carried him herself in a case and had placed him herself on the lawn of the datcha des Iles, that he might continue to watch over her happiness and over the life of her Feodor. And in order that he should not be bored, eternally smoking his pipe all alone, she had surrounded him with a group of little porcelain genii, after the fashion of the Jardins des Iles. Lord! how that young Frenchman had frightened her, rising suddenly like that, without warning, on the lawn. She had believed for a moment that it was the domovoi-doukh himself rising to stretch his legs. Happily he had spoken at once and she had recognized his voice. And besides, her domovoi surely would not speak French. Ah! Matrena Petrovna breathed freely now. It seemed to her, this night, that there were two little familiar genii watching over the house. And that was worth more than all the police in the world, surely. How wily that little fellow was to order all those men away. There was something it was necessary to know; it was necessary therefore that nothing should be in the way of learning it. As things were now, the mystery could operate without suspicion or interference. Only one man watched it, and he had not the air of watching. Certainly Rouletabille had not the air of constantly watching anything. He had the manner, out in the night, of an easy little man in porcelain, neither more nor less, yet he could see everything—if anything were there to see—and he could hear everything—if there were anything to hear. One passed beside him without suspecting him, and men might talk to each other without an idea that he heard them, and even talk to themselves according to the habit people have sometimes when they think themselves quite alone. All the guests had departed thus, passing close by him, almost brushing him, had exchanged their "Adieus," their "Au revoirs," and all their final, drawn-out farewells. That dear little living domovoi certainly was a rogue! Oh, that dear little domovoi who had been so affected by the tears of Matrena Petrovna! The good, fat, sentimental, heroic woman longed to hear, just then, his reassuring voice.

"It is I. Here I am," said the voice of her little living familiar spirit at that instant, and she felt her skirt grasped. She waited for what he should say. She felt no fear. Yet she had supposed he was outside the house. Still, after all, she was not too astonished that he was within. He was so adroit! He had entered behind her, in the shadow of her skirts, on all-fours, and had slipped away without anyone noticing him, while she was speaking to her enormous, majestic schwitzar.

"So you were here?" she said, taking his hand and pressing it nervously in hers.

"Yes, yes. I have watched you closing the house. It is a task well-done, certainly. You have not forgotten anything."

"But where were you, dear little demon? I have been into all the corners, and my hands did not touch you."

"I was under the table set with hors-d'oeuvres in the sitting-room."

"Ah, under the table of zakouskis! I have forbidden them before now to spread a long hanging cloth there, which obliges me to kick my foot underneath casually in order to be sure there is no one beneath. It is imprudent, very imprudent, such table-cloths. And under the table of zakouskis have you been able to see or hear anything?"

"Madame, do you think that anyone could possibly see or hear anything in the villa when you are watching it alone, when the

99

general is asleep and your step-daughter is preparing for bed?"

"No. No. I do not believe so. I do not. No, oh, Christ!"

They talked thus very low in the dark, both seated in a corner of the sofa, Rouletabille's hand held tightly in the burning hands of Matrena Petrovna.

She sighed anxiously. "And in the garden— have you heard anything?"

"I heard the officer Boris say to the officer Michael, in French, 'Shall we return at once to the villa?' The other replied in Russian in a way I could see was a refusal. Then they had a discussion in Russian which I, naturally, could not understand. But from the way they talked I gathered that they disagreed and that no love was lost between them."

"No, they do not love each other. They both love Natacha."

"And she, which one of them does she love? It is necessary to tell me."

"She pretends that she loves Boris, and I believe she does, and yet she is very friendly with Michael and often she goes into nooks and corners to chat with him, which makes Boris mad with jealousy. She has forbidden Boris to speak to her father about their marriage, on the pretext that she does not wish to leave her father now, while each day, each minute the general's life is in danger."

"And you, madame—do you love your step-daughter?" brutally inquired the reporter.

"Yes—sincerely," replied Matrena Petrovna, withdrawing her hand from those of Rouletabille.

"And she—does she love you?"

"I believe so, monsieur, I believe so sincerely. Yes, she loves me, and there is not any reason why she should not love me. I believe—understand me thoroughly, because it comes from my heart—that we all here in this house love one another. Our friends are old proved friends. Boris has been orderly to my husband for a very long time. We do not share any of his too-modern ideas, and there were many discussions on the duty of soldiers at the time of the massacres. I reproached him with being as womanish as we were in going down on his knees to the general behind Natacha and me, when it became necessary to kill all those poor moujiks of Presnia. It was not his role. A soldier is a soldier. My husband raised him roughly and ordered him, for his pains, to march at the head of the troops. It was right. What else could he do? The general already had enough to fight against, with the whole revolution, with his conscience, with the natural pity in his heart of a brave man, and with the tears and insupportable moanings, at such a moment, of his daughter and his wife. Boris understood and obeyed him, but, after the death of the poor students, he behaved again like a woman in composing those verses on the heroes of the barricades; don't you think so? Verses that Natacha and he learned by heart, working together, when they were surprised at it by the general. There was a terrible scene. It was before the next-to-the-last attack. The general then had the use of both legs. He stamped his feet and fairly shook the house."

"Madame," said Rouletabille, "a propos of the attacks, you must tell me about the third."

As he said this, leaning toward her, Matrena Petrovna shouted "Listen!" that made him rigid in the night with ear alert.

What had she heard? For him, he had heard nothing.

"You hear nothing?" she whispered to him with an effort. "A tick-tack?"

"No, I hear nothing."

"You know—like the tick-tack of a clock. Listen."

"How can you hear the tick-tack? I've noticed that no clocks are running here."

"Don't you understand? It is so that we shall be able to hear the tick-tack better."

"Oh, yes, I understand. But I do not hear anything."

"For myself, I think I hear the tick-tack all the time since the last attempt. It haunts my ears, it is frightful, to say to one's self:

There is clockwork somewhere, just about to reach the death-tick—and not to know where, not to know where! When the police were here I made them all listen, and I was not sure even when they had all listened and said there was no tick-tack. It is terrible to hear it in my ear any moment when I least expect it. Tick-tack! Tick-tack! It is the blood beating in my ear, for instance, hard, as if it struck on a sounding-board. Why, here are drops of perspiration on my hands! Listen!"

"Ah, this time someone is talking—is crying," said the young man.

"Sh-h-h!" And Rouletabille felt the rigid hand of Matrena Petrovna on his arm. "It is the general. The general is dreaming!"

She drew him into the dining-room, into a corner where they could no longer hear the moanings. But all the doors that communicated with the dining-room, the drawing-room and the sitting-room remained open behind him, by the secret precaution of Rouletabille.

He waited while Matrena, whose breath he heard come hard, was a little behind. In a moment, quite talkative, and as though she wished to distract Rouletabille's attention from the sounds above, the broken words and sighs, she continued:

"See, you speak of clocks. My husband has a watch which strikes. Well, I have stopped his watch because more than once I have been startled by hearing the tick-tack of his watch in his waistcoat-pocket. Koupriane gave me that advice one day when he was here and had pricked his ears at the noise of the pendulums, to stop all my watches and clocks so that there would be no chance of confusing them with the tick-tack that might come from an infernal machine planted in some corner. He spoke from experience, my dear little monsieur, and it was by his order that all the clocks at the Ministry, on the Naberjnaia, were stopped, my dear little friend. The Nihilists, he told me, often use clockworks to set off their machines at the time they decide on. No one can guess all the inventions that they have, those brigands. In the same way, Koupriane advised me to take away all the draught-boards from the fireplaces. By that precaution they were enabled to avoid a terrible disaster at the Ministry near the Pont-des-chantres, you know, petit demovoi? They saw a bomb just as it was being lowered into the fire-place of the minister's cabinet. (note 1) The Nihilists held it by a cord and were up on the roof letting it down the chimney. One of them was caught, taken to Schlusselbourg and hanged. Here you can see that all the

---

1. Actual attack on Witte.

draught-boards of the fireplaces are cleared away."

"Madame," interrupted Rouletabille (Matrena Petrovna did not know that no one ever succeeded in distracting Rouletabille's attention), "madame, someone moans still, upstairs."

"Oh, that is nothing, my little friend. It is the general, who has bad nights. He cannot sleep without a narcotic, and that gives him a fever. I am going to tell you now how the third attack came about. And then you will understand, by the Virgin Mary, how it is I have yet, always have, the tick-tack in my ears.

"One evening when the general had got to sleep and I was in my own room, I heard distinctly the tick-tack of clockwork operating. All the clocks had been stopped, as Koupriane advised, and I had made an excuse to send Feodor's great watch to the repairer. You can understand how I felt when I heard that tick-tack. I was frenzied. I turned my head in all directions, and decided that the sound came from my husband's chamber. I ran there. He still slept, man that he is! The tick-tack was there. But where? I turned here and there like a fool. The chamber was in darkness and it seemed absolutely impossible for me to light a lamp because I thought I could not take the time for fear the infernal machine would go off in those few seconds. I threw myself on the floor and listened under the bed. The noise came from above. But where? I sprang to the fireplace, hoping that, against my orders, someone had started the mantel-clock. No, it was not that! It seemed to me now that the tick-tack came from the bed itself, that the machine was in the bed. The general awaked just then and cried to me, 'What is it, Matrena? What are you doing?' And he raised himself in bed, while I cried, 'Listen! Hear the tick-tack. Don't you hear the tick-tack?' I threw myself upon him and gathered him up in my arms to carry him, but I trembled too much, was too weak from fear, and fell back with him onto the bed, crying, 'Help!' He thrust me away and said roughly, 'Listen.' The frightful tick-tack was behind us now, on the table. But there was nothing on the table, only the night-light, the glass with the potion in it, and a gold vase where I had placed with my own hands that morning a cluster of grasses and wild flowers that Ermolai had brought that morning on his return from the Orel country. With one bound I was on the table and at the flowers. I struck my fingers among the grasses and the flowers, and felt a resistance. The tick-tack was in the bouquet! I took the bouquet in both hands, opened the window and threw it as far as I could into the garden. At the same moment the bomb burst with a terrible noise, giving me quite a deep wound in the hand. Truly, my dear little domovoi, that day we had been very near death, but God and the Little Father watched over us."

And Matrena Petrovna made the sign of the cross.

"All the windows of the house were broken. In all, we escaped with the fright and a visit from the glazier, my little friend, but I certainly believed that all was over."

"And Mademoiselle Natacha?" inquired Rouletabille. "She must also have been terribly frightened, because the whole house must have rocked."

"Surely. But Natacha was not here that night. It was a Saturday. She had been invited to the soiree du 'Michel' by the parents of Boris Nikolaievitch, and she slept at their house, after supper at the Ours, as had been planned. The next day, when she learned the danger the general had escaped, she trembled in every limb. She threw herself in her father's arms, weeping, which was natural enough, and declared that she never would go away from him again. The general told her how I had managed. Then she pressed me to her heart, saying that she never would forget such an action, and that she loved me more than if I were truly her mother. It was all in vain that during the days following we sought to understand how the infernal machine had been placed in the bouquet of wild flowers. Only the general's friends that you saw this evening, Natacha and I had entered the general's chamber during the day or in the evening. No servant, no chamber-maid, had been on that floor. In the day-time as well as all night long that entire floor is closed and I have the keys. The door of the servants' staircase which opens onto that floor, directly into the general's chamber, is always locked and barred on the inside with iron. Natacha and I do the chamber work. There is no way of taking greater precautions. Three police agents watched over us night and day. The night of the bouquet two had spent their time watching around the house, and the third lay on the sofa in the veranda. Then, too, we found all the doors and windows of the villa shut tight. In such circumstances you can judge whether my anguish was not deeper than any I had known hitherto. Because to whom, henceforth, could we trust ourselves? what and whom could we believe? what and whom could we watch? From that day, no other person but Natacha and me have the right to go to the first floor. The general's chamber was forbidden to his friends. Anyway, the general improved, and soon had the pleasure of receiving them himself at his table. I carry the general down and take him to his room again on my back. I do not wish anyone to help. I am strong enough for that. I feel that I could carry him to the end of the world if that would save him. Instead of three police, we had ten; five outside, five inside. The days went well enough, but the nights were frightful, because the shadows of the police that I encountered always made me fear that I was face to face with the Nihilists. One night I almost strangled one with my hand. It was after that incident that we arranged with Koupriane that the agents who watched at night, inside, should stay placed in the veranda, after having, at the end of the evening, made complete examination of everything. They were not to leave the veranda unless they heard a suspicious noise or I called to them. And it was after that arrangement that the incident of the floor happened, that has puzzled so both Koupriane and me."

"Pardon, madame," interrupted Rouletabille, "but the agents, during the examination of everything, never went to the bedroom floor?"

"No, my child, there is only myself and Natacha, I repeat, who, since the bouquet, go there."

"Well, madame, it is necessary to take me there at once."

"At once!"

"Yes, into the general's chamber."

"But he is sleeping, my child. Let me tell you exactly how the affair of the floor happened, and you will know as much of it as I and as Koupriane."

"To the general's chamber at once."

She took both his hands and pressed them nervously. "Little friend! Little friend! One hears there sometimes things which are the secret of the night! You understand me?"

"To the general's chamber, at once, madame."

Abruptly she decided to take him there, agitated, upset as she was by ideas and sentiments which held her without respite between the wildest inquietude and the most imprudent audacity.

IV

"The Youth of Moscow is Dead"

Rouletabille let himself be led by Matrena through the night, but he stumbled and his awkward hands struck against various things. The ascent to the first floor was accomplished in profound silence. Nothing broke it except that restless moaning which had so affected the young man just before.

The tepid warmth, the perfume of a woman's boudoir, then, beyond, through two doors opening upon the dressing-room which lay between Matrena's chamber and Feodor's, the dim luster of a night-lamp showed the bed where was stretched the sleeping tyrant of Moscow. Ah, he was frightening to see, with the play of faint yellow light and diffused shadows upon him. Such heavy-arched eyebrows, such an aspect of pain and menace, the massive jaw of a savage come from the plains of Tartary to be the Scourge of God, the stiff, thick, spreading beard. This was a form akin to the gallery of old nobles at Kasan, and young Rouletabille imagined him as none other than Ivan the Terrible himself. Thus appeared as he slept the excellent Feodor Feodorovitch, the easy, spoiled father of the family table, the friend of the advocate celebrated for his feats with knife and fork and of the bantering timber-merchant and amiable bear-hunter, the joyous Thaddeus and Athanase; Feodor, the faithful spouse of Matrena Petrovna and the adored papa of Natacha, a brave man who was so unfortunate as to have nights of cruel sleeplessness or dreams more frightful still.

At that moment a hoarse sigh heaved his huge chest in an uneven rhythm, and

Rouletabille, leaning in the doorway of the dressing-room, watched—but it was no longer the general that he watched, it was something else, lower down, beside the wall, near the door, and it was that which set him tiptoeing so lightly across the floor that it gave no sound. There was no slightest sound in the chamber, except the heavy breathing lifting the rough chest. Behind Rouletabille Matrena raised her arms, as though she wished to hold him back, because she did not know where he was going. What was he doing? Why did he stoop thus beside the door and why did he press his thumb all along the floor at the doorway? He rose again and returned. He passed again before the bed, where rumbled now, like the bellows of a forge, the respiration of the sleeper. Matrena grasped Rouletabille by the hand. And she had already hurried him into the dressing-room when a moan stopped them.

"The youth of Moscow is dead!"

It was the sleeper speaking. The mouth which had given the stringent orders moaned. And the lamentation was still a menace. In the haunted sleep thrust upon that man by the inadequate narcotic the words Feodor Feodorovitch spoke were words of mourning and pity. This perfect fiend of a soldier, whom neither bullets nor bombs could intimidate, had a way of saying words which transformed their meaning as they came from his terrible mouth. The listeners could not but feel absorbed in the tones of the brutal victor.

Matrena Petrovna and Rouletabille had leant their two shadows, blended one into the other, against the open doorway just beyond the gleam of the night-lamp, and they heard with horror:

"The youth of Moscow is dead! They have cleared away the corpses. There is nothing but ruin left. The Kremlin itself has shut its gates—that it may not see. The youth of Moscow is dead!"

Feodor Feodorovitch's fist shook above his bed; it seemed that he was about to strike, to kill again, and Rouletabille felt Matrena trembling against him, while he trembled as well before the fearful vision of the killer in the Red Week!

Feodor heaved an immense sigh and his breast descended under the bed-clothes, the fist relaxed and fell, the great head lay over on its ear. There was silence. Had he repose at last? No, no. He sighed, he choked anew, he tossed on his couch like the damned in torment, and the words written by his daughter—by his daughter—blazed in his eyes, which now were wide open—words written on the wall, that he read on the wall, written in blood.

"The youth of Moscow is dead!
They had gone so young into the fields
and into the mines,
And they had not found a single corner of
the Russian land where there
were not moanings.
Now the youth of Moscow is dead and
no more moanings are heard,
Because those for whom all youth died
do not dare even to moan any more.

But—what? The voice of Feodor lost its threatening tone. His breath came as from a weeping child. And it was with sobs in his throat that he said the last verse, the verse written by his daughter in the album, in red letters:

"The last barricade had standing there
the girl of eighteen winters, the virgin of
Moscow, flower of the snow.
Who gave her kisses to the workmen struck
by the bullets from the soldiers of the Czar;

"She aroused the admiration of the very
soldiers who, weeping, killed her:
"What killing! All the houses shuttered,
the windows with heavy eyelids of plank
in order not to see!—
"And the Kremlin itself has closed its gates—
that it may not see.
"The youth of Moscow is dead!"

"Feodor! Feodor!"

She had caught him in her arms, holding him
fast, comforting him while still he raved,
"The youth of Moscow is dead," and appeared
to thrust away with insensate gestures a
crowd of phantoms. She crushed him to her
breast, she put her hands over his mouth to
make him stop, but he, saying, "Do you hear?
Do you hear? What do they say? They say
nothing, now. What a tangle of bodies under
the sleigh, Matrena! Look at those frozen
legs of those poor girls we pass, sticking out

in all directions, like logs, from under their icy, blooded skirts. Look, Matrena!"

And then came further delirium uttered in Russian, which was all the more terrible to Rouletabille because he could not comprehend it.

Then, suddenly, Feodor became silent and thrust away Matrena Petrovna.

"It is that abominable narcotic," he said with an immense sigh. "I'll drink no more of it. I do not wish to drink it."

With one hand he pointed to a large glass on the table beside him, still half full of a soporific mixture with which he moistened his lips each time he woke; with the other hand he wiped the perspiration from his face. Matrena Petrovna stayed trembling near him, suddenly overpowered by the idea that he might discover there was someone there behind the door, who had seen and heard the sleep of General Trebassof! Ah, if he learned that, everything was over. She might say her prayers; she should die.

But Rouletabille was careful to give no sign. He barely breathed. What a nightmare! He understood now the emotion of the general's friends when Natacha had sung in her low, sweet voice, "Good-night. May your eyes have rest from tears and calm re-enter your heart oppressed." The friends had certainly been made aware, by Matrena's anxious talking, of the general's insomnia, and they could not repress their tears as they listened to the poetic wish of charming Natacha. "All the same," thought Rouletabille, "no one could imagine what I have just seen. They are not dead for everyone in the world, the youths of Moscow, and every night I know now a chamber where in the glow of the night-lamp they rise—they rise—they rise!" and the young man frankly, naively regretted to have intruded where he was; to have penetrated, however unintentionally, into an affair which, after all, concerned only the many dead and the one living. Why had he come to put himself between the dead and the living? It might be said to him: "The living has done his whole heroic duty," but the dead, what else was it that they had done?

Ah, Rouletabille cursed his curiosity, for—he saw it now—it was the desire to approach the mystery revealed by Koupriane and to penetrate once more, through all the besetting dangers, an astounding and perhaps monstrous enigma, that had brought him to the threshold of the datcha des Iles, which had placed him in the trembling hands of Matrena Petrovna in promising her his help. He had shown pity, certainly, pity for the delirious distress of that heroic woman. But there had been more curiosity than pity in his motives. And now he must pay, because it was too late now to withdraw, to say casually, "I wash my hands of it." He had sent away the police and he alone remained between the general and the vengeance of the dead! He might desert, perhaps! That one idea brought him to himself, roused all his spirit. Circumstances had brought him into a camp that he must defend at any cost, unless he was afraid!

The general slept now, or, at least, with eyelids closed simulated sleep, doubtless in order to reassure poor Matrena who, on her knees beside his pillow, had retained the hand of her terrible husband in her own. Shortly she rose and rejoined Rouletabille in her chamber. She took him then to a little guest-chamber where she urged him to get some sleep. He replied that it was she who needed rest. But, agitated still by what had just happened, she babbled:

"No, no! after such a scene I would have nightmares myself as well. Ah, it is dreadful!

Appalling! Appalling! Dear little monsieur, it is the secret of the night. The poor man! Poor unhappy man! He cannot tear his thoughts away from it. It is his worst and unmerited punishment, this translation that Natacha has made of Boris's abominable verses. He knows them by heart, they are in his brain and on his tongue all night long, in spite of narcotics, and he says over and over again all the time, 'It is my daughter who has written that!—my daughter!—my daughter!' It is enough to wring all the tears from one's body—that an aide-de-camp of a general, who himself has killed the youth of Moscow, is allowed to write such verses and that Natacha should take it upon herself to translate them into lovely poetic French for her album. It is hard to account for what they do nowadays, to our misery."

She ceased, for just then they heard the floor creak under a step downstairs. Rouletabille stopped Matrena short and drew his revolver.

He wished to creep down alone, but he had not time. As the floor creaked a second time, Matrena's anguished voice called down the staircase in Russian, "Who is there?" and immediately the calm voice of Natacha answered something in the same language. Then Matrena, trembling more and more, and very much excited keeping steadily to the same place as though she had been nailed to the step of the stairway, said in French, "Yes, all is well; your father is resting. Good-night, Natacha." They heard Natacha's step cross the drawing-room and the sitting-room. Then the door of her chamber closed. Matrena and Rouletabille descended, holding their breath. They reached the dining-room and Matrena played her dark-lantern on the sofa where the general always reclined. The sofa was in its usual place on the carpet. She pushed it back and raised the carpet, laying the floor bare. Then she got onto her knees and examined the floor minutely. She rose, wiping the perspiration from her brow, put the carpet hack in place, adjusted the sofa and dropped upon it with a great sigh.

"Well?" demanded Rouletabille.

"Nothing at all," said she.

"Why did you call so openly?"

"Because there was no doubt that it could only be my step-daughter on the ground-floor at that hour."

"And why this anxiety to examine the floor again?"

"I entreat you, my dear little child, do not see in my acts anything mysterious, anything hard to explain. That anxiety you speak of never leaves me. Whenever I have the chance I examine the flooring."

"Madame," demanded the young man, "what was your daughter doing in this room?"

"She came for a glass of mineral water; the bottle is still on the table."

"Madame, it is necessary that you tell me precisely what Koupriane has only hinted to me, unless I am entirely mistaken. The first time that you thought to examine the floor, was it after you heard a noise on the ground-floor such as has just happened?"

"Yes. I will tell you all that is necessary. It was the night after the attempt with the bouquet, my dear little monsieur, my dear little domovoi; it seemed to me I heard a noise on the ground-floor. I hurried downstairs and saw nothing suspicious at first. Everything was shut tight. I opened the door of Natacha's chamber softly. I wished to ask her if she had heard anything. But she was so fast asleep that I had not the heart to awaken her. I opened the door of the veranda, and all the police—all, you understand—slept soundly. I took another turn around the furniture, and, with my lantern in my hand, I was just going out of the dining-room when I noticed that the carpet on the floor was disarranged at one corner. I got down and my hand struck a great fold of carpet near the general's sofa. You would have said that the sofa had been rolled carelessly, trying to replace it in the position it usually occupied. Prompted by a sinister presentiment, I pushed away the sofa and I lifted the carpet. At first glance I saw nothing, but when I examined things closer I saw that a strip of wood did not lie well with the others on the floor. With a knife I was able to lift that strip and I found that two nails which had fastened it to the beam below had been freshly pulled out. It was just so I could raise the end of the board a little without being able to slip my hand under. To lift it any more it would be necessary to pull at least half-a-dozen nails. What could it mean? Was I on the point of discovering some new terrible and mysterious plan? I let the board fall back into place. I spread the carpet back again carefully, put the sofa in its place, and in the morning sent for Koupriane."

Rouletabille interrupted.

"You had not, madame, spoken to anyone of this discovery?"

"To no one."

"Not even to your step-daughter?"

"No," said the husky voice of Matrena, "not even to my step-daughter."

"Why?" demanded Rouletabille.

"Because," replied Matrena, after a moment's hesitation, "there were already enough frightening things about the house. I would not have spoken to my daughter any more than I would have said a word to the general. Why add to the disquiet they already suffered so much, in case nothing developed?"

"And what did Koupriane say?"

"We examined the floor together, secretly. Koupriane slipped his hand under more easily than I had done, and ascertained that under the board, that is to say between the beam and the ceiling of the kitchen, there was a hollow where any number of things might be placed. For the moment the board was still too little released for any maneuver to be possible. Koupriane, when he rose, said to me, 'You have happened, madame, to interrupt the person in her operations. But we are prepared henceforth. We know what she does and she is unaware that we know. Act as though you had not noticed anything; do not speak of it to anyone whatever—and watch. Let the general continue to sit in his usual place and let no one suspect that we have discovered the beginnings of this attempt. It is the only way we can plan so that they will continue. All the same,' he added, 'I will give my agents orders to patrol the ground-floor anew during the night. I would be risking too much to let the person continue her work each night. She might continue it so well that she would be able to accomplish it—you understand me? But by day you arrange that the rooms on the ground-floor be free from time to time—not for long, but from time to time.' I don't know why, but what he said and the way he said it frightened me more than ever. However, I carried out his program. Then, three days later, about eight o'clock, when the night watch was not yet started, that is to say at the moment when the police were still all out in the garden or walking around the house, outside, and when I had left the the ground-floor perfectly free while I helped the general to bed, I felt drawn even against myself suddenly to the dining-room. I lifted the carpet and examined the floor. Three more nails had been drawn from the board, which lifted more easily now, and under it, I could see that the normal cavity had been made wider still!"

When she had said this, Matrena stopped, as if, overcome, she could not tell more.

"Well?" insisted Rouletabille.

"Well, I replaced things as I found them and made rapid inquiries of the police and their chief; no one had entered the ground-floor. You understand me?—no one at all. Neither had anyone come out from it."

"How could anyone come out if no one had entered?"

"I wish to say," said she with a sob, "that Natacha during this space of time had been in her chamber, in her chamber on the ground-floor."

"You appear to be very disturbed, madame, at this recollection. Can you tell me further, and precisely, why you are agitated?" "You understand me, surely," she said, shaking her head.

"If I understand you correctly, I have to understand that from the previous time you examined the floor until the time that you noted three more nails drawn out, no other person could have entered the dining-room but you and your step-daughter Natacha."

Matrena took Rouletabille's hand as though she had reached an important decision.

"My little friend," moaned she, "there are things I am not able to think about and which I can no longer entertain when Natacha embraces me. It is a mystery more frightful than all else. Koupriane tells me that he is sure, absolutely sure, of the agents he kept here; my sole consolation, do you see, my little friend can tell you frankly, now that you have sent away those men—my sole consolation since that day has been that Koupriane is less sure of his men than I am of Natacha."

She broke down and sobbed.

When she was calmed, she looked for Rouletabille, and could not find him.
Then she wiped her eyes, picked up her dark-lantern, and, furtively, crept to her post beside the general.

For that day these are the points in Rouletabille's notebook:

"Topography: Villa surrounded by a large garden on three sides. The fourth side gives directly onto a wooded field that stretches to the river Neva. On this side the level of the ground is much lower, so low that the sole window opening in that wall (the window of Natacha's sitting-room on the ground-floor) is as high from the ground as though it were on the next floor in any other part of the house. This window is closed by iron shutters, fastened inside by a bar of iron.

"Friends: Athanase Georgevitch, Ivan Petrovitch, Thaddeus the timber-merchant (peat boots), Michael and Boris (fine shoes). Matrena, sincere love, blundering heroism. Natacha unknown. Against Natacha: Never there during the attacks. At Moscow at the time of the bomb in the sleigh, no one knows where she was, and it is she who should have accompanied the general (detail furnished by Koupriane that Matrena generously kept back). The night of the bouquet is the only night Natacha has slept away from the house. Coincidence of the disappearance of the nails and the presence all alone on the ground-floor of Natacha, in case, of course, Matrena did not pull them out herself. For Natacha: Her eyes when she looks at her father."

And this bizarre phrase:

"We mustn't be rash. This evening I have not yet spoken to Matrena Petrovna about the little hat-pin. That little hat-pin is the greatest relief of my life."

V

By Rouletabille's Order the General Promenades

Good morning, my dear little familiar spirit. The general slept splendidly the latter part of the night. He did not touch his narcotic. I am sure it is that dreadful mixture that gives him such frightful dreams. And you, my dear little friend, you have not slept an instant. I know it. I felt you going everywhere about the house like a little mouse. Ah, it seems good, so good. I slept so peacefully, hearing the subdued movement of your little steps. Thanks for the sleep you have given me, little friend."

Matrena talked on to Rouletabille, whom she had found the morning after the nightmare tranquilly smoking his pipe in the garden.

"Ah, ah, you smoke a pipe. Now you do certainly look exactly like a dear little domovoi-doukh. See how much you are alike. He smokes just like you. Nothing new, eh? You do not look very bright this morning. You are worn out. I have just arranged the little guest-chamber for you, the only one we have, just behind mine. Your bed is waiting for you. Is there anything you need? Tell me. Everything here is at your service."

"I'm not in need of anything, madame," said the young man smilingly, after this outpouring of words from the good, heroic dame.

"How can you say that, dear child? You will make yourself sick. I want you to understand that I wish you to rest. I want to be a mother to you, if you please, and you must obey me, my child. Have you had breakfast yet this morning? If you do not have breakfast promptly mornings, I will think you are annoyed. I am so annoyed that you have heard the secret of the night. I have been afraid that you would want to leave at once and for good, and that you would have mistaken ideas about the general. There is not a better man in the world than Feodor, and he must have a good, a very good conscience to dare, without fail, to perform such terrible duties as those at Moscow, when he is so good at heart. These things are easy enough for wicked people, but for good men, for good men who can reason it out, who know what they do and that they are condemned to death into the bargain, it is terrible, it is terrible! Why, I told him the moment things began to go wrong in Moscow, 'You know what to expect, Feodor. Here is a dreadful time to get through—make out you are sick.' I believed he was going to strike me, to kill me on the spot. 'I! Betray the Emperor in such a moment! His Majesty, to whom I owe everything! What are you thinking of, Matrena Petrovna!' And he did not speak to me after that for two days. It was only when he saw I was growing very ill that he pardoned me, but he had to be plagued with my jeremiads and the appealing looks of Natacha without end in his own home each time we heard any shooting in the street. Natacha attended the lectures of the Faculty, you know. And she knew many of them, and even some of those who were being killed on the barricades. Ah, life was not easy for him in his own home, the poor general! Besides, there was also Boris, whom I love as well, for that matter, as my own child, because I shall be very happy to see him married to Natacha—there was poor Boris who always came home from the attacks paler than a corpse and who could not keep from moaning with us."

"And Michael?" questioned Rouletabille.

"Oh, Michael only came towards the last. He is a new orderly to the general. The government at St. Petersburg sent him, because of course they couldn't help learning that Boris rather lacked zeal in repressing the students and did not encourage the general in being as severe as was necessary for the safety of the Empire. But Michael, he has a heart of stone; he knows nothing but the countersign and massacres fathers and mothers, crying, 'Vive le Tsar!' Truly, it seems his heart can only be touched by the sight of Natacha. And that again has caused a good deal of anxiety to Feodor and me. It has caught us in a useless complication that we would have liked to end by the prompt marriage of Natacha and Boris. But Natacha, to our great surprise, has not wished it to be so. No, she has not wished it, saying that there is always time to think of her wedding and that she is in no hurry to leave us. Meantime she entertains herself with this Michael as if she did not fear his passion, and neither has Michael the desperate air of a man who knows the definite engagement of Natacha and Boris. And my step-daughter is not a coquette. No, no. No one can say she is a coquette. At least, no one had been able to say it up to the time that Michael arrived. Can it be that she is a coquette? They are mysterious, these young girls, very mysterious, above all when they have that calm and tranquil look that Natacha always has; a face, monsieur, as you have noticed perhaps, whose beauty is rather passive whatever one says and does, excepting when the volleys in the streets kill her young comrades of the schools. Then I have seen her almost faint, which proves she has a great heart under her tranquil beauty. Poor Natacha! I have seen her excited as I over the life of her father. My little friend, I have seen her searching in the middle of the night, with me, for infernal machines under the furniture, and then she has expressed the opinion that it is nervous, childish, unworthy of us to act like that, like timid beasts under the sofas, and she has left me to search by myself. True, she never quits the general. She is more reassured, and is reassuring to him, at his side. It has an excellent moral effect on him, while I walk about and search like a beast. And she has become as fatalistic as he, and now she sings verses to the guzla, like Boris, or talks in corners with Michael, which makes the two enraged each with the other. They are curious, the young women of St. Petersburg and Moscow, very curious. We were not like that in our time, at Orel. We did not try to enrage people. We would have received a box on the ears if we had."

Natacha came in upon this conversation, happy, in white voile, fresh and smiling like a girl who had passed an excellent night. She asked after the health of the young man very prettily and embraced Matrena, in truth as one embraces a much-beloved mother. She complained again of Matrena's night-watch.

"You have not stopped it, mamma; you have not stopped it, eh? You are not going to be a little reasonable at last? I beg of you! What has given me such a mother! Why don't you sleep? Night is made for sleep. Koupriane has upset you. All the terrible things are over in Moscow. There is no occasion to think of them any more. That Koupriane makes himself important with his police-agents and obsesses us all. I am convinced that the affair of the bouquet was the work of his police."

"Mademoiselle," said Rouletabille, "I have just had them all sent away, all of them— because I think very much the same as you do."

"Well, then, you will be my friend, Monsieur Rouletabille I promise you, since you have done that. Now that the police are gone we have nothing more to fear. Nothing.

I tell you, mamma; you can believe me and not weep any more, mamma dear."

"Yes, yes; kiss me. Kiss me again!" repeated Matrena, drying her eyes. "When you kiss me I forget everything. You love me like your own mother, don't you?"

"Like my mother. Like my own mother."

"You have nothing to hide from me?—tell me, Natacha."

"Nothing to hide."

"Then why do you make Boris suffer so? Why don't you marry him?"

"Because I don't wish to leave you, mamma dear."

She escaped further parley by jumping up on the garden edge away from Khor, who had just been set free for the day.

"The dear child," said Matrena; "the dear little one, she little knows how much pain she has caused us without being aware of it, by her ideas, her extravagant ideas. Her father said to me one day at Moscow, 'Matrena Petrovna, I'll tell you what I think—Natacha is the victim of the wicked books that have turned the brains of all these poor rebellious students. Yes, yes; it would be better for her and for us if she did not know how to read, for there are moments—my word!—when she talks very wildly, and I have said to myself more than once that with such ideas her place is not in our salon hut behind a barricade. All the same,' he added after reflection, 'I prefer to find her in the salon where I can embrace her than behind a barricade where I would kill her like a mad dog.' But my husband, dear little monsieur, did not say what he really thinks, for he loves his daughter more than all the rest of the world put together, and there are things that even a general, yes, even a governor-general, would not be able to do without violating both divine and human laws. He suspects Boris also of setting Natacha's wits awry. We really have to consider that when they are married they will read everything they have a mind to. My husband has much more real respect for Michael Korsakoff because of his impregnable character and his granite conscience. More than once he has said, 'Here is the aide I should have had in the worst days of Moscow. He would have spared me much of the individual pain.' I can understand how that would please the general, but how such a tigerish nature succeeds in appealing to Natacha, how it succeeds in not actually revolting her, these young girls of the capital, one never can tell about them—they get away from all your notions of them."

Rouletabille inquired:

"Why did Boris say to Michael, 'We will return together'? Do they live together?"

"Yes, in the small villa on the Krestowsky Ostrov, the isle across from ours, that you can see from the window of the sitting-room. Boris chose it because of that. The orderlies wished to have camp-beds prepared for them right here in the general's house, by a natural devotion to him; but I opposed it, in order to keep them both from Natacha, in whom, of course, I have the most complete confidence, but one cannot be sure about the extravagance of men nowadays."

Ermolai came to announce the petit-dejeuner. They found Natacha already at table and she poured them coffee and milk, eating away all the time at a sandwich of anchovies and caviare.

"Tell me, mamma, do you know what gives me such an appetite? It is the thought of the way poor Koupriane must have taken this dismissal of his men. I should like to go to see him."

"If you see him," said Rouletabille, "it is unnecessary to tell him that the general will go for a long promenade among the isles this afternoon, because without fail he would send us an escort of gendarmes."

"Papa! A promenade among the islands? Truly? Oh, that is going to be lovely!"

Matrena Petrovna sprang to her feet.

"Are you mad, my dear little domovoi, actually mad?"

"Why? Why? It is fine. I must run and tell papa."

"Your father's room is locked," said Matrena brusquely.

"Yes, yes; he is locked in. You have the key. Locked away until death! You will kill him. It will be you who kills him."

She left the table without waiting for a reply and went and shut herself also in her chamber.

Matrena looked at Rouletabille, who continued his breakfast as though nothing had happened.

"Is it possible that you speak seriously?" she demanded, coming over and sitting down beside him. "A promenade! Without the police, when we have received again this morning a letter saying now that before forty-eight hours the general will be dead!"

"Forty-eight hours," said Rouletabille, soaking his bread in his chocolate, "forty-eight hours? It is possible. In any case, I know they will try something very soon."

"My God, how is it that you believe that? You speak with assurance."

"Madame, it is necessary to do everything I tell you, to the letter."

"But to have the general go out, unless he is guarded—how can you take such a responsibility? When I think about it, when I really think about it, I ask myself how you have dared send away the police. But here, at least, I know what to do in order to feel a little safe, I know that downstairs with Gniagnia and Ermolai we have nothing to fear. No stranger can approach even the basement. The provisions are brought from the lodge by our dvornicks whom we have had sent from my mother's home in the

Orel country and who are as devoted to us as bull-dogs. Not a bottle of preserves is taken into the kitchens without having been previously opened outside. No package comes from any tradesman without being opened in the lodge. Here, within, we are able to feel a little safe, even without the police—but away from here—outside!"

"Madame, they are going to try to kill your husband within forty-eight hours. Do you desire me to save him perhaps for a long time—for good, perhaps?"

"Ah, listen to him! Listen to him, the dear little domovoi! But what will Koupriane say? He will not permit any venturing beyond the villa; none, at least for the moment. Ah, now, how he looks at me, the dear little domovoi! Oh, well, yes. There, I will do as you wish."

"Very well, come into the garden with me."

She accompanied him, leaning on his arm.

"Here's the idea," said Rouletabille. "This afternoon you will go with the general in his rolling-chair. Everybody will follow. Everyone, you understand, Madame—understand me thoroughly, I mean to say that everyone who wishes to come must be invited to. Only those who wish to remain behind will do so. And do not insist. Ah, now, I see, you understand me. Why do you tremble?"

"But who will guard the house?"

"No one. Simply tell the servant at the lodge to watch from the lodge those who enter the villa, but simply from the lodge, without interfering with them, and saying nothing to them, nothing."

"I will do as you wish. Do you want me to announce our promenade beforehand?"

"Why, certainly. Don't be uneasy; let everybody have the good news."

"Oh, I will tell only the general and his friends, you may be sure."

"Now, dear Madame, just one more word. Do not wait for me at luncheon."

"What! You are going to leave us?" she cried instantly, breathless. "No, no. I do not wish it. I am willing to do without the police, but I am not willing to do without you. Everything might happen in your absence. Everything! Everything!" she repeated with singular energy. "Because, for me, I cannot feel sure as I should, perhaps. Ah, you make me say these things. Such things! But do not go."

"Do not be afraid; I am not going to leave you, madame."

"Ah, you are good! You are kind, kind! Caracho! (Very well.)"

"I will not leave you. But I must not be at luncheon. If anyone asks where I am, say that I have my business to look after, and have gone to interview political personages in the city."

"There's only one political personage in Russia," replied Matrena Petrovna bluntly; "that is the Tsar."

"Very well; say I have gone to interview the Tsar."

"But no one will believe that. And where will you be?"

"I do not know myself. But I will be about the house."

"Very well, very well, dear little domovoi."

She left him, not knowing what she thought about it all, nor what she should think—her head was all in a muddle.

In the course of the morning Athanase Georgevitch and Thaddeus Tchnitchnikof arrived. The general was already in the veranda. Michael and Boris arrived shortly after, and inquired in their turn how he had passed the night without the police. When they were told that Feodor was going for a promenade that afternoon they applauded his decision. "Bravo! A promenade a la strielka (to the head of the island) at the hour when all St. Petersburg is driving there. That is fine. We will all be there." The general made them stay for luncheon. Natacha appeared for the meal, in rather melancholy mood. A little before luncheon she had held a double conversation in the garden with Michael and Boris. No one ever could have known what these three young people had said if some stenographic notes in Rouletabille's memorandum-book did not give us a notion; the reporter had overheard, by accident surely, since all self-respecting reporters are quite incapable of eavesdropping.

The memorandum notes:

Natacha went into the garden with a book, which she gave to Boris, who pressed her hand lingeringly to his lips. "Here is your book; I return it to you. I don't want any more of them, the ideas surge so in my brain. It makes my head ache. It is true, you are right, I don't love novelties. I can satisfy myself with Pouchkine perfectly. The rest are all one to me. Did you pass a good night?"

Boris (good-looking young man, about thirty years old, blonde, a little effeminate, wistful. A curious appurtenance in the military household of so vigorous a general). "Natacha, there is not an hour that I can call truly good if I spend it away from you, dear, dear Natacha."

"I ask you seriously if you have passed a good night?"

She touched his hand a moment and looked into his eyes, but he shook his head.

"What did you do last night after you reached home?" she demanded insistently. "Did you stay up?"

"I obeyed you; I only sat a half-hour by the window looking over here at the villa, and then I went to bed."

"Yes, it is necessary you should get your rest. I wish it for you as for everyone else. This feverish life is impossible. Matrena Petrovna is getting us all ill, and we shall be prostrated."

"Yesterday," said Boris, "I looked at the villa for a half-hour from my window. Dear, dear villa, dear night when I can feel you breathing, living near me. As if you had been against my heart. I could have wept because I could hear Michael snoring in his chamber. He seemed happy. At last, I heard nothing more, there was nothing more to hear but the double chorus of frogs in the pools of the island. Our pools, Natacha, are like the enchanted lakes of the Caucasus which are silent by day and sing at evening; there are innumerable throngs of frogs which sing on the same chord, some of them on a major and some on a minor. The chorus speaks from pool to pool, lamenting and moaning across the fields and gardens, and re-echoing like AEolian harps placed opposite one another."

"Do AEolian harps make so much noise, Boris?"

"You laugh? I don't find you yourself half the time. It is Michael who has changed you, and I am out of it. (Here they spoke in Russian.) I shall not be easy until I am your husband. I can't understand your manner with Michael at all."

(Here more Russian words which I do not understand.)

"Speak French; here is the gardener," said Natacha.

"I do not like the way you are managing our lives. Why do you delay our marriage? Why?"

(Russian words from Natacha. Gesture of desperation from Boris.)

"How long? You say a long time? But that says nothing—a long time. How long? A year? Two years? Ten years? Tell me, or I will kill myself at your feet. No, no; speak or I will kill Michael. On my word! Like a dog!"

"I swear to you, by the dear head of your mother, Boris, that the date of our marriage does not depend on Michael."

(Some words in Russian. Boris, a little consoled, holds her hand lingeringly to his lips.)

Conversation between Michael and Natacha in the garden:

"Well? Have you told him?"

"I ended at last by making him understand that there is not any hope. None. It is necessary to have patience. I have to have it myself."

"He is stupid and provoking."

"Stupid, no. Provoking, yes, if you wish. But you also, you are provoking."

"Natacha! Natacha!"

(Here more Russian.) As Natacha started to leave, Michael placed his hand on her shoulder, stopped her and said, looking her direct in the eyes:

"There will be a letter from Annouchka this evening, by a messenger at five o'clock." He made each syllable explicit. "Very important and requiring an immediate reply."

These notes of Rouletabille's are not followed by any commentary.

After luncheon the gentlemen played poker until half-past four, which is the "chic" hour for the promenade to the head of the island. Rouletabille had directed Matrena to start exactly at a quarter to five. He appeared in the meantime, announcing that he had just interviewed the mayor of St. Petersburg, which made Athanase laugh, who could not understand that anyone would come clear from Paris to talk with men like that. Natacha came from her chamber to join them for the promenade. Her father told her she looked too worried.

They left the villa. Rouletabille noted that the dvornicks were before the gate and that the schwitzar was at his post, from which he could detect everyone who might enter or leave the villa. Matrena pushed the rolling-chair herself. The general was radiant. He had Natacha at his right and at his left Athanase and Thaddeus. The two orderlies followed, talking with Rouletabille, who had monopolized them. The conversation turned on the devotion of Matrena Petrovna, which they placed above the finest heroic traits in the women of antiquity, and also on

Natacha's love for her father. Rouletabille made them talk.

Boris Mourazoff explained that this exceptional love was accounted for by the fact that Natacha's own mother, the general's first wife, died in giving birth to their daughter, and accordingly Feodor Feodorovitch had been both father and mother to his daughter. He had raised her with the most touching care, not permitting anyone else, when she was sick, to have the care of passing the nights by her bedside.

Natacha was seven years old when Feodor Feodorovitch was appointed governor of Orel. In the country near Orel, during the summer, the general and his daughter lived on neighborly terms near the family of old Petroff, one of the richest fur merchants in Russia. Old Petroff had a daughter, Matrena, who was magnificent to see, like a beautiful field-flower. She was always in excellent humor, never spoke ill of anyone in the neighborhood, and not only had the fine manners of a city dame but a great, simple heart, which she lavished on the little Natacha.

The child returned the affection of the beautiful Matrena, and it was on seeing them always happy to find themselves together that Trebassof dreamed of reestablishing his fireside. The nuptials were quickly arranged, and the child, when she learned that her good Matrena was to wed her papa, danced with joy. Then misfortune came only a few weeks before the ceremony. Old Petroff, who speculated on the Exchange for a long time without anyone knowing anything about it, was ruined from top to bottom. Matrena came one evening to apprise Feodor Feodorovitch of this sad news and return his pledge to him. For all response Feodor placed Natacha in Matrena's arms.

"Embrace your mother," he said to the child, and to Matrena, "From today I consider you my wife, Matrena Petrovna. You should obey me in all things. Take that reply to your father and tell him my purse is at his disposition."

The general was already, at that time, even before he had inherited the Cheremaieff, immensely rich. He had lands behind Nijni as vast as a province, and it would have been difficult to count the number of moujiks who worked for him on his property. Old Pretroff gave his daughter and did not wish to accept anything in exchange. Feodor wished to settle a large allowance on his wife; her father opposed that, and Matrena sided with him in the matter against her husband, because of Natacha. "It all belongs to the little one," she insisted. "I accept the position of her mother, but on the condition that she shall never lose a kopeck of her inheritance."

"So that," concluded Boris, "if the general died tomorrow she would be poorer than Job."

"Then the general is Matrena's sole resource," reflected Rouletabille aloud.

"I can understand her hanging onto him," said Michael Korsakoff, blowing the smoke of his yellow cigarette. "Look at her. She watches him like a treasure."

"What do you mean, Michael Nikolaievitch?" said Boris, curtly. "You believe, do you, that the devotion of Matrena Petrovna is not disinterested. You must know her very poorly to dare utter such a thought."

"I have never had that thought, Boris Alexandrovitch," replied the other in a tone curter still. "To be able to imagine that anyone who lives in the Trebassofs' home could have such a thought needs an ass's head, surely."

"We will speak of it again, Michael Nikolaievitch."

"At your pleasure, Boris Alexandrovitch."

They had exchanged these latter words tranquilly continuing their walk and negligently smoking their yellow tobacco. Rouletabille was between them. He did not regard them; he paid no attention even to their quarrel; he had eyes only for Natacha, who just now quit her place beside her father's wheel-chair and passed by them with a little nod of the head, seeming in haste to retrace the way back to the villa.

"Are you leaving us?" Boris demanded of her.

"Oh, I will rejoin you immediately. I have forgotten my umbrella."

172

"But I will go and get it for you," proposed Michael.

"No, no. I have to go to the villa; I will return right away."

She was already past them. Rouletabille, during this, looked at Matrena Petrovna, who looked at him also, turning toward the young man a visage pale as wax. But no one else noted the emotion of the good Matrena, who resumed pushing the general's wheel-chair.

Rouletabille asked the officers, "Was this arrangement because the first wife of the general, Natacha's mother, was rich?"

"No. The general, who always had his heart in his hand," said Boris, "married her for her great beauty. She was a beautiful girl of the Caucasus, of excellent family besides, that Feodor Feodorovitch had known when he was in garrison at Tiflis."

"In short," said Rouletabille, "the day that General Trebassof dies Madame Trebassof, who now possesses everything, will have nothing, and the daughter, who now has nothing, will have everything."

"Exactly that," said Michael.

"That doesn't keep Matrena Petrovna and Natacha Feodorovna from deeply loving each other," observed Boris.

The little party drew near the "Point." So far the promenade had been along pleasant open country, among the low meadows traversed by fresh streams, across which tiny bridges had been built, among bright gardens guarded by porcelain dwarfs, or in the shade of small weeds from the feet of whose trees the newly-cut grass gave a seasonal fragrance. All was reflected in the pools—which lay like glass whereon a scene-painter had cut the green hearts of the pond-lily leaves. An adorable country glimpse which seemed to have been created centuries back for the amusement of a queen and preserved, immaculately trimmed and cleaned, from generation to generation, for the eternal charm of such an hour as this on the banks of the Gulf of Finland.

Now they had reached the bank of the Gulf, and the waves rippled to the prows of the light ships, which dipped gracefully like huge and rapid sea-gulls, under the pressure of their great white sails.

Along the roadway, broader now, glided, silently and at walking pace, the double file of luxurious equipages with impatient horses, the open carriages in which the great personages of the court saw the view and let themselves be seen. Enormous coachmen held the reins high. Lively young women, negligently reclining against the cushions, displayed their new Paris toilettes, and kept young officers on horseback busy with salutes. There were all kinds of uniforms. No talking was heard. Everyone was kept busy looking. There rang in the pure, thin air only the noise of the champing bits and the tintinnabulation of the bells attached to the hairy Finnish ponies' collars. And all that, so beautiful, fresh, charming and clear, and silent, it all seemed more a dream than even that which hung in the pools, suspended between the crystal of the air and the crystal of the water. The transparence of the sky and the transparence of the gulf blended their two unrealities so that one could not note where the horizons met.

Rouletabille looked at the view and looked at the general, and in all his young vibrating soul there was a sense of infinite sadness, for he recalled those terrible words in the night: "They have gone into all the corners of the Russian land, and they have not found a single corner of that land where there are not moanings." "Well," thought he, "they have not come into this corner, apparently. I don't know anything lovelier or happier in the world." No, no, Rouletabille, they have not come here. In every country there is a corner of happy life, which the poor are ashamed to approach, which they know nothing of, and of which merely the sight would turn famished mothers enraged, with their thin bosoms, and, if it is not more beautiful than that, certainly no part of the earth is made so atrocious to live in for some, nor so happy for others as in this Scythian country, the boreal country of the world.

Meanwhile the little group about the general's rolling-chair had attracted attention. Some passers-by saluted, and the news spread quickly that General Trebassof had come for a promenade to "the Point." Heads turned as carriages passed; the general, noticing how much excitement his presence produced, begged Matrena Petrovna to push his chair into an adjacent by-path, behind a shield of trees where he would be able to enjoy the spectacle in peace.

He was found, nevertheless, by Koupriane, the Chief of Police, who was looking for him. He had gone to the datcha and been told there that the general, accompanied by his friends and the young Frenchman, had gone for a turn along the gulf. Koupriane had left his carriage at the datcha, and taken the shortest route after them.

He was a fine man, large, solid, clear-eyed. His uniform showed his fine build to advantage. He was generally liked in St. Petersburg, where his martial bearing and his well-known bravery had given him a sort of popularity in society, which, on the other hand, had great disdain for Gounsovski, the head of the Secret Police, who was known to be capable of anything underhanded and had been accused of sometimes playing into the hands of the Nihilists, whom he disguised as agents-provocateurs, without anybody really doubting it, and he had to fight against these widespread political suspicions.

Well-informed men declared that the death of the previous "prime minister," who had been blown up before Varsovie station when he was on his way to the Tsar at Peterhof, was Gounsovski's work and that in this he was the instrument of the party at court which had sworn the death of the minister which inconvenienced it. (note 1) On the other hand, everyone regarded Koupriane as incapable of participating in any such horrors and that he contented himself with honest performance of his obvious duties, confining himself to ridding the streets of its troublesome elements, and sending to Siberia as many as he could of the hot-heads,

---

1. Rumored cause of Plehve's assassination.

without lowering himself to the compromises which, more than once, had given grounds for the enemies of the empire to maintain that it was difficult to say whether the chiefs of the Russian police played the part of the law or that of the revolutionary party, even that the police had been at the end of a certain time of such mixed procedure hardly able to decide themselves which they did.

This afternoon Koupriane appeared very nervous. He paid his compliments to the general, grumbled at his imprudence, praised him for his bravery, and then at once picked out Rouletabille, whom he took aside to talk to.

"You have sent my men back to me," said he to the young reporter. "You understand that I do not allow that. They are furious, and quite rightly. You have given publicly as explanation of their departure—a departure which has naturally astonished, stupefied the general's friends—the suspicion of their possible participation in the last attack. That is abominable, and I will not permit it. My men have not been trained in the methods of Gounsovski, and it does them a cruel injury, which I resent, for that matter, personally, to treat them this way. But let that go, as a matter of sentiment, and return to the simple fact itself, which proves your excessive imprudence, not to say more, and which involves you, you alone, in a responsibility of which you certainly have not measured the importance. All in all, I consider that you have strangely abused the complete authority that I gave you upon the Emperor's orders. When I learned what you had done I went to find the Tsar, as was my duty, and told him the whole thing. He was more astonished than can be expressed. He directed me to go myself to find out just how things were and to furnish the general the guard you had removed. I arrive at the isles and not only find the villa open like a mill where anyone may enter, but I am informed, and then I see, that the general is promenading in the midst of the crowd, at the mercy of the first miserable venturer. Monsieur Rouletabille, I am not satisfied. The Tsar is not satisfied. And, within an hour, my men will return to assume their guard at the datcha."

Rouletabille listened to the end. No one ever had spoken to him in that tone. He was red, and as ready to burst as a child's balloon blown too hard. He said:

"And I will take the train this evening."

"You will go?"

"Yes, and you can guard your general all alone. I have had enough of it. Ah, you are not satisfied! Ah, the Tsar is not satisfied! It is too bad. No more of it for me. Monsieur, I am not satisfied, and I say Good-evening to you. Only do not forget to send me from here every three or four days a letter which will keep me informed of the health of the general, whom I love dearly. I will offer up a little prayer for him."

Thereupon he was silent, for he caught the glance of Matrena Petrovna, a glance so desolated, so imploring, so desperate, that the poor woman inspired him anew with great pity. Natacha had not returned. What was the young girl doing at that moment? If Matrena really loved Natacha she must be suffering atrociously. Koupriane spoke; Rouletabille did not hear him, and he had already forgotten his own anger. His spirit was wrapped in the mystery.

"Monsieur," Koupriane finished by saying, tugging his sleeve, "do you hear me? I pray you at least reply to me. I offer all possible excuses for speaking to you in that tone. I reiterate them. I ask your pardon. I pray you to explain your conduct, which appeared imprudent to me but which, after all, should have some reason. I have to explain to the Emperor. Will you tell me? What ought I to say to the Emperor?"

"Nothing at all," said Rouletabille. "I have no explanation to give you or the Emperor, or to anyone. You can offer him my utmost homage and do me the kindness to vise my passport for this evening."

And he sighed:

"It is too bad, for we were just about to see something interesting."

Koupriane looked at him. Rouletabille had not quitted Matrena Petrovna's eyes, and her pallor struck Koupriane.

"Just a minute," continued the young man. "I'm sure there is someone who will miss me—that brave woman there. Ask her which she prefers, all your police, or her dear little domovoi. We are good friends already. And—don't forget to present my condolences to her when the terrible moment has come."

It was Koupriane's turn to be troubled.

He coughed and said:

"You believe, then, that the general runs a great immediate danger?"

"I do not only believe it, monsieur, I am sure of it. His death is a matter of hours for the poor dear man. Before I go I shall not fail to tell him, so that he can prepare himself comfortably for the great journey and ask pardon of the Lord for the rather heavy hand he has laid on these poor men of Presnia."

"Monsieur Rouletabille, have you discovered something?"

"Good Lord, yes, I have discovered something, Monsieur Koupriane. You don't suppose I have come so far to waste my time, do you?"

"Something no one else knows?"

"Yes, Monsieur Koupriane, otherwise I shouldn't have troubled to feel concerned. Something I have not confided to anyone, not even to my note-book, because a note-book, you know, a note-book can always be lost. I just mention that in case you had any idea of having me searched before my departure."

"Oh, Monsieur Rouletabille!"

"Eh, eh, like the way the police do in your country; in mine too, for that matter. Yes, that's often enough seen. The police, furious because they can't hit a clue in some case that interests them, arrest a reporter who knows more than they do, in order to make him talk. But—nothing of that sort with me, monsieur. You might have me taken to your famous 'Terrible Section,' I'd not open my mouth, not even in the famous rocking-chair, not even under the blows of clenched fists."

"Monsieur Rouletabille, what do you take us for? You are the guest of the Tsar."

"Ah, I have the word of an honest man. Very well, I will treat you as an honest man. I will tell you what I have discovered. I don't wish through any false pride to keep you in darkness about something which may perhaps—I say perhaps—permit you to save the general."

"Tell me. I am listening."

"But it is perfectly understood that once I have told you this you will give me my passport and allow me to depart?"

"You feel that you couldn't possibly," inquired Koupriane, more and more troubled, and after a moment of hesitation, "you couldn't possibly tell me that and yet remain?"

"No, monsieur. From the moment you place me under the necessity of explaining each of my movements and each of my acts, I prefer to go and leave to you that 'responsibility' of which you spoke just now, my dear Monsieur Koupriane."

Astonished and disquieted by this long conversation between Rouletabille and the Head of Police, Matrena Petrovna continually turned upon them her anguished glance, which always insensibly softened as it rested on Rouletabille. Koupriane read there all the hope that the brave woman had in the young reporter, and he read also in Rouletabille's eye all the extraordinary confidence that the mere boy had in himself. As a last consideration had he not already something in hand in circumstances where all the police of the world had admitted themselves vanquished? Koupriane pressed Rouletabille's hand and said just one word to him:

"Remain."

Having saluted the general and Matrena affectionately, and a group of friends in one courteous sweep, he departed, with thoughtful brow.

During all this time the general, enchanted with the promenade, told stories of the Caucasus to his friends, believing himself young again and re-living his nights as sub-lieutenant at Tills. As to Natacha, no one had seen her. They retraced the way to the villa along deserted by-paths. Koupriane's call made occasion for Athanase Georgevitch and Thaddeus, and the two officers also, to say that he was the only honest man in all the Russian police, and that Matrena Petrovna was a great woman to have dared rid herself of the entire clique of agents, who are often more revolutionary than the Nihilists themselves. Thus they arrived at the datcha.

The general inquired for Natacha, not understanding why she had left him thus during his first venture out. The schwitzar replied that the young mistress had returned to the house and had left again about a quarter of an hour later, taking the way that the party had gone on their promenade, and he had not seen her since.

Boris spoke up:

"She must have passed on the other side of the carriages while we were behind the trees, general, and not seeing us she has gone on her way, making the round of the island, over as far as the Barque."

The explanation seemed the most plausible one.

"Has anyone else been here?" demanded Matrena, forcing her voice to be calm. Rouletabille saw her hand tremble on the handle of the rolling-chair, which she had not quitted for a second during all the promenade, refusing aid from the officers, the friends, and even from Rouletabille.

"First there came the Head of Police, who told me he would go and find you, Barinia, and right after, His Excellency the Marshal of the Court. His Excellency will return, although he is very pressed for time, before he takes the train at seven o'clock for Krasnoie-Coelo."

All this had been said in Russian, naturally, but Matrena translated the words of the schwitzar into French in a low voice for Rouletabille, who was near her. The general during this time had taken Rouletabille's hand and pressed it affectionately, as if, in that mute way, to thank him for all the young man had done for them. Feodor himself also had confidence, and he was grateful for the freer air that he was being allowed to breathe. It seemed to him that he was emerging from prison. Nevertheless, as the promenade had been a little fatiguing, Matrena ordered him to go and rest immediately. Athanase and Thaddeus took their leave. The two officers were already at the end of the garden, talking coldly, and almost confronting one another, like wooden soldiers. Without doubt they were arranging the conditions of an encounter to settle their little difference at once.

The schwitzar gathered the general into his great arms and carried him into the veranda. Feodor demanded five minutes' respite before he was taken upstairs to his chamber. Matrena Petrovna had a light luncheon brought at his request. In truth, the good woman trembled with impatience and hardly dared move without consulting Rouletabille's face. While the general talked with Ermolai, who passed him his tea, Rouletabille made a sign to Matrena that she understood at once. She joined the young man in the drawing-room.

"Madame," he said rapidly, in a low voice, "you must go at once to see what has happened there."

He pointed to the dining-room.

"Very well."

It was pitiful to watch her.

"Go, madame, with courage."

"Why don't you come with me?"

"Because, madame, I have something to do elsewhere. Give me the keys of the next floor."

"No, no. What for?"

"Not a second's delay, for the love of Heaven. Do what I tell you on your side, and let me do mine. The keys! Come, the keys!"

He snatched them rather than took them, and pointed a last time to the dining-room with a gesture so commanding that she did not hesitate further. She entered the dining-room, shaking, while he bounded to the upper floor. He was not long. He took only time to open the doors, throw a glance into the general's chamber, a single glance, and to return, letting a cry of joy escape him, borrowed from his new and very limited accomplishment of Russian, "Caracho!"

How Rouletabille, who had not spent half a second examining the general's chamber, was able to be certain that all went well on that side, when it took Matrena—and that how many times a day!—at least a quarter of an hour of ferreting in all the corners each time she explored her house before she was even inadequately reassured, was a question. If that dear heroic woman had been with him during this "instant information" she would have received such a shock that, with all confidence gone, she would have sent for Koupriane immediately, and all his agents, reinforced by the personnel of the Okrana (Secret Police). Rouletabille at once rejoined the general, whistling. Feodor and Ermolai were deep in conversation about the Orel country. The young man did not disturb them. Then, soon, Matrena reappeared. He saw her come in quite radiant. He handed back her keys, and she took them mechanically. She was overjoyed and did not try to hide it. The general himself noticed it, and asked what had made her so.

"It is my happiness over our first promenade since we arrived at the datcha des Iles," she explained. "And now you must go upstairs to bed, Feodor. You will pass a good night, I am sure."

"I can sleep only if you sleep, Matrena."

"I promise you. It is quite possible now that we have our dear little domovoi. You know, Feodor, that he smokes his pipe just like the dear little porcelain domovoi."

"He does resemble him, he certainly does," said Feodor. "That makes us feel happy, but I wish him to sleep also."

"Yes, yes," smiled Rouletabille, "everybody will sleep here. That is the countersign. We have watched enough. Since the police are gone we can all sleep, believe me, general."

"Eh, eh, I believe you, on my word, easily enough. There were only they in the house capable of attempting that affair of the bouquet. I have thought that all out, and now I am at ease. And anyway, whatever happens, it is necessary to get sleep, isn't it? The chances of war! Nichevo!" He pressed Rouletabille's hand, and Matrena Petrovna took, as was her habit, Feodor Feodorovitch on her back and lugged him to his chamber. In that also she refused aid from anyone. The general clung to his wife's neck during the ascent and laughed like a child. Rouletabille remained in the hallway, watching the garden attentively. Ermolai walked out of the villa and crossed the garden, going to meet a personage in uniform whom the young man recognized immediately as the grand-marshal of the court, who had introduced him to the Tsar.

Ermolai informed him that Madame Matrena was engaged in helping her husband retire, and the marshal remained at the end of the garden where he had found Michael and Boris talking in the kiosque. All three remained there for some time in conversation, standing by a table where General and Madame Trebassof sometimes dined when they had no guests. As they talked the marshal played with a box of white cardboard tied with a pink string. At this moment Matrena, who had not been able to resist the desire to talk for a moment with Rouletabille and tell him how happy she was, rejoined the young man.

"Little domovoi," said she, laying her hand on his shoulder, "you have not watched on this side?"

She pointed in her turn to the dining-room.

"No, no. You have seen it, madame, and I am sufficiently informed."

"Perfectly. There is nothing. No one has worked there! No one has touched the board. I knew it. I am sure of it. It is dreadful what we have thought about it! Oh, you do not know how relieved and happy I am. Ah, Natacha, Natacha, I have not loved you in vain. (She pronounced these words in accents of great beauty and tragic sincerity.) When I saw her leave us, my dear, ah, my legs sank under me. When she said, 'I have forgotten something; I must hurry back,' I felt I had not the strength to go a single step. But now I certainly am happy, that weight at least is off my heart, off my heart, dear little domovoi, because of you, because of you."

She embraced him, and then ran away, like one possessed, to resume her post near the general.

Notes in Rouletabille's memorandum-book:
The affair of the little cavity under the
floor not having been touched again proves
nothing for or against Natacha (even though
that excellent Matrena Petrovna thinks
so). Natacha could very well have been
warned by the too great care with which
Madame Matrena watched the floor. My
opinion, since I saw Matrena lift the carpet
the first time without any real precaution,
is that they have definitely abandoned the
preparation of that attack and are trying
to account for the secret becoming known.
What Matrena feels so sure of is that the
trap I laid by the promenade to the Point
was against Natacha particularly. I knew
beforehand that Natacha would absent
herself during the promenade. I'm not
looking for anything new from Natacha, but
what I did need was to be sure that Matrena
didn't detest Natacha, and that she had not
faked the preparations for an attack under
the floor in such a way as to throw almost

certain suspicion on her step-daughter. I am sure about that now. Matrena is innocent of such a thing, the poor dear soul. If Matrena had been a monster the occasion was too good. Natacha's absence, her solitary presence for a quarter of an hour in the empty villa, all would have urged Matrena, whom I sent alone to search under the carpet in the dining-room, to draw the last nails from the board if she was really guilty of having drawn the others. Natacha would have been lost then! Matrena returned sincerely, tragically happy at not having found anything new, and now I have the material proof that I needed. Morally and physically Matrena is removed from it. So I am going to speak to her about the hat-pin. I believe that the matter is urgent on that side rather than on the side of the nails in the floor.

VI

THE MYSTERIOUS HAND

After the departure of Matrena, Rouletabille turned his attention to the garden. Neither the marshal of the court nor the officers were there any longer. The three men had disappeared. Rouletabille wished to know at once where they had gone. He went rapidly to the gate, named the officers and the marshal to Ermolai, and Ermolai made a sign that they had passed out. Even as he spoke he saw the marshal's carriage disappear around a corner of the road. As to the two officers, they were nowhere on the roadway. He was surprised that the marshal should have gone without seeing Matrena or the general or himself, and, above all, he was disquieted by the disappearance of the orderlies. He gathered from the gestures of Ermolai that they had passed before the lodge only a few minutes after the marshal's departure. They had gone together. Rouletabille set himself to follow them, traced their steps in the soft earth of the roadway and soon they crossed onto the grass. At this point the tracks through the massed ferns became very difficult to follow. He hurried along, bending close to the ground over such traces as he could see, which continually led him astray, but which conducted him finally to the thing that he sought. A noise of voices made him raise his head and then throw himself behind a tree. Not twenty steps from him Natacha and Boris were having an animated conversation. The young officer held himself erect directly in front of her, frowning and impatient. Under the uniform cloak that he had wrapped about him without having bothered to use the sleeves, which were tossed up over his chest, Boris had his arms crossed. His entire attitude indicated hauteur, coldness and disdain for what he was hearing. Natacha never appeared calmer or more mistress of herself. She talked to him rapidly and mostly in a low voice. Sometimes a word in Russian sounded, and then she resumed her care to speak low. Finally she ceased, and Boris, after a short silence, in which he had seemed to reflect deeply, pronounced distinctly these words in French, pronouncing them syllable by syllable, as though to give them additional force:

"You ask a frightful thing of me."

"It is necessary to grant it to me," said the young girl with singular energy. "You understand, Boris Alexandrovitch! It is necessary."

Her gaze, after she had glanced penetratingly all around her and discovered nothing suspicious, rested tenderly on the young officer, while she murmured, "My Boris!"

The young man could not resist either the sweetness of that voice, nor the captivating charm of that glance. He took the hand she extended toward him and kissed it passionately. His eyes, fixed on Natacha, proclaimed that he granted everything that she wished and admitted himself vanquished. Then she said, always with that adorable gaze upon him, "This evening!" He replied, "Yes, yes. This evening! This evening!" upon which Natacha withdrew her hand and made a sign to the officer to leave, which he promptly obeyed. Natacha remained there still a long time, plunged in thought. Rouletabille had already taken the road back to the villa. Matrena Petrovna was watching for his return, seated on the first step of the landing on the great staircase which ran up from the veranda. When she saw him she ran to him. He had already reached the dining-room.

"Anyone in the house?" he asked.

"No one. Natacha has not returned, and. . ."

"Your step-daughter is coming in now. Ask her where she has been, if she has seen the orderlies, and if they said they would return this evening, in case she answers that she has seen them."

"Very well, little domovoi doukh. The orderlies left without my seeing when they went."

"Ah," interrupted Rouletabille, "before she arrives, give me all her hat-pins."

"What!"

"I say, all her hat-pins. Quickly!"

Matrena ran to Natacha's chamber and returned with three enormous hat-pins with beautifully-cut stones in them.

"These are all?"

"They are all I have found. I know she has two others. She has one on her head, or two, perhaps; I can't find them."

"Take these back where you found them," said the reporter, after glancing at them.

Matrena returned immediately, not understanding what he was doing.

"And now, your hat-pins. Yes, your hat-pins."

"Oh, I have only two, and here they are," said she, drawing them from the toque she had been wearing and had thrown on the sofa when she re-entered the house.

Rouletabille gave hers the same inspection.

"Thanks. Here is your step-daughter."

Natacha entered, flushed and smiling.

"Ah, well," said she, quite breathless, "you may boast that I had to search for you. I made the entire round, clear past the Barque. Has the promenade done papa good?"

"Yes, he is asleep," replied Matrena. "Have you met Boris and Michael?"

She appeared to hesitate a second, then replied:

"Yes, for an instant."

"Did they say whether they would return this evening?"

"No," she replied, slightly troubled. "Why all these questions?"

She flushed still more.

"Because I thought it strange," parried Matrena, "that they went away as they did, without saying goodby, without a word, without inquiring if the general needed them. There is something stranger yet. Did you see Kaltsof with them, the grand-marshal of the court?"

"No."

"Kaltsof came for a moment, entered the garden and went away again without seeing us, without saying even a word to the general."

"Ah," said Natacha.

With apparent indifference, she raised her arms and drew out her hat-pins. Rouletabille watched the pin without a word. The young girl hardly seemed aware of their presence. Entirely absorbed in strange thoughts, she replaced the pin in her hat and went to hang it in the veranda, which served also as vestibule. Rouletabille never quitted her eyes. Matrena watched the reporter with a stupid glance. Natacha crossed the drawing-room and entered her chamber by passing through her little sitting-room, through which all entrance to her chamber had to be made. That little room, though, had three doors. One opened into Natacha's chamber, one into the drawing-room, and the third into the little passage in a corner of the house where was the stairway by which the servants passed from the kitchens to the ground-floor and the upper floor. This passage had also a door giving directly upon the drawing-room. It was certainly a poor arrangement for serving the dining-room, which was on the other side of the drawing-room and behind the veranda, such a chance laying-out of a house as one often sees in the off-hand planning of many places in the country.

Alone again with Rouletabille, Matrena noticed that he had not lost sight of the corner of the veranda where Natacha had hung her hat. Beside this hat there was a toque that Ermolai had brought in. The old servant had found it in some corner of the garden or the conservatory where he had been. A hat-pin stuck out of that toque also.

"Whose toque is that?" asked Rouletabille. "I haven't seen it on the head of anyone here."

"It is Natacha's," replied Matrena.

She moved toward it, but the young man held her back, went into the veranda himself, and, without touching it, standing on tiptoe, he examined the pin. He sank back on his heels and turned toward Matrena. She caught a glimpse of fleeting emotion on the face of her little friend.

"Explain to me," she said.

But he gave her a glance that frightened her, and said low:

"Go and give orders right away that dinner be served in the veranda. All through dinner it is absolutely necessary that the door of Natacha's sitting-room, and that of the stairway passage, and that of the veranda giving on the drawing-room remain open all the time. Do you understand me? As soon as you have given your orders go to the general's chamber and do not quit the general's bedside, keep it in view. Come down to dinner when it is announced, and do not bother yourself about anything further."

So saying, he filled his pipe, lighted it with a sort of sigh of relief, and, after a final order to Matrena, "Go," he went into the garden, puffing great clouds. Anyone would have said he hadn't smoked in a week. He appeared not to be thinking but just idly enjoying himself. In fact, he played like a child with Milinki,

Matrena's pet cat, which he pursued behind the shrubs, up into the little kiosque which, raised on piles, lifted its steep thatched roof above the panorama of the isles that Rouletabille settled down to contemplate like an artist with ample leisure.

The dinner, where Matrena, Natacha and Rouletabille were together again, was lively. The young man having declared that he was more and more convinced that the mystery of the bomb in the bouquet was simply a play of the police, Natacha reinforced his opinion, and following that they found themselves in agreement on about everything else. For himself, the reporter during that conversation hid a real horror which had seized him at the cynical and inappropriate tranquillity with which the young lady received all suggestions that accused the police or that assumed the general no longer ran any immediate danger. In short, he worked, or at least believed he

214

worked, to clear Natacha as he had cleared Matrena, so that there would develop the absolute necessity of assuming a third person's intervention in the facts disclosed so clearly by Koupriane where Matrena or Natacha seemed alone to be possible agents. As he listened to Natacha Rouletabille commenced to doubt and quake just as he had seen Matrena do. The more he looked into the nature of Natacha the dizzier he grew. What abysmal obscurities were there in her nature!

Nothing interesting happened during dinner. Several times, in spite of Rouletabille's obvious impatience with her for doing it, Matrena went up to the general. She returned saying, "He is quiet. He doesn't sleep. He doesn't wish anything. He has asked me to prepare his narcotic. It is too bad. He has tried in vain, he cannot get along without it."

"You, too, mamma, ought to take something to make you sleep. They say morphine is very good."

"As for me," said Rouletabille, whose head for some few minutes had been dropping now toward one shoulder and now toward another, "I have no need of any narcotic to make me sleep. If you will permit me, I will get to bed at once."

"Eh, my little domovoi doukh, I am going to carry you there in my arms."

Matrena extended her large round arms ready to take Rouletabille as though he had been a baby.

"No, no. I will get up there all right alone," said Rouletabille, rising stupidly and appearing ashamed of his excessive sleepiness.

"Oh, well, let us both accompany him to his chamber," said Natacha, "and I will wish papa good-night. I'm eager for bed myself. We will all make a good night of it. Ermolai and Gniagnia will watch with the schwitzar in the lodge. Things are reasonably arranged now."

They all ascended the stairs. Rouletabille did not even go to see the general, but threw himself on his bed. Natacha got onto the bed beside her father, embraced him a dozen times, and went downstairs again. Matrena followed behind her, closed doors and windows, went upstairs again to close the door of the landing-place and found Rouletabille seated on his bed, his arms crossed, not appearing to have any desire for sleep at all. His face was so strangely pensive also that the anxiety of Matrena, who had been able to make nothing out of his acts and looks all day, came back upon her instantly in greater force than ever. She touched his arm in order to be sure that he knew she was there.

"My little friend," she said, "will you tell me now?"

"Yes, madame," he replied at once. "Sit in that chair and listen to me. There are things you must know at once, because we have reached a dangerous hour."

"The hat-pins first. The hat-pins!"

Rouletabille rose lightly from the bed and, facing her, but watching something besides her, said:

"It is necessary you should know that someone almost immediately is going to renew the attempt of the bouquet."

Matrena sprang to her feet as quickly as though she had been told there was a bomb in the seat of her chair. She made herself sit down again, however, in obedience to Rouletabille's urgent look commanding absolute quiet.

"Renew the attempt of the bouquet!" she murmured in a stifled voice. "But there is not a flower in the general's chamber."

"Be calm, madame. Understand me and answer me: You heard the tick-tack from the bouquet while you were in your own chamber?"

"Yes, with the doors open, naturally."

"You told me the persons who came to say good-night to the general. At that time there was no noise of tick-tack?"

"No, no."

"Do you think that if there had been any tick-tack then you would have heard it, with all those persons talking in the room?"

"I hear everything. I hear everything."

"Did you go downstairs at the same time those people did?"

"No, no; I remained near the general for some time, until he was sound asleep."

"And you heard nothing?"

"Nothing."

"You closed the doors behind those persons?"

"Yes, the door to the great staircase. The door of the servants' stairway was condemned a long time ago; it has been locked by me, I alone have the key and on the inside of the door opening into the general's chamber there is also a bolt which is always shot. All the other doors of the chambers have been condemned by me. In order to enter any of the four rooms on this floor it is necessary now to pass by the door of my chamber, which gives on the main staircase."

"Perfect. Then, no one has been able to enter the apartment. No one had been in the apartment for at least two hours excepting you and the general, when you heard the clockwork. From that the only conclusion is that only the general and you could have started it going."

"What are you trying to say?" Matrena demanded, astounded.

"I wish to prove to you by this absurd conclusion, madame, that it is necessary never—never, you understand? Never— to reason solely upon even the most evident external evidence when those seemingly-conclusive appearances are in conflict with certain moral truths that also are clear as the light of day. The light of day for me, madame, is that the general does not desire to commit suicide and, above all, that he would not choose the strange method of suicide by clockwork. The light of day for me is that you adore your husband and that you are ready to sacrifice your life for his."

"Now!" exclaimed Matrena, whose tears, always ready in emotional moments, flowed freely. "But, Holy Mary, why do you speak to me without looking at me? What is it? What is it?"

"Don't turn! Don't make a movement! You hear—not a move! And speak low, very low. And don't cry, for the love of God!"

"But you say at once... the bouquet! Come to the general's room!"

222

"Not a move. And continue listening to me without interrupting," said he, still inclining his ear, and still without looking at her. "It is because these things were as the light of day to me that I say to myself, 'It is impossible that it should be impossible for a third person not to have placed the bomb in the bouquet. Someone is able to enter the general's chamber even when the general is watching and all the doors are locked.'"

"Oh, no. No one could possibly enter. I swear it to you."

As she swore it a little too loudly, Rouletabille seized her arm so that she almost cried out, but she understood instantly that it was to keep her quiet.

"I tell you not to interrupt me, once for all."

"But, then, tell me what you are looking at like that."

"I am watching the corner where someone is going to enter the general's chamber when everything is locked, madame. Do not move!"

Matrena, her teeth chattering, recalled that when she entered Rouletabille's chamber she had found all the doors open that communicated with the chain of rooms: the young man's chamber with hers, the dressing-room and the general's chamber. She tried, under Rouletabille's look, to keep calm, but in spite of all the reporter's exhortations she could not hold her tongue.

"But which way? Where will they enter?"

"By the door."

"Which door?"

"That of the chamber giving on the servants' stair-way."

"Why, how? The key! The bolt!"

"They have made a key."

"But the bolt is drawn this side."

"They will draw it back from the other side."

"What! That is impossible."

Rouletabille laid his two hands on Matrena's strong shoulders and repeated, detaching each syllable, "They will draw it back from the other side."

"It is impossible. I repeat it."

"Madame, your Nihilists haven't invented anything. It is a trick much in vogue with sneak thieves in hotels. All it needs is a little hole the size of a pin bored in the panel of the door above the bolt."

"God!" quavered Matrena. "I don't understand what you mean by your little hole. Explain to me, little domovoi."

"Follow me carefully, then," continued Rouletabille, his eyes all the time fixed elsewhere. "The person who wishes to enter sticks through the hole a brass wire that he has already given the necessary curve to and which is fitted on its end with a light point of steel curved inward. With such an instrument it is child's play, if the hole has been made where it ought to be, to touch the bolt on the inside from the outside, pick the knob on it, withdraw it, and open the door if the bolt is like this one, a small door-bolt."

"Oh, oh, oh," moaned Matrena, who paled visibly. "And that hole?"

"It exists."

"You have discovered it?"

"Yes, the first hour I was here."

"Oh, domovoi! But how did you do that when you never entered the general's chamber until tonight?"

"Doubtless, but I went up that servants' staircase much earlier than that. And I will tell you why. When I was brought into the villa the first time, and you watched me, bidden behind the door, do you know what I was watching myself, while I appeared to be solely occupied digging out the caviare? The fresh print of boot-nails which left the carpet near the table, where someone had spilled beer (the beer was still running down the cloth). Someone had stepped in the beer. The boot-print was not clearly visible excepting there. But from there it went to the door of the servants' stairway and mounted the stairs. That boot was too fine to be mounting a stairway reserved to servants and that Koupriane told me had been condemned, and it was that made me notice it in a moment; but just then you entered."

"You never told me anything about it. Of course if I had known there was a boot-print. . ."

"I didn't tell you anything about it because I had my reasons for that, and, anyway, the trace dried while I was telling you about my journey."

"Ah, why not have told me later?"

"Because I didn't know you yet."

"Subtle devil! You will kill me. I can no longer. . . Let us go into the general's chamber. We will wake him."

"Remain here. Remain here. I have not told you anything. That boot-print preoccupied me, and later, when I could get away from the dining-room, I was not easy until I had climbed that stairway myself and gone to see that door, where I discovered what I have just told you and what I am going to tell you now."

"What? What? In all you have said there has been nothing about the hat-pins."

"We have come to them now."

"And the bouquet attack, which is going to happen again? Why? Why?"

"This is it. When this evening you let me go to the general's chamber, I examined the bolt of the door without your suspecting it. My opinion was confirmed. It was that way that the bomb was brought, and it is by that way that someone has prepared to return."

"But how? You are sure the little hole is the way someone came? But what makes you think that is how they mean to return? You know well enough that, not having succeeded in the general's chamber, they are at work in the dining-room."

"Madame, it is probable, it is certain that they have given up the work in the dining-room since they have commenced this very day working again in the general's chamber. Yes, someone returned, returned that way, and I was so sure of that, of the forthcoming return, that I removed the police in order to be able to study everything more at my ease. Do you understand now my confidence and why I have been able to assume so heavy a responsibility? It is because I knew I had only one thing to watch: one little hat-pin. It is not difficult, madame, to watch a single little hat-pin."

"A mistake," said Matrena, in a low voice. "Miserable little domovoi who told me nothing, me whom you let go to sleep on my mattress, in front of that door that might open any moment."

"No, madame. For I was behind it!"

"Ah, dear little holy angel! But what were you thinking of! That door has not been watched this afternoon. In our absence it could have been opened. If someone has placed a bomb during our absence!"

"That is why I sent you at once in to the dining-room on that search that I thought would be fruitless, dear madame. And that is why I hurried upstairs to the bedroom. I went to the stairway door instantly. I had prepared for proof positive if anyone had pushed it open even half a millimeter. No, no one had touched the door in our absence.

"Ah, dear heroic little friend of Jesus! But listen to me. Listen to me, my angel. Ah, I don't know where I am or what I say. My brain is no more than a flabby balloon punctured with pins, with little holes of hat-pins. Tell me about the hat-pins. Right off! No, at first, what is it that makes you believe—good God!—that someone will return by that door? How can you see that, all that, in a poor little hat-pin?"

"Madame, it is not a single hat-pin hole; there are two of them.

"Two hat-pin holes?"

"Yes, two. An old one and a new one. One quite new. Why this second hole? Because the old one was judged a little too narrow and they wished to enlarge it, and in enlarging it they broke off the point of a hat-pin in it. Madame, the point is there yet, filling up the little old hole and the piece of metal is very sharp and very bright."

"Now I understand the examination of the hat-pins. Then it is so easy as that to get through a door with a hat-pin?"

"Nothing easier, especially if the panel is of pine. Sometimes one happens to break the point of a pin in the first hole. Then of necessity one makes a second. In order to commence the second hole, the point of the pin being broken, they have used the point of a pen-knife, then have finished the hole with the hat-pin. The second hole is still nearer the bolt than the first one. Don't move like that, madame."

"But they are going to come! They are going to come!"

"I believe so."

"But I can't understand how you can remain so quiet with such a certainty. Great heavens! what proof have you that they have not been there already?"

"Just an ordinary pin, madame, not a hat-pin this time. Don't confuse the pins. I will show you in a little while."

"He will drive me distracted with his pins, dear light of my eyes! Bounty of Heaven! God's envoy! Dear little happiness-bearer!"

In her transport she tried to take him in her trembling arms, but he waved her back. She caught her breath and resumed:

"Did the examination of all the hat-pins tell you anything?"

"Yes. The fifth hat-pin of Mademoiselle Natacha's, the one in the toque out in the veranda, has the tip newly broken off."

234

"O misery!" cried Matrena, crumpling in her chair.

Rouletabille raised her.

"What would you have? I have examined your own hat-pins. Do you think I would have suspected you if I had found one of them broken? I would simply have thought that someone had used your property for an abominable purpose, that is all."

"Oh, that is true, that is true. Pardon me. Mother of Christ, this boy crazes me! He consoles me and he horrifies me. He makes me think of such dreadful things, and then he reassures me. He does what he wishes with me. What should I become without him?"

And this time she succeeded in taking his head in her two hands and kissing him passionately. Rouletabille pushed her back roughly.

"You keep me from seeing," he said.

She was in tears over his rebuff. She understood now. Rouletabille during all this conversation had not ceased to watch through the open doors of Matrena's room and the dressing-room the farther fatal door whose brass bolt shone in the yellow light of the night-lamp.

At last he made her a sign and the reporter, followed by Matrena, advanced on tip-toe to the threshold of the general's chamber, keeping close to the wall. Feodor Feodorovitch slept. They heard his heavy breath, but he appeared to be enjoying peaceful sleep. The horrors of the night before had fled. Matrena was perhaps right in attributing the nightmares to the narcotic prepared for him each night, for the glass from which he drank it when he felt he could not sleep was still full and obviously had not been touched. The bed of the general was so placed that whoever occupied it, even if they were wide awake, could not see the door giving on the servants' stairway. The little table where the glass and various phials were placed and which had borne the dangerous bouquet, was placed near the bed, a little back of it, and nearer the door. Nothing would have been easier than for someone who could open the door to stretch an arm and place the infernal machine among the wild flowers, above all, as could easily be believed, if he had waited for that treachery until the heavy breathing of the general told them outside that he was fast asleep, and if, looking through the key-hole, he had made sure Matrena was occupied in her own chamber. Rouletabille, at the threshold, glided to one side, out of the line of view from the hole, and got down on all fours. He crawled toward the door. With his head to the floor he made sure that the little ordinary pin which he had placed on guard that evening, stuck in the floor against the door, was still erect, having thus additional proof that the door had not been moved. In any other case the pin would have lain flat on the floor. He crept back, rose to his feet, passed into the dressing-room and, in a corner, had a rapid conversation in a low voice with Matrena.

"You will go," said he, "and take your mattress into the corner of the dressing-room where you can still see the door but no one can see you by looking through the key-hole. Do that quite naturally, and then go to your rest. I will pass the night on the mattress, and I beg you to believe that I will be more comfortable there than on a bed of staircase wood where I spent the night last night, behind the door."

"Yes, but you will fall asleep. I don't wish that."

"What are you thinking, madame?"

"I don't wish it. I don't wish it. I don't wish to quit the door where the eye is. And since I'm not able to sleep, let me watch."

He did not insist, and they crouched together on the mattress. Rouletabille was squatted like a tailor at work; but Matrena remained on all-fours, her jaw out, her eyes fixed, like a bulldog ready to spring. The minutes passed by in profound silence, broken only by the irregular breathing and puffing of the general. His face stood out pallid and tragic on the pillow; his mouth was open and, at times, the lips moved. There was fear at any moment of nightmare or his awakening. Unconsciously he threw an arm over toward the table where the glass of narcotic stood. Then he lay still again and snored lightly.

The night-lamp on the mantelpiece caught queer yellow reflections from the corners of the furniture, from the gilded frame of a picture on the wall and from the phials and glasses on the table. But in all the chamber Matrena Petrovna saw nothing, thought of nothing but the brass bolt which shone there on the door. Tired of being on her knees, she shifted, her chin in her hands, her gaze steadily fixed. As time passed and nothing happened she heaved a sigh. She could not have said whether she hoped for or dreaded the coming of that something new which Rouletabille had indicated. Rouletabille felt her shiver with anguish and impatience.

As for him, he had not hoped that anything would come to pass until toward dawn, the moment, as everyone knows, when deep sleep is most apt to vanquish all watchfulness and all insomnia. And as he waited for that moment he had not budged any more than a Chinese ape or the dear little porcelain domovoi doukh in the garden. Of course it might be that it was not to happen this night.

Suddenly Matrena's hand fell on Rouletabille's. His imprisoned hers so firmly that she understood she was forbidden to make the least movement. And both, with necks extended, ears erect, watched like beasts, like beasts on the scent.

Yes, yes, there had been a slight noise in the lock. A key turned, softly, softly, in the lock, and then—silence; and then another little noise, a grinding sound, a slight grating of wire, above, then on the bolt; upon the bolt which shone in the subdued glow of the night-lamp. The bolt softly, very softly, slipped slowly.

Then the door was pushed slowly, so slowly. It opened.

Through the opening the shadow of an arm stretched, an arm which held in its fingers something which shone. Rouletabille felt Matrena ready to bound. He encircled her, he pressed her in his arms, he restrained her in silence, and he had a horrible fear of hearing her suddenly shout, while the arm stretched out, almost touched the pillow on the bed where the general continued to sleep a sleep of peace such as he had not known for a long time.

VII

ARSENATE OF SODA

The mysterious hand held a phial and poured the entire contents into the potion. Then the hand withdrew as it had come, slowly, prudently, slyly, and the key turned in the lock and the bolt slipped back into place.

Like a wolf, Rouletabille, warning Matrena for a last time not to budge, gained the landing-place, bounded towards the stairs, slid down the banister right to the veranda, crossed the drawing-room like a flash, and reached the little sitting-room without having jostled a single piece of furniture. He noticed nothing, saw nothing. All around was undisturbed and silent.

The first light of dawn filtered through the blinds. He was able to make out that the only closed door was the one to Natacha's chamber. He stopped before that door, his heart beating, and listened. But no sound came to his ear. He had glided so lightly over the carpet that he was sure he had not been heard. Perhaps that door would open. He waited. In vain. It seemed to him there was nothing alive in that house except his heart. He was stifled with the horror that he glimpsed, that he almost touched, although that door remained closed. He felt along the wall in order to reach the window, and pulled aside the curtain. Window and blinds of the little room giving on the Neva were closed. The bar of iron inside was in its place. Then he went to the passage, mounted and descended the narrow servants' stairway, looked all about, in all the rooms, feeling everywhere with silent hands, assuring himself that no lock had been tampered with. On his return to the veranda, as he raised his head, he saw at the top of the main staircase a figure wan as death, a spectral apparition amid the shadows of the passing night, who leaned toward him. It was Matrena Petrovna. She came down, silent as a phantom and he no longer recognized her voice when she demanded of him, "Where? I require that you tell me. Where?"

"I have looked everywhere," he said, so low that Matrena had to come nearer to understand his whisper. "Everything is shut tight. And there is no one about."

Matrena looked at Rouletabille with all the power of her eyes, as though she would discover his inmost thoughts, but his clear glance did not waver, and she saw there was nothing he wished to hide. Then Matrena pointed her finger at Natacha's chamber.

"You have not gone in there?" she inquired.

He replied, "It is not necessary to enter there."

"I will enter there, myself, nevertheless," said she, and she set her teeth.

He barred her way with his arms spread out.

"If you hold the life of someone dear," said he, "don't go a step farther."

"But the person is in that chamber. The person is there! It is there you will find out!" And she waved him aside with a gesture as though she were sleepwalking.

To recall her to the reality of what he had said to her and to make her understand what he desired, he had to grip her wrist in the vice of his nervous hand.

"The person is not there, perhaps," he said, shaking his head. "Understand me now."

But she did not understand him. She said:

"Since the person is nowhere else, the person must be there."

But Rouletabille continued obstinately:

"No, no. Perhaps he is gone."

"Gone! And everything locked on the inside!"

"That is not a reason," he replied.

But she could not follow his thoughts any further. She wished absolutely to make her way into Natacha's chamber. The obsession of that was upon her.

"If you enter there," said he, "and if (as is most probable) you don't find what you seek there, all is lost! And as to me, I give up the whole thing."

She sank in a heap onto a chair.

"Don't despair," he murmured. "We don't know for sure yet."

She shook her poor old head dejectedly.

"We know that only she is here, since no one has been able to enter and since no one has been able to leave."

That, in truth, filled her brain, prevented her from discerning in any corner of her mind the thought of Rouletabille. Then the impossible dialogue resumed.

"I repeat that we do not know but that the person has gone," repeated the reporter, and demanded her keys.

"Foolish," she said. "What do you want them for?"

"To search outside as we have searched inside."

"Why, everything is locked on the inside!"

"Madame, once more, that is no reason that the person may not be outside."

He consumed five minutes opening the door of the veranda, so many were his precautions. She watched him impatiently.

He whispered to her:

"I am going out, but don't you lose sight of the little sitting-room. At the least movement call me; fire a revolver if you need to."

He slipped into the garden with the same precautions for silence. From the corner that she kept to, through the doors left open, Matrena could follow all the movements of the reporter and watch Natacha's chamber at the same time. The attitude of Rouletabille continued to confuse her beyond all expression. She watched what he did as if she thought him besotted. The dyernick on guard out in the roadway also watched the young man through the bars of the gate in consternation, as though he thought him a fool. Along the paths of beaten earth or cement which offered no chance for footprints Rouletabille hurried silently. Around him he noted that the grass of the lawn had not been trodden. And then he paid no more attention to his steps. He seemed to study attentively the rosy color in the east, breathing the delicacy of dawning morning in the Isles, amid the silence of the earth, which still slumbered.

Bare-headed, face thrown back, hands behind his back, eyes raised and fixed, he made a few steps, then suddenly stopped as if he had been given an electric shock. As soon as he seemed to have recovered from that shock he turned around and went a few steps back to another path, into which he advanced, straight ahead, his face high, with the same fixed look that he had had up to the time he so suddenly stopped, as if something or someone advised or warned him not to go further. He continually worked back toward the house, and thus he traversed all the paths that led from the villa, but in all these excursions he took pains not to place himself in the field of vision from Natacha's window, a restricted field because of its location just around an abutment of the building. To ascertain about this window he crept on all-fours up to the garden-edge that ran along the foot of the wall and had sufficient proof that no one had jumped out that way. Then he went to rejoin Matrena in the veranda.

"No one has come into the garden this morning," said he, "and no one has gone out of the villa into the garden. Now I am going to look outside the grounds. Wait here; I'll be back in five minutes."

He went away, knocked discreetly on the window of the lodge and waited some seconds. Ermolai came out and opened the gate for him. Matrena moved to the threshold of the little sitting-room and watched Natacha's door with horror. She felt her legs give under her, she could not stand up under the diabolic thought of such a crime. Ah, that arm, that arm! reaching out, making its way, with a little shining phial in its hand. Pains of Christ! What could there be in the damnable books over which Natacha and her companions pored that could make such abominable crimes possible? Ah, Natacha, Natacha! it was from her that she would have desired the answer, straining her almost to stifling on her rough bosom and strangling her with her own strong hand that she might not hear the response. Ah, Natacha, Natacha, whom she had loved so much! She sank to the floor, crept across the carpet to the door, and lay there, stretched like a beast, and buried her head in her arms while she wept over her daughter. Natacha, Natacha, whom she had cherished as her own child, and who did not hear her. Ah, what use that the little fellow had gone to search outside when the whole truth lay behind this door? Thinking of him, she was embarrassed lest he should find her in that animalistic posture, and she rose to her knees and worked her way over to the window that looked out upon the Neva. The angle of the slanting blinds let her see well enough what passed outside, and what she saw made her spring to her feet. Below her the reporter was going through the same incomprehensible maneuvers that she had seen him do in the garden. Three pathways led to the little road that ran along the wall of the villa by the bank of the Neva. The young man, still with his hands behind his back and with his face up, took them one after the other. In the first he stopped at the first step. He didn't take more than two steps in the second. In the third, which cut obliquely toward the right and seemed to run to the bank nearest Krestowsky Ostrow, she saw him advance slowly at first, then more quickly among the small trees and hedges. Once only he stopped and looked closely at the trunk of a tree against which he seemed to pick out something invisible, and then he continued to the bank. There he sat down on a stone and appeared to reflect, and then suddenly he cast off his jacket and trousers, picked out a certain place on the bank across from him, finished undressing and plunged into the stream. She saw at once that he swam like a porpoise, keeping beneath and showing his head from time to time, breathing, then diving below the surface again. He reached Krestowsky Ostrow in a clump of reeds. Then he disappeared. Below him, surrounded by trees, could be seen the red tiles of the villa which sheltered Boris and Michael. From that villa a person could see the window of the sitting-room in General Trebassof's residence, but not what might occur along the bank of the river just below its walls. An isvotchick drove along the distant route of Krestowsky, conveying in his carriage a company of young officers and young women who had been feasting and who sang as they rode; then deep silence ensued. Matrena's eyes searched for Rouletabille, but could not find him. How long was he going to stay hidden like that? She pressed her face against the chill window. What was she waiting for? She waited perhaps for someone to make a move on this side, for the door near her to open and the traitorous figure of The Other to appear.

A hand touched her carefully. She turned.

Rouletabille was there, his face all scarred by red scratches, without collar or neck-tie, having hastily resumed his clothes. He appeared furious as he surprised her in his disarray. She let him lead her as though she were a child. He drew her to his room and closed the door.

"Madame," he commenced, "it is impossible to work with you. Why in the world have you wept not two feet from your step-daughter's door? You and your Koupriane, you commence to make me regret the Faubourg Poissoniere, you know. Your step-daughter has certainly heard you. It is lucky that she attaches no importance at all to your nocturnal phantasmagorias, and that she has been used to them a long time. She has more sense than you, Mademoiselle Natacha has. She sleeps, or at least she pretends to sleep, which leaves everybody in peace. What reply will you give her if it happens that she asks you the reason today for your marching and counter-marching up and down the sitting-room and complains that you kept her from sleeping?"

Matrena only shook her old, old head.

"No, no, she has not heard me. I was there like a shadow, like a shadow of myself. She will never hear me. No one hears a shadow."

Rouletabille felt returning pity for her and spoke more gently.

"In any case, it is necessary, you must understand, that she should attach no more importance to what you have done tonight than to the things she knows of your doing other nights. It is not the first time, is it, that you have wandered in the sitting-room? You understand me? And tomorrow, madame, embrace her as you always have."

"No, not that," she moaned. "Never that. I could not."

"Why not?"

Matrena did not reply. She wept. He took her in his arms like a child consoling its mother.

"Don't cry. Don't cry. All is not lost. Someone did leave the villa this morning."

"Oh, little domovoi! How is that? How is that? How did you find that out?"

"Since we didn't find anything inside, it was certainly necessary to find something outside."

"And you have found it?"

"Certainly."

"The Virgin protect you!"

"SHE is with us. She will not desert us. I will even say that I believe she has a special guardianship over the Isles. She watches over them from evening to morning."

"What are you saying?"

"Certainly. You don't know what we call in France 'the watchers of the Virgin'?"

"Oh, yes, they are the webs that the dear little beasts of the good God spin between the trees and that..."

"Exactly. You understand me and you will understand further when you know that in the garden the first thing that struck me across the face as I went into it was these watchers of the Virgin spun by the dear little spiders of the good God. At first when I felt them on my face I said to myself, 'Hold on, no one has passed this way,' and so I went to search other places. The webs stopped me everywhere in the garden. But, outside the garden, they kept out of the way and let me pass undisturbed down a pathway which led to the Neva. So then I said to myself, 'Now, has the Virgin by accident overlooked her work in this pathway? Surely not. Someone has ruined it.' I found the shreds of them hanging to the bushes, and so I reached the river."

"And you threw yourself into the river, my dear angel. You swim like a little god."

"And I landed where the other landed. Yes, there were the reeds all freshly broken. And I slipped in among the bushes."

"Where to?"

"Up to the Villa Krestowsky, madame—where they both live."

"Ah, it was from there someone came?"

There was a silence between them.

She questioned:

"Boris?"

"Someone who came from the villa and who returned there. Boris or Michael, or another. They went and returned through the reeds. But in coming they used a boat; they returned by swimming."

Her customary agitation reasserted itself.

She demanded ardently:

"And you are sure that he came here and that he left here?"

"Yes, I am sure of it."

"How?"

"By the sitting-room window."

"It is impossible, for we found it locked."

"It is possible, if someone closed it behind him."

"Ah!"

She commenced to tremble again, and, falling back into her nightmarish horror, she no longer wasted fond expletives on her domovoi as on a dear little angel who had just rendered a service ten times more precious to her than life. While he listened patiently, she said brutally:

"Why did you keep me from throwing myself on him, from rushing upon him as he opened the door? Ah, I would have, I would have... we would know."

"No. At the least noise he would have closed the door. A turn of the key and he would have escaped forever. And he would have been warned."

"Careless boy! Why then, if you knew he was going to come, didn't you leave me in the bedroom and you watch below yourself?"

"Because so long as I was below he would not have come. He only comes when there is no one downstairs."

"Ah, Saints Peter and Paul pity a poor woman. Who do you think it is, then? Who do you think it is? I can't think any more. Tell me, tell me that. You ought to know—you know everything. Come—who? I demand the truth. Who? Still some agent of the Committee, of the Central Committee? Still the Nihilists?"

"If it was only that!" said Rouletabille quietly.

"You have sworn to drive me mad! What do you mean by your 'if it was only that'?"

Rouletabille, imperturbable, did not reply.

"What have you done with the potion?" said he.

"The potion? The glass of the crime! I have locked it in my room, in the cupboard—safe, safe!"

"Ah, but, madame, it is necessary to replace it where you took it from."

"What!"

"Yes, after having poured the poison into a phial, to wash the glass and fill it with another potion."

"You are right. You think of everything. If the general wakes and wants his potion, he must not be suspicious of anything, and he must be able to have his drink."

"It is not necessary that he should drink."

"Well, then, why have the drink there?"

"So that the person can be sure, madame, that if he has not drunk it is simply because he has not wished to. A pure chance, madame, that he is not poisoned. You understand me this time?"

"Yes, yes. O Christ! But how now, if the general wakes and wishes to drink his narcotic?"

"Tell him I forbid it. And here is another thing you must do. When—Someone—comes into the general's chamber, in the morning, you must quite openly and naturally throw out the potion, useless and vapid, you see, and so Someone will have no right to be astonished that the general continues to enjoy excellent health."

"Yes, yes, little one; you are wiser than King Solomon. And what will I do with the phial of poison?"

"Bring it to me."

"Right away."

She went for it and returned five minutes later.

"He is still asleep. I have put the glass on the table, out of his reach. He will have to call me."

"Very good. Then push the door to, close it; we have to talk things over."

"But if someone goes back up the servants' staircase?"

"Be easy about that. They think the general is poisoned already. It is the first care-free moment I have been able to enjoy in this house."

"When will you stop making me shake with horror, little demon! You keep your secret well, I must say. The general is sleeping better than if he really were poisoned. But what shall we do about Natacha? I dare ask you that—you and you alone."

"Nothing at all."

"How—nothing?"

"We will watch her..."

"Ah, yes, yes."

"Still, Matrena, you let me watch her by myself."

"Yes, yes, I promise you. I will not pay any attention to her. That is promised. That is promised. Do as you please. Why, just now, when I spoke of the Nihilists to you, did you say, 'If it were only that!'? You believe, then, that she is not a Nihilist? She reads such things—things like on the barricades. . ."

"Madame, madame, you think of nothing but Natacha. You have promised me not to watch her; promise me not to think about her."

"Why, why did you say, 'If it was only that!'?"

"Because, if there were only Nihilists in your affair, dear madame, it would be too simple, or, rather, it would have been more simple. Can you possibly believe, madame, that simply a Nihilist, a Nihilist who was only a Nihilist, would take pains that his bomb exploded from a vase of flowers?—that it would have mattered where, so long as it overwhelmed the general? Do you imagine that the bomb would have had less effect behind the door than in front of it? And the little cavity under the floor, do you believe that a genuine revolutionary, such as you have here in Russia, would amuse himself by penetrating to the villa only to draw out two nails from a board, when one happens to give him time between two visits to the dining-room? Do you suppose that a revolutionary who wished to avenge the dead of Moscow and who could succeed in getting so far as the door behind which General Trebassof slept would amuse himself by making a little hole with a pin in order to draw back the bolt and amuse himself by pouring poison into a glass? Why, in such a case, he would have thrown his bomb outright, whether it blew him up along with the villa, or he was arrested on the spot, or had to submit to the martyrdom of the dungeons in the Fortress of SS. Peter and Paul, or be hung at Schlusselburg. Isn't that what always happens? That is the way he would have done, and not have acted like a hotel-rat! Now, there is someone in your home (or who comes to your home) who acts like a hotel-rat because he does not wish to be seen, because he does not wish to be discovered, because he does not wish to be taken in the act. Now, the moment that he fears nothing so much as to be taken in the act, so that he plays all these tricks of legerdemain, it is certain that his object lies beyond the act itself, beyond the bomb, beyond the poison. Why all this necessity for bombs of deferred explosion, for clockwork placed where it will be confused with other things, and not on a bare staircase forbidden to everybody, though you visit it twenty times a day?"

"But this man comes in as he pleases by day and by night? You don't answer. You know who he is, perhaps?"

270

"I know him, perhaps, but I am not sure who it is yet."

"You are not curious, little domovoi doukh! A friend of the house, certainly, and who enters the house as he wishes, by night, because someone opens the window for him. And who comes from the Krestowsky Villa! Boris or Michael! Ah, poor miserable Matrena! Why don't they kill poor Matrena? Their general! Their general! And they are soldiers— soldiers who come at night to kill their general. Aided by—by whom? Do you believe that? You? Light of my eyes! you believe that! No, no, that is not possible! I want you to understand, monsieur le domovoi, that I am not able to believe anything so horrible. No, no, by Jesus Christ Who died on the Cross, and Who searches our hearts, I do not believe that Boris—who, however, has very advanced ideas, I admit—it is necessary not to forget that; very advanced; and who composes very advanced verses also, as I have always told him—I will not believe that Boris is capable of such a fearful crime. As to Michael, he is an honest man, and my daughter, my Natacha, is an honest girl. Everything looks very bad, truly, but I do not suspect either Michael or Boris or my pure and beloved Natacha (even though she has made a translation into French of very advanced verses, certainly most improper for the daughter of a general). That is what lies at the bottom of my mind, the bottom of my heart—you have understood me perfectly, little angel of paradise? Ah, it is you the general owes his life to, that Matrena owes her life. Without you this house would already be a coffin. How shall I ever reward you? You wish for nothing! I annoy you! You don't even listen to me! A coffin—we would all be in our coffins! Tell me what you desire. All that I have belongs to you!"

"I desire to smoke a pipe.

"Ah, a pipe! Do you want some yellow perfumed tobacco that I receive every month from Constantinople, a treat right from the harem? I will get enough for you, if you like it, to smoke ten thousand pipes full."

"I prefer caporal," replied Rouletabille. "But you are right. It is not wise to suspect anybody. See, watch, wait. There is always time, once the game is caught, to say whether it is a hare or a wild boar. Listen to me, then, my good mamma. We must know first what is in the phial. Where is it?"

"Here it is."

She drew it from her sleeve. He stowed it in his pocket.

"You wish the general a good appetite, for me. I am going out. I will be back in two hours at the latest. And, above all, don't let the general know anything. I am going to see one of my friends who lives in the Aptiekarski pereolek." (note 1)

"Depend on me, and get back quickly for love of me. My blood clogs in my heart when you are not here, dear servant of God."

She mounted to the general's room and came down at least ten times to see if Rouletabille had not returned. Two hours later he was around the villa, as he had promised. She could not keep herself from running to meet him, for which she was scolded.

"Be calm. Be calm. Do you know what was in the phial?"

"No."

"Arsenate of soda, enough to kill ten people."

---

1. The little street of the apothecaries.

"Holy Mary!"

"Be quiet. Go upstairs to the general."

Feodor Feodorovitch was in charming humor. It was his first good night since the death of the youth of Moscow. He attributed it to his not having touched the narcotic and resolved, once more, to give up the narcotic, a resolve Rouletabille and Matrena encouraged. During the conversation there was a knock at the door of Matrena's chamber. She ran to see who was there, and returned with Natacha, who wished to embrace her father. Her face showed traces of fatigue. Certainly she had not passed as good a night as her father, and the general reproached her for looking so downcast.

"It is true. I had dreadful dreams. But you, papa, did you sleep well? Did you take your narcotic?"

"No, no, I have not touched a drop of my potion."

"Yes, I see. Oh, well, that is all right; that is very good. Natural sleep must be coming back. . ."

Matrena, as though hypnotized by Rouletabille, had taken the glass from the table and ostentatiously carried it to the dressing-room to throw it out, and she delayed there to recover her self-possession.

Natacha continued:

"You will see, papa, that you will be able to live just like everyone else finally. The great thing was to clear away the police, the atrocious police; wasn't it, Monsieur Rouletabille?"

"I have always said, for myself, that I am entirely of Mademoiselle Natacha's mind.

You can be entirely reassured now, and I shall leave you feeling reassured. Yes, I must think of getting my interviews done quickly, and departing. Ah well, I can only say what I think. Run things yourselves and you will not run any danger. Besides, the general gets much better, and soon I shall see you all in France, I hope. I must thank you now for your friendly hospitality."

"Ah, but you are not going? You are not going!" Matrena had already set herself to protest with all the strenuous torrent of words in her poor desolated heart, when a glance from the reporter cut short her despairing utterances.

"I shall have to remain a week still in the city. I have engaged a chamber at the Hotel de France. It is necessary. I have so many people to see and to receive. I will come to make you a little visit from time to time."

"You are then quite easy," demanded the general gravely, "at leaving me all alone?"

"Entirely easy. And, besides, I don't leave you all alone. I leave you with Madame Trebassof and Mademoiselle. I repeat: All three of you stay as I see you now. No more police, or, in any case, the fewest possible."

"He is right, he is right," repeated Natacha again.

At this moment there were fresh knocks at the door of Matrena's chamber. It was Ermolai, who announced that his Excellency the Marshal of the Court, Count Keltzof, wished to see the general, acting for His Majesty.

"Go and receive the Count, Natacha, and tell him that your father will be downstairs in a moment."

Natacha and Rouletabille went down and found the Count in the drawing-room. He was a magnificent specimen, handsome and big as one of the Swiss papal guard. He seemed watchful in all directions and all among the furniture, and was quite evidently disquieted. He advanced immediately to meet the young lady, inquiring the news.

"It is all good news," replied Natacha. "Everybody here is splendid. The general is quite gay. But what news have you, monsieur le marechal? You appear preoccupied."

The marshal had pressed Rouletabille's hand.

"And my grapes?" he demanded of Natacha.

"How, your grapes? What grapes?"

"If you have not touched them, so much the better. I arrived here very anxious. I brought you yesterday, from Krasnoie-Coelo, some of the Emperor's grapes that Feodor Feodorovitch enjoyed so much. Now this morning I learned that the eldest son of Doucet, the French head-gardener of the Imperial conservatories at Krasnoie, had died from eating those grapes, which he had taken from those gathered for me to bring here. Imagine my dismay. I knew, however, that at the general's table, grapes would not be eaten without having been washed, but I reproached myself for not having taken the precaution of leaving word that Doucet recommend that they be washed thoroughly. Still, I don't suppose it would matter. I couldn't see how my gift could be dangerous, but when I learned of little Doucet's death this morning, I jumped into the first train and came straight here."

"But, your Excellency," interrupted Natacha, "we have not seen your grapes."

"Ah, they have not been served yet? All the better. Thank goodness!"

"The Emperor's grapes are diseased, then?" interrogated Rouletabille. "Phylloxera pest has got into the conservatories?"

"Nothing can stop it, Doucet told me. So he didn't want me to leave last evening until he had washed the grapes. Unfortunately, I was pressed for time and I took them as they were, without any idea that the mixture they spray on the grapes to protect them was so deadly. It appears that in the vineyard country they have such accidents every year. They call it, I think, the. . . the mixture. . ."

"The Bordeaux mixture," was heard in Rouletabille's trembling voice "And do you know what it is, Your Excellency, this Bordeaux mixture?"

"Why, no."

At this moment the general came down the stairs, clinging to the banister and supported by Matrena Petrovna.

"Well," continued Rouletabille, watching Natacha, "the Bordeaux mixture which covered the grapes you brought the general yesterday was nothing more nor less than arsenate of soda."

"Ah, God!" cried Natacha.

As for Matrena Petrovna, she uttered a low exclamation and let go the general, who almost fell down the staircase. Everybody rushed. The general laughed. Matrena, under the stringent look of Rouletabille, stammered that she had suddenly felt faint. At last they were all together in the veranda. The general settled back on his sofa and inquired:

"Well, now, were you just saying something, my dear marshal, about some grapes you have brought me?"

"Yes, indeed," said Natacha, quite frightened, "and what he said isn't pleasant at all. The son of Doucet, the court gardener, has just been poisoned by the same grapes that monsieur le marschal, it appears, brought you."

"Where was this? Grapes? What grapes? I haven't seen any grapes!" exclaimed Matrena. "I noticed you, yesterday, marshal, out in the garden, but you went away almost immediately, and I certainly was surprised that you did not come in. What is this story?"

"Well, we must clear this matter up. It is absolutely necessary that we know what happened to those grapes."

"Certainly," said Rouletabille, "they could cause a catastrophe."

"If it has not happened already," fretted the marshal.

"But how? Where are they? Whom did you give them to?"

"I carried them in a white cardboard box, the first one that came to hand in Doucet's place. I came here the first time and didn't find you. I returned again with the box, and the general was just lying down. I was pressed for my train and Michael Nikolaievitch and Boris Alexandrovitch were in the garden, so I asked them to execute my commission, and I laid the box down near them on the little garden table, telling them not to forget to tell you it was necessary to wash the grapes as Doucet expressly recommended."

"But it is unbelievable! It is terrible!" quavered Matrena. "Where can the grapes be? We must know."

"Absolutely," approved Rouletabille.

"We must ask Boris and Michael," said Natacha. "Good God! surely they have not eaten them! Perhaps they are sick."

"Here they are," said the general. All turned. Michael and Boris were coming up the steps. Rouletabille, who was in a shadowed corner under the main staircase, did not lose a single play of muscle on the two faces which for him were two problems to solve. Both faces were smiling; too smiling, perhaps.

"Michael! Boris! Come here," cried Feodor Feodorovitch. "What have you done with the grapes from monsieur le marechal?"

They both looked at him upon this brusque interrogation, seemed not to understand, and then, suddenly recalling, they declared very naturally that they had left them on the garden table and had not thought about them.

"You forgot my caution, then?" said Count Kaltzof severely.

"What caution?" said Boris. "Oh, yes, the washing of the grapes. Doucet's caution."

"Do you know what has happened to Doucet with those grapes? His eldest son is dead, poisoned. Do you understand now why we are anxious to know what has become of my grapes?"

"But they ought to be out there on the table," said Michael.

"No one can find them anywhere," declared Matrena, who, no less than Rouletabille, watched every change in the countenances of the two officers. "How did it happen that you went away yesterday evening without saying good-bye, without seeing us, without troubling yourselves whether or not the general might need you?"

"Madame," said Michael, coldly, in military fashion, as though he replied to his superior officer himself, "we have ample excuse to offer you and the general. It is necessary that we make an admission, and the general will pardon us, I am sure. Boris and I, during the promenade, happened to quarrel. That quarrel was in full swing when we reached here and we were discussing the way to end it most promptly when monsieur le marechal entered the garden. We must make that our excuse for giving divided attention to what he had to say. As soon as he was gone we had only one thought, to get away from here to settle our difference with arms in our hands."

"Without speaking to me about it!" interrupted Trehassof. "I never will pardon that."

"You fight at such a time, when the general is threatened! It is as though you fought between yourselves in the face of the enemy. It is treason!" added Matrena.

"Madame," said Boris, "we did not fight. Someone pointed out our fault, and I offered my excuses to Michael Nikolaievitch, who generously accepted them. Is that not so, Michael Nikolaievitch?"

"And who is this that pointed out your fault?" demanded the marshal.

"Natacha."

"Bravo, Natacha. Come, embrace me, my daughter."

The general pressed his daughter effusively to his broad chest.

"And I hope you will not have further disputing," he cried, looking over Natacha's shoulder.

"We promise you that, General," declared Boris. "Our lives belong to you."

"You did well, my love. Let us all do as well. I have passed an excellent night, messieurs. Real sleep! I have had just one long sleep."

"That is so," said Matrena slowly. "The general had no need of narcotic. He slept like a child and did not touch his potion."

"And my leg is almost well."

"All the same, it is singular that those grapes should have disappeared," insisted the marshal, following his fixed idea.

"Ermolai," called Matrena.

The old servant appeared.

"Yesterday evening, after these gentlemen had left the house, did you notice a small white box on the garden table?"

"No, Barinia."

"And the servants? Have any of them been sick? The dvornicks? The schwitzar? In the kitchens? No one sick? No? Go and see; then come and tell me."

He returned, saying, "No one sick."

Like the marshal, Matrena Petrovna and Feodor Feodorovitch looked at one another, repeating in French, "No one sick! That is strange!"

Rouletabille came forward and gave the only explanation that was plausible—for the others.

"But, General, that is not strange at all. The grapes have been stolen and eaten by some domestic, and if the servant has not been sick it is simply that the grapes monsieur le marechal brought escaped the spraying of the Bordeaux mixture. That is the whole mystery."

"The little fellow must be right," cried the delighted marshal.

"He is always right, this little fellow," beamed Matrena, as proudly as though she had brought him into the world.

But "the little fellow," taking advantage of the greetings as Athanase Georgevitch and Ivan Petrovitch arrived, left the villa, gripping in his pocket the phial which held what is required to make grapes flourish or to kill a general who is in excellent health. When he had gone a few hundred steps toward the bridges one must cross to go into the city, he was overtaken by a panting dvornick, who brought him a letter that had just come by courier. The writing on the envelope was entirely unknown to him. He tore it open and read, in excellent French:

"Request to M. Joseph Rouletabille not to mix in matters that do not concern him. The second warning will be the last." It was signed: "The Central Revolutionary Committee."

"So, ho!" said Rouletabille, slipping the paper into his pocket, "that's the line it takes, is it! Happily I have nothing more to occupy myself with at all. It is Koupriane's turn now! Now to go to Koupriane's!"

On this date, Rouletabille's note-book: "Natacha to her father: 'But you, papa, have you had a good night? Did you take your narcotic?'

"Fearful, and (lest I confuse heaven and hell) I have no right to take any further notes." (note 1)

---

1. As a matter of fact, after this day no more notes are found in Rouletabille's memorandum-book. The last one is that above, bizarre and romantic, and necessary, as Sainclair, the Paris advocate and friend of Rouletabille, indicates opposite it in the papers from which we have taken all the details of this story.

VIII

The Little Chapel of the Guards

Rouletabille took a long walk which led him to the Troitsky Bridge, then, re-descending the Naberjnaia, he reached the Winter Palace. He seemed to have chased away all preoccupation, and took a child's pleasure in the different aspects of the life that characterizes the city of the Great Peter. He stopped before the Winter Palace, walked slowly across the square where the prodigious monolith of the Alexander Column rises from its bronze socket, strolled between the palace and the colonnades, passed under an immense arch: everything seemed Cyclopean to him, and he never had felt so tiny, so insignificant. None the less he was happy in his insignificance, he was satisfied with himself in the presence of these colossal things; everything pleased him this morning. The speed of the isvos, the bickering humor of the osvotchicks, the elegance of the women, the fine presences of the officers and their easy naturalness under their uniforms, so opposed to the wooden posturing of the Berlin military men whom he had noticed at the "Tilleuls" and in the Friederichstrasse between two trains. Everything enchanted him—the costume even of the moujiks, vivid blouses, the red shirts over the trousers, the full legs and the boots up to the knees, even the unfortunates who, in spite of the soft atmosphere, were muffled up in sheepskin coats, all impressed him favorably, everything appeared to him original and congenial.

Order reigned in the city. The guards were polite, decorative and superb in bearing. The passers-by in that quarter talked gayly among themselves, often in French, and had manners as civilized as anywhere in the world. Where, then, was the Bear of the North? He never had seen bears so well licked. Was it this very city that only yesterday was in revolution? This was certainly the Alexander Park where troops a few weeks before had fired on children who had sought refuge in the trees, like sparrows. Was this the very pavement where the Cossacks had left so many bodies? Finally he saw before him the Nevsky Prospect, where the bullets rained like hail not long since upon a people dressed for festivities and very joyous. Nichevo! Nichevo! All that was so soon forgotten. They forgot yesterday as they forget tomorrow. The Nihilists? Poets, who imagined that a bomb could accomplish anything in that Babylon of the North more important than the noise of its explosion! Look at these people who pass. They have no more thought for the old attack than for those now preparing in the shadow of the "tracktirs." Happy men, full of serenity in this bright quarter, who move about their affairs and their pleasures in the purest air, the lightest, the most transparent on earth. No, no; no one knows the joy of mere breathing if he has not breathed the air there, the finest in the north of the world, which gives food and drink of beautiful white eau-de-vie and yellow pivo, and strikes the blood and makes one a beast vigorous and joyful and fatalistic, and mocks at the Nihilists and, as well, at the ten thousand eyes of the police staring from under the porches of houses, from under the skulls of dvornicks— all police, the dvornicks; all police, also the joyous concierges with extended hands. Ah, ah, one mocks at it all in such air, provided one has roubles in one's pockets, plenty of roubles, and that one is not besotted by reading those extraordinary books that preach the happiness of all humanity to students and to poor girl-students too. Ah, ah, seed of the Nihilists, all that! These poor little fellows and poor little girls who have their heads turned by lectures that they cannot digest! That is all the trouble, the digestion. The digestion is needed. Messieurs the commercial travelers for champagne, who talk together importantly in the lobbies of the Grand Morskaia Hotel and who have studied the Russian people even in the most distant cities where champagne is sold, will tell you that over any table of hors-d'oeuvres, and will regulate the whole question of the Revolution between two little glasses of vodka, swallowed properly, quickly, elbow up, at a single draught, in the Russian manner. Simply an affair of digestion, they tell you. Who is the fool that would dare compare a young gentleman who has well digested a bottle of champagne or two, and another young man who has poorly digested the lucubrations of, who shall we say?—the lucubrations of the economists? The economists? The economists! Fools who compete which can make the most violent statements! Those who read them and don't understand them go off like a bomb! Your health! Nichevo! The world goes round still, doesn't it?

Discussion political, economic, revolutionary, and other in the room where they munch hors-d'oeuvres! You will hear it all as you pass through the hotel to your chamber, young Rouletabille. Get quickly now to the home of Koupriane, if you don't wish to arrive there at luncheon-time; then you would have to put off these serious affairs until evening.

The Department of Police. Massive entrance, heavily guarded, a great lobby, halls with swinging doors, many obsequious schwitzars on the lookout for tips, many poor creatures sitting against the walls on dirty benches, desks and clerks, brilliant boots and epaulets of gay young officers who are telling tales of the Aquarium with great relish.

"Monsieur Rouletabille! Ah, yes. Please be seated. Delighted, M. Koupriane will be very happy to receive you, but just at this moment he is at inspection. Yes, the inspection of the police dormitories in the barracks. We will take you there. His own idea! He doesn't neglect anything, does he? A great Chief. Have you seen the police-guards' dormitory? Admirable! The first dormitories of the world. We say that without wishing to offend France. We love France. A great nation! I will take you immediately to M. Koupriane. I shall be delighted."

"I also," said Rouletabille, who put a rouble into the honorable functionary's hand.

"Permit me to precede you."

Bows and salutes. For two roubles he would have walked obsequiously before him to the end of the world.

"These functionaries are admirable," thought Rouletabille as he was led to the barracks. He felt he had not paid too much for the services of a personage whose uniform was completely covered with lace. They tramped, they climbed, they descended. Stairways, corridors. Ah, the barracks at last. He seemed to have entered a convent. Beds very white, very narrow, and images of the Virgin and saints everywhere, monastic neatness and the most absolute silence. Suddenly an order sounded in the corridor outside, and the police-guard, who sprang from no one could tell where, stood to attention at the head of their beds. Koupriane and his aide appeared. Koupriane looked at everything closely, spoke to each man in turn, called them by their names, inquired about their needs, and the men stammered replies, not knowing what to answer, reddening like children. Koupriane observed Rouletabille. He dismissed his aide with a gesture. The inspection was over. He drew the young man into a little room just off the dormitory. Rouletabille, frightened, looked about him. He found himself in a chapel. This little chapel completed the effect of the guards' dormitory. It was all gilded, decorated in marvelous colors, thronged with little ikons that bring happiness, and, naturally, with the portrait of the Tsar, the dear Little Father.

"You see," said Koupriane, smiling at Rouletabille's amazement, "we deny them nothing. We give them their saints right here in their quarters." Closing the door, he drew a chair toward Rouletabille and motioned him to sit down. They sat before the little altar loaded with flowers, with colored paper and winged saints.

"We can talk here without being disturbed," he said. "Yonder there is such a crowd of people waiting for me. I'm ready to listen."

"Monsieur," said Rouletabille, "I have come to give you the report of my mission here, and to terminate my connection with it. All that is left for clearing this obscure affair is to arrest the guilty person, with which I have nothing to do. That concerns you. I simply inform you that someone tried to poison the general last night by pouring arsenate of soda into his sleeping-potion, which I bring you in this phial, arsenate which was secured most probably by washing it from grapes brought to General Trebassof by the marshal of the court, and which disappeared without anyone being able to say how."

"Ah, ah, a family affair, a plot within the family. I told you so," murmured Koupriane.

"The affair at least has happened within the family, as you think, although the assassin came from outside. Contrary to what you may be able to believe, he does not live in the house."

"Then how does he get there?" demanded Koupriane.

"By the window of the room overlooking the Neva. He has often come that way. And that is the way he returns also, I am sure. It is there you can take him if you act with prudence."

"How do you know he often comes that way?"

"You know the height of the window above the little roadway. To reach it he uses a water-trough, whose iron rings are bent, and also the marks of a grappling-iron that he carries with him and uses to hoist himself to the window are distinctly visible on the ironwork of the little balcony outside. The marks are quite obviously of different dates."

"But that window is closed."

"Someone opens it for him."

"Who, if you please?"

"I have no desire to know."

"Eh, yes. It necessarily is Natacha. I was sure that the Villa des Iles had its viper. I tell you she doesn't dare leave her nest because she knows she is watched. Not one of her movements outside escapes us! She knows it. She has been warned. The last time she ventured outside alone was to go into the old quarters of Derewnia. What has she to do in such a rotten quarter? I ask you that. And she turned in her tracks without seeing anyone, without knocking at a single door, because she saw that she was followed. She isn't able to get to see them outside, therefore she has to see them inside."

"They are only one, and always the same one."

"Are you sure?"

"An examination of the marks on the wall and on the pipe doesn't leave any doubt of it, and it is always the same grappling-iron that is used for the window."

"The viper!"

"Monsieur Koupriane, Mademoiselle Natacha seems to preoccupy you exceedingly. I did not come here to talk about Mademoiselle Natacha. I came to point out to you the route used by the man who comes to do the murder."

"Eh, yes, it is she who opens the way."

"I can't deny that."

"The little demon! Why does she take him into her room at night? Do you think perhaps there is some love-affair. . .?"

"I am sure of quite the opposite."

"I too. Natacha is not a wanton. Natacha has no heart. She has only a brain. And it doesn't take long for a brain touched by Nihilism to get so it won't hesitate at anything."

Koupriane reflected a minute, while Rouletabille watched him in silence.

"Have we solely to do with Nihilism?" resumed Koupriane. "Everything you tell me inclines me more and more to my idea: a family affair, purely in the family. You know, don't you, that upon the general's death Natacha will be immensely rich?"

"Yes, I know it," replied Rouletabille, in a voice that sounded singular to the ear of the Chief of Police and which made him raise his head.

"What do you know?"

"I? Nothing," replied the reporter, this time in a firmer tone. "I ought, however, to say this to you: I am sure that we are dealing with Nihilism. . ."

"What makes you believe it?"

"This."

And Rouletabille handed Koupriane the message he had received that same morning.

"Oh, oh," cried Koupriane. "You are under watch! Look out."

"I have nothing to fear; I'm not bothering myself about anything further. Yes, we have an affair of the revolutionaries, but not of the usual kind. The way they are going about it isn't like one of their young men that the Central Committee arms with a bomb and who is sacrificed in advance."

"Where are the tracks that you have traced?"

"Right up to the little Krestowsky Villa."

Koupriane bounded from his chair.

"Occupied by Boris. Parbleu! Now we have them. I see it all now. Boris, another cracked brain! And he is engaged. If he plays the part of the Revolutionaries, the affair would work out big for him."

"That villa," said Rouletabille quietly, "is also occupied by Michael Korosakoff."

"He is the most loyal, the most reliable soldier of the Tsar."

"No one is ever sure of anything, my dear Monsieur Koupriane."

"Oh, I am sure of a man like that."

"No man is ever sure of any man, my dear Monsieur Koupriane."

"I am, in every case, for those I employ."

"You are wrong."

"What do you say?"

"Something that can serve you in the enterprise you are going to undertake, because I trust you can catch the murderer right in his nest. To do that, I'll not conceal from you that I think your agents will have to be enormously clever. They will have to watch the datcha des Iles at night, without anyone possibly suspecting it. No more maroon coats with false astrakhan trimmings, eh? But Apaches, Apaches on the wartrail, who blend themselves with the ground, with the trees, with the stones in the roadway. But among those Apaches don't send that agent of your Secret Service who watched the window while the assassin climbed to it."

"What?"

"Why, these climbs that you can read the proofs of on the wall and on the iron forgings of the balcony went on while your agents, night and day, were watching the villa. Have you noticed, monsieur, that it was always the same agent who took the post at night, behind the villa, under the window? General Trebassof 's book in which he kept a statement of the exact disposal of each of your men during the period of siege was most instructive on that point. The other posts changed in turn, but the same agent, when he was among the guard, demanded always that same post, which was not disputed by anybody, since it is no fun to pass the hours of the night behind a wall, in an empty field. The others much preferred to roll away the time watching in the villa or in front of the lodge, where vodka and Crimean wine, kwass and pivo, kirsch and tchi, never ran short. That agent's name is Touman."

"Touman! Impossible! He is one of the best agents from Kiew. He was recommended by Gounsovski."

Rouletabille chuckled.

"Yes, yes, yes," grumbled the Chief of Police. "Someone always laughs when his name is mentioned."

Koupriane had turned red. He rose, opened the door, gave a long direction in Russian, and returned to his chair.

"Now," said he, "go ahead and tell me all the details of the poison and the grapes the marshal of the court brought. I'm listening."

Rouletabille told him very briefly and without drawing any deductions all that we already know. He ended his account as a man dressed in a maroon coat with false astrakhan was introduced. It was the same man Rouletabille had met in General Trebassof's drawing-room and who spoke French. Two gendarmes were behind him. The door had been closed. Koupriane turned toward the man in the coat.

"Touman," he said, "I want to talk to you. You are a traitor, and I have proof. You can confess to me, and I will give you a thousand roubles and you can take yourself off to be hanged somewhere else."

The man's eyes shrank, but he recovered himself quickly. He replied in Russian.

"Speak French. I order it," commanded Koupriane.

"I answer, Your Excellency," said Touman firmly, "that I don't know what Your Excellency means."

"I mean that you have helped a man get into the Trebassof villa by night when you were on guard under the window of the little sitting-room. You see that there is no use deceiving us any longer. I play with you frankly, good play, good money. The name of that man, and you have a thousand roubles."

"I am ready to swear on the ikon of. . ."

"Don't perjure yourself."

"I have always loyally served. . ."

"The name of that man."

"I still don't know yet what Your Excellency means."

"Oh, you understand me," replied Koupriane, who visibly held in an anger that threatened to break forth any moment. "A man got into the house while you were watching. . ."

"I never saw anything. After all, it is possible. There were some very dark nights. I went back and forth."

"You are not a fool. The name of that man."

"I assure you, Excellency. . ."

"Strip him."

"What are you going to do?" cried Rouletabille.

But already the two guards had thrown themselves on Touman and had drawn off his coat and shirt. The man was bare to the waist.

"What are you going to do? What are you going to do?"

"Leave them alone," said Koupriane, roughly pushing Rouletabille back.

Seizing a whip which hung at the waist of the guards he struck Touman a blow across the shoulders that drew blood. Touman, mad with the outrage and the pain, shouted, "Yes, it is true! I brag of it!"

Koupriane did not restrain his rage. He showered the unhappy man with blows, having thrown Rouletabille to the end of the room when he tried to interfere. And while he proceeded with the punishment the Chief of Police hurled at the agent who had betrayed him an accompaniment of fearful threats, promising him that before he was hanged he should rot in the bottom-most dungeon of Peter and Paul, in the slimy pits lying under the Neva. Touman, between the two guards who held him, and who sometimes received blows on the rebound that were not intended for them, never uttered a complaint. Outside the invectives of Koupriane there was heard only the swish of the cords and the cries of Rouletabille, who continued to protest that it was abominable, and called the Chief of Police a savage. Finally the savage stopped. Gouts of blood had spattered all about.

"Monsieur," said Rouletabille, who supported himself against the wall. "I shall complain to the Tsar."

"You are right," Koupriane replied, "but I feel relieved now. You can't imagine the harm this man can have done to us in the weeks he has been here."

Touman, across whose shoulders they had thrown his coat and who lay now across a chair, found strength to look up and say:

"It is true. You can't do me as much harm as I have done you, whether you think so or not. All the harm that can be done me by you and yours is already accomplished. My name is not Touman, but Matiev. Listen. I had a son that was the light of my eyes. Neither my son nor I had ever been concerned with politics. I was employed in Moscow. My son was a student. During the Red Week we went out, my son and I, to see a little of what was happening over in the Presnia quarter. They said everybody had been killed over there! We passed before the Presnia gate. Soldiers called to us to stop because they wished to search us. We opened our coats. The soldiers saw my son's student waistcoat and set up a cry. They unbuttoned the vest, drew a note-book out of his pocket and they found a workman's song in it that had been published in the Signal. The soldiers didn't know how to read. They believed the paper was a proclamation, and they arrested my son. I demanded to be arrested with him. They pushed me away. I ran to the governor's house. Trebassof had me thrust away from his door with blows from the butt-ends of his Cossacks' guns. And, as I persisted, they kept me locked up all that night and the morning of the next day. At noon I was set free. I demanded my son and they replied they didn't know what I was talking about. But a soldier that I recognized as having arrested my son the evening before pointed out a van that was passing, covered with a tarpaulin and surrounded by Cossacks. 'Your son is there,' he said; 'they are taking him to the graves.' Mad with despair, I ran after the van. It went to the outskirts of Golountrine cemetery. There I saw in the white snow a huge grave, wide, deep. I shall see it to my last minute. Two vans had already stopped near the hole. Each van held thirteen corpses. The vans were dumped into the trench and the soldiers commenced to sort the bodies into rows of six. I watched for my son. At last I recognized him in a body that half hung over the edge of the trench. Horrors of suffering were stamped in the expression of his face. I threw myself beside him. I said that I was his father. They let me embrace him a last time and count his wounds. He had fourteen. Someone had stolen the gold chain that had hung about his neck and held the picture of his mother, who died the year before. I whispered into his ear, I swore to avenge him. Forty-eight hours later I had placed myself at the disposition of the Revolutionary Committee. A week had not passed before Touman, whom, it seems, I resemble and who was one of the Secret Service agents in Kiew, was assassinated in the train that was taking him to St. Petersburg. The assassination was kept a secret. I received all his papers and I took his place with you. I was doomed beforehand and I asked nothing better, so long as I might last until after the execution of Trebassof. Ah, how I longed to kill him with my own hands! But another had already been assigned the duty and my role was to help him. And do you suppose I am going to tell you the name of that other? Never! And if you discover that other, as you have discovered me, another will come, and another, and another, until Trebassof has paid for his crimes. That is all I have to say to you, Koupriane. As for you, my little fellow," added he, turning to Rouletabille, "I wouldn't give much for your bones. Neither of you will last long. That is my consolation."

Koupriane had not interrupted the man. He looked at him in silence, sadly.

"You know, my poor man, you will be hanged now?" he said.

"No," growled Rouletabille.
"Monsieur Koupriane, I'll bet you my purse that he will not be hanged."

"And why not?" demanded the Chief of rolice, while, upon a sign from him, they took away the false Touman.

"Because it is I who denounced him."

"What a reason! And what would you like me to do?"

"Guard him for me; for me alone, do you understand?"

"In exchange for what?"

"In exchange for the life of General Trebassof, if I must put it that way."

"Eh? The life of General Trebassof! You speak as if it belonged to you, as if you could dispose of it."

Rouletabille laid his hand on Koupriane's arm.

"Perhaps that's so," said he.

"Would you like me to tell you one thing, Monsieur Rouletabille? It is that General Trebassof 's life, after what has just escaped the lips of this Touman, who is not Touman, isn't worth any more than—than yours if you remain here. Since you are disposed not to do anything more in this affair, take the train, monsieur, take the train, and go."

Rouletabille walked back and forth, very much worked up; then suddenly he stopped short.

"Impossible," he said. "It is impossible. I cannot; I am not able to go yet."

"Why?"

"Good God, Monsieur Koupriane, because I have to interview the President of the Duma yet, and complete my little inquiry into the politics of the cadets."

"Oh, indeed!"

Koupriane looked at him with a sour grin.

"What are you going to do with that man?" demanded Rouletabille.

"Have him fixed up first."

"And then?"

"Then take him before the judges."

"That is to say, to the gallows?" "Certainly."

"Monsieur Koupriane, I offer it to you again. Life for life. Give me the life of that poor devil and I promise you General Trebassof's."

"Explain yourself."

"Not at all. Do you promise me that you will maintain silence about the case of that man and that you will not touch a hair of his head?"

Koupriane looked at Rouletabille as he had looked at him during the altercation they had on the edge of the Gulf. He decided the same way this time.

"Very well," said he. "You have my word. The poor devil!"

"You are a brave man, Monsieur Koupriane, but a little quick with the whip..."

"What would you expect? One's work teaches that."

"Good morning. No, don't trouble to show me out. I am compromised enough already," said Rouletabille, laughing.

"Au revoir, and good luck! Get to work interviewing the President of the Duma," added Koupriane knowingly, with a great laugh.

But Rouletabille was already gone.

"That lad," said the Chief of Police aloud to himself, "hasn't told me a bit of what he knows."

IX

ANNOUCHKA

And now it's between us two, Natacha,"
murmured Rouletabille as soon as he was
outside. He hailed the first carriage that
passed and gave the address of the datcha
des Iles. When he got in he held his head
between his hands; his face burned, his jaws
were set. But by a prodigious effort of his
will he resumed almost instantly his calm,
his self-control. As he went back across the
Neva, across the bridge where he had felt
so elated a little while before, and saw the
isles again he sighed heavily. "I thought
I had got it all over with, so far as I was
concerned, and now I don't know where it
will stop." His eyes grew dark for a moment
with somber thoughts and the vision of
the Lady in Black rose before him; then he

shook his head, filled his pipe, lighted it, dried a tear that had been caused doubtless by a little smoke in his eye, and stopped sentimentalizing. A quarter of an hour later he gave a true Russian nobleman's fist-blow in the back to the coachman as an intimation that they had reached the Trebassof villa. A charming picture was before him. They were all lunching gayly in the garden, around the table in the summer-house. He was astonished, however, at not seeing Natacha with them. Boris Mourazoff and Michael Korsakoff were there. Rouletabille did not wish to be seen. He made a sign to Ermolai, who was passing through the garden and who hurried to meet him at the gate.

"The Barinia," said the reporter, in a low voice and with his finger to his lips to warn the faithful attendant to caution.

In two minutes Matrena Petrovna joined Rouletabille in the lodge.

"Well, where is Natacha?" he demanded hurriedly as she kissed his hands quite as though she had made an idol of him.

"She has gone away. Yes, out. Oh, I did not keep her. I did not try to hold her back. Her expression frightened me, you can understand, my little angel. My, you are impatient! What is it about? How do we stand? What have you decided? I am your slave. Command me. Command me. The keys of the villa?"

"Yes, give me a key to the veranda; you must have several. I must be able to get into the house tonight if it becomes necessary."

She drew a key from her gown, gave it to the young man and said a few words in Russian to Ermolai, to enforce upon him that he must obey the little domovoi-doukh in anything, day or night.

"Now tell me where Natacha has gone."

"Boris's parents came to see us a little while ago, to inquire after the general. They have taken Natacha away with them, as they often have done. Natacha went with them readily enough. Little domovoi, listen to me, listen to Matrena Petrovna—Anyone would have said she was expecting it!"

"Then she has gone to lunch at their house?"

"Doubtless, unless they have gone to a cafe. I don't know. Boris's father likes to have the family lunch at the Barque when it is fine. Calm yourself, little domovoi. What ails you? Bad news, eh? Any bad news?"

"No, no; everything is all right. Quick, the address of Boris's family."

"The house at the corner of La Place St. Isaac and la rue de la Poste."

"Good. Thank you. Adieu."

He started for the Place St. Isaac, and picked up an interpreter at the Grand Morskaia Hotel on the way. It might be useful to have him. At the Place St. Isaac he learned the Morazoffs and Natacha Trebassof had gone by train for luncheon at Bergalowe, one of the nearby stations in Finland.

"That is all," said he, and added apart to himself, "And perhaps that is not true."

He paid the coachman and the interpreter, and lunched at the Brasserie de Vienne nearby. He left there a half-hour later, much calmer. He took his way to the Grand Morskaia Hotel, went inside and asked the schwitzar:

"Can you give me the address of Mademoiselle Annouchka?"

"The singer of the Krestowsky?"

"That is who I mean."

"She had luncheon here. She has just gone away with the prince."

Without any curiosity as to which prince, Rouletabille cursed his luck and again asked for her address.

"Why, she lives in an apartment just across the way."

Rouletabille, feeling better, crossed the street, followed by the interpreter that he had engaged. Across the way he learned on the landing of the first floor that Mademoiselle Annouchka was away for the day. He descended, still followed by his interpreter, and recalling how someone had told him that in Russia it was always profitable to be generous,

he gave five roubles to the interpreter
and asked him for some information
about Mademoiselle Annouchka's life in
St. Petersburg. The interpreter whispered:

"She arrived a week ago, but has not spent a
single night in her apartment over there."

He pointed to the house they had just left,
and added:

"Merely her address for the police."

"Yes, yes," said Rouletabille, "I understand.
She sings this evening, doesn't she?"

"Monsieur, it will be a wonderful debut."

"Yes, yes, I know. Thanks."

All these frustrations in the things he had
undertaken that day instead of disheartening
him plunged him deep into hard thinking. He

returned, his hands in his pockets, whistling softly, to the Place St. Isaac, walked around the church, keeping an eye on the house at the corner, investigated the monument, went inside, examined all its details, came out marveling, and finally went once again to the residence of the Mourazoffs, was told that they had not yet returned from the Finland town, then went and shut himself in his room at the hotel, where he smoked a dozen pipes of tobacco. He emerged from his cloud of smoke at dinner-time.

At ten that evening he stepped out of his carriage before the Krestowsky. The establishment of Krestowsky, which looms among the Isles much as the Aquarium does, is neither a theater, nor a music-hall, nor a cafe-concert, nor a restaurant, nor a public garden; it is all of these and some other things besides. Summer theater, winter theater, open-air theater, hall for spectacles, scenic mountain, exercise-ground, diversions of all sorts, garden promenades, cafes, restaurants, private dining-rooms, everything is combined here that can amuse, charm, lead to the wildest orgies, or provide those who never think of sleep till toward three or four o'clock of a morning the means to await the dawn with patience. The most celebrated companies of the old and the new world play there amid an enthusiasm that is steadily maintained by the foresight of the managers: Russian and foreign dancers, and above all the French chanteuses, the little dolls of the cafes-concerts, so long as they are young, bright, and elegantly dressed, may meet their fortune there. If there is no such luck, they are sure at least to find every evening some old beau, and often some officer, who willingly pays twenty-five roubles for the sole pleasure of having a demoiselle born on the banks of the Seine for his companion at the supper-table. After their turn at the singing, these women display their graces and their eager smiles in the promenades of the garden or among the tables where the champagne-drinkers sit. The head-liners, naturally, are not driven to this wearying perambulation, but can go away to their rest if they are so inclined. However, the management is appreciative if they accept the invitation of some dignitary of the army, of administration, or of finance, who seeks the honor of hearing from the chanteuse, in a private room and with a company of friends not disposed to melancholy, the Bohemian songs of the Vieux Derevnia. They sing, they loll, they talk of Paris, and above all they drink. If sometimes the little fete ends rather roughly, it is the friendly and affectionate champagne that is to blame, but usually the orgies remain quite innocent, of a character that certainly might trouble the temperance societies but need not make M. le Senateur Berenger feel involved.

A war whose powder fumes reeked still, a revolution whose last defeated growls had not died away at the period of these events, had not at all diminished the nightly gayeties of Kretowsky. Many of the young men who displayed their uniforms that evening and called their "Nichevo" along the brilliantly lighted paths of the public gardens, or filled the open-air tables, or drank vodka at the buffets, or admired the figures of the wandering soubrettes, had come here on the eve of their departure for the war and had returned with the same child-like, enchanted smile, the same ideal of futile joy, and kissed their passing comrades as gayly as ever. Some of them had a sleeve lying limp now, or walked with a crutch, or even on a wooden leg, but it was, all the same, "Nichevo!"

The crowd this evening was denser than ordinarily, because there was the chance to hear Annouchka again for the first time since the somber days of Moscow. The students were ready to give her an ovation, and no one opposed it, because, after all, if she sang now it was because the police were willing at last. If the Tsar's government had granted her her life, it was not in order to compel her to die of hunger. Each earned a livelihood as was possible. Annouchka only knew how to sing and dance, and so she must sing and dance!

When Rouletabille entered the Krestowsky Gardens, Annouchka had commenced her number, which ended with a tremendous "Roussalka." Surrounded by a chorus of male and female dancers in the national dress and with red boots, striking tambourines with their fingers, then suddenly taking a rigid pose to let the young woman's voice, which was of rather ordinary register, come out, Annouchka had centered the attention of the immense audience upon herself. All the other parts of the establishment were deserted, the tables had been removed, and a panting crowd pressed about the open-air theater.

Rouletabille stood up on his chair at the moment tumultuous "Bravos" sounded from a group of students. Annouchka bowed toward them, seeming to ignore the rest of the audience, which had not dared declare itself yet. She sang the old peasant songs arranged to present-day taste, and interspersed them with dances. They had an enormous success, because she gave her whole soul to them and sang with her voice sometimes caressing, sometimes menacing, and sometimes magnificently desperate, giving much significance to words which on paper had not aroused the suspicions of the censor. The taste of the day was obviously still a taste for the revolution, which retained its influence on the banks of the Neva. What she was doing was certainly very bold, and apparently she realized how audacious she was, because, with great adroitness, she would bring out immediately after some dangerous phrase a patriotic couplet which everybody was anxious to applaud. She succeeded by such means in appealing to all the divergent groups of her audience and secured a complete triumph for herself. The students, the revolutionaries, the radicals and the cadets acclaimed the singer, glorifying not only her art but also and beyond everything else the sister of the engineer Volkousky, who had been doomed to perish with her brother by the bullets of the Semenovsky regiment. The friends of the Court on their side could not forget that it was she who, in front of the Kremlin, had struck aside the arm of Constantin Kochkarof, ordered by the Central Revolutionary Committee to assassinate the Grand Duke Peter Alexandrovitch as he drove up to the governor's house in his sleigh. The bomb burst ten feet away, killing Constantin Kochkarof himself. It may be that before death came he had time to hear Annouchka cry to him, "Wretch! You were told to kill the prince, not to assassinate his children."

As it happened, Peter Alexandrovitch held on his knees the two little princesses, seven and eight years old. The Court had wished to recompense her for that heroic act. Annouchka had spit at the envoy of the Chief of Police who called to speak to her of money. At the Hermitage in Moscow, where she sang then, some of her admirers had warned her of possible reprisals on the part of the revolutionaries. But the revolutionaries gave her assurance at once that she had nothing to fear. They approved her act and let her know that they now counted on her to kill the Grand Duke some time when he was alone; which had made Annouchka laugh. She was an enfant terrible, whose friends no one knew, who passed for very wise, and whose lines of intrigue were inscrutable. She enjoyed making her hosts in the private supper-rooms quake over their meal. One day she had said bluntly to one of the most powerful tchinovnicks of Moscow: "You, my old friend, you are president of the Black Hundred. Your fate is sealed. Yesterday you were condemned to death by the delegates of the Central Committee at Presnia. Say your prayers." The man reached for champagne. He never finished his glass. The dvornicks carried him out stricken with apoplexy. Since the time she saved the little grand-duchesses the police had orders to allow her to act and talk as she pleased. She had been mixed up in the deepest plots against the government. Those who lent the slightest countenance to such plottings and were not of the police simply disappeared. Their friends dared not even ask for news of them. The only thing not in doubt about them was that they were at hard labor somewhere in the mines of the Ural Mountains. At the moment of the revolution Annouchka had a brother who was an engineer on the Kasan-Moscow line. This Volkousky was one of the leaders on the Strike Committee. The authorities had an eye on him. The revolution started. He, with the help of his sister, accomplished one of those formidable acts which will carry their memory as heroes to the farthest posterity. Their work accomplished, they were taken by Trebassof's soldiers. Both were condemned to death. Volkousky was executed first, and the sister was taking her turn when an officer of the government arrived on horseback to stop the firing. The Tsar, informed of her intended fate, had sent a pardon by telegraph. After that she disappeared. She was supposed to have gone on some tour across Europe, as was her habit, for she spoke all the languages, like a true Bohemian. Now she had reappeared in all her joyous glory at Krestowsky. It was certain, however, that she had not forgotten her brother. Gossips said that if the government and the police showed themselves so long-enduring they found it to their interest to do so. The open, apparent life Annouchka led was less troublesome to them than her hidden activities would be. The lesser police who surrounded the Chief of the St. Petersburg Secret Service, the famous Gounsovski, had meaning smiles when the matter was discussed. Among them Annouchka had the ignoble nickname, "Stool-pigeon."

Rouletabille must have been well aware of all these particulars concerning Annouchka, for he betrayed no astonishment at the great interest and the strong emotion she aroused. From the corner where he was he could see only a bit of the stage, and he was standing on tiptoes to see the singer when he felt his coat pulled. He turned. It was the jolly advocate, well known for his gastronomic feats, Athanase Georgevitch, along with the jolly Imperial councilor, Ivan Petrovitch, who motioned him to climb down.

"Come with us; we have a box."

Rouletabille did not need urging, and he was soon installed in the front of a box where he could see the stage and the public both. Just then the curtain fell on the first part of Annouchka's performance. The friends were soon rejoined by Thaddeus Tchitchnikoff, the great timber-merchant, who came from behind the scenes.

"I have been to see the beautiful Onoto," announced the Lithuanian with a great satisfied laugh. "Tell me the news. All the girls are sulking over Annouchka's success."

"Who dragged you into the Onoto's dressing-room then?" demanded Athanase.

"Oh, Gounsovski himself, my dear. He is very amateurish, you know."

"What! do you knock around with Gounsovski?"

"On my word, I tell you, dear friends, he isn't a bad acquaintance. He did me a little service at Bakou last year. A good acquaintance in these times of public trouble."

"You are in the oil business now, are you?"

"Oh, yes, a little of everything for a livelihood. I have a little well down Bakou way, nothing big; and a little house, a very small one for my small business."

"What a monopolist Thaddeus is," declared Athanase Georgevitch, hitting him a formidable slap on the thigh with his enormous hand. "Gounsovski has come himself to keep an eye on Annouchka's debut, eh? Only he goes into Onoto's dressing-room, the rogue."

"Oh, he doesn't trouble himself. Do you know who he is to have supper with? With Annouchka, my dears, and we are invited."

"How's that?" inquired the jovial councilor.

"It seems Gounsovski influenced the minister to permit Annouchka's performance by declaring he would be responsible for it all. He required from Annouchka solely that she have supper with him on the evening of her debut."

"And Annouchka consented?"

"That was the condition, it seems. For that matter, they say that Annouchka and Gounsovski don't get along so badly together. Gounsovski has done Annouchka many a good turn. They say he is in love with her."

"He has the air of an umbrella merchant," snorted Athanase Georgevitch.

"Have you seen him at close range?" inquired Ivan.

"I have dined at his house, though it is nothing to boast of, on my word."

"That is what he said," replied Thaddeus. "When he knew we were here together, he said to me: 'Bring him, he is a charming fellow who plies a great fork; and bring that dear man Ivan Petrovitch, and all your friends.'"

"Oh, I only dined at his house," grumbled Athanase, "because there was a favor he was going to do me."

"He does services for everybody, that man," observed Ivan Petrovitch.

"Of course, of course; he ought to," retorted Athanase. "What is a chief of Secret Service for if not to do things for everybody? For everybody, my dear friends, and a little for himself besides. A chief of Secret Service has to be in with everybody, with everybody and his father, as La Fontaine says (if you know that author), if he wants to hold his place. You know what I mean."

Athanase laughed loudly, glad of the chance to show how French he could be in his allusions, and looked at Rouletabille to see if he had been able to catch the tone of the conversation; but Rouletabille was too much occupied in watching a profile wrapped in a mantilla of black lace, in the Spanish fashion, to repay Athanase's performance with a knowing smile.

"You certainly have naive notions. You think a chief of Secret Police should be an ogre," replied the advocate as he nodded here and there to his friends.

"Why, certainly not. He needs to be a sheep in a place like that, a thorough sheep. Gounsovski is soft as a sheep. The time I dined with him he had mutton streaked with fat. He is just like that. I am sure he is mainly layers of fat. When you shake hands you feel as though you had grabbed a piece of fat. My word! And when he eats he wags his jaw fattishly. His head is like that, too; bald, you know, with a cranium like fresh lard. He speaks softly and looks at you like a kid looking to its mother for a juicy meal."

"But—why—it is Natacha!" murmured the lips of the young man.

"Certainly it is Natacha, Natacha herself," exclaimed Ivan Petrovitch, who had used his glasses the better to see whom the young French journalist was looking at. "Ah, the dear child! she has wanted to see Annouchka for a long time."

"What, Natacha! So it is. So it is. Natacha! Natacha!" said the others. "And with Boris Mourazoff 's parents."

"But Boris is not there," sniggered Thaddeus Tehitchnikoff.

"Oh, he can't be far away. If he was there we would see Michael Korsakoff too. They keep close on each other's heels."

"How has she happened to leave the general? She said she couldn't bear to be away from him."

"Except to see Annouchka," replied Ivan. "She wanted to see her, and talked so about it when I was there that even Feodor Feodorovitch was rather scandalized at her and Matrena Petrovna reproved her downright rudely. But what a girl wishes the gods bring about. That's the way."

"That's so, I know," put in Athanase. "Ivan Petrovitch is right. Natacha hasn't been able to hold herself in since she read that Annouchka was going to make her debut at

Krestowsky. She said she wasn't going to die without having seen the great artist."

"Her father had almost drawn her away from that crowd," affirmed Ivan, "and that was as it should be. She must have fixed up this affair with Boris and his parents."

"Yes, Feodor certainly isn't aware that his daughter's idea was to applaud the heroine of Kasan station. She is certainly made of stern stuff, my word," said Athanase.

"Natacha, you must remember, is a student," said Thaddeus, shaking his head; "a true student. They have misfortunes like that now in so many families. I recall, apropos of what Ivan said just now, how today she asked Michael Korsakoff, before me, to let her know where Annouchka would sing. More yet, she said she wished to speak to that artist if it were possible. Michael frowned on that idea, even before me. But Michael couldn't refuse her, any more than the others. He can reach Annouchka easier than anyone else. You remember it was he who rode hard and arrived in time with the pardon for that beautiful witch; she ought not to forget him if she cared for her life."

"Anyone who knows Michael Nikolaievitch knows that he did his duty promptly," announced Athanase Georgevitch crisply. "But he would not have gone a step further to save Annouchka. Even now he won't compromise his career by being seen at the home of a woman who is never from under the eyes of Gounsovski's agents and who hasn't been nicknamed 'Stool-pigeon' for nothing."

"Then why do we go to supper tonight with Annouchka?" asked Ivan.

"That's not the same thing. We are invited by Gounsovski himself. Don't forget that, if stories concerning it drift about some day, my friends," said Thaddeus.

"For that matter, Thaddeus, I accept the invitation of the honorable chief of our admirable Secret Service because I don't wish to slight him. I have dined at his house already. By sitting opposite him at a public table here I feel that I return that politeness. What do you say to that?"

"Since you have dined with him, tell us what kind of a man he is aside from his fattish qualities," said the curious councilor. "So many things are said about him. He certainly seems to be a man it is better to stand in with than to fall out with, so I accept his invitation. How could you manage to refuse it, anyway?"

"When he first offered me hospitality," explained the advocate, "I didn't even know him. I never had been near him. One day a police agent came and invited me to dinner by command—or, at least, I understood it wasn't wise to refuse the invitation, as you said, Ivan Petrovitch. When I went to his house I thought I was entering a fortress, and inside I thought it must be an umbrella shop. There were umbrellas everywhere, and goloshes. True, it was a day of pouring rain. I was struck by there being no guard with a big revolver in the antechamber. He had a little, timid schwitzar there, who took my umbrella, murmuring 'barine' and bowing over and over again. He conducted me through very ordinary rooms quite unguarded to an average sitting-room of a common kind. We dined with Madame Gounsovski, who appeared fattish like her husband, and three or four men whom I had never seen anywhere. One servant waited on us. My word!

"At dessert Gounsovski took me aside and told me I was unwise to 'argue that way.'

I asked him what he meant by that. He took my hands between his fat hands and repeated, 'No, no, it is not wise to argue like that.' I couldn't draw anything else out of him. For that matter, I understood him, and, you know, since that day I have cut out certain side passages unnecessary in my general law pleadings that had been giving me a reputation for rather too free opinions in the papers. None of that at my age! Ah, the great Gounsovski! Over our coffee I asked him if he didn't find the country in pretty strenuous times. He replied that he looked forward with impatience to the month of May, when he could go for a rest to a little property with a small garden that he had bought at Asnieres, near Paris. When he spoke of their house in the country Madame Gounsovski heaved a sigh of longing for those simple country joys. The month of May brought tears to her eyes. Husband and wife looked at one another with real tenderness. They had not the air of thinking for one second: tomorrow or the day after, before our country happiness comes, we may find ourselves stripped of everything. No! They were sure of their happy vacation and nothing seemed able to disquiet them under their fat. Gounsovski has done everybody so many services that no one really wishes him ill, poor man. Besides, have you noticed, my dear old friends, that no one ever tries to work harm to chiefs of Secret Police? One goes after heads of police, prefects of police, ministers, grand-dukes, and even higher, but the chiefs of Secret Police are never, never attacked. They can promenade tranquilly in the streets or in the gardens of Krestowsky or breathe the pure air of the Finland country or even the country around Paris. They have done so many little favors for this one and that, here and there, that no one wishes to do them the least injury. Each person always thinks, too, that others have been less well served than he. That is the secret of the thing, my friends, that is the secret. What do you say?"

The others said: "Ah, ah, the good Gounsovski. He knows. He knows. Certainly, accept his supper. With Annouchka it will be fun."

"Messieurs," asked Rouletabille, who continued to make discoveries in the audience, "do you know that officer who is seated at the end of a row down there in the orchestra seats? See, he is getting up."

"He? Why, that is Prince Galitch, who was one of the richest lords of the North Country. Now he is practically ruined."

"Thanks, gentlemen; certainly it is he. I know him," said Rouletabille, seating himself and mastering his emotion.

"They say he is a great admirer of Annouchka," hazarded Thaddeus. Then he walked away from the box.

"The prince has been ruined by women," said Athanase Georgevitch, who pretended to know the entire chronicle of gallantries in the empire.

"He also has been on good terms with Gounsovski," continued Thaddeus.

"He passes at court, though, for an unreliable. He once made a long visit to Tolstoi."

"Bah! Gounsovski must have rendered some signal service to that imprudent prince," concluded Athanase. "But for yourself, Thaddeus, you haven't said what you did with Gounsovski at Bakou."

(Rouletabille did not lose a word of what was being said around him, although he never lost sight of the profile hidden in the black mantle nor of Prince Galitch, his personal enemy, (note 1) who reappeared, it seemed to him, at a very critical moment.)

"I was returning from Balakani in a drojki," said Thaddeus Tchitchnikoff, "and I was drawing near Bakou after having seen the debris of my oil shafts that had been burned by the Tartars, when I met Gounsovski in the road, who, with two of his friends, found themselves badly off with one of the wheels of their carriage broken. I stopped. He explained to me that he had a Tartar coachman, and that this coachman having seen an Armenian on the road before him, could find nothing better to do than run full tilt into the Armenian's equipage. He had

---

1. as told in "The Lady In Black."

reached over and taken the reins from him, but a wheel of the carriage was broken." (Rouletabille quivered, because he caught a glance of communication between Prince Galitch and Natacha, who was leaning over the edge of her box.) "So I offered to take Gounsovski and his friends into my carriage, and we rode all together to Bakou after Gounsovski, who always wishes to do a service, as Athanase Georgevitch says, had warned his Tartar coachman not to finish the Armenian." (Prince Galitch, at the moment the orchestra commenced the introductory music for Annouchka's new number, took advantage of all eyes being turned toward the rising curtain to pass near Natacha's seat. This time he did not look at Natacha, but Rouletabille was sure that his lips had moved as he went by her.)

Thaddeus continued: "It is necessary to explain that at Bakou my little house is one of the first before you reach the quay. I had some Armenian employees there. When arrived, what do you suppose I saw? A file of soldiers with cannon, yes, with a cannon, on my word, turned against my house and an officer saying quietly, 'there it is. Fire!'" (Rouletabille made yet another discovery— two, three discoveries. Near by, standing back of Natacha's seat, was a figure not unknown to the young reporter, and there, in one of the orchestra chairs, were two other men whose faces he had seen that same morning in Koupriane's barracks. Here was where a memory for faces stood him in good stead. He saw that he was not the only person keeping close watch on Natacha.) "When I heard what the officer said," Thaddeus went on, "I nearly dropped out of the drojki. I hurried to the police commissioner. He explained the affair promptly, and I was quick to understand. During my absence one of my Armenian employees had fired at a Tartar who was passing. For that matter, he had killed him. The governor was informed and had ordered the house to be bombarded, for an example, as had been done with several others. I found Gounsovski and told him the trouble in two words. He said it wasn't necessary for him to interfere in the affair, that I had only to talk to the officer. 'Give him a good present, a hundred roubles, and he will leave your house. I went back to the officer and took him aside; he said he wanted to do anything that he could for me, but that the order was positive to bombard the house. I reported his answer to Gounsovski, who told me: 'Tell him then to turn the muzzle of the cannon the other way and bombard the building of the chemist across the way, then he can always say that he mistook which house was intended.' I did that, and he had them turn the cannon. They bombarded the chemist's place, and I got out of the whole thing for the hundred roubles. Gounsovski, the good fellow, may be a great lump of fat and be like an umbrella merchant, but I have always been grateful to him from the bottom of my heart, you can understand, Athanase Georgevitch."

"What reputation has Prince Galitch at the court?" inquired Rouletabille all at once.

"Oh, oh!" laughed the others. "Since he went so openly to visit Tolstoi he doesn't go to the court any more."

"And—his opinions? What are his opinions?"

"Oh, the opinions of everybody are so mixed nowadays, nobody knows."

Ivan Petrovitch said, "He passes among some people as very advanced and very much compromised."

"Yet they don't bother him?" inquired Rouletabille.

"Pooh, pooh," replied the gay Councilor of Empire, "it is rather he who tries to mix with them."

Thaddeus stooped down and said, "They say that he can't be reached because of the hold he has over a certain great personage in the court, and it would be a scandal—a great scandal."

"Be quiet, Thaddeus," interrupted Athanase Georgevitch, roughly. "It is easy to see that you are lately from the provinces to speak so recklessly, but if you go on this way I shall leave."

"Athanase Georgevitch is right; hang onto your mouth, Thaddeus," counseled Ivan Petrovitch.

The talkers all grew silent, for the curtain was rising. In the audience there were mysterious allusions being made to this second number of Annouchka, but no one seemed able to say what it was to be, and it was, as a matter of fact, very simple. After the whirl-wind of dances and choruses and all the splendor with which she had been accompanied the first time, Annouchka appeared as a poor Russian peasant in a scene representing the barren steppes, and very simply she sank to her knees and recited her evening prayers. Annouchka was singularly beautiful. Her aquiline nose with sensitive nostrils, the clean-cut outline of her eyebrows, her look that now was almost tender, now menacing, always unusual, her pale rounded cheeks and the entire expression of her face showed clearly the strength of new ideas, spontaneity, deep resolution and, above all, passion. The prayer was passionate. She had an admirable contralto voice which affected the audience strangely from its very first notes. She asked God for daily bread for everyone in the immense Russian land, daily bread for the flesh and for the spirit, and she stirred the tears of everyone there, to which-ever party they belonged. And when, as her last note sped across the desolate steppe and she rose and walked toward the miserable hut, frantic bravos from a delirious audience told her the prodigious emotions she had aroused. Little Rouletabille, who, not understanding the words, nevertheless caught the spirit of that prayer, wept. Everybody wept. Ivan Petrovitch, Athanase Georgevitch, Thaddeus Tchitchnikoff were standing up, stamping their feet and clapping their hands like enthusiastic boys. The students, who could be easily distinguished by the uniform green edging they wore on their coats, uttered insensate cries. And suddenly there rose the first strains of the national hymn. There was hesitation at first, a wavering. But not for long. Those who had been dreading some counter-demonstration realized that no objection could possibly be raised to a prayer for the Tsar. All heads uncovered and the Bodje Taara Krari mounted, unanimously, toward the stars.

Through his tears the young reporter never gave up his close watch on Natacha. She had half risen, and, sinking back, leaned on the edge of the box. She called, time and time again, a name that Rouletabille could not hear in the uproar, but that he felt sure was "Annouchka! Annouchka!" "The reckless girl," murmured Rouletabille, and, profiting by the general excitement, he left the box without being noticed. He made his way through the crowd toward Natacha, whom he had sought futilely since morning. The audience, after clamoring in vain for a repetition of the prayer by Annouchka, commenced to disperse, and the reporter was swept along with them for a few moments. When he reached the range of boxes he saw that Natacha and the family she had been with were gone. He looked on all sides without seeing the object of his search and like a madman commenced to run through the passages, when a sudden idea struck his blood cold. He inquired where the exit for the artists was and as soon as it was pointed out, he hurried there. He was not mistaken. In the front line of the crowd that waited to see Annouchka come out he recognized Natacha, with her head enveloped in the black mantle so that none should see her face. Besides, this corner of the garden was in a half-gloom. The police barred the way; he could not approach as near Natacha as he wished. He set himself to slip like a serpent through the crowd. He was not separated from Natacha by more than four or five persons when a great jostling commenced. Annouchka was coming out. Cries rose: "Annouchka! Annouchka!" Rouletabille threw himself on his knees and on all-fours succeeded in sticking his head through into the way kept by the police for Annouchka's passage. There, wrapped in a great red mantle, his hat on his arm, was a man Rouletabille immediately recognized. It was Prince Galitch. They were hurrying to escape the impending pressure of the crowd. But Annouchka as she passed near Natacha stopped just a second—a movement that did not escape Rouletabille—and, turning toward her said just the one word, "Caracho." Then she passed on. Rouletabille got up and forced his way back, having once more lost Natacha. He searched for her. He ran to the carriage-way and arrived just in time to see her seated in a carriage with the Mourazoff family. The carriage started at once in the direction of the datcha des Iles. The young man remained standing there, thinking. He made a gesture as though he were ready now to let luck take its course. "In the end," said he, "it will be better so, perhaps," and then, to himself, "Now to supper, my boy."

He turned in his tracks and soon was established in the glaring light of the restaurant. Officers standing, glass in hand, were saluting from table to table and waving a thousand compliments with grace that was almost feminine.

He heard his name called joyously, and recognized the voice of Ivan Petrovitch. The three boon companions were seated over a bottle of champagne resting in its ice-bath and were being served with tiny pates while they waited for the supper-hour, which was now near.

Rouletabille yielded to their invitation readily enough, and accompanied them when the head-waiter informed Thaddeus that the gentlemen were desired in a private room. They went to the first floor and were ushered into a large apartment whose balcony opened on the hall of the winter-theater, empty now. But the apartment was already occupied. Before a table covered with a shining service Gounsovski did the honors.

He received them like a servant, with his head down, an obsequious smile, and his back bent, bowing several times as each of the guests were presented to him. Athanase had described him accurately enough, a mannikin in fat. Under the vast bent brow one could hardly see his eyes, behind the blue glasses that seemed always ready to fall as he inclined too far his fat head with its timid and yet all-powerful glance. When he spoke in his falsetto voice, his chin dropped in a fold over his collar, and he had a steady gesture with the thumb and index finger of his right hand to retain the glasses from sliding down his short, thick nose.

Behind him there was the fine, haughty silhouette of Prince Galitch. He had been invited by Annouchka, for she had consented to risk this supper only in company with three or four of her friends, officers who could not be further compromised by this affair, as they were already under the eye of

374

the Okrana (Secret Police) despite their high birth. Gounsovski had seen them come with a sinister chuckle and had lavished upon them his marks of devotion.

He loved Annouchka. It would have sufficed to have surprised just once the jealous glance he sent from beneath his great blue glasses when he gazed at the singer to have understood the sentiments that actuated him in the presence of the beautiful daughter of the Black Land.

Annouchka was seated, or, rather, she lounged, Oriental fashion, on the sofa which ran along the wall behind the table. She paid attention to no one. Her attitude was forbidding, even hostile. She indifferently allowed her marvelous black hair that fell in two tresses over her shoulder to be caressed by the perfumed hands of the beautiful Onoto, who had heard her this evening for the first time and had thrown herself with enthusiasm into her arms after the last number. Onoto was an artist too, and the pique she felt at first over Annouchka's success could not last after the emotion aroused by the evening prayer before the hut. "Come to supper," Annouchka had said to her.

"With whom?" inquired the Spanish artist.

"With Gounsovski."

"Never."

"Do come. You will help me pay my debt and perhaps he will be useful to you as well. He is useful to everybody."

Decidedly Onoto did not understand this country, where the worst enemies supped together.

Rouletabille had been monopolized at once by Prince Galitch, who took him into a corner and said:

"What are you doing here?"

"Do I inconvenience you?" asked the boy.

The other assumed the amused smile of the great lord.

"While there is still time," he said, "believe me, you ought to start, to quit this country. Haven't you had sufficient notice?"

"Yes," replied the reporter. "And you can dispense with any further notice from this time on."

He turned his back.

"Why, it is the little Frenchman from the Trebassof villa," commenced the falsetto voice of Gounsovski as he pushed a seat towards the young man and begged him to sit between him and Athanase Georgevitch, who was already busy with the hors-d'oeuvres.

"How do you do, monsieur?" said the beautiful, grave voice of Annouchka.

Rouletabille saluted.

"I see that I am in a country of acquaintances," he said, without appearing disturbed.

He addressed a lively compliment to Annouchka, who threw him a kiss.

"Rouletabille!" cried la belle Onoto. "Why, then, he is the little fellow who solved the mystery of the Yellow Room."

"Himself."

"What are you doing here?"

"He came to save the life of General Trebassof," sniggered Gounsovski. "He is certainly a brave little young man."

"The police know everything," said Rouletabille coldly. And he asked for champagne, which he never drank.

The champagne commenced its work. While Thaddeus and the officers told each other stories of Bakou or paid compliments to the women, Gounsovski, who was through with raillery, leaned toward Rouletabille and gave that young man fatherly counsel with great unction.

"You have undertaken, young man, a noble task and one all the more difficult because General Trebassof is condemned not only by his enemies but still more by the ignorance of Koupriane. Understand me thoroughly:

Koupriane is my friend and a man whom I esteem very highly. He is good, brave as a warrior, but I wouldn't give a kopeck for his police. He has mixed in our affairs lately by creating his own secret police, but I don't wish to meddle with that. It amuses us. It's the new style, anyway; everybody wants his secret police nowadays. And yourself, young man, what, after all, are you doing here? Reporting? No. Police work? That is our business and your business. I wish you good luck, but I don't expect it. Remember that if you need any help I will give it you willingly. I love to be of service. And I don't wish any harm to befall you."

"You are very kind, monsieur," was all Rouletabille replied, and he called again for champagne.

Several times Gounsovski addressed remarks to Annouchka, who concerned herself with her meal and had little answer for him.

"Do you know who applauded you the most this evening?"

"No," said Annouchka indifferently.

"The daughter of General Trebassof."

"Yes, that is true, on my word," cried Ivan Petrovitch.

"Yes, yes, Natacha was there," joined in the other friends from the datcha des Iles.

"For me, I saw her weep," said Rouletabille, looking at Annouchka fixedly.

But Annouchka replied in an icy tone:

"I do not know her."

"She is unlucky in having a father..." Prince Galitch commenced.

"Prince, no politics, or let me take my leave," clucked Gounsovski. "Your health, dear Annouchka."

"Your health, Gounsovski. But you have no worry about that."

"Why?" demanded Thaddeus Tchitchnikoff in equivocal fashion.

"Because he is too useful to the government," cried Ivan Petrovitch.

"No," replied Annouchka; "to the revolutionaries."

All broke out laughing. Gounsovski recovered his slipping glasses by his usual quick movement and sniggered softly, insinuatingly, like fat boiling in the pot:

"So they say. And it is my strength."

"His system is excellent," said the prince. "As he is in with everybody, everybody is in with the police, without knowing it."

"They say. . . ah, ah. . . they say. . ." (Athanase was choking over a little piece of toast that he had soaked in his soup) "they say that he has driven away all the hooligans and even all the beggars of the church of Kasan."

Thereupon they commenced to tell stories of the hooligans, street-thieves who since the recent political troubles had infested St. Petersburg and whom nobody, could get rid of without paying for it.

Athanase Georgevitch said:

"There are hooligans that ought to have existed even if they never have. One of them stopped a young girl before Varsovie station. The girl, frightened, immediately held out her purse to him, with two roubles and fifty kopecks in it. The hooligan took it all. 'Goodness,' cried she, 'I have nothing now to take my train with.' 'How much is it?' asked the hooligan. 'Sixty kopecks.' 'Sixty kopecks! Why didn't you say so?' And the bandit, hanging onto the two roubles, returned the fifty-kopeck piece to the trembling child and added a ten-kopeck piece out of his own pocket."

"Something quite as funny happened to me two winters ago, at Moscow," said la belle Onoto. "I had just stepped out of the door when I was stopped by a hooligan. 'Give me twenty kopecks,' said the hooligan. I was so frightened that I couldn't get my purse open. 'Quicker,' said he. Finally I gave him twenty kopecks. 'Now,' said he then, 'kiss my hand.' And I had to kiss it, because he held his knife in the other."

"Oh, they are quick with their knives," said Thaddeus. "As I was leaving Gastinidvor once I was stopped by a hooligan who stuck a huge carving-knife under my nose. 'You can have it for a rouble and a half,' he said. You can believe that I bought it without any haggling. And it was a very good bargain. It was worth at least three roubles. Your health, belle Onoto."

"I always take my revolver when I go out," said Athanase. "It is more prudent. I say this before the police. But I would rather be arrested by the police than stabbed by the hooligans."

"There's no place any more to buy revolvers," declared Ivan Petrovitch. "All such places are closed."

Gounsovski settled his glasses, rubbed his fat hands and said:

"There are some still at my locksmith's place. The proof is that today in the little

Kaniouche my locksmith, whose name is Smith, went into the house of the grocer at the corner and wished to sell him a revolver. It was a Browning. 'An arm of the greatest reliability,' he said to him, 'which never misses fire and which works very easily.' Having pronounced these words, the locksmith tried his revolver and lodged a ball in the grocer's lung. The grocer is dead, but before he died he bought the revolver. 'You are right,' he said to the locksmith; 'it is a terrible weapon.' And then he died."

The others laughed heartily. They thought it very funny. Decidedly this great Gounsovski always had a funny story. Who would not like to be his friend? Annouchka had deigned to smile. Gounsovski, in recognition, extended his hand to her like a mendicant. The young woman touched it with the end of her fingers, as if she were placing a twenty-kopeck piece in the hand of a hooligan, and withdrew from it with disgust.

Then the doors opened for the Bohemians. Their swarthy troupe soon filled the room. Every evening men and women in their native costumes came from old Derevnia, where they lived all together in a sort of ancient patriarchal community, with customs that had not changed for centuries; they scattered about in the places of pleasure, in the fashionable restaurants, where they gathered large sums, for it was a fashionable luxury to have them sing at the end of suppers, and everyone showered money on them in order not to be behind the others. They accompanied on guzlas, on castanets, on tambourines, and sang the old airs, doleful and languorous, or excitable and breathless as the flight of the earliest nomads in the beginnings of the world.

When they had entered, those present made place for them, and Rouletabille, who for some moments had been showing marks of fatigue and of a giddiness natural enough in a young man who isn't in the habit of drinking the finest champagnes, profited by the diversion to get a corner of the sofa not far from Prince Galitch, who occupied the place at Annouchka's right.

"Look, Rouletabaille is asleep," remarked la belle Onoto.

"Poor boy!" said Annouchka.

And, turning toward Gounsovski:

"Aren't you soon going to get him out of our way? I heard some of our brethren the other day speaking in a way that would cause pain to those who care about his health."

"Oh, that," said Gounsovski, shaking his head, "is an affair I have nothing to do with. Apply to Koupriane. Your health, belle Annouchka."

But the Bohemians swept some opening chords for their songs, and the singers took everybody's attention, everybody excepting Prince Galitch and Annouchka, who, half turned toward one another, exchanged some words on the edge of all this musical uproar. As for Rouletabille, he certainly must have been sleeping soundly not to have been waked by all that noise, melodious as it was. It is true that he had—apparently—drunk a good deal and, as everyone knows, in Russia drink lays out those who can't stand it. When the Bohemians had sung three times Gounsovski made a sign that they might go to charm other ears, and slipped into the hands of the chief of the band a twenty-five rouble note. But Onoto wished to give her mite, and a regular collection commenced. Each one threw roubles into the plate held out by a little swarthy Bohemian girl with crow-black hair, carelessly combed, falling over her forehead, her eyes and her face, in so droll a fashion that one would have said the little thing was a weeping-willow soaked in ink. The plate reached Prince Galitch, who futilely searched his pockets.

"Bah!" said he, with a lordly air, "I have no money. But here is my pocket-book; I will give it to you for a souvenir of me, Katharina."

Thaddeus and Athanase exclaimed at the generosity of the prince, but Annouchka said:

"The prince does as he should, for my friends can never sufficiently repay the hospitality that that little thing gave me in her dirty hut when I was in hiding, while your famous department was deciding what to do about me, my dear Gounsovski."

"Eh," replied Gounsovski, "I let you know that all you had to do was to take a fine apartment in the city."

Annouchka spat on the ground like a teamster, and Gounsovski from yellow turned green.

"But why did you hide yourself that way, Annouchka?" asked Onoto as she caressed the beautiful tresses of the singer.

"You know I had been condemned to death, and then pardoned. I had been able to leave Moscow, and I hadn't any desire to be re-taken here and sent to taste the joys of Siberia."

"But why were you condemned to death?"

"Why, she doesn't know anything!" exclaimed the others.

"Good Lord, I'm just back from London and Paris—how should I know anything! But to have been condemned to death! That must have been amusing."

"Very amusing," said Annouchka icily. "And if you have a brother whom you love, Onoto, think how much more amusing it must be to have him shot before you."

"Oh, my love, forgive me!"

"So you may know and not give any pain to your Annouchka in the future, I will tell you, madame, what happened to our dear friend," said Prince Galitch.

"We would do better to drive away such terrible memories," ventured Gounsovski, lifting his eyelashes behind his glasses, but he bent his head as Annouchka sent him a blazing glance.

"Speak, Galitch."

The Prince did as she said.

"Annouchka had a brother, Vlassof, an engineer on the Kasan line, whom the Strike Committee had ordered to take out a train as the only means of escape for the leaders of the revolutionary troops when Trebassof's soldiers, aided by the Semenowsky regiment, had become masters of the city. The last resistance took place at the station. It was necessary to get started. All the ways were guarded by the military. There were soldiers everywhere! Vlassof said to his comrades, 'I will save you;' and his comrades saw him mount the engine with a woman. That woman was—well, there she sits. Vlassof 's fireman had been killed the evening before, on a barricade; it was Annouchka who took his place. They busied themselves and the train started like a shot. On that curved line, discovered at once, easy to attack, under a shower of bullets, Vlassof developed a speed of ninety versts an hour. He ran the indicator up to the explosion point. The lady over there continued to pile coal into the furnace. The danger came to be less from the military and more from an explosion at any moment. In the midst of the balls Vlassof kept his usual coolness. He sped not only with the firebox open but with the forced draught. It was a miracle that the engine was not smashed against the curve of the embankment. But they got past. Not a man was hurt. Only a woman was wounded. She got a ball in the chest."

"There!" cried Annouchka.

With a magnificent gesture she flung open her white and heaving chest, and put her finger on a scar that Gounsovski, whose fat began to melt in heavy drops of sweat about his temples, dared not look at.

"Fifteen days later," continued the prince, "Vlassof entered an inn at Lubetszy. He didn't know it was full of soldiers. His face never altered. They searched him. They found a revolver and papers on him. They knew whom they had to do with. He was a good prize. Vlassof was taken to Moscow and condemned to be shot. His sister, wounded as she was, learned of his arrest and joined him. 'I do not wish,' she said to him, 'to leave you to die alone.' She also was condemned. Before the execution the soldiers offered to bandage their eyes, but both refused, saying they preferred to meet death face to face. The orders were to shoot all the other condemned revolutionaries first, then Vlassof, then his sister. It was in vain that Vlassof asked to die last. Their comrades in execution sank to their knees, bleeding from their death wounds. Vlassof embraced his sister and walked to the place of death. There he addressed the soldiers: 'Now you have to carry out your duty according to the oath you have taken. Fulfill it honestly as I have fulfilled mine. Captain, give the order.' The volley sounded. Vlassof remained erect, his arms crossed on his breast, safe and sound. Not a ball had touched him. The soldiers did not wish to fire at him. He had to summon them again to fulfill their duty, and obey their chief. Then they fired again, and he fell. He looked at his sister with his eyes full of horrible suffering. Seeing that he lived, and wishing to appear charitable, the captain, upon Annouchka's prayers, approached and cut short his sufferings by firing a revolver into his ear. Now it was Annouchka's turn. She knelt by the body of her brother, kissed his bloody lips, rose and said, 'I am ready.' As the guns were raised, an officer came running, bearing the pardon of the Tsar. She did not wish it, and she whom they had not bound when she was to die had to be restrained when she learned she was to live."

Prince Galitch, amid the anguished silence of all there, started to add some words of comment to his sinister recital, but Annouchka interrupted:

"The story is ended," said she. "Not a word, Prince. If I asked you to tell it in all its horror, if I wished you to bring back to us the atrocious moment of my brother's death, it is so that monsieur" (her fingers pointed to Gounsovski) "shall know well, once for all, that if I have submitted for some hours now to this promiscuous company that has been imposed upon me, now that I have paid the debt by accepting this abominable supper, I have nothing more to do with this purveyor of bagnios and of hangman's ropes who is here."

"She is mad," he muttered. "She is mad. What has come over her? What has happened? Only today she was so, so amiable."

And he stuttered, desolately, with an embarrassed laugh:

"Ah, the women, the women! Now what have I done to her?"

"What have you done to me, wretch? Where are Belachof, Bartowsky and Strassof? And Pierre Slutch? All the comrades who swore with me to revenge my brother? Where are they? On what gallows did you have them hung? What mine have you buried them in? And still you follow your slavish task. And my friends, my other friends, the poor comrades of my artist life, the inoffensive young men who have not committed any other crime than to come to see me too often when I was lively, and who believed they could talk freely in my dressing-room—where are they? Why have they left me, one by one? Why have they disappeared? It is you, wretch, who watched them, who spied on them, making me, I haven't any doubt, your horrible accomplice, mixing me up in your beastly work, you dog! You knew what they call me. You have known it for a long time, and you may well laugh over it. But I, I never knew until this evening; I never learned until this evening all I owe to you. 'Stool pigeon! Stool pigeon!' I! Horror! Ah, you dog, you dog! Your mother, when you were brought into the world, your mother..." Here she hurled at him the most offensive insult that a Russian can offer a man of that race.

She trembled and sobbed with rage, spat in fury, and stood up ready to go, wrapped in her mantle like a great red flag. She was the statue of hate and vengeance. She was horrible and terrible. She was beautiful. At the final supreme insult, Gounsovski started and rose to his feet as though he had received an actual blow in the face. He did not look at Annouchka, but fixed his eyes on Prince Galitch. His finger pointed him out:

"There is the man," he hissed, "who has told you all these fine things."

"Yes, it is I," said the Prince, tranquilly.

"Caracho!" barked Gounsovski, instantaneously regaining his coolness.

"Ah, yes, but you'll not touch him," clamored the spirited girl of the Black Land; "you are not strong enough for that."

"I know that monsieur has many friends at court," agreed the chief of the Secret Service with an ominous calm. "I don't wish ill to monsieur. You speak, madame, of the way some of your friends have had to be sacrificed. I hope that some day you will be better informed, and that you will understand I saved all of them I could."

"Let us go," muttered Annouchka. "I shall spit in his face."

"Yes, all I could," replied the other, with his habitual gesture of hanging on to his glasses.

400

"And I shall continue to do so. I promise you not to say anything more disagreeable to the prince than as regards his little friend the Bohemian Katharina, whom he has treated so generously just now, doubtless because Boris Mourazoff pays her too little for the errands she runs each morning to the villa of Krestowsky Ostrow."

At these words the Prince and Annouchka both changed countenance. Their anger rose. Annouchka turned her head as though to arrange the folds of her cloak. Galitch contented himself with shrugging his shoulders impatiently and murmuring:

"Still some other abomination that you are concocting, monsieur, and that we don't know how to reply to."

After which he bowed to the supper-party, took Annouchka's arm and had her move before him. Gounsovski bowed, almost bent in two. When he rose he saw before him the three astounded and horrified figures of Thaddeus Tchitchnikoff, Ivan Petrovitch and Athanase Georgevitch.

"Messieurs," he said to them, in a colorless voice which seemed not to belong to him, "the time has come for us to part. I need not say that we have supped as friends and that, if you wish it to be so, we can forget everything that has been said here."

The three others, frightened, at once protested their discretion. He added, roughly this time, "Service of the Tsar," and the three stammered, "God save the Tsar!" After which he saw them to the door. When the door had closed after them, he said, "My little Annouchka, you mustn't reckon without me." He hurried toward the sofa, where Rouletabille was lying forgotten, and gave him a tap on the shoulder.

"Come, get up. Don't act as though you were asleep. Not an instant to lose. They are going to carry through the Trebassof affair this evening."

Rouletabille was already on his legs.

"Oh, monsieur," said he, "I didn't want you to tell me that. Thanks all the same, and good evening."

He went out.

Gounsovski rang. A servant appeared.

"Tell them they may now open all the rooms on this corridor; I'll not hold them any longer." Thus had Gounsovski kept himself protected.

Left alone, the head of the Secret Service wiped his brow and drank a great glass of iced water which he emptied at a draught. Then he said:

"Koupriane will have his work cut out for him this evening; I wish him good luck. As to them, whatever happens, I wash my hands of them."

And he rubbed his hands.

X

A DRAMA IN THE NIGHT

At the door of the Krestowsky Rouletabille, who was in a hurry for a conveyance, jumped into an open carriage where la belle Onoto was already seated. The dancer caught him on her knees.

"To Eliaguine, fast as you can," cried the reporter for all explanation.

"Scan! Scan! (Quickly, quickly)" repeated Onoto.

She was accompanied by a vague sort of person to whom neither of them paid the least attention.

"What a supper! You waked up at last, did you?" quizzed the actress. But Rouletabille, standing up behind the enormous coachman, urged the horses and directed the route of the carriage. They bolted along through the night at a dizzy pace. At the corner of a bridge he ordered the horses stopped, thanked his companions and disappeared.

"What a country! What a country! Caramba!" said the Spanish artist.

The carriage waited a few minutes, then turned back toward the city.

Rouletabille got down the embankment and slowly, taking infinite precautions not to reveal his presence by making the least noise, made his way to where the river is widest. Seen through the blackness of the night the blacker mass of the Trebassof villa loomed like an enormous blot, he stopped. Then he glided like a snake through the reeds, the grass, the ferns. He was at the back of the villa, near the river, not far from the little path where he had discovered the passage of the assassin, thanks to the broken cobwebs. At that moment the moon rose and the birch-trees, which just before had been like great black staffs, now became white tapers which seemed to brighten that sinister solitude.

The reporter wished to profit at once by the sudden luminance to learn if his movements had been noticed and if the approaches to the villa on that side were guarded. He picked up a small pebble and threw it some distance from him along the path. At the unexpected noise three or four shadowy heads were outlined suddenly in the white light of the moon, but disappeared at once, lost again in the dark tufts of grass.

He had gained his information.

The reporter's acute ear caught a gliding in his direction, a slight swish of twigs; then all at once a shadow grew by his side and he felt the cold of a revolver barrel on his temple. He said "Koupriane," and at once a hand seized his and pressed it.

The night had become black again. He murmured: "How is it you are here in person?"

The Prefect of Police whispered in his ear:

"I have been informed that something will happen tonight. Natacha went to Krestowsky and exchanged some words with Annouchka there. Prince Galitch is involved, and it is an affair of State."

"Natacha has returned?" inquired Rouletabille.

"Yes, a long time ago. She ought to be in bed. In any case she is pretending to be abed. The light from her chamber, in the window over the garden, has been put out."

"Have you warned Matrena Petrovna?"

"Yes, I have let her know that she must keep on the sharp look-out tonight."

"That's a mistake. I shouldn't have told her anything. She will take such extra precautions that the others will be instantly warned."

"I have told her she should not go to the ground-floor at all this night, and that she must not leave the general's chamber."

"That is perfect, if she will obey you."

"You see I have profited by all your information. I have followed your instructions. The road from the Krestowsky is under surveillance."

"Perhaps too much. How are you planning?"

"We will let them enter. I don't know whom I have to deal with. I want to strike a sure blow. I shall take him in the act. No more doubt after this, you trust me."

"Adieu."

"Where are you going?"

"To bed. I have paid my debt to my host. I have the right to some repose now. Good luck!"

But Koupriane had seized his hand.

"Listen."

With a little attention they detected a light stroke on the water. If a boat was moving at this time for this bank of the Neva and wished to remain hidden, the right moment had certainly been chosen. A great black cloud covered the moon; the wind was light. The boat would have time to get from one bank to the other without being discovered. Rouletabille waited no longer. On all-fours he ran like a beast, rapidly and silently, and rose behind the wall of the villa, where he made a turn, reached the gate, aroused the dvornicks and demanded Ermolai, who opened the gate for him.

"The Barinia?" he said.

Ermolai pointed his finger to the bedroom floor.

"Caracho!"

Rouletabille was already across the garden and had hoisted himself by his fingers to the window of Natacha's chamber, where he listened. He plainly heard Natacha walking about in the dark chamber. He fell back lightly onto his feet, mounted the veranda steps and opened the door, then closed it so lightly that Ermolai, who watched him from outside not two feet away, did not hear the slightest grinding of the hinges. Inside the villa Rouletabille advanced on tiptoe. He found the door of the drawing-room open. The door of the sitting-room had not been closed, or else had been reopened. He turned in his tracks, felt in the dark for a chair and sat down, with his hand on his revolver in his pocket, waiting for the events that would not delay long now. Above he heard distinctly from time to time the movements of Matrena Petrovna. And this would evidently give a sense of security to those who needed to have the ground-floor free this night. Rouletabille imagined that the doors of the rooms on the ground-floor had been left open so that it would be easier for those who would be below to hear what was happening upstairs. And perhaps he was not wrong.

Suddenly there was a vertical bar of pale light from the sitting-room that overlooked the Neva. He deduced two things: first, that the window was already slightly open, then that the moon was out from the clouds again. The bar of light died almost instantly, but Rouletabille's eyes, now used to the obscurity, still distinguished the open line of the window. There the shade was less deep. Suddenly he felt the blood pound at his temples, for the line of the open window grew larger, increased, and the shadow of a man gradually rose on the balcony. Rouletabille drew his revolver.

The man stood up immediately behind one of the shutters and struck a light blow on the glass. Placed as he was now he could be seen no more. His shadow mixed with the shadow of the shutter. At the noise on the glass Natacha's door had opened cautiously, and she entered the sitting-room. On tiptoe she went quickly to the window and opened it. The man entered. The little light that by now was commencing to dawn was enough to show Rouletabille that Natacha still wore the toilette in which he had seen her that same evening at Krestowsky. As for the man, he tried in vain to identify him; he was only a dark mass wrapped in a mantle. He leaned over and kissed Natacha's hand. She said only one word: "Scan!" (Quickly).

But she had no more than said it before, under a vigorous attack, the shutters and the two halves of the window were thrown wide, and silent shadows jumped rapidly onto the balcony and sprang into the villa. Natacha uttered a shrill cry in which Rouletabille believed still he heard more of despair than terror, and the shadows threw themselves on the man; but he, at the first alarm, had thrown himself upon the carpet and had slipped from them between their legs. He regained the balcony and jumped from it as the others turned toward him. At least, it was so that Rouletabille believed he saw the mysterious struggle go in the half-light, amid most impressive silence, after that frightened cry of Natacha's. The whole affair had lasted only a few seconds, and the man was still hanging over the balcony, when from the bottom of the hall a new person sprang. It was Matrena Petrovna.

Warned by Koupriane that something would happen that night, and foreseeing that it would happen on the ground-floor where she was forbidden to be, she had found nothing better to do than to make her faithful maid go secretly to the bedroom floor, with orders to walk about there all night, to make all think she herself was near the general, while she remained below, hidden in the dining-room.

Matrena Petrovna now threw herself out onto the balcony, crying in Russian, "Shoot! Shoot!" In just that moment the man was hesitating whether to risk the jump and perhaps break his neck, or descend less rapidly by the gutter-pipe. A policeman fired and missed him, and the man, after firing back and wounding the policeman, disappeared. It was still too far from dawn for them to see clearly what happened below, where the barking of Brownings alone was heard. And there could be nothing more sinister than the revolver-shots unaccompanied by cries in the mists of the morning. The man, before he disappeared, had had only time by a quick kick to throw down one of the two ladders which had been used by the police in climbing; down the other one all the police in a bunch, even to the wounded one, went sliding, falling, rising, running after the shadow which fled still, discharging the Browning steadily; other shadows rose from the river-bank, hovering in the mist. Suddenly Koupriane's voice was heard shouting orders, calling upon his agents to take the quarry alive or dead. From the balcony Matrena Petrovna cried out also, like a savage, and Rouletabille tried in vain to keep her quiet. She was delirious at the thought "The Other" might escape yet. She fired a revolver, she also, into the group, not knowing whom she might wound. Rouletabille grabbed her arm and as she turned on him angrily she observed Natacha, who, leaning until she almost fell over the balcony, her lips trembling with delirious utterance, followed as well as she could the progress of the struggle, trying to understand what happened below, under the trees, near the Neva, where the tumult by now extended. Matrena Petrovna pulled her back by the arms. Then she took her by the neck and threw her into the drawing-room in a heap. When she had almost strangled her step-daughter, Matrena Petrovna saw that the general was there. He appeared in the pale glimmerings of dawn like a specter. By what miracle had Feodor Feodorovitch been able to descend the stairs and reach there? How had it been brought about? She saw him tremble with anger or with wretchedness under the folds of the soldier's cape that floated about him. He demanded in a hoarse voice, "What is it?"

Matrena Petrovna threw herself at his feet, made the orthodox sign of the Cross, as if she wished to summon God to witness, and then, pointing to Natacha, she denounced his daughter to her husband as she would have pointed her out to a judge.

"The one, Feodor Feodorovitch, who has wished more than once to assassinate you, and who this night has opened the datcha to your assassin is your daughter."

The general held himself up by his two hands against the wall, and, looking at Matrena and Natacha, who now were both upon the floor before him like suppliants, he said to Matrena:

"It is you who assassinate me."

"Me! By the living God!" babbled Matrena Petrovna desperately. "If I had been able to keep this from you, Jesus would have been good! But I say no more to crucify you. Feodor Feodorovitch, question your daughter, and if what I have said is not true, kill me, kill me as a lying, evil beast. I will say thank you, thank you, and I will die happier than if what I have said was true. Ah, I long to be dead! Kill me!"

Feodor Feodorovitch pushed her back with his stick as one would push a worm in his path. Without saying anything further, she rose from her knees and looked with her haggard eyes, with her crazed face, at Rouletabille, who grasped her arm. If she had had her hands still free she would not have hesitated a second in wreaking justice upon herself under this bitter fate of alienating Feodor. And it seemed frightful to Rouletabille that he should be present at one of those horrible family dramas the issue of which in the wild times of Peter the Great would have sent the general to the hangman either as a father or as a husband.

The general did not deign even to consider for any length of time Matrena's delirium. He said to his daughter, who shook with sobs on the floor, "Rise, Natacha Feodorovna." And Feodor's daughter understood that her father never would believe in her guilt. She drew herself up towards him and kissed his hands like a happy slave.

At this moment repeated blows shook the veranda door. Matrena, the watch-dog, anxious to die after Feodor's reproach, but still at her post, ran toward what she believed to be a new danger. But she recognized Koupriane's voice, which called on her to open. She let him in herself.

"What is it?" she implored.

"Well, he is dead."

A cry answered him. Natacha had heard.

"But who—who—who?" questioned Matrena breathlessly.

Koupriane went over to Feodor and grasped his hands.

"General," he said, "there was a man who had sworn your ruin and who was made an instrument by your enemies. We have just killed that man."

"Do I know him?" demanded Feodor.

"He is one of your friends, you have treated him like a son."

"His name?"

"Ask your daughter, General."

Feodor turned toward Natacha, who burned Koupriane with her gaze, trying to learn what this news was he brought—the truth or a ruse.

"You know the man who wished to kill me, Natacha?"

"No," she replied to her father, in accents of perfect fury. "No, I don't know any such man."

"Mademoiselle," said Koupriane, in a firm, terribly hostile voice, "you have yourself, with your own hands, opened that window tonight; and you have opened it to him many other times besides. While everyone else here does his duty and watches that no person shall be able to enter at night the house where sleeps General Trebassof, governor of Moscow, condemned to death by the Central Revolutionary Committee now reunited at Presnia, this is what you do; it is you who introduce the enemy into this place."

"Answer, Natacha; tell me, yes or no, whether you have let anybody into this house by night."

"Father, it is true."

Feodor roared like a lion:

"His name!"

"Monsieur will tell you himself," said Natacha, in a voice thick with terror, and she pointed to Koupriane. "Why does he not tell you himself the name of that person? He must know it, if the man is dead."

"And if the man is not dead," replied Feodor, who visibly held onto himself, "if that man, whom you helped to enter my house this night, has succeeded in escaping, as you seem to hope, will you tell us his name?"

"I could not tell it, Father."

"And if I prayed you to do so?"

Natacha desperately shook her head.

"And if I order you?"

"You can kill me, Father, but I will not pronounce that name."

"Wretch!"

He raised his stick toward her. Thus Ivan the Terrible had killed his son with a blow of his boar-spear.

But Natacha, instead of bowing her head beneath the blow that menaced her, turned toward Koupriane and threw at him in accents of triumph:

"He is not dead. If you had succeeded in taking him, dead or alive, you would already have his name."

Koupriane took two steps toward her, put his hand on her shoulder and said:

"Michael Nikolaievitch."

"Michael Korsakoff!" cried the general.

Matrena Petrovna, as if revolted by that suggestion, stood upright to repeat:

"Michael Korsakoff!"

The general could not believe his ears, and was about to protest when he noticed that his daughter had turned away and was trying to flee to her room. He stopped her with a terrible gesture.

"Natacha, you are going to tell us what Michael Korsakoff came here to do tonight."

"Feodor Feodorovitch, he came to poison you."

It was Matrena who spoke now and whom nothing could have kept silent, for she saw in Natacha's attempt at flight the most sinister confession. Like a vengeful fury she told over with cries and terrible gestures what she had experienced, as if once more stretched before her the hand armed with the poison, the mysterious hand above the pillow of her poor invalid, her dear, rigorous tyrant; she told them about the preceding night and all her terrors, and from her lips, by her voluble staccato utterance that ominous recital had grotesque emphasis. Finally she told all that she had done, she and the little Frenchman, in order not to betray their suspicions to The Other, in order to take finally in their own trap all those who for so many days and nights schemed for the death of Feodor Feodorovitch. As she ended she pointed out Rouletabille to Feodor and cried, "There is the one who has saved you."

Natacha, as she listened to this tragic recital, restrained herself several times in order not to interrupt, and Rouletabille, who was watching her closely, saw that she had to use almost superhuman efforts in order to achieve that. All the horror of what seemed to be to her as well as to Feodor a revelation of Michael's crime did not subdue her, but seemed, on the contrary, to restore to her in full force all the life that a few seconds earlier had fled from her. Matrena had hardly finished her cry, "There is the one who has saved you," before Natacha cried in her turn, facing the reporter with a look full of the most frightful hate, "There is the one who has been the death of an innocent man!" She turned to her father. "Ah, papa, let me, let me say that Michael Nikolaievitch, who came here this evening, I admit, and whom, it is true, I let into the house, that Michael Nikolaievitch did not come here yesterday, and that the man who has tried to poison you is certainly someone else."

At these words Rouletabille turned pale, but he did not let himself lose self-control. He replied simply:

"No, mademoiselle, it was the same man."

428

And Koupriane felt compelled to add:

"Anyway, we have found the proof of Michael Nikolaievitch's relations with the revolutionaries."

"Where have you found that?" questioned the young girl, turning toward the Chief of Police a face ravished with anguish.

"At Krestowsky, mademoiselle."

She looked a long time at him as though she would penetrate to the bottom of his thoughts.

"What proofs?" she implored.

"A correspondence which we have placed under seal."

"Was it addressed to him? What kind of correspondence?"

"If it interests you, we will open it before you."

"My God! My God!" she gasped. "Where have you found this correspondence? Where? Tell me where!"

"I will tell you. At the villa, in his chamber. We forced the lock of his bureau."

She seemed to breathe again, but her father took her brutally by the arm.

"Come, Natacha, you are going to tell us what that man was doing here tonight."

"In her chamber!" cried Matrena Petrovna.

Natacha turned toward Matrena:

"What do you believe, then? Tell me now."

"And I, what ought I to believe?" muttered Feodor. "You have not told me yet. You did not know that man had relations with my enemies. You are innocent of that, perhaps. I wish to think so. I wish it, in the name of Heaven I wish it. But why did you receive him? Why? Why did you bring him in here, as a robber or as a..."

"Oh, papa, you know that I love Boris, that I love him with all my heart, and that I would never belong to anyone but him."

"Then, then, then.—speak!"

The young girl had reached the crisis.

"Ah, Father, Father, do not question me! You, you above all, do not question me now. I can say nothing! There is nothing I can tell you. Excepting that I am sure—sure, you understand—that Michael Nikolaievitch did not come here last night."

"He did come," insisted Rouletabille in a slightly troubled voice.

"He came here with poison. He came here to poison your father, Natacha," moaned Matrena Petrovna, who twined her hands in gestures of sincere and naive tragedy.

"And I," replied the daughter of Feodor ardently, with an accent of conviction which made everyone there vibrate, and particularly Rouletabille, "and I, I tell you it was not he, that it was not he, that it could not possibly be he. I swear to you it was another, another."

"But then, this other, did you let him in as well?" said Koupriane.

"Ah, yes, yes. It was I. It was I. It was I who left the window and blinds open. Yes, it is I who did that. But I did not wait for the other, the other who came to assassinate.

432

As to Michael Nikolaievitch, I swear to you, my father, by all that is most sacred in heaven and on earth, that he could not have committed the crime that you say. And now— kill me, for there is nothing more I can say."

"The poison," replied Koupriane coldly, "the poison that he poured into the general's potion was that arsenate of soda which was on the grapes the Marshal of the Court brought here. Those grapes were left by the Marshal, who warned Michael Nikolaievitch and Boris Alexandrovitch to wash them. The grapes disappeared. If Michael is innocent, do you accuse Boris?"

Natacha, who seemed to have suddenly lost all power for defending herself, moaned, begged, railed, seemed dying.

"No, no. Don't accuse Boris. He has nothing to do with it. Don't accuse Michael. Don't accuse anyone so long as you don't know.

But these two are innocent. Believe me. Believe me. Ah, how shall I say it, how shall I persuade you! I am not able to say anything to you. And you have killed Michael. Ah, what have you done, what have you done!"

"We have suppressed a man," said the icy voice of Koupriane, "who was merely the agent for the base deeds of Nihilism."

She succeeded in recovering a new energy that in her depths of despair they would have supposed impossible. She shook her fists at Koupriane:

"It is not true, it is not true. These are slanders, infamies! The inventions of the police! Papers devised to incriminate him. There is nothing at all of what you said you found at his house. It is not possible. It is not true."

"Where are those papers?" demanded the curt voice of Feodor. "Bring them here at once, Koupriane; I wish to see them."

Koupriane was slightly troubled, and this did not escape Natacha, who cried:

"Yes, yes, let him give us them, let him bring them if he has them. But he hasn't," she clamored with a savage joy. "He has nothing. You can see, papa, that he has nothing. He would already have brought them out. He has nothing. I tell you he has nothing. Ah, he has nothing! He has nothing!"

And she threw herself on the floor, weeping, sobbing, "He has nothing, he has nothing!" She seemed to weep for joy.

"Is that true?" demanded Feodor Feodorovitch, with his most somber manner.

"Is it true, Koupriane, that you have nothing?"

"It is true, General, that we have found nothing. Everything had already been carried away."

But Natacha uttered a veritable torrent of glee:

"He has found nothing! Yet he accuses him of being allied with the revolutionaries. Why? Why? Because I let him in? But I, am I a revolutionary? Tell me. Have I sworn to kill papa? I? I? Ah, he doesn't know what to say. You see for yourself, papa, he is silent. He has lied. He has lied."

"Why have you made this false statement, Koupriane?"

"Oh, we have suspected Michael for some time, and truly, after what has just happened, we cannot have any doubt."

"Yes, but you declared you had papers, and you have not. That is abominable procedure, Koupriane," replied Feodor sternly. "I have heard you condemn such expedients many times."

"General! We are sure, you hear, we are absolutely sure that the man who tried to poison you yesterday and the man today who is dead are one and the same."

"And what reason have you for being so sure? It is necessary to tell it," insisted the general, who trembled with distress and impatience.

"Yes, let him tell now."

"Ask monsieur," said Koupriane.

They all turned to Rouletabille.

The reporter replied, affecting a coolness that perhaps he did not entirely feel:

"I am able to state to you, as I already have before Monsieur the Prefect of Police, that one, and only one, person has left the traces of his various climbings on the wall and on the balcony."

"Idiot!" interrupted Natacha, with a passionate disdain for the young man. "And that satisfies you?"

The general roughly seized the reporter's wrist:

"Listen to me, monsieur. A man came here this night. That concerns only me. No one has any right to be astonished excepting myself. I make it my own affair, an affair between my daughter and me. But you, you have just told us that you are sure that man is an assassin. Then, you see, that calls for something else. Proofs are necessary, and I want the proofs at once. You speak of traces; very well, we will go and examine those traces together. And I wish for your sake, monsieur, that I shall be as convinced by them as you are."

Rouletabille quietly disengaged his wrist and replied with perfect calm:

"Now, monsieur, I am no longer able to prove anything to you."

"Why?"

"Because the ladders of the police agents have wiped out all my proofs, monsieur.

"So now there remains for us only your word, only your belief in yourself. And if you are mistaken?"

"He would never admit it, papa," cried Natacha. "Ah, it is he who deserves the fate Michael Nikolaievitch has met just now. Isn't it so? Don't you know it? And that will be your eternal remorse! Isn't there something that always keeps you from admitting that you are mistaken? You have had an innocent man killed. Now, you know well enough, you know well that I would not have admitted Michael Nikolaievitch here if I had believed he was capable of wishing to poison my father."

"Mademoiselle," replied Rouletabille, not lowering his eyes under Natacha's thunderous regard, "I am sure of that."

He said it in such a tone that Natacha continued to look at him with incomprehensible anguish in her eyes. Ah, the baffling of those two regards, the mute scene between those two young people, one of whom wished to make himself understood and the other afraid beyond all other things of being thoroughly understood. Natacha murmured:

"How he looks at me! See, he is the demon; yes, yes, the little domovoi, the little domovoi. But look out, poor wretch; you don't know what you have done."

She turned brusquely toward Koupriane:

"Where is the body of Michael Nikolaievitch?" said she. "I wish to see it. I must see it."

Feodor Feodorovitch had fallen, as though asleep, upon a chair. Matrena Petrovna dared not approach him. The giant appeared hurt to the death, disheartened forever. What neither bombs, nor bullets, nor poison had been able to do, the single idea of his daughter's co-operation in the work of horror plotted about him—or rather the impossibility he faced of understanding

Natacha's attitude, her mysterious conduct, the chaos of her explanations, her insensate cries, her protestations of innocence, her accusations, her menaces, her prayers and all her disorder, the avowed fact of her share in that tragic nocturnal adventure where Michael Nikolaievitch found his death, had knocked over Feodor Feodorovitch like a straw. One instant he sought refuge in some vague hope that Koupriane was less assured than he pretended of the orderly's guilt. But that, after all, was only a detail of no importance in his eyes. What alone mattered was the significance of Natacha's act, and the unhappy girl seemed not to be concerned over what he would think of it. She was there to fight against Koupriane, Rouletabille and Matrena Petrovna, defending her Michael Nikolaievitch, while he, the father, after having failed to overawe her just now, was there in a corner suffering agonizedly.

Koupriane walked over to him and said:

"Listen to me carefully, Feodor Feodorovitch. He who speaks to you is Head of the Police by the will of the Tsar, and your friend by the grace of God. If you do not demand before us, who are acquainted with all that has happened and who know how to keep any necessary secret, if you do not demand of your daughter the reason for her conduct with Michael Nikolaievitch, and if she does not tell you in all sincerity, there is nothing more for me to do here. My men have already been ordered away from this house as unworthy to guard the most loyal subject of His Majesty; I have not protested, but now I in my turn ask you to prove to me that the most dangerous enemy you have had in your house is not your daughter."

These words, which summed up the horrible situation, came as a relief for Feodor. Yes, they must know. Koupriane was right. She must speak. He ordered his daughter to tell everything, everything.

Natacha fixed Koupriane again with her look of hatred to the death, turned from him and repeated in a firm voice:

"I have nothing to say."

"There is the accomplice of your assassins," growled Koupriane then, his arm extended.

Natacha uttered a cry like a wounded beast and fell at her father's feet. She gathered them within her supplicating arms. She pressed them to her breasts. She sobbed from the bottom of her heart. And he, not comprehending, let her lie there, distant, hostile, somber. Then she moaned, distractedly, and wept bitterly, and the dramatic atmosphere in which she thus suddenly enveloped Feodor made it all sound like those cries of an earlier time when the all-powerful, punishing father appeared in the women's apartments to punish the culpable ones.

"My father! Dear Father! Look at me! Look at me! Have pity on me, and do not require me to speak when I must be silent forever. And believe me! Do not believe these men! Do not believe Matrena Petrovna. And am I not your daughter? Your very own daughter! Your Natacha Feodorovna! I cannot make things dear to you. No, no, by the Holy Virgin Mother of Jesus I cannot explain. By the holy ikons, it is because I must not. By my mother, whom I have not known and whose place you have taken, oh, my father, ask me nothing more! Ask me nothing more! But take me in your arms as you did when I was little; embrace me, dear father; love me. I never have had such need to be loved. Love me! I am miserable. Unfortunate me, who cannot even kill myself before your eyes to prove my innocence and my love. Papa, Papa! What will your arms be for in the days left you to live, if you no longer wish to press me to your heart? Papa! Papa!"

She laid her head on Feodor's knees. Her hair had come down and hung about her in a magnificent disorderly mass of black.

"Look in my eyes! Look in my eyes! See how they love you, Batouchka! Batouchka! My dear Batouchka!"

Then Feodor wept. His great tears fell upon Natacha's tears. He raised her head and demanded simply in a broken voice:

"You can tell me nothing now? But when will you tell me?"

Natacha lifted her eyes to his, then her look went past him toward heaven, and from her lips came just one word, in a sob:

"Never."

Matrena Petrovna, Koupriane and the reporter shuddered before the high and terrible thing that happened then. Feodor had taken his daughter's face between his hands. He looked long at those eyes raised toward heaven, the mouth which had just uttered the word "Never," then, slowly, his rude lips went to the tortured, quivering lips of the girl. He held her close. She raised her head wildly, triumphantly, and cried, with arm extended toward Matrena Petrovna:

"He believes me! He believes me! And you would have believed me also if you had been my real mother."

Her head fell back and she dropped unconscious to the floor. Feodor fell to his knees, tending her, deploring her, motioning the others out of the room.

"Go away! All of you, go! All! You, too, Matrena Petrovna. Go away!"

They disappeared, terrified by his savage gesture.

In the little datcha across the river at Krestowsky there was a body. Secret Service agents guarded it while they waited for their chief. Michael Nikolaievitch had come there to die, and the police had reached him just at his last breath. They were behind him as, with the death-rattle in his throat, he pulled himself into his chamber and fell in a heap. Katharina the Bohemian was there. She bent her quick-witted, puzzled head over his death agony. The police swarmed everywhere, ransacking, forcing locks, pulling drawers from the bureau and tables, emptying the cupboards. Their search took in everything, even to ripping the mattresses, and not respecting the rooms of Boris Mourazoff, who was away this night. They searched thoroughly, but they found absolutely nothing they were looking for in Michael's rooms. But they accumulated a multitude of publications that belonged to Boris: Western books, essays on political economy, a history of the French Revolution, and verses that a man ought to hang for. They put them all under seal. During the search Michael died in Katharina's arms. She had held him close, after opening his clothes over the chest, doubtless to make his last breaths easier. The unfortunate officer had received a bullet at the back of the head just after he had plunged into the Neva from the rear of the Trebassof datcha and started to swim across. It was a miracle that he had managed to keep going. Doubtless he hoped to die in peace if only he could reach his own house. He apparently had believed he could manage that once he had broken through his human bloodhounds. He did not know he was recognized and his place of retreat therefore known.

Now the police had gone from cellar to garret. Koupriane came from the Trebassof villa and joined them, Rouletabille followed him. The reporter could not stand the sight of that body, that still had a lingering warmth, of the great open eyes that seemed to stare at him, reproaching him for this violent death. He turned away in distaste, and perhaps a little in fright. Koupriane caught the movement.

"Regrets?" he queried.

"Yes," said Rouletabille. "A death always must be regretted. None the less, he was a criminal. But I'm sincerely sorry he died before he had been driven to confess, even though we are sure of it."

"Being in the pay of the Nihilists, you mean? That is still your opinion?" asked Koupriane.

"Yes."

"You know that nothing has been found here in his rooms. The only compromising papers that have been found belong to Boris Mourazoff."

"Why do you say that?"

"Oh—nothing."

Koupriane questioned his men further. They replied categorically. No, nothing had been found that directly incriminated anybody; and suddenly Rouletabille noted that the conversation of the police and their chief had grown more animated. Koupriane had become angry and was violently reproaching them. They excused themselves with vivid gesture and rapid speech.

Koupriane started away. Rouletabille followed him. What had happened?

As he came up behind Koupriane, he asked the question. In a few curt words, still hurrying on, Koupriane told the reporter he had just learned that the police had left the little Bohemian Katharina alone for a moment with the expiring officer. Katharina acted as housekeeper for Michael and Boris. She knew the secrets of them both. The first thing any novice should have known was to keep a constant eye upon her, and now no one knew where she was. She must be searched for and found at once, for she had opened Michael's shirt, and therein probably lay the reason that no papers were found on the corpse when the police searched it. The absence of papers, of a portfolio, was not natural.

The chase commenced in the rosy dawn of the isles. Already blood-like tints were on the horizon. Some of the police cried that they had the trail. They ran under the trees, because it was almost certain she had taken the narrow path leading to the bridge that joins Krestowsky to Kameny-Ostrow. Some indications discovered by the police who swarmed to right and left of the path confirmed this hypothesis. And no carriage in sight! They all ran on, Koupriane among the first. Rouletabille kept at his heels, but he did not pass him. Suddenly there were cries and calls among the police. One pointed out something below gliding upon the sloping descent. It was little Katharina. She flew like the wind, but in a distracted course. She had reached Kameny-Ostrow on the west bank. "Oh, for a carriage, a horse!" clamored Koupriane, who had left his turn-out at Eliaguine. "The proof is there. It is the final proof of everything that is escaping us!"

Dawn was enough advanced now to show the ground clearly. Katharina was easily discernible as she reached the Eliaguine bridge. There she was in Eliaguine-Ostrow. What was she doing there? Was she going to the Trebassof villa? What would she have to say to them? No, she swerved to the right. The police raced behind her. She was still far ahead, and seemed untiring. Then she disappeared among the trees, in the thicket, keeping still to the right. Koupriane gave a cry of joy. Going that way she must be taken. He gave some breathless orders for the island to be barred. She could not escape now! She could not escape! But where was she going? Koupriane knew that island better than anybody. He took a short cut to reach the other side, toward which Katharina seemed to be heading, and all at once he nearly fell over the girl, who gave a squawk of surprise and rushed away, seeming all arms and legs.

"Stop, or I fire!" cried Koupriane, and he drew his revolver. But a hand grabbed it from him.

"Not that!" said Rouletabille, as he threw the revolver far from them. Koupriane swore at him and resumed the chase. His fury multiplied his strength, his agility; he almost reached Katharina, who was almost out of breath, but Rouletabille threw himself into the Chief 's arms and they rolled together upon the grass. When Koupriane rose, it was to see Katharina mounting in mad haste the stairs that led to the Barque, the floating restaurant of the Strielka. Cursing Rouletabille, but believing his prey easily captured now, the Chief in his turn hurried to the Barque, into which Katharina had disappeared. He reached the bottom of the stairs. On the top step, about to descend from the festive place, the form of Prince Galitch appeared. Koupriane received the sight like a blow stopping him short in his ascent. Galitch had an exultant air which Koupriane did not mistake. Evidently he had arrived too late. He felt the certainty of it in profound discouragement. And this appearance of the prince on the Barque explained convincingly enough the reason for Katharina's flight here.

If the Bohemian had filched the papers or the portfolio from the dead, it was the prince now who had them in his pocket.

Koupriane, as he saw the prince about to pass him, trembled. The prince saluted him and ironically amused himself by inquiring:

"Well, well, how do you do, my dear Monsieur Koupriane. Your Excellency has risen in good time this morning, it seems to me. Or else it is I who start for bed too late."

"Prince," said Koupriane, "my men are in pursuit of a little Bohemian named Katharina, well known in the restaurants where she sings. We have seen her go into the Barque. Have you met her by any chance?"

"Good Lord, Monsieur Koupriane, I am not the concierge of the Barque, and I have not noticed anything at all, and nobody. Besides, I am naturally a little sleepy. Pardon me."

"Prince, it is not possible that you have not seen Katharina."

"Oh, Monsieur the Prefect of Police, if I had seen her I would not tell you about it, since you are pursuing her. Do you take me for one of your bloodhounds? They say you have them in all classes, but I insist that I haven't enlisted yet. You have made a mistake, Monsieur Koupriane."

The prince saluted again. But Koupriane still stood in his way.

"Prince, consider that this matter is very serious. Michael Nikolaievitch, General Trebassof's orderly, is dead, and this little girl has stolen his papers from his body.

All persons who have spoken with Katharina will be under suspicion. This is an affair of State, monsieur, which may reach very far. Can you swear to me that you have not seen, that you have not spoken to Katharina?"

The prince looked at Koupriane so insolently that the Prefect turned pale with rage. Ah, if he were able—if he only dared!—but such men as this were beyond him. Galitch walked past him without a word of answer, and ordered the schwitzar to call him a carriage.

"Very well," said Koupriane, "I will make my report to the Tsar."

Galitch turned. He was as pale as Koupriane.

"In that case, monsieur," said he, "don't forget to add that I am His Majesty's most humble servant."

The carriage drew up. The prince stepped in. Koupriane watched him roll away, raging at heart and with his fists doubled. Just then his men came up.

"Go. Search," he said roughly, pointing into the Barque.

They scattered through the establishment, entering all the rooms. Cries of irritation and of protest arose. Those lingering after the latest of late suppers were not pleased at this invasion of the police. Everybody had to rise while the police looked under the tables, the benches, the long table-cloths. They went into the pantries and down into the hold. No sign of Katharina. Suddenly Koupriane, who leaned against a netting and looked vaguely out upon the horizon, waiting for the outcome of the search, got a start. Yonder, far away on the other side of the river, between a little wood and the Staria Derevnia, a light boat drew to the shore, and a little black spot jumped from it like a flea. Koupriane recognized the little black spot as Katharina. She was safe. Now he could not reach her. It would be useless to search the maze of the Bohemian quarter, where her country-people lived in full control, with customs and privileges that had never been infringed. The entire Bohemian population of the capital would have risen against him. It was Prince Galitch who had made him fail. One of his men came to him:

"No luck," said he. "We have not found Katharina, but she has been here nevertheless. She met Prince Galitch for just a minute, and gave him something, then went over the other side into a canoe."

"Very well," and the Prefect shrugged his shoulders. "I was sure of it."

He felt more and more, exasperated. He went down along the river edge and the first person he saw was Rouletabille, who waited for him without any impatience, seated philosophically on a bench.

"I was looking for you," cried the Prefect. "We have failed. By your fault! If you had not thrown yourself into my arms—"

"I did it on purpose," declared the reporter.

"What! What is that you say? You did it on purpose?"

Koupriane choked with rage.

"Your Excellency," said Rouletabille, taking him by the arm, "calm yourself. They are watching us. Come along and have a cup of tea at Cubat's place. Easy now, as though we were out for a walk."

"Will you explain to me?"

"No, no, Your Excellency. Remember that I have promised you General Trebassof 's life in exchange for your prisoner's. Very well; by throwing myself in your arms and keeping you from reaching Katharina, I saved the general's life. It is very simple."

"Are you laughing at me? Do you think you can mock me?"

But the prefect saw quickly that Rouletabille was not fooling and had no mockery in his manner.

"Monsieur," he insisted, "since you speak seriously, I certainly wish to understand—"

"It is useless," said Rouletabille. "It is very necessary that you should not understand."

"But at least. . ."

"No, no, I can't tell you anything."

"When, then, will you tell me something to explain your unbelievable conduct?"

Rouletabille stopped in his tracks and declared solemnly:

"Monsieur Koupriane, recall what Natacha Feodorovna as she raised her lovely eyes to heaven, replied to her father, when he, also, wished to understand: 'Never.'"

XI

The Poison Continues

At ten o'clock that morning Rouletabille
went to the Trebassof villa, which had its
guard of secret agents again, a double guard,
because Koupriane was sure the Nihilists
would not delay in avenging Michael's death.
Rouletabille was met by Ermolai, who would
not allow him to enter. The faithful servant
uttered some explanation in Russian, which
the young man did not understand, or,
rather, Rouletabille understood perfectly
from his manner that henceforth the
door of the villa was closed to him. In
vain he insisted on seeing the general,
Matrena Petrovna and Mademoiselle Natacha.
Ermolai made no reply but "Niet, niet, niet."
The reporter turned away without having
seen anyone, and walked away deeply

depressed. He went afoot clear into the city, a long promenade, during which his brain surged with the darkest forebodings. As he passed by the Department of Police he resolved to see Koupriane again. He went in, gave his name, and was ushered at once to the Chief of Police, whom he found bent over a long report that he was reading through with noticeable agitation.

"Gounsovski has sent me this," he said in a rough voice, pointing to the report. "Gounsovski, 'to do me a service,' desires me to know that he is fully aware of all that happened at the Trebassof datcha last night. He warns me that the revolutionaries have decided to get through with the general at once, and that two of them have been given the mission to enter the datcha in any way possible. They will have bombs upon their bodies and will blow the bombs and themselves up together as soon as they are beside the general. Who are the two victims designated for this horrible vengeance, and who have light-heartedly accepted such a death for themselves as well as for the general? That is what we don't know. That is what we would have known, perhaps, if you had not prevented me from seizing the papers that Prince Galitch has now," Koupriane finished, turning hostilely toward Rouletabille.

Rouletabille had turned pale.

"Don't regret what happened to the papers," he said. "It is I who tell you not to. But what you say doesn't surprise me. They must believe that Natacha has betrayed them."

"Ah, then you admit at last that she really is their accomplice?"

"I haven't said that and I don't admit it. But I know what I mean, and you, you can't. Only, know this one thing, that at the present moment I am the only person able to save you in this horrible situation. To do that I must see Natacha at once. Make her understand this, while I wait at my hotel for word. I'll not leave it."

Rouletabille saluted Koupriane and went out.

Two days passed, during which Rouletabille did not receive any word from either Natacha or Koupriane, and tried in vain to see them. He made a trip for a few hours to Finland, going as far as Pergalovo, an isolated town said to be frequented by the revolutionaries, then returned, much disturbed, to his hotel, after having written a last letter to Natacha imploring an interview. The minutes passed very slowly for him in the hotel's vestibule, where he had seemed to have taken up a definite residence.

Installed on a bench, he seemed to have become part of the hotel staff, and more than one traveler took him for an interpreter. Others thought he was an agent of the Secret Police appointed to study the faces of those arriving and departing. What was he waiting for, then? Was it for Annouchka to return for a luncheon or dinner in that place that she sometimes frequented? And did he at the same time keep watch upon Annouchka's apartments just across the way? If that was so, he could only bewail his luck, for Annouchka did not appear either at her apartments or the hotel, or at the Krestowsky establishment, which had been obliged to suppress her performance. Rouletabille naturally thought, in the latter connection, that some vengeance by Gounsovski lay back of this, since the head of the Secret Service could hardly forget the way he had been treated. The reporter could see already the poor singer, in spite of all her safeguards and the favor of the Imperial family, on the road to the Siberian steppes or the dungeons of Schlusselbourg.

"My, what a country!" he murmured.

But his thoughts soon quit Annouchka
and returned to the object of his main
preoccupation. He waited for only one thing,
and for that as soon as possible—to have
a private interview with Natacha. He had
written her ten letters in two days, but
they all remained unanswered. It was an
answer that he waited for so patiently in the
vestibule of the hotel—so patiently, but so
nervously, so feverishly.

When the postman entered, poor
Rouletabille's heart beat rapidly. On
that answer he waited for depended the
formidable part he meant to play before
quitting Russia. He had accomplished nothing
up to now, unless he could play his part in
this later development.

But the letter did not come. The postman
left, and the schwitzar, after examining all

470

the mail, made him a negative sign. Ah, the servants who entered, and the errand-boys, how he looked at them! But they never came for him. Finally, at six o'clock in the evening of the second day, a man in a frock-coat, with a false astrakhan collar, came in and handed the concierge a letter for Joseph Rouletabille. The reporter jumped up. Before the man was out the door he had torn open the letter and read it. The letter was not from Natacha. It was from Gounsovski. This is what it said:

"My dear Monsieur Joseph Rouletabille, if it will not inconvenience you, I wish you would come and dine with me today. I will look for you within two hours. Madame Gounsovski will be pleased to make your acquaintance. Believe me your devoted Gounsovski."

Rouletabille considered, and decided:

"I will go. He ought to have wind of what is being plotted, and as for me, I don't know where Annouchka has gone. I have more to learn from him than he has from me. Besides, as Athanase Georgevitch said, one may regret not accepting the Head of the Okrana's pleasant invitation."

From six o'clock to seven he still waited vainly for Natacha's response. At seven o'clock, he decided to dress for the dinner. Just as he rose, a messenger arrived. There was still another letter for Joseph Rouletabille. This time it was from Natacha, who wrote him:

"General Trebassof and my step-mother will be very happy to have you come to dinner today. As for myself, monsieur, you will pardon me the order which has closed to you for a number of days a dwelling where you have rendered services which I shall not forget all my life."

The letter ended with a vague polite formula. With the letter in his hand the reporter sat in thought. He seemed to be asking himself, "Is it fish or flesh?" Was it a letter of thanks or of menace? That was what he could not decide. Well, he would soon know, for he had decided to accept that invitation. Anything that brought him and Natacha into communication at the moment was a thing of capital importance to him. Half-an-hour later he gave the address of the villa to an isvotchick, and soon he stepped out before the gate where Ermolai seemed to be waiting for him.

Rouletabille was so occupied by thought of the conversation he was going to have with Natacha that he had completely forgotten the excellent Monsieur Gounsovski and his invitation.

The reporter found Koupriane's agents making a close-linked chain around the grounds and each watching the other. Matrena had not wished any agent to be in house. He showed Koupriane's pass and entered.

Ermolai ushered Rouletabille in with shining face. He seemed glad to have him there again. He bowed low before him and uttered many compliments, of which the reporter did not understand a word. Rouletabille passed on, entered the garden and saw Matrena Petrovna there walking with her step-daughter. They seemed on the best of terms with each other. The grounds wore an air of tranquillity and the residents seemed to have totally forgotten the somber tragedy of the other night. Matrena and Natacha came smilingly up to the young man, who inquired after the general. They both turned and pointed out Feodor Feodorovitch, who waved to him from the height of the kiosk, where it seemed the table had been spread.

They were going to dine out of doors this fine night.

"Everything goes very well, very well indeed, dear little domovoi," said Matrena. "How glad it is to see you and thank you. If you only knew how I suffered in your absence, I who know how unjust my daughter was to you. But dear Natacha knows now what she owes you. She doesn't doubt your word now, nor your clear intelligence, little angel. Michael Nikolaievitch was a monster and he was punished as he deserved. You know the police have proof now that he was one of the Central Revolutionary Committee's most dangerous agents. And he an officer! Whom can we trust now!"

"And Monsieur Boris Mourazoff, have you seen him since?" inquired Rouletabille.

"Boris called to see us today, to say good-by, but we did not receive him, under the orders of the police. Natacha has written to tell him of Koupriane's orders. We have received letters from him; he is quitting St. Petersburg.

"What for?"

"Well, after the frightful bloody scene in his little house, when he learned how Michael Nikolaievitch had found his death, and after he himself had undergone a severe grilling from the police, and when he learned the police had sacked his library and gone through his papers, he resigned, and has resolved to live from now on out in the country, without seeing anyone, like the philosopher and poet he is. So far as I am concerned, I think he is doing absolutely right. When a young man is a poet, it is useless to live like a soldier. Someone has said that, I don't know the name now, and when one has ideas that may upset other people, surely they ought to live in solitude."

Rouletabille looked at Natacha, who was as pale as her white gown, and who added no word to her mother's outburst. They had drawn near the kiosk. Rouletabille saluted the general, who called to him to come up and, when the young man extended his hand, he drew him abruptly nearer and embraced him. To show Rouletabille how active he was getting again, Feodor Feodorovitch marched up and down the kiosk with only the aid of a stick. He went and came with a sort of wild, furious gayety.

"They haven't got me yet, the dogs. They haven't got me! And one (he was thinking of Michael) who saw me every day was here just for that. Very well. I ask you where he is now. And yet here I am! An attack! I'm always here! But with a good eye; and I begin to have a good leg. We shall see. Why, I recollect how, when I was at Tiflis, there was an insurrection in the Caucasus. We fought. Several times I could feel the swish of bullets past my hair. My comrades fell around me like flies. But nothing happened to me, not a thing. And here now! They will not get me, they will not get me. You know how they plan now to come to me, as living bombs. Yes, they have decided on that. I can't press a friend's hand any more without the fear of seeing him explode. What do you think of that? But they won't get me. Come, drink my health. A small glass of vodka for an appetizer. You see, young man, we are going to have zakouskis here. What a marvelous panorama! You can see everything from here. If the enemy comes," he added with a singular loud laugh, "we can't fail to detect him."

Certainly the kiosk did rise high above the garden and was completely detached, no wall being near. They had a clear view. No branches of trees hung over the roof and no tree hid the view. The rustic table of rough wood was covered with a short cloth and was spread with zakouskis. It was a meal under the open sky, a seat and a glass in the clear azure. The evening could not have been softer and clearer. And, as the general felt so gay, the repast would have promised to be most agreeable, if Rouletabille had not noticed that Matrena Petrovna and Natacha were uneasy and downcast. The reporter soon saw, too, that all the general's joviality was a little excessive. Anyone would have said that Feodor Feodorovitch spoke to distract himself, to keep himself from thinking. There was sufficient excuse for him after the outrageous drama of the other night. Rouletabille noticed further that the general never looked at his daughter, even when he spoke to her. There was too formidable a mystery lying between them for restraint not to increase day by day. Rouletabille involuntarily shook his head, saddened by all he saw. His movement was surprised by Matrena Petrovna, who pressed his hand in silence.

"Well, now," said the general, "well, now my children, where is the vodka?"

Among all the bottles which graced the table the general looked in vain for his flask of vodka. How in the world could he dine if he did not prepare for that important act by the rapid absorption of two or three little glasses of white wine, between two or three sandwiches of caviare!

"Ermolai must have left it in the wine-chest," said Matrena.

The wine-closet was in the dining-room. She rose to go there, but Natacha hurried before her down the little flight of steps, crying, "Stay there, mamma. I will go."

"Don't you bother, either. I know where it is," cried Rouletabille, and hurried after Natacha.

She did not stop. The two young people arrived in the dining-room at the same time. They were there alone, as Rouletabille had foreseen. He stopped Natacha and planted himself in front of her.

"Why, mademoiselle, did you not answer me earlier?"

"Because I don't wish to have any conversation with you."

"If that was so, you would not have come here, where you were sure I would follow."

She hesitated, with an emotion that would have been incomprehensible to all others perhaps, but was not to Rouletabille.

"Well, yes, I wished to say this to you: Don't write to me any more. Don't speak to me. Don't see me. Go away from here, monsieur; go away. They will have your life. And if you have found out anything, forget it. Ah, on the head of your mother, forget it, or you are lost. That is what I wished to tell you. And now, you go."

She grasped his hand in a quick sympathetic movement that she seemed instantly to regret.

"You go away," she repeated.

Rouletabille still held his place before her. She turned from him; she did not wish to hear anything further.

"Mademoiselle," said he, "you are watched closer than ever. Who will take Michael Nikolaievitch's place?"

"Madman, be silent! Hush!"

"I am here."

He said this with such simple bravery that tears sprang to her eyes.

"Dear man! Poor man! Dear brave man!" She did not know what to say. Her emotion checked all utterance. But it was necessary for her to enable him to understand that there was nothing he could do to help her in her sad straits.

"No. If they knew what you have just said, what you have proposed now, you would be dead tomorrow. Don't let them suspect. And above all, don't try to see me anywhere. Go back to papa at once. We have been here too long. What if they learn of it?—and they learn everything! They are everywhere, and have ears everywhere."

"Mademoiselle, just one word more, a single word. Do you doubt now that Michael tried to poison your father?"

"Ah, I wish to believe it. I wish to. I wish to believe it for your sake, my poor boy."

Rouletabille desired something besides "I wish to believe it for your sake, my poor boy." He was far from being satisfied. She saw him turn pale. She tried to reassure him while her trembling hands raised the lid of the wine-chest.

"What makes me think you are right is that I have decided myself that only one and the same person, as you said, climbed to the window of the little balcony. Yes, no one can doubt that, and you have reasoned well."

But he persisted still.

"And yet, in spite of that, you are not entirely sure, since you say, 'I wish to believe it, my poor boy.'"

"Monsieur Rouletabille, someone might have tried to poison my father, and not have come by way of the window."

"No, that is impossible."

"Nothing is impossible to them."

And she turned her head away again.

"Why, why," she said, with her voice entirely changed and quite indifferent, as if she wished to be merely 'the daughter of the house' in conversation with the young man, "the vodka is not in the wine chest, after all. What has Ermolai done with it, then?"

She ran over to the buffet and found the flask.

"Oh, here it is. Papa shan't be without it, after all."

Rouletabille was already into the garden again.

"If that is the only doubt she has," he said to himself, "I can reassure her. No one could come, excepting by the window. And only one came that way."

The young girl had rejoined him, bringing the flask. They crossed the garden together to the general, who was whiling away the time as he waited for his vodka explaining to Matrena Petrovna the nature of "the constitution." He had spilt a box of matches on the table and arranged them carefully.

"Here," he cried to Natacha and Rouletabille. "Come here and I will explain to you as well what this Constitution amounts to."

The young people leaned over his demonstration curiously and all eyes in the kiosk were intent on the matches.

"You see that match," said
Feodor Feodorovitch. "It is the Emperor.
And this other match is the Empress;
this one is the Tsarevitch; and that one is
the Grand-duke Alexander; and these are
the other granddukes. Now, here are the
ministers and there the principal governors,
and then the generals; these here are the
bishops."

The whole box of matches was used up, and
each match was in its place, as is the way in
an empire where proper etiquette prevails in
government and the social order.

"Well," continued the general, "do you
want to know, Matrena Petrovna, what
a constitution is? There! That is the
Constitution."

The general, with a swoop of his hand, mixed
all the matches. Rouletabille laughed, but the
good Matrena said:

"I don't understand, Feodor."

"Find the Emperor now."

Then Matrena understood. She laughed heartily, she laughed violently, and Natacha laughed also. Delighted with his success, Feodor Feodorovitch took up one of the little glasses that Natacha had filled with the vodka she brought.

"Listen, my children," said he. "We are going to commence the zakouskis. Koupriane ought to have been here before this."

Saying this, holding still the little glass in his hand, he felt in his pocket with the other for his watch, and drew out a magnificent large watch whose ticking was easily heard.

"Ah, the watch has come back from the repairer," Rouletabille remarked smilingly to Matrena Petrovna. "It looks like a splendid one."

"It has very fine works," said the general. "It was bequeathed to me by my grandfather. It marks the seconds, and the phases of the moon, and sounds the hours and half-hours."

Rouletabille bent over the watch, admiring it.

"You expect M. Koupriane for dinner?" inquired the young man, still examining the watch.

"Yes, but since he is so late, we'll not delay any longer. Your healths, my children," said the general as Rouletabille handed him back the watch and he put it in his pocket.

"Your health, Feodor Feodorovitch," replied Matrena Petrovna, with her usual tenderness.

Rouletabille and Natacha only touched their lips to the vodka, but Feodor Feodorovitch and Matrena drank theirs in the Russian fashion, head back and all at a draught, draining it to the bottom and flinging the contents to the back of the throat. They had no more than performed this gesture when the general uttered an oath and tried to expel what he had drained so heartily. Matrena Petrovna spat violently also, looking with horror at her husband.

"What is it? What has someone put in the vodka?" cried Feodor.

"What has someone put in the vodka?" repeated Matrena Petrovna in a thick voice, her eyes almost starting from her head.

The two young people threw themselves upon the unfortunates. Feodor's face had an expression of atrocious suffering.

"We are poisoned," cried the general, in the midst of his chokings. "I am burning inside."

Almost mad, Natacha took her father's head in her hands. She cried to him:

"Vomit, papa; vomit!"

"We must find an emetic," cried Rouletabille, holding on to the general, who had almost slipped from his arms.

Matrena Petrovna, whose gagging noises were violent, hurried down the steps of the kiosk, crossed the garden as though wild-fire were behind her, and bounded into the veranda. During this time the general succeeded in easing himself, thanks to Rouletabille, who had thrust a spoon to the root of his tongue. Natacha could do nothing but cry, "My God, my God, my God!" Feodor held onto his stomach, still crying, "I'm burning, I'm burning!" The scene was frightfully tragic and funny at the same time. To add to the burlesque, the general's watch in his pocket struck eight o'clock. Feodor Feodorovitch stood up in a final supreme effort. "Oh, it is horrible!" Matrena Petrovna showed a red, almost violet face as she came back; she distorted it, she choked, her mouth twitched, but she brought something, a little packet that she waved, and from which, trembling frightenedly, she shook a powder into the first two empty glasses, which were on her side of the table and were those she and the general had drained. She still had strength to fill them with water, while Rouletabille was almost overcome by the general, whom he still had in his arms, and Natacha concerned herself with nothing but her father, leaning over him as though to follow the progress of the terrible poison, to read in his eyes if it was to be life or death. "Ipecac," cried Matrena Petrovna, and she made the general drink it. She did not drink until after him.

The heroic woman must have exerted superhuman force to go herself to find the saving antidote in her medicine-chest, even while the agony pervaded her vitals.

Some minutes later both could be considered saved. The servants, Ermolai at their head, were clustered about. Most of them had been at the lodge and they had not, it appeared, heard the beginning of the affair, the cries of Natacha and Rouletabille. Koupriane arrived just then. It was he who worked with Natacha in getting the two to bed. Then he directed one of his agents to go for the nearest doctors they could find.

This done, the Prefect of Police went toward the kiosk where he had left Rouletabille. But Rouletabille was not to be found, and the flask of vodka and the glasses from which they had drunk were gone also. Ermolai was near-by, and he inquired of the servant for the young Frenchman. Ermolai replied that he had just gone away, carrying the flask and the glasses. Koupriane swore. He shook Ermolai and even started to give him a blow with the fist for permitting such a thing to happen before his eyes without making a protest.

Ermolai, who had his own haughtiness, dodged Koupriane's fist and replied that he had wished to prevent the young Frenchman, but the reporter had shown him a police-paper on which Koupriane himself had declared in advance that the young Frenchman was to do anything he pleased.

XII

PERE ALEXIS

Koupriane jumped into his carriage and hurried toward St. Petersburg. On the way he spoke to three agents who only he knew were posted in the neighborhood of Eliaguine. They told him the route Rouletabille had taken. The reporter had certainly returned into the city. He hurried toward Troitski Bridge. There, at the corner of the Naberjnaia, Koupriane saw the reporter in a hired conveyance. Rouletabille was pounding his coachman in the back, Russian fashion, to make him go faster, and was calling with all his strength one of the few words he had had time to learn, "Naleva, naleva" (to the left). The driver was forced to understand at last, for there was no other way to turn than to the left.

If he had turned to the right (naprava) he would have driven into the river. The conveyance clattered over the pointed flints of a neighborhood that led to a little street, Aptiekarski-Pereoulok, at the corner of the Katharine canal. This "alley of the pharmacists" as a matter of fact contained no pharmacists, but there was a curious sign of a herbarium, where Rouletabille made the driver stop. As the carriage rolled under the arch Rouletabille recognized Koupriane. He did not wait, but cried to him, "Ah, here you are. All right; follow me." He still had the flask and the glasses in his hands. Koupriane couldn't help noticing how strange he looked. He passed through a court with him, and into a squalid shop.

"What," said Koupriane, "do you know Pere Alexis?"

They were in the midst of a curious litter. Clusters of dried herbs hung from the

496

ceiling, and all among them were clumps of old boots, shriveled skins, battered pans, scrap-iron, sheep-skins, useless touloupes, and on the floor musty old clothes, moth-eaten furs, and sheep-skin coats that even a moujik of the swamps would not have deigned to wear. Here and there were old teeth, ragged finery, dilapidated hats, and jars of strange herbs ranged upon some rickety shelving. Between the set of scales on the counter and a heap of little blocks of wood used for figuring the accounts of this singular business were ungilded ikons, oxidized silver crosses, and Byzantine pictures representing scenes from the Old and New Testaments. Jars of alcohol with what seemed to be the skeletons of frogs swimming in them filled what space was left. In a corner of this large, murky room, under the vault of mossed stone, a small altar stood and the light burned in a hanging glass of oil before the holy images. A man was praying before the altar. He wore the costume of old Russia, the caftan of green cloth, buttoned at the shoulder and tucked in at the waist by a narrow belt. He had a bushy beard and his hair fell to his shoulders. When he had finished his prayer he rose, perceived Rouletabille and came over to take his hand. He spoke French to the reporter:

"Well, here you are again, lad. Do you bring poison again today? This will end by being found out, and the police. . ."

Just then he discerned Koupriane's form in the shadow, drew close to make out who it was, and fell to his knees as he saw who it was. Rouletabille tried to raise him, but he insisted on prostrating himself. He was sure the Prefect of Police had come to his house to hang him. Finally he was reassured by Rouletabille's positive assertions and the great chief 's robust laugh. The Prefect wished to know how the young man came to be acquainted with the "alchemist" of the police. Rouletabille told him in a few words.

Maitre Alexis, in his youth, went to France afoot, to study pharmacy, because of his enthusiasm for chemistry. But he always remained countrified, very much a Russian peasant, a semi-Oriental bear, and did not achieve his degree. He took some certificates, but the examinations were too much for him. For fifty years he lived miserably as a pharmacist's assistant in the back of a disreputable shop in the Notre Dame quarter. The proprietor of the place was implicated in the famous affair of the gold ingots, which started Rouletabille's reputation, and was arrested along with his assistant, Alexis. It was Rouletabille who proved, clear as day, that poor Alexis was innocent, and that he had never been cognizant of his master's evil ways, being absorbed in the depths of his laboratory in trying to work out a naive alchemy which fascinated him, though the world of chemistry had passed it by centuries ago. At the trial Alexis was acquitted, but found himself in the street. He shed what tears remained in his body upon the neck of the reporter, assuring him of paradise if he got him back to his own country, because he desired only the one thing more of life, that he might see his birth-land before he died. Rouletabille advanced the necessary means and sent him to St. Petersburg. There he was picked up at the end of two days by the police, in a petty gambling-game, and thrown into prison, where he promptly had a chance to show his talents. He cured some of his companions in misery, and even some of the guards. A guard who had an injured leg, whose healing he had despaired of, was cured by Alexis. Then there was found to be no actual charge against him. They set him free and, moreover, they interested themselves in him. They found meager employment for him in the Stchoukine-dvor, an immense popular bazaar. He accumulated a few roubles and installed himself on his own account at the back of a court in the Aptiekarski-Pereoulok, where he gradually piled up a heap of old odds and ends that no one wanted even in the Stchoukine-dvor. But he was happy, because behind his shop he had installed a little laboratory where he continued for his pleasure his experiments in alchemy and his study of plants. He still proposed to write a book that he had already spoken of in France to Rouletabille, to prove the truth of "Empiric Treatment of Medicinal Herbs, the Science of Alchemy, and the Ancient Experiments in Sorcery." Between times he continued to cure anyone who applied to him, and the police in particular. The police guards protected him and used him. He had splendid plasters for them after "the scandal," as they called the October riots. So when the doctors of the quarter tried to prosecute him for illegal practice, a deputation of police-guards went to Koupriane, who took the responsibility and discontinued proceedings against him. They regarded him as under protection of the saints, and Alexis soon came to be regarded himself as something of a holy man. He never failed every Christmas and Easter to send his finest images to Rouletabille, wishing him all prosperity and saying that if ever he came to St. Petersburg he should be happy to receive him at Aptiekarski-Pereoulok, where he was established in honest labor. Pere Alexis, like all the true saints, was a modest man.

When Alexis had recovered a little from his emotion Rouletabille said to him:

"Pere Alexis, I do bring you poison again, but you have nothing to fear, for His Excellency the Chief of Police is with me. Here is what we want you to do. You must tell us what poison these four glasses have held, and what poison is still in this flask and this little phial."

"What is that little phial?" demanded Koupriane, as he saw Rouletabille pull a small, stoppered bottle out of his pocket.

The reporter replied, "I have put into this bottle the vodka that was poured into Natacha's glass and mine and that we barely touched."

"Someone has tried to poison you!" exclaimed Pere Alexis.

"No, not me," replied Rouletabille, in bored fashion. "Don't think about that. Simply do what I tell you. Then analyze these two napkins, as well."

And he drew from his coat two soiled napkins.

"Well," said Koupriane, "you have thought of everything."

"They are the napkins the general and his wife used."

"Yes, yes, I understand that," said the Chief of Police.

"And you, Alexis, do you understand?" asked the reporter. "When can we have the result of your analysis?

"In an hour, at the latest."

"Very well," said Koupriane. "Now I need not tell you to hold your tongue. I am going to leave one of my men here. You will write us a note that you will seal, and he will bring it to head-quarters. Sure you understand? In an hour?"

"In an hour, Excellency."

They went out, and Alexis followed them, bowing to the floor. Koupriane had

Rouletabille get into his carriage. The young man did as he was told. One would have said he did not know where he was or what he did. He made no reply to the chief's questions.

"This Pere Alexander," resumed Koupriane, "is a character, really quite a figure. And a bit of a schemer, I should say. He has seen how Father John of Cronstadt succeeded, and he says to himself, 'Since the sailors had their Father John of Cronstadt, why shouldn't the police-guard have their Father Alexis of Aptiekarski-Pereoulok?'"

But Rouletabille did not reply at all, and Koupriane wound up by demanding what was the matter with him.

"The matter is," replied Rouletabille, unable longer to conceal his anguish, "that the poison continues."

"Does that astonish you?" returned Koupriane. "It doesn't me."

Rouletabille looked at him and shook his head. His lips trembled as he said, "I know what you think. It is abominable. But the thing I have done certainly is more abominable still."

"What have you done, then, Monsieur Rouletabille?"

"Perhaps I have caused the death of an innocent man."

"So long as you aren't sure of it, you would better not fret about it, my dear friend."

"It is enough that the doubt has arisen," said the reporter, "almost to kill me;" and he heaved so gloomy a sigh that the excellent Monsieur Koupriane felt pity for the lad. He tapped him on the knee.

"Come, come, young man, you ought to know one thing by this time—'you can't make omelettes without breaking eggs,' as they say, I think, in Paris."

Rouletabille turned away from him with horror in his heart. If there should be another, someone besides Michael! If it was another hand than his that appeared to Matrena and him in the mysterious night! If Michael Nikolaievitch had been innocent! Well, he would kill himself, that was all. And those horrible words that he had exchanged with Natacha rose in his memory, singing in his ears as though they would deafen him.

"Do you doubt still?" he had asked her, "that Michael tried to poison your father?"

And Natacha had replied, "I wish to believe it! I wish to believe it, for your sake, my poor boy." And then he recalled her other words, still more frightful now! "Couldn't someone have tried to poison my father and not have come by the window?" He had faced such a hypothesis with assurance then—but now, now that the poison continued, continued within the house, where he believed himself so fully aware of all people and things— continued now that Michael Nikolaievitch was dead—ah, where did it come from, this poison?—and what was it? Pere Alexis would hurry his analysis if he had any regard for poor Rouletabille.

For Rouletabille to doubt, and in an affair where already there was one man dead through his agency, was torment worse than death.

When they arrived at police-headquarters, Rouletabille jumped from Koupriane's carriage and without saying a word hailed an empty isvotchick that was passing. He had himself driven back to Pere Alexis. His doubt mastered his will; he could not bear to wait away. Under the arch of Aptiekarski-Pereoulok he saw once more the man Koupriane had placed there with the order to bring him Alexis's message. The man looked at him in astonishment. Rouletabille crossed the court and entered the dingy old room once more. Pere Alexis was not there, naturally, engaged as he was in his laboratory. But a person whom he did not recognize at first sight attracted the reporter's attention. In the half-light of the shop a melancholy shadow leaned over the ikons on the counter. It was only when he straightened up, with a deep sigh, and a little light, deflected and yellow from passing through window-panes that had known no touch of cleaning since they were placed there, fell faintly on the face, that Rouletabille ascertained he was face to face with Boris Mourazoff. It was indeed he, the erstwhile brilliant officer whose elegance and charm the reporter had admired as he saw him at beautiful Natacha's feet in the datcha at Eliaguine. Now, no more in uniform, he had thrown over his bowed shoulders a wretched coat, whose sleeves swayed listlessly at his sides, in accord with his mood of languid desperation, a felt hat with the rim turned down hid a little the misery in his face in these few days, these not-many hours, how he was changed! But, even as he was, he still concerned Rouletabille. What was he doing there? Was he not going to go away, perhaps? He had picked up an ikon from the counter and carried it over to the window to examine its oxidized silver, giving such close attention to it that the reporter hoped he might reach the door of the laboratory without being noticed. He already had his hand on the knob of that door, which was behind the counter, when he heard his name called.

"It is you, Monsieur Rouletabille," said the low, sad voice of Boris. "What has brought you here, then?"

"Well, well, Monsieur Boris Mourazoff, unless I'm mistaken? I certainly didn't expect to find you here in Pere Alexis's place."

"Why not, Monsieur Rouletabille? One can find anything here in Pere Alexis's stock. See; here are two old ikons in wood, carved with sculptures, which came direct from Athos, and can't be equaled, I assure you, either at Gastini-Dvor nor even at Stchoukine-Dvor."

"Yes, yes, that is possible," said Rouletabille, impatiently. "Are you an amateur of such things?" he added, in order to say something.

"Oh, like anybody else. But I was going to tell you, Monsieur Rouletabille, I have resigned my commission. I have resolved to retire from the world; I am going on a long voyage." (Rouletabille thought: 'Why not have gone at once?') "And before going, I have come here to supply myself with some little gifts to send those of my friends I particularly care for, although now, my dear Monsieur Rouletabille, I don't care much for anything."

"You look desolate enough, monsieur."

Boris sighed like a child.

"How could it be otherwise?" he said. "I loved and believed myself beloved. But it proved to be—nothing, alas!"

"Sometimes one only imagines things," said Rouletabille, keeping his hand on the door.

"Oh, yes," said the other, growing more and more melancholy. "So a man suffers. He is his own tormentor; he himself makes the wheel on which, like his own executioner, he binds himself."

"It is not necessary, monsieur; it is not necessary," counseled the reporter.

"Listen," implored Boris in a voice that showed tears were not far away. "You are still a child, but still you can see things. Do you believe Natacha loves me?"

"I am sure of it, Monsieur Boris; I am sure of it."

"I am sure of it, too. But I don't know what to think now. She has let me go, without trying to detain me, without a word of hope."

"And where are you going like that?"

"I am returning to the Orel country, where I first saw her."

"That is good, very good, Monsieur Boris. At least there you are sure to see her again. She goes there every year with her parents for a few weeks. It is a detail you haven't overlooked, doubtless."

"Certainly I haven't. I will tell you that that prospect decided my place of retreat."

"See!"

"God gives me nothing, but He opens His treasures, and each takes what he can."

"Yes, yes; and Mademoiselle Natacha, does she know it is to Orel you have decided to retire?"

"I have no reason for concealing it from her, Monsieur Rouletabille."

"So far so good. You needn't feel so desolate, my dear Monsieur Boris. All is not lost. I will say even that I see a future for you full of hope."

"Ah, if you are able to say that truthfully, I am happy indeed to have met you. I will never forget this rope you have flung me when all the waters seemed closing over my head. 'What do you advise, then?"

"I advise you to go to Orel, monsieur, and as quickly as possible."

"Very well. You must have reasons for saying that. I obey you, monsieur, and go."

As Boris started towards the entrance-arch, Rouletabille slipped into the laboratory. Old Alexis was bent over his retorts. A wretched lamp barely lighted his obscure work. He turned at the noise the reporter made.

"Ah!—you, lad!"

"'Well?"

"Oh, nothing so quick. Still, I have already analyzed the two napkins, you know."

"Yes? The stains? Tell me, for the love of God!"

"Well, my boy, it is arsenate of soda again."

Rouletabille, stricken to the heart, uttered a low cry and everything seemed to dance around him. Pere Alexis in the midst of all the strange laboratory instruments seemed Satan himself, and he repulsed the kindly arms stretched forth to sustain him; in the gloom, where danced here and there the little blue flames from the crucibles, lively as flickering tongues, he believed he saw Michael Nikolaievitch's ghost come to cry, "The arsenate of soda continues, and I am dead." He fell against the door, which swung open, and he rolled as far as the counter, and struck his face against it. The shock, that might well have been fatal, brought him out of his intense nightmare and made him instantly himself again. He rose, jumped over the heap of boots and fol-de-rols, and leaped

516

to the court. There Boris grabbed him by his coat. Rouletabille turned, furious:

"What do you want? You haven't started for the Orel yet?"

"Monsieur, I am going, but I will be very grateful if you will take these things yourself to—to Natacha." He showed him, still with despairing mien, the two ikons from Mount Athos, and Rouletabille took them from him, thrust them in his pocket, and hurried on, crying, "I understand."

Outside, Rouletabille tried to get hold of himself, to recover his coolness a little. Was it possible that he had made a mortal error? Alas, alas, how could he doubt it now! The arsenate of soda continued. He made a superhuman effort to ward off the horror of that, even momentarily—the death of innocent Michael Nikolaievitch— and to think of nothing except the immediate consequences, which must be carefully considered if he wished to avoid some new catastrophe. Ah, the assassin was not discouraged. And that time, what a piece of work he had tried! What a hecatomb if he had succeeded! The general, Matrena Petrovna, Natacha and Rouletabille himself (who almost regretted, so far as he was concerned, that it had not succeeded)— and Koupriane! Koupriane, who should have been there for luncheon. What a bag for the Nihilists! That was it, that was it. Rouletabille understood now why they had not hesitated to poison everybody at once: Koupriane was among them.

Michael Nikolaievitch would have been avenged!

The attempt had failed this time, but what might they not expect now! From the moment he believed Michael Nikolaievitch no longer guilty, as he had imagined, Rouletabille fell into a bottomless abyss.

Where should he go? After a few moments he made the circuit of the Rotunda, which serves as the market for this quarter and is the finest ornament of Aptiekarski-Pereoulok. He made the circuit without knowing it, without stopping for anything, without seeing or understanding anything. As a broken-winded horse makes its way in the treadmill, so he walked around with the thought that he also was lost in a treadmill that led him nowhere. Rouletabille was no longer Rouletabille.

XIII

THE LIVING BOMBS

At random—because now he could only act at random—he returned to the datcha. Great disorder reigned there. The guard had been doubled. The general's friends, summoned by Trebassof, surrounded the two poisoned sufferers and filled the house with their bustling devotion and their protestations of affection. However, an insignificant doctor from the common quarter of the Vasili-Ostrow, brought by the police, reassured everybody. The police had not found the general's household physician at home, but promised the immediate arrival of two specialists, whom they had found instead. In the meantime they had picked up on the way this little doctor, who was gay and talkative as a magpie. He had enough to do looking after Matrena Petrovna, who had been so sick that her husband, Feodor Feodorovitch, still trembled, "for the first time in his life," as the excellent Ivan Petrovitch said.

The reporter was astonished at not finding Natacha either in Matrena's apartment or Feodor's. He asked Matrena where her step-daughter was. Matrena turned a frightened face toward him. When they were alone, she said:

"We do not know where she is. Almost as soon as you left she disappeared, and no one has seen her since. The general has asked for her several times. I have had to tell him Koupriane took her with him to learn the details from her of what happened."

"She is not with Koupriane," said Rouletabille.

"Where is she? This disappearance is more than strange at the moment we were dying, when her father—O God! Leave me, my child; I am stifling; I am stifling."

Rouletabille called the temporary doctor and withdrew from the chamber. He had come with the idea of inspecting the house room by room, corner by corner, to make sure whether or not any possibility of entrance existed that he had not noticed before, an entrance would-be poisoners were continuing to use. But now a new fact confronted him and overshadowed everything: the disappearance of Natacha. How he lamented his ignorance of the Russian language—and not one of Koupriane's men knew French. He might draw something out of Ermolai.

Ermolai said he had seen Natacha just outside the gate for a moment, looking up and down the road. Then he had been called to the general, and so knew nothing further.

That was all the reporter could gather from the gestures rather than the words of the old servant.

An additional difficulty now was that twilight drew on, and it was impossible for the reporter to discern Natacha's foot-prints. Was it true that the young girl had fled at such a moment, immediately after the poisoning, before she knew whether her father and mother were entirely out of danger? If Natacha were innocent, as Rouletabille still wished to believe, such an attitude was simply incomprehensible. And the girl could not but be aware she would increase Koupriane's suspicions. The reporter had a vital reason for seeing her immediately, a vital reason for all concerned, above all in this moment when the Nihilists were culminating their plans, a vital reason for her and for him, equally menaced with death, to talk with her and to renew the propositions he had made a few minutes before the poisoning and which she had not wished to hear him talk about, in fearful pity for him or in defiance of him. Where was Natacha? He thought maybe she was trying to rejoin Annouchka, and there were reasons for that, both if she were innocent and if she were guilty. But where was Annouchka? Who could say! Gounsovski perhaps. Rouletabille jumped into an isvo, returning from the Point empty, and gave Gounsovski's address. He deigned then to recall that he had been invited that same day to dine with the Gounsovskis. They would no longer be expecting him. He blamed himself.

They received him, but they had long since finished dinner.

Monsieur and Madame Gounsovski were playing a game of draughts under the lamp. Rouletabille as he entered the drawing-room recognized the shining, fattish bald head of the terrible man. Gounsovski came to him, bowing, obsequious, his fat hands held out. He was presented to Madame Gounsovski, who was besprinkled with jewels over her black silk gown. She had a muddy skin and magnificent eyes. She also was tentatively effusive. "We waited for you, monsieur," she said, smirking timidly, with the careful charm of a woman a little along in years who relies still on infantine graces. As the recreant young man offered his apologies, "Oh, we know you are much occupied, Monsieur Rouletabille. My husband said that to me only a moment ago. But he knew you would come finally. In the end one always accepts my husband's invitation." She said this with a fat smile of importance.

Rouletabille turned cold at this last phrase. He felt actual fear in the presence of these two figures, so atrociously commonplace, in their horrible, decent little drawing-room.

Madame continued:

"But you have had rather a bad dinner already, through that dreadful affair at General Trebassof 's. Come into the dining-room." "Ah, so someone has told you?" said Rouletabille. "No, no, thanks; I don't need anything more. You know what has happened?"

"If you had come to dinner, perhaps nothing would have happened at all, you know," said Gounsovski tranquilly, seating himself again on the cushions and considering his game of draughts through his glasses. "Anyway, congratulations to Koupriane for being away from there through his fear."

For Gounsovski there was only Koupriane! The life or death of Trebassof did not occupy his mind. Only the acts and movements of the Prefect of Police had power to move him. He ordered a waiting-maid who glided into the apartment without making more noise than a shadow to bring a small stand loaded with zakouskis and bottles of champagne close to the game-table, and he moved one of his pawns, saying, "You will permit me? This move is mine. I don't wish to lose it."

Rouletabille ventured to lay his hand on the oily, hairy fist which extended from a dubious cuff.

"What is this you tell me? How could you have foreseen it?"

"It was easy to foresee everything," replied Gounsovski, offering cigars, "to foresee everything from the moment Matiew's place was filled by Priemkof."

"Well?" questioned Rouletabille, recalling with some inquietude the sight of the whipping in the guards' chapel.

"Well, this Priemkof, between ourselves," (and he bent close to the reporter's ear) "is no better, as a police-guard for Koupriane than Matiew himself. Very dangerous. So when I learned that he took Matiew's place at the datcha des Iles, I thought there was sure to be some unfortunate happening. But it was no affair of mine, was it? Koupriane would have been able to say to me, 'Mind your own business.' I had gone far enough in warning him of the 'living bombs.' They had been denounced to us by the same agency that enabled us to seize the two living bombs (women, if you please!) who were going to the military tribunal at Cronstadt after the rebellion in the fleet. Let him recall that. That ought to make him reflect. I am a brave man. I know he speaks ill of me; but I don't wish him any harm. The interests of the Empire before all else between us! I wouldn't talk to you as I do if I didn't know the Tsar honors you with his favor. Then I invited you to dinner. As one dines one talks. But you did not come. And, while you were dining down there and while Priemkof was on guard at the datcha, that annoying affair Madame Gounsovski has spoken about happened."

Rouletabille had not sat down, in spite of Madame Gounsovski's insistences. He took the box of cigars brusquely out of the hand of the Chief of the Secret Service, who had continued tendering them, for this detail of hospitality only annoyed his mood, which had been dark enough for hours and was now deepened by what the other had just said. He comprehended only one thing, that a man named Priemkof, whom he had never heard spoken of, as determined as Matiew to destroy the general, had been entrusted by Koupriane with the guard of the datcha des Iles. It was necessary to warn Koupriane instantly.

"How is it that you have not done so already, yourself, Monsieur Gounsovski? Why wait to speak about it to me? It is unimaginable."

530

"Pardon, pardon," said Gounsovski, smiling softly behind his goggles; "it is not the same thing."

"No, no, it is not the same thing," seconded the lady with the black silk, brilliant jewels and flabby chin. "We speak here to a friend in the course of dinner-talk, to a friend who is not of the police. We never denounce anybody."

"We must tell you. But sit down now," Gounsovski still insisted, lighting his cigar. "Be reasonable. They have just tried to poison him, so they will take time to breathe before they try something else. Then, too, this poison makes me think they may have given up the idea of living bombs. Then, after all, what is to be will be."

"Yes, yes," approved the ample dame. "The police never have been able to prevent what was bound to happen. But, speaking of this Priemkof, it remains between us, eh? Between just us?"

"Yes, we must tell you now," Gounsovski slipped in softly, "that it will be much better not to let Koupriane know that you got the information from me. Because then, you understand, he would not believe you; or, rather, he would not believe me. That is why we take these precautions of dining and smoking a cigar. We speak of one thing and another and you do as you please with what we say. But, to make them useful, it is absolutely necessary, I repeat, to be silent about their source." (As he said that, Gounsovski gave Rouletabille a piercing glance through his goggles, the first time Rouletabille had seen such a look in his eyes. He never would have suspected him capable of such fire.) "Priemkof," continued Gounsovski in a low voice, using his handkerchief vigorously, "was employed here in my home and we separated on bad terms, through his fault, it is necessary to say. Then he got into Koupriane's confidence by saying the worst he could of us, my dear little monsieur."

"But what could he say?—servants' stories! my dear little monsieur," repeated the fat dame, and rolled her great magnificent black eyes furiously. "Stories that have been treated as they deserved at Court, certainly. Madame Daquin, the wife of His Majesty's head-cook, whom you certainly know, and the nephew of the second Maid of Honor to the Empress, who stands very well with his aunt, have told us so; servants' stories that might have ruined us but have not produced any effect on His Majesty, for whom we would give our lives, Christ knows. Well, you understand now that if you were to say to Koupriane, 'Gaspadine Gounsovski has spoken ill to me of Priemkof,' he would not care to hear a word further. Still, Priemkof is in the scheme for the living bombs, that is all I can tell you; at least, he was before the affair of the poisoning. That poisoning is certainly very astonishing, between us. It does not appear to have come from without, whereas the living bombs will have to come from without. And Priemkof is mixed up in it."

"Yes, yes," approved Madame Gounsovski again, "he is committed to it. There have been stories about him, too. Other people as well as he can tell tales; it isn't hard to do. He has got to make some showing now if he is to keep in with Annouchka's clique."

"Koupriane, our dear Koupriane," interrupted Gounsovski, slightly troubled at hearing his wife pronounce Annouchka's name, "Koupriane ought to be able to understand that this time Priemkof must bring things off, or he is definitely ruined."

"Priemkof knows it well enough," replied Madame as she re-filled the glasses, "but

Koupriane doesn't know it; that is all we can tell you. Is it enough? All the rest is mere gossip."

It certainly was enough for Rouletabille; he had had enough of it! This idle gossip and these living bombs! These pinchbecks, these whispering tale-tellers in their bourgeois, countrified setting; these politico-police combinations whose grotesque side was always uppermost; while the terrible side, the Siberian aspect, prisons, black holes, hangings, disappearances, exiles and deaths and martyrdoms remained so jealously hidden that no one ever spoke of them! All that weight of horror, between a good cigar and "a little glass of anisette, monsieur, if you won't take champagne." Still, he had to drink before he left, touch glasses in a health, promise to come again, whenever he wished—the house was open to him. Rouletabille knew it was open to anybody— anybody who had a tale to tell, something that would send some other person to prison or to death and oblivion. No guard at the entrance to check a visitor—men entered Gounsovski's house as the house of a friend, and he was always ready to do you a service, certainly!

He accompanied the reporter to the stairs. Rouletabille was just about to risk speaking of Annouchka to him, in order to approach the subject of Natacha, when Gounsovski said suddenly, with a singular smile:

"By the way, do you still believe in Natacha Trebassof?"

"I shall believe in her until my death," Rouletabille thrust back; "but I admit to you that at this moment I don't know where she has gone."

"Watch the Bay of Lachtka, and come to tell me tomorrow if you will believe in her always," replied Gounsovski, confidentially, with a horrid sort of laugh that made the reporter hurry down the stairs.

And now here was Priemkof to look after! Priemkof after Matiew! It seemed to the young man that he had to contend against all the revolutionaries not only, but all the Russian police as well—and Gounsovski himself, and Koupriane! Everybody, everybody! But most urgent was Priemkof and his living bombs. What a strange and almost incomprehensible and harassing adventure this was between Nihilism and the Russian police. Koupriane and Gounsovski both employed a man they knew to be a revolutionary and the friend of revolutionaries. Nihilism, on its side, considered this man of the police force as one of its own agents. In his turn, this man, in order to maintain his perilous equilibrium, had to do work for both the police and the revolutionaries, and accept whatever either gave him to do as it came, because it was necessary he should give them assurances of his fidelity. Only imbeciles, like Gapone, let themselves be hanged or ended by being executed, like Azef, because of their awkward slips. But a Priemkof, playing both branches of the police, had a good chance of living a long time, and a Gounsovski would die tranquilly in his bed with all the solaces of religion.

However, the young hearts hot with sincerity, sheathed with dynamite, are mysteriously moved in the atrocious darkness of Holy Russia, and they do not know where they will be sent, and it is all one to them, because all they ask is to die in a mad spiritual delirium of hate and love—living bombs! (note 1)

——————

1. In the trial after the revolt at Cronstadt two young women were charged with wearing bombs as false bosoms.

At the corner of Aptiekarski-Pereoulok Rouletabille came in the way of Koupriane, who was leaving for Pere Alexis's place and, seeing the reporter, stopped his carriage and called that he was going immediately to the datcha.

"You have seen Pere Alexis?"

"Yes," said Koupriane. "And this time I have it on you. What I told you, what I foresaw, has happened. But have you any news of the sufferers? Apropos, rather a curious thing has happened. I met Kister on the Nevsky just now."

"The physician?"

"Yes, one of Trebassof 's physicians whom I had sent an inspector to his house to fetch to the datcha, as well as his usual associate, Doctor Litchkof. Well, neither Litchkof nor he had been summoned. They didn't know anything had happened at the datcha. They had not seen my inspector. I hope he has met some other doctor on the way and, in view of the urgency, has taken him to the datcha."

"That is what has happened," replied Rouletabille, who had turned very pale. "Still, it is strange these gentlemen had not been notified, because at the datcha the Trebassofs were told that the general's usual doctors were not at home and so the police had summoned two others who would arrive at once."

Koupriane jumped up in the carriage.

"But Kister and Litchkof had not left their houses. Kister, who had just met Litchkof, said so. What does this mean?"

"Can you tell me," asked Rouletabille, ready now for the thunder-clap that his question invited, "the name of the inspector you ordered to bring them?"

"Priemkof, a man with my entire confidence."

Koupriane's carriage rushed toward the Isles. Late evening had come. Alone on the deserted route the horses seemed headed for the stars; the carriage behind seemed no drag upon them. The coachman bent above them, arms out, as though he would spring into the ether. Ah, the beautiful night, the lovely, peaceful night beside the Neva, marred by the wild gallop of these maddened horses!

"Priemkof! Priemkof! One of Gounsovski's men! I should have suspected him," railed Koupriane after Rouletabille's explanations. "But now, shall we arrive in time?"

They stood up in the carriage, urging the coachman, exciting the horses: "Scan! Scan!

Faster, douriak!" Could they arrive before the "living bombs"? Could they hear them before they arrived? Ah, there was Eliaguine!

They rushed from the one bank to the other as though there were no bridges in their insensate course. And their ears were strained for the explosion, for the abomination now to come, preparing slyly in the night so hypocritically soft under the cold glance of the stars. Suddenly, "Stop, stop!" Rouletabille cried to the coachman.

"Are you mad!" shouted Koupriane.

"We are mad if we arrive like madmen. That would make the catastrophe sure. There is still a chance. If we wish not to lose it, then we must arrive easily and calmly, like friends who know the general is out of danger."

"Our only chance is to arrive before the bogus doctors. Either they aren't there, or it already is all over. Priemkof must have been surprised at the affair of the poisoning, but he has seized the opportunity; fortunately he couldn't find his accomplices immediately."

"Here is the datcha, anyway. In the name of heaven, tell your driver to stop the horses here. If the 'doctors' are already there it is we who shall have killed the general."

"You are right."

Koupriane moderated his excitement and that of his driver and horses, and the carriage stopped noiselessly, not far from the datcha. Ermolai came toward them.

"Priemkof?" faltered Koupriane.

"He has gone again, Excellency."

"How—gone again?"

"Yes, but he has brought the doctors."

Koupriane crushed Rouletabille's wrist. The doctors were there!

"Madame Trebassof is better," continued Ermolai, who understood nothing of their emotion. "The general is going to meet them and take them to his wife himself."

"Where are they?"

"They are waiting in the drawing-room."

"Oh, Excellency, keep cool, keep cool, and all is not lost," implored the reporter.

Rouletabille and Koupriane slipped carefully into the garden. Ermolai followed them.

"There?" inquired Koupriane.

"There," Ermolai replied.

From the corner where they were, and looking through the veranda, they could see the "doctors" as they waited.

They were seated in chairs side by side, in a corner of the drawing-room from where they could see every-thing in the room and a part of the garden, which they faced, and could hear everything. A window of the first-floor was open above their heads, so that they could hear any noise from there. They could not be surprised from any side, and they held every door in view. They were talking softly and tranquilly, looking straight before them. They appeared young. One had a pleasant face, pale but smiling, with rather long, curly hair; the other was more angular, with haughty bearing and grave face, an eagle nose and glasses. Both wore long black coats buttoned over their calm chests.

Koupriane and the reporter, followed by Ermolai, advanced with the greatest precaution across the lawn. Screened by the wooden steps leading to the veranda and by the vine-clad balustrade, they got near enough to hear them. Koupriane gave eager ear to the words of these two young men, who might have been so rich in the many years of life that naturally belonged to them, and who were about to die so horrible a death in destroying all about them. They spoke of what time it was, of the softness of the night and the beauty of the sky; they spoke of the shadows under the birch-trees, of the gulf shining in the late evening's fading golden light, of the river's freshness and the sweetness of springtime in the North. That is what they talked about. Koupriane murmured, "The assassins!"

Now it was necessary to decide on action, and that necessity was horrible. A false movement, an awkwardness, and the "doctors" would be warned, and everything lost. They must have the bombs under their coats; there were certainly at least two "living bombs." Their chests, as they breathed, must heave to and fro and their hearts beat against an impending explosion.

Above on the bedroom floor, they heard the rapid arranging of the room, steps on the floor and a confusion of voices; shadows passed across the window-space. Koupriane rapidly interrogated Ermolai and learned that all the general's friends were there. The two doctors had arrived only a couple of minutes before the Prefect of Police and the reporter. The little doctor of Vassili-Ostrow had already gone, saying there was nothing more for him to do when two such celebrated specialists had arrived. However, in spite of their celebrity, no one had ever heard the names they gave. Koupriane believed the little doctor was an accomplice. The most necessary thing was to warn those in the room above. There was immediate danger that someone would come downstairs to find the doctors and take them to the general, or that the general would come down himself to meet them. Evidently that was what they were waiting for. They wished to die in his arms, to make sure that this time he did not escape them! Koupriane directed Ermolai to go into the veranda and speak in a commonplace way to them at the threshold of the drawing-room door, saying that he would go upstairs and see if he might now escort them to Madame Trebassof 's room. Once in the room above, he could warn the others not to do anything but wait for Koupriane; then Ermolai was to come down and say to the men, "In just a moment, if you please."

Ermolai crept back as far as the lodge, and then came quite normally up the path, letting the gravel crunch under his countrified footsteps. He was an intelligent man, and grasped with extraordinary coolness the importance of the plan of campaign. Easily and naturally he mounted the veranda steps, paused at the threshold of the drawing-room, made the remark he had been told to make, and went upstairs. Koupriane and Rouletabille now watched the bedroom windows. The flitting shadows there suddenly became motionless. All moving about ceased; no more steps were heard, nothing. And that sudden silence made the two "doctors" raise their faces toward the ceiling. Then they exchanged an aroused glance. This change in the manner of things above was dangerous. Koupriane muttered, "The idiots!" It was such a blow for those upstairs to learn they walked over a mine ready to explode that it evidently had paralyzed their limbs. Happily Ermolai came down almost immediately and said to the "doctors" in his very best domestic manner:

"Just a second, messieurs, if you please."

He did it still with utter naturalness. And he returned to the ledge before he rejoined Koupriane and Rouletabille by way of the lawn. Rouletabille, entirely cool, quite master of himself, as calm now as Koupriane was nervous, said to the Prefect of Police:

"We must act now, and quickly. They are commencing to be suspicious. Have you a plan?"

"Here is all I can see," said Koupriane. "Have the general come down by the narrow servants' stairway, and slip out of the house from the window of Natacha's sitting-room, with the aid of a twisted sheet. Matrena Petrovna will come to speak to them during this time; that will keep them patient until the general is out of danger. As soon as Matrena has withdrawn into the garden, I will call my men, who will shoot them from a distance."

"And the house itself? And the general's friends?"

"Let them try to get away, too, by the servants' stairway and jump from the window after the general. We must try something. Say that I have them at the muzzle of my revolver."

"Your plan won't work," said Rouletabille, "unless the door of Natacha's sitting-room that opens on the drawing-room is closed."

"It is. I can see from here."

"And unless the door of the little passage-way before that staircase that opens into the drawing-room is closed also, and you cannot see it from here."

"That door is open," said Ermolai.

Koupriane swore. But he recovered himself promptly.

"Madame Trebassof will close the door when she speaks to them."

"It's impracticable," said the reporter. "That will arouse their suspicions more than ever. Leave it to me; I have a plan."

"What?"

"I have time to execute it, but not to tell you about it. They have already waited too long. I shall have to go upstairs, though. Ermolai will need to go with me, as with a friend of the family."

"I'll go too."

"That would give the whole show away, if they saw you, the Prefect of Police."

"Why, no. If they see me—and they know I ought to be there—as soon as I show myself to them they will conclude I don't know anything about it."

"You are wrong."

"It is my duty. I should be near the general to defend him until the last."

Rouletabille shrugged his shoulders before this dangerous heroism, but he did not stop to argue. He knew that his plan must succeed at once, or in five minutes at the latest there would be only ruins, the dead and the dying in the datcha des Iles.

Still he remained astonishingly calm. In principle he had admitted that he was going to die. The only hope of being saved which remained to them rested entirely upon their keeping perfectly cool and upon the patience of the living bombs. Would they still have three minutes' patience?

Ermolai went ahead of Koupriane and Rouletabille. At the moment they reached the foot of the veranda steps the servant said loudly, repeating his lesson:

"Oh, the general is waiting for you, Excellency. He told me to have you come to him at once. He is entirely well and Madame Trebassof also."

When they were in the veranda, he added:

"She is to see also, at once, these gentlemen, who will be able to tell her there is no more danger."

And all three passed while Koupriane and Rouletabille vaguely saluted the two conspirators in the drawing-room. It was a decisive moment. Recognizing Koupriane, the two Nihilists might well believe themselves discovered, as the reporter had said, and precipitate the catastrophe. However, Ermolai, Koupriane and Rouletabille climbed the stairs to the bedroom like automatons, not daring to look behind them, and expecting the end each instant. But neither stirred. Ermolai went down again, by Rouletabille's order, normally, naturally, tranquilly. They went into Matrena Petrovna's chamber. Everybody was there. It was a gathering of ghosts.

Here was what had happened above. That the "doctors" still remained below, that they had not been received instantly, in brief, that the catastrophe had been delayed up to now was due to Matrena Petrovna, whose watchful love, like a watch-dog, was always ready to scent danger. These two "doctors" whose names she did not know, who arrived so late, and the precipitate departure of the little doctor of

Vassili-Ostrow aroused her watchfulness. Before allowing them to come upstairs to the general she resolved to have a look at them herself downstairs. She arose from her bed for that; and now her presentiment was justified. When she saw Ermolai, sober and mysterious, enter with Koupriane's message, she knew instinctively, before he spoke, that there were bombs in the house. When Ermolai did speak it was a blow for everybody. At first she, Matrena Perovna, had been a frightened, foolish figure in the big flowered dressing-gown belonging to Feodor that she had wrapped about her in her haste. When Ermolai left, the general, who knew she only trembled for him, tried to reassure her, and, in the midst of the frightened silence of all of them, said a few words recalling the failure of all the previous attempts. But she shook her head and trembled, shaking with fear for him, in agony at the thought that she could do nothing there above those living bombs but

556

wait for them to burst. As to the friends, already their limbs were ruined, absolutely ruined, in very truth. For a moment they were quite incapable of moving. The jolly Councilor of Empire, Ivan Petrovitch, had no longer a lively tale to tell, and the abominable prospect of "this horrible mix-up" right at hand rendered him much less gay than in his best hours at Cubat's place. And poor Thaddeus Tchitchnikoff was whiter than the snow that covers old Lithuania's fields when the winter's chase is on. Athanase Georgevitch himself was not brilliant, and his sanguine face had quite changed, as though he had difficulty in digesting his last masterpiece with knife and fork. But, in justice to them, that was the first instantaneous effect. No one could learn like that, all of a sudden, that they were about to die in an indiscriminate slaughter without the heart being stopped for a little. Ermolai's words had turned these amiable loafers into waxen statues, but, little by little, their hearts commenced to beat again and each suggested some way of preventing the disaster—all of them sufficiently incoherent—while Matrena Petrovna invoked the Virgin and at the same time helped Feodor Feodorovitch adjust his sword and buckle his belt; for the general wished to die in uniform.

Athanase Georgevitch, his eyes sticking out of his head and his body bent as though he feared the Nihlists just below him might perceive his tall form—through the floor, no doubt—proposed that they should throw themselves out of the window, even at the cost of broken legs. The saddened Councilor of Empire declared that project simply idiotic, for as they fell they would be absolutely at the disposal of the Nihilists, who would be attracted by the noise and would make a handful of dust of them with a single gesture through the window. Thaddeus Tchitchnikoff, who couldn't think of anything at all, blamed Koupriane and the rest of the police for not having devised something. Why hadn't they already got rid of these Nihilists? After the frightened silence they had kept at first, now they all spoke at once, in low voices, hoarse and rapid, with shortened breath, making wild movements of the arms and head, and walked here and there in the chamber quite without motive, but very softly on tiptoe, going to the windows, returning, listening at the doors, peering through the key-holes, exchanging absurd suggestions, full of the wildest imaginings. "If we should... if... if,"—everybody speaking and everybody making signs for the others to be quiet. "Lower! If they hear us, we are lost." And Koupriane, who did not come, and his police, who themselves had brought two assassins into the house, and were not able now to make them leave without having everybody jump! They were certainly lost. There was nothing left but to say their prayers. They turned to the general and Matrena Petrovna, who were wrapped in a close embrace. Feodor had taken the poor disheveled head of the good Matrena between his hands and pressed it upon his shoulders as he embraced her. He said, "Rest quietly against my heart, Matrena Petrovna. Nothing can happen to us except what God wills."

At that sight and that remark the others grew ashamed of their confusion. The harmony of that couple embracing in the presence of death restored them to themselves, to their courage, and their "Nitchevo." Athanase Georgevitch, Ivan Petrovitch and Thaddeus Tchitchnikoff repeated after Matrena Petrovna, "As God wills." And then they said "Nitchevo! Nitchevo! (note 1) We will all die with you, Feodor Feodorovitch." And they all kissed

------

1. "What does it matter!"

one another and clasped one another in their arms, their eyes dim with love one for another, as at the end of a great banquet when they had eaten and drunk heavily in honor of one another.

"Listen. Someone is coming up the stairs," whispered Matrena, with her keen ear, and she slipped from the restraint of her husband.

Breathless, they all hurried to the door opening on the landing, but with steps as light "as though they walked on eggs." All four of them were leaning over there close by the door, hardly daring to breathe. They heard two men on the stairs. Were they Koupriane and Rouletabille, or were they the others? They had revolvers in their hands and drew back a little when the footsteps sounded near the door. Behind them Trebassof was quietly seated in his chair. The door was opened and Koupriane and Rouletabille perceived these death-like figures, motionless and mute. No one dared to speak or make a movement until the door had been closed. But then:

"Well? Well? Save us! Where are they? Ah, my dear little domovoi-doukh, save the general, for the love of the Virgin!"

"Tsst! tsst! Silence."

Rouletabille, very pale, but calm, spoke:

"The plan is simple. They are between the two staircases, watching the one and the other. I will go and find them and make them mount the one while you descend by the other."

"Caracho! That is simple enough. Why didn't we think of it sooner? Because everybody lost his head except the dear little domovoi-doukh!" But here something happened Rouletabille had not counted on. The general rose and said, "You have forgotten one thing, my young friend; that is that General Trebassof will not descend by the servants' stairway."

His friends looked at him in stupefaction, and asked if he had gone mad.

"What is this you say, Feodor?" implored Matrena.

"I say," insisted the general, "that I have had enough of this comedy, and that since Monsieur Koupriane has not been able to arrest these men, and since, on their side, they don't seem to decide to do their duty, I shall go myself and put them out of my house."

He started a few steps, but had not his cane and suddenly he tottered. Matrena Petrovna jumped to him and lifted him in her arms as though he were a feather.

"Not by the servants' stairway, not by the servants' stairway," growled the obstinate general.

"You will go," Matrena replied to him, "by the way I take you."

And she carried him back into the apartment while she said quickly to Rouletabille:

"Go, little domovoi! And God protect us!"

Rouletabille disappeared at once through the door to the main staircase, and the group attended by Koupriane, passed through the dressing-room and the general's chamber, Matrena Petrovna in the lead with her precious burden. Ivan Petrovitch had his hand already on the famous bolt which locked the door to the servants' staircase when they all turned at the sound of a quick step behind them. Rouletabille had returned.

"They are no longer in the drawing-room."

"Not in the drawing-room! Where are they, then?"

Rouletabille pointed to the door they were about to open.

"Perhaps behind that door. Take care!"

All drew back.

"But Ermolai ought to know where they are," exclaimed Koupriane. "Perhaps they have gone, finding out they were discovered."

"They have assassinated Ermolai."

"Assassinated Ermolai!"

"I have seen his body lying in the middle of the drawing-room as I leaned over the top of the banister. But they were not in the room, and I was afraid you would run into them, for they may well be hidden in the servants' stairway."

"Then open the window, Koupriane, and call your men to deliver us."

"I am quite willing," replied Koupriane coldly, "but it is the signal for our deaths."

"Well, why do they wait so to make us die?" muttered Feodor Feodorovitch. "I find them very tedious about it, for myself. What are you doing, Ivan Petrovitch?"

The spectral figure of Ivan Petrovitch, bent beside the door of the stairway, seemed to be hearing things the others could not catch, but which frightened them so that they fled from the general's chamber in disorder.

Ivan Petrovitch was close on them, his eyes almost sticking from his head, his mouth babbling:

"They are there! They are there!"

Athanase Georgevitch open a window wildly and said:

"I am going to jump."

But Thaddeus Tchitchnikofl' stopped him with a word. "For me, I shall not leave Feodor Feodorovitch."

Athanase and Ivan both felt ashamed, and trembling, but brave, they gathered round the general and said, "We will die together, we will die together. We have lived with Feodor Feodorovitch, and we will die with him."

"What are they waiting for? What are they waiting for?" grumbled the general.

Matrena Petrovna's teeth chattered.
"They are waiting for us to go down," said Koupraine.

"Very well, let us do it. This thing must end," said Feodor.

"Yes, yes," they all said, for the situation was becoming intolerable; "enough of this. Go on down. Go on down. God, the Virgin and Saints Peter and Paul protect us. Let us go."

The whole group, therefore, went to the main staircase, with the movements of drunken men, fantastic waving of the arms, mouths speaking all together, saying things no one but themselves understood. Rouletabille had already hurriedly preceded them, was down the staircase, had time to throw a glance into the drawing-room, stepped over Ermolai's huge corpse, entered Natacha's sitting-room and her chamber, found all these places deserted and bounded back into the veranda at the moment the others commenced to descend the steps around Feodor Feodorovitch. The reporter's eyes searched all the dark corners and had perceived nothing suspicious when, in the veranda, he moved a chair. A shadow detached itself from it and glided under the staircase. Rouletabille cried to the group on the stairs.

"They are under the staircase!"

Then Rouletabille confronted a sight that he could never forget all his life.

At this cry, they all stopped, after an instinctive move to go back. Feodor Feodorovitch, who was still in Matrena Petrovna's arms, cried:

"Vive le Tsar!"

And then, those whom the reporter half expected to see flee, distracted, one way and another, or to throw themselves madly from the height of the steps, abandoning Feodor and Matrena, gathered themselves instead by a spontaneous movement around the general, like a guard of honor, in battle, around the flag. Koupriane marched ahead. And they insisted also upon descending the terrible steps slowly, and sang the Bodje tsara Krani, the national anthem!

With an overwhelming roar, which shocked earth and sky and the ears of Rouletabille, the entire house seemed lifted in the air; the staircase rose amid flame and smoke, and the group which sang the Bodje tsara Krani disappeared in a horrible apotheosis.

XIV

THE MARSHES

They ascertained the next day that there had been two explosions, almost simultaneous, one under each staircase. The two Nihilists, when they felt themselves discovered, and watched by Ermolai, had thrown themselves silently on him as he turned his back in passing them, and strangled him with a piece of twine. Then they separated each to watch one of the staircases, reasoning that Koupriane and General Trebassof would have to decide to descend.

The datcha des Iles was nothing now but a smoking ruin. But from the fact that the living bombs had exploded separately the destructive effect was diffused, and although there were numerous wounded, as in the case of the attack on the Stolypine datcha, at least no one was killed outright; that is, excepting the two Nihilists, of whom no trace could be found save a few rags.

Rouletabille had been hurled into the garden and he was glad enough to escape so, a little shaken, but without a scratch. The group composed of Feodor and his friends were strangely protected by the lightness of the datcha's construction. The iron staircase, which, so to speak, almost hung to the two floors, being barely attached at top and bottom, raised under them and then threw them off as it broke into a thousand pieces, but only after, by its very yielding, it had protected them from the first force of the bomb. They had risen from the ruins without mortal wounds. Koupriane had a hand badly burned, Athanase Georgevitch had his nose and cheeks seriously hurt, Ivan Petrovitch lost an ear; the most seriously injured was Thaddeus Tchitchnikoff, both of whose legs were broken. Extraordinarily enough, the first person who appeared, rising from the midst of the wreckage, was Matrena Petrovna, still holding Feodor in her arms. She had escaped with a few burns and the general, saved again by the luck of the soldier whom Death does not want, was absolutely uninjured. Feodor gave shouts of joy. They strove to quiet him, because, after all, around him some poor wretches had been badly hurt, as well as poor Ermolai, who lay there dead. The domestics in the basement had been more seriously wounded and burned because the main force of the explosion had gone downwards; which had probably saved the personages above.

Rouletabille had been taken with the other victims to a neighboring datcha; but as soon as he had shaken himself free of that terrible nightmare he escaped from the place. He really regretted that he was not dead. These successive waves of events had swamped him; and he accused himself alone of all this disaster. With acutest anxiety he had inquired about the condition of each of "his victims." Feodor had not been wounded, but now he was almost delirious, asking every other minute as the hours crept on for Natacha, who had not reappeared. That unhappy girl Rouletabille had steadily believed innocent. Was she a culprit? "Ah, if she had only chosen to! If she had had confidence," he cried, raising anguished hands towards heaven, "none of all this need have happened. No one would have attacked and no one would ever again attack the life of Trebassof. For I was not wrong in claiming before Koupriane that the general's life was in my hand, and I had the right to say to him, 'Life for life! Give me Matiew's and I will give you the general's.' And now there has been one more fruitless attempt to kill Feodor Feodorovitch and it is Natacha's fault—that I swear, because she would not listen to me. And is Natacha implicated in it? O my God" Rouletabille asked this vain question of the Divinity, for he expected no more help in answering it on earth.

Natacha! Innocent or guilty, where was she? What was she doing? to know that! To know if one were right or wrong—and if one were wrong, to disappear, to die!

Thus the unhappy Rouletabille muttered as he walked along the bank of the Neva, not far from the ruins of the poor datcha, where the joyous friends of Feodor Feodorovitch would have no more good dinners, never; so he soliloquized, his head on fire.

And, all at once, he recovered trace of the young girl, that trace lost earlier, a trace left at her moment of flight, after the poisoning and before the explosion. And had he not in that a terrible coincidence? Because the poison might well have been only in preparation for the final attack, the pretext for the tragic arrival of the two false doctors. Natacha, Natacha, the living mystery surrounded already by so many dead!

Not far from the ruins of the datcha Rouletabille soon made sure that a group of people had been there the night before, coming from the woods near-by, and returning to them. He was able to be sure of this because the boundaries of the datcha had been guarded by troops and police as soon as the explosion took place, under orders to keep back the crowd that hurried to Eliaguine. He looked attentively at the grass, the ferns, the broken and trampled twigs. Certainly a struggle had occurred there. He could distinguish clearly in the soft earth of a narrow glade the prints of Natacha's two little boots among all the large footprints.

He continued his search with his heart heavier and heavier, he had a presentiment that he was on the point of discovering a new misfortune. The footprints passed steadily under the branches along the side of the Neva. From a bush he picked a shred of white cloth, and it seemed to him a veritable battle had taken place there. Torn branches strewed the grass. He went on. Very close to the bank he saw by examination of the soil, where there was no more trace of tiny heels and little soles, that the woman who had been found there was carried, and carried, into a boat, of which the place of fastening to the bank was still visible.

"They have carried off Natacha," he cried in a surge of anguish. "bungler that I am, that is my fault too—all my fault—all my fault! They wished to avenge Michael Nikolaievitch's death, for which they hold Natacha responsible, and they have kidnapped her."

His eyes searched the great arm of the river for a boat. The river was deserted. Not a sail, nothing visible on the dead waters! "What shall I do? What shall I do? I must save her."

He resumed his course along the river. Who could give him any useful information? He drew near a little shelter occupied by a guard. The guard was speaking to an officer. Perhaps he had noticed something during his watch that evening along the river. That branch of the river was almost always deserted after the day was over. A boat plying between these shores in the twilight would certainly attract attention. Rouletabille showed the guard the paper Koupriane had given him in the beginning, and with the officer (who turned out to be a police officer) as interpreter, he asked his questions. As a matter of fact the guard had been sufficiently puzzled by the doings and comings of a light boat which, after disappearing for an instant, around the bend of the river, had suddenly rowed swiftly out again and accosted a sailing-yacht which appeared at the opening of the gulf. It was one of those small but rapid and elegant sailing craft such as are seen in the Lachtka regattas.

Lachtka! "The Bay of Lachtka!"

The word was a ray of light for the reporter, who recalled now the counsel Gounsovski had given him. "Watch the Bay of Lachtka, and tell me then if you still believe Natacha is innocent!" Gounsovski must have known when he said this that Natacha had embarked in company with the Nihilists, but evidently he was ignorant that she had gone with them under compulsion, as their prisoner.

Was it too late to save Natacha? In any case, before he died, he would try in every way possible, so as at least to have kept her as much as he could from the disaster for which he held himself responsible. He ran to the Barque, near the Point.

His voice was firm as he hailed the canoe of the floating restaurant where, thanks to him, Koupriane had been thwarted in impotent anger. He had himself taken to just below Staria-Derevnia and jumped out at the spot where he saw little Katharina disappear a few days before. He landed in the mud and climbed on hands and knees up the slope of a roadway which followed the bank. This bank led to the Bay of Lachtka, not far from the frontier of Finland.

On Rouletabille's left lay the sea, the immense gulf with slight waves; to his right was the decaying stretch of the marsh. Stagnant water stretching to the horizon, coarse grass and reeds, an extraordinary tangle of water-plants, small ponds whose greenish scum did not stir under the stiff breeze, water that was heavy and dirty.

Along this narrow strip of land thrust thus between the marsh, the sky and the sea, he hurried, with many tumbling, his eyes fixed on the deserted gulf. Suddenly he turned his head at a singular noise. At first he didn't see anything, but heard in the distance a vague clamoring while a sort of vapor commenced to rise from the marsh. And then he noticed, nearer him, the high marsh grasses undulating. Finally he saw a countless flock rising from the bed of the marshes. Beasts, groups of beasts, whose horns one saw like bayonets, jostled each other trying to keep to the firm land. Many of them swam and on the backs of some were naked men, stark naked, with hair falling to their shoulders and streaming behind them like manes. They shouted war-cries and waved their clubs. Rouletabille stopped short before this prehistoric invasion. He would never have imagined that a few miles from the Nevsky Prospect he could have found himself in the midst of such a spectacle. These savages had not even a loin-cloth. Where did they come from with their herd? From what remote place in the world or in old and gone history had they emerged? What was this new invasion? What prodigious slaughter-house awaited these unruly herds? They made a noise like thunder in the marsh. Here were a thousand unkempt haunches undulating in the marsh like the ocean as a storm approaches. The stark-naked men jumped along the route, waving their clubs, crying gutturally in a way the beasts seemed to understand. They worked their way out from the marsh and turned toward the city, leaving behind, to swathe the view of them a while and then fade away, a pestilential haze that hung like an aura about the naked, long-haired men. It was terrible and magnificent. In order not to be shoved into the water, Rouletabille had climbed a small rock that stood beside the route, and had waited there as though petrified himself. When the barbarians had finally passed by he climbed down again, but the route had become a bog of trampled filth.

Happily, he heard the noise of a primitive conveyance behind him. It was a telega. Curiously primitive, the telega is four-wheeled, with two planks thrown crudely across the axle-trees. Rouletabille gave the man who was seated in it three roubles, and jumped into the planks beside him, and the two little Finnish horses, whose manes hung clear to the mud, went like the wind. Such crude conveyances are necessary on such crude roads, but it requires a strong constitution to make a journey on them. Still, the reporter felt none of the jolting, he was so intent on the sea and the coast of Lachtka Bay. The vehicle finally reached a wooden bridge, across a murky creek. As the day commenced to fade colorlessly, Rouletabille jumped off onto the shore and his rustic equipage crossed to the Sestroriesk side. It was a corner of land black and somber as his thoughts that he surveyed now. "Watch the Bay of Lachtka!" The reporter knew that this desolate plain, this impenetrable marsh, this sea which offered the fugitive refuge in innumerable fords, had always been a useful retreat for Nihilistic adventurers. A hundred legends circulated in St. Petersburg about the mysteries of Lachtka marshes. And that gave him his last hope. Maybe he would be able to run across some revolutionaries to whom he could explain about Natacha, as prudently as possible; he might even see Natacha herself. Gounsovski could not have spoken vain words to him.

Between the Lachtkrinsky marsh and the strand he perceived on the edge of the forests which run as far as Sestroriesk a little wooden house whose walls were painted a reddish-brown, and its roof green. It was not the Russian isba, but the Finnish touba. However, a Russian sign announced it to be a restaurant. The young man had to take only a few steps to enter it. He was the only customer there. An old man, with glasses and a long gray beard, evidently the proprietor of the establishment, stood behind the counter, presiding over the zakouskis. Rouletabille chose some little sandwiches which he placed on a plate. He took a bottle of pivo and made the man understand that later, if it were possible, he would like a good hot supper. The other made a sign that he understood and showed him into an adjoining room which was used for diners. Rouletabille was quite ready enough to die in the face of his failures, but he did not wish to perish from hunger.

A table was placed beside a window looking out over the sea and over the entrance to the bay. It could not have been better and, with his eye now on the horizon, now on the estuary near-by, he commenced to eat with gloomy avidity. He was inclined to feel sorry for himself, to indulge in self-pity. "Just the same, two and two always make four," he said to himself; "but in my calculations perhaps I have forgotten the surd. Ah, there was a time when I would not have overlooked anything. And even now I haven't overlooked anything, if Natacha is innocent!" Having literally scoured the plate, he struck the table a great blow with his fist and said: "She is!"

Just then the door opened. Rouletabille supposed the proprietor of the place was entering.

It was Koupriane.

He rose, startled. He could not imagine by what mystery the Prefect of Police had made his way there, but he rejoiced from the bottom of his heart, for if he was trying to rescue Natacha from the hands of the revolutionaries Koupriane would be a valuable ally. He clapped the Prefect on the shoulder.

"Well, well!" he said, almost joyfully. "I certainly did not expect you here. How is your wound?"

"Nitchevo! Not worth speaking about; it's nothing."

"And the general and—! Ah, that frightful night! And those two unfortunates who—?"

"Nitchevo! Nitchevo!"

"And poor Ermolai!"

"Nitchevo! Nitchevo! It is nothing."

Rouletabille looked him over. The Prefect of Police had an arm in a sling, but he was bright and shining as a new ten-rouble piece, while he, poor Rouletabille, was so abominably soiled and depressed. Where did he come from? Koupriane understood his look and smiled.

"Well, I have just come from the Finland train; it is the best way."

"But what can you have come here to do, Excellency?"

"The same thing as you."

"Bah!" exclaimed Rouletabille, "do you mean to say that you have come here to save Natacha?"

"How—to save her! I come to capture her."

"To capture her?"

"Monsieur Rouletabille, I have a very fine little dungeon in Saints Peter and Paul fortress that is all ready for her."

"You are going to throw Natacha into a dungeon!"

"The Emperor's order, Monsieur Rouletabille. And if you see me here in person it is simply because His Majesty requires that the thing be done as respectfully and discreetly as possible."

"Natacha in prison!" cried the reporter, who saw in horror all obstacles rising before him at one and the same time. "For what reasons, pray?"

"The reason is simple enough. Natacha Feodorovna is the last word in wickedness and doesn't deserve anybody's pity. She is the accomplice of the revolutionaries and the instigator of all the crimes against her father."

"I am sure that you are mistaken, Excellency. But how have you been guided to her?"

"Simply by you."

"By me?"

"Yes, we lost all trace of Natacha. But, as you had disappeared also, I made up my mind that you could only be occupied in searching for her, and that by finding you I might have the chance to lay my hands on her."

"But I haven't seen any of your men?"

"Why, one of them brought you here."

"Me?"

"Yes, you. Didn't you climb onto a telega?"

"Ah, the driver."

"Exactly. I had arranged to have him meet me at the Sestroriesk station. He pointed out the place where you dropped off, and here I am."

The reporter bent his head, red with chagrin. Decidedly the sinister idea that he was responsible for the death of an innocent man and all the ills which had followed out of it had paralyzed his detective talents. He recognized it now. What was the use of struggling! If anyone had told him that he would be played with that way sometime, he, Rouletabille! he would have laughed heartily enough—then. But now, well, he wasn't capable of anything further. He was his own most cruel enemy. Not only was Natacha in the hands of the revolutionaries through his fault, by his abominable error, but worse yet, in the very moment when he wished to save her, he foolishly, naively, had conducted the police to the very spot where they should have been kept away. It was the depth of his humiliation; Koupriane really pitied the reporter.

"Come, don't blame yourself too much," said he. "We would have found Natacha without you; Gounsovski notified us that she was going to embark in the Bay of Lachtka this evening with Priemkof."

"Natacha with Priemkof!" exclaimed Rouletabille. "Natacha with the man who introduced the two living bombs into her father's house! If she is with him, Excellency, it is because she is his prisoner, and that alone will be sufficient to prove her innocence. I thank the Heaven that has sent you here."

Koupriane swallowed a glass of vodka, poured another after it, and finally deigned to translate his thought:

"Natacha is the friend of these precious men and we will see them disembark hand in hand."

"Your men, then, haven't studied the traces of the struggle that 'these precious men' have had on the banks of the Neva before they carried away Natacha?"

"Oh, they haven't been hoodwinked. As a matter of fact, the struggle was quite too visible not to have been done for appearances' sake. What a child you are! Can't you see that Natacha's presence in the datcha had become quite too dangerous for that charming young girl after the poisoning of her father and step-mother failed and at the moment when her comrades were preparing to send General Trebassof a pleasant little gift of dynamite? She arranged to get away and yet to appear kidnapped. It is too simple."

Rouletabille raised his head.

"There is something simpler still to imagine than the culpability of Natacha. It is that Priemkof schemed to pour the poison into the flask of vodka, saying to himself that if the poison didn't succeed at least it would make the occasion for introducing his dynamite into the house in the pockets of the 'doctors' that they would go to find."

Koupriane seized Rouletabille's wrist and threw some terrible words at him, looking into the depths of his eyes:

"It was not Priemkof who poured the poison, because there was no poison in the flask."

Rouletabille, as he heard this extraordinary declaration, rose, more startled than he had ever been in the course of this startling campaign.

If there was no poison in the flask, the poison must have been poured directly into the glasses by a person who was in the kiosk! Now, there were only four persons in the kiosk: the two who were poisoned and Natacha and himself, Rouletabille. And that kiosk was so perfectly isolated that it was impossible for any other persons than the four who were there to pour poison upon the table.

"But it is not possible!" he cried.

"It is so possible that it is so. Pere Alexis declared that there is no poison in the flask, and I ought to tell you that an analysis I had made after his bears him out. There was no poison, either, in the small bottle you took to Pere Alexis and into which you yourself had poured the contents of Natacha's glass and yours; no trace of poison excepting in two of the four glasses, arsenate of soda was found only on the soiled napkins of Trebassof and his wife and in the two glasses they drank from."

"Oh, that is horrible," muttered the stupefied reporter; "that is horrible, for then the poisoner must be either Natacha or me."

"I have every confidence in you," declared Koupriane with a great laugh of satisfaction, striking him on the shoulder. "And I arrest Natacha, and you who love logic ought to be satisfied now."

Rouletabille hadn't a word more to say. He sat down again and let his head fall into his hands, like one sleep has seized.

"Ah, our young girls; you don't know them. They are terrible, terrible!" said Koupriane, lighting a big cigar. "Much more terrible than the boys. In good families the boys still enjoy themselves; but the girls—they read! It goes to their heads. They are ready for anything; they know neither father nor mother. Ah, you are a child, you cannot comprehend. Two lovely eyes, a melancholy air, a soft, low voice, and you are captured—you believe you have before you simply an inoffensive, good little girl. Well, Rouletabille, here is what I will tell you for your instruction. There was the time of the Tchipoff attack; the revolutionaries who were assigned to kill Tchipoff were disguised as coachmen and footmen. Everything had been carefully prepared and it would seem that no one could have discovered the bombs in the place they had been stored. Well, do you know the place where those bombs were found? In the rooms of the governor, of Wladmir's daughter! Exactly, my little friend, just there! The rooms of the governor's daughter, Mademoiselle Alexeieiv. Ah, these young girls! Besides, it was this same Mademoiselle Alexeieiv who, so prettily, pierced the brain of an honest Swiss merchant who had the misfortune to resemble one of our ministers. If we had hanged that charming young girl earlier, my dear Monsieur Rouletabille, that last catastrophe might have been avoided. A good rope around the neck of all these little females—it is the only way, the only way!"

A man entered. Rouletabille recognized the driver of the telega. There were some rapid words between the Chief and the agent. The man closed the shutters of the room, but through the interstices they would be able to see what went on outside. Then the agent left; Koupriane, as he pushed aside the table that was near the window, said to the reporter:

"You had better come to the window; my man has just told me the boat is drawing near. You can watch an interesting sight. We are sure that Natacha is still aboard. The yacht, after the explosion at the datcha, took up two men who put off to it in a canoe, and since then it has simply sailed back and forth in the gulf. We have taken our precautions in Finland the same as here and it is here they are going to try to disembark. Keep an eye on them."

Koupriane was at his post of observation. Evening slowly fell. The sky was growing grayish-black, a tint that blended with the slate-colored sea. To those on the bank, the sound of the men about to die came softly across the water. There was a sail far out. Between the strand and the touba where Koupriane watched, was a ridge, a window, which, however, did not hide the shore or the bay from the prefect of police, because at the height where he was his glance passed at an angle above it. But from the sea this ridge entirely hid anyone who lay in ambush behind it. The reporter watched fifty moujiks flat on their stomachs crawling up the ridge, behind two of their number whose heads alone topped the ridge. In the line of gaze taken by those two heads was the white sail, looming much larger now. The yacht was heeled in the water and glided with real elegance, heading straight on. Suddenly, just when they supposed she was coming straight to shore, the sails fell and a canoe was dropped over the side. Four men got into it; then a woman jumped lightly down a little gangway into the canoe. It was Natacha. Koupriane had no difficulty in recognizing her through the gathering darkness.

"Ah, my dear Monsieur Rouletabille," said he, "see your prisoner of the Nihilists. Notice how she is bound. Her thongs certainly are causing her great pain. These revolutionaries surely are brutes!"

The truth was that Natacha had gone quite readily to the rudder and while the others rowed she steered the light boat to the place on the beach that had been pointed out to her. Soon the prow of the canoe touched the sands. There did not seem to be a soul about, and that was the conclusion the men in the canoe who stood up looking around, seemed to reach. They jumped out, and then it was Natacha's turn. She accepted the hand held out to her, talking pleasantly with the men all the time. She even turned to press the hand of one of them. The group came up across the beach. All this time the watchers in the little eating-house could see the false moujiks, who had wriggled on their stomachs to the very edge of the ridge, holding themselves ready to spring.

Behind his shutter, Koupriane could not restrain an exclamation of triumph; he gradually identified some of the figures in the group, and muttered:

"Eh! eh! There is Priemkof himself and the others. Gounsovski is right and he certainly is well-informed; his system is decidedly a good one. What a net-full!"

He hardly breathed as he watched the outcome. He could discern elsewhere, beside the bay, flat on the ground, concealed by the slightest elevation of the soil, other false moujiks. The wood of Sestroriesk was watched in the same way. The group of revolutionaries who strolled behind Natacha stopped to confer. In three—maybe two—minutes, they would be surrounded—cut off, taken in the trap. Suddenly a gunshot sounded in the night, and the group, with startled speed, turned in their tracks and made silently for the sea, while from all directions poured the concealed agents and threw themselves into the pursuit, jostling each other and crying after the fugitives. But the cries became cries of rage, for the group of revolutionaries gained the beach. They saw Natacha, who was held up by Priemkof himself, reject the aid of the Nihilist, who did not wish to abandon her, in order that he might save himself. She made him go and seeing that she was going to be taken, stopped short and waited for the enemy stoically, with folded arms. Meanwhile, her three companions succeeded in throwing themselves into the canoe and plied the oars hard while Koupriane's men, in the water up to their chests, discharged their revolvers at the fugitives. The men in the canoe, fearing to wound Natacha, made no reply to the firing. The yacht had sails up by the time they drew alongside, and made off like a bird toward the mysterious fords of Finland, audaciously hoisting the black flag of the Revolution.

Meantime, Koupriane's agents, trembling before his anger, gathered at the eating-house. The Prefect of Police let his fury loose on them and treated them like the most infamous of animals. The capture of Natacha was little comfort. He had planned for the whole bag, and his men's stupidity took away all his self-control. If he had had a whip at hand he would have found prompt solace for his mined hopes. Natacha, standing in a corner, with her face singularly calm, watched this extraordinary scene that was like a menagerie in which the tamer himself had become a wild beast. From another corner, Rouletabille kept his eyes fixed on Natacha who ignored him. Ah, that girl, sphinx to them all! Even to him who thought a while ago that he could read things invisible to other vulgar men in her features, in her eyes! The impassive face of that girl whose father they had tried to assassinate only a few hours before and who had just pressed the hand of Priemkof, the assassin! Once she turned her head slightly toward Rouletabille. The reporter then looked towards her with increased eagerness, his eyes burning, as though he would say: "Surely, Natacha, you are not the accomplice of your father's assassins; surely it was not you who poured the poison!"

But Natacha's glance passed the reporter coldly over. Ah, that mysterious, cold mask, the mouth with its bitter, impudent smile, an atrocious smile which seemed to say to the reporter: "If it is not I who poured the poison, then it is you!"

It was the visage common enough to the daughters whom Koupriane had spoken of a little while before, "the young girls who read" and, their reading done, set themselves to accomplish some terrible thing, some thing because of which, from time to time, they place stiff ropes around the necks of these young females.

Finally, Koupriane's frenzy wore itself out and he made a sign. The men filed out in dismal silence. Two of them remained to guard Natacha. From outside came the sounds of a carriage from Sestroriesk ready to convey the girl to the Dungeons of Sts. Peter and Paul. A final gesture from the Prefect of Police and the rough bands of the two guards seized the prisoner's frail wrists. They hustled her along, thrust her outside, jamming her against the doorway, venting thus their anger at the reproaches of their chief. A few seconds later the carriage departed, not to stop until the fortress was reached with the trickling tombs under the bed of the river where young girls about to die are confined— who have read too much, without entirely understanding, as Monsieur Kropotkine says.

Koupriane prepared to leave in turn. Rouletabille stopped him.

"Excellency, I wish you to tell me why you have shown such anger to your men just now."

"They are brute beasts," cried the Chief of Police, quite beside himself again. "They have made me miss the biggest catch of my life. They threw themselves on the group two minutes too early. Some of them fired a gun that they took for the signal and that served to warn the Nihilists. But I will let them all rot in prison until I learn which one fired that shot."

"You needn't look far for that," said Rouletabille. "I did it."

"You! Then you must have gone outside the touba?"

"Yes, in order to warn them. But still I was a little late, since you did take Natacha."

Koupriane's eyes blazed.

"You are their accomplice in all this," he hurled at the reporter, "and I am going to the Tsar for permission to arrest you."

"Hurry, then, Excellency," replied the reporter coldly, "because the Nihilists, who also think they have a little account to settle with me, may reach me before you."

And he saluted.

XV

"I Have Been Waiting for You"

At the hotel a note from Gounsovski: "Don't forget this time to come tomorrow to have luncheon with me. Warmest regards from Madame Gounsovski." Then a horrible, sleepless night, shaken with echoes of explosions and the clamor of the wounded; and the solemn shade of Pere Alexis, stretching out toward Rouletabille a phial of poison and saying, "Either Natacha or you!" Then, rising among the shades the bloody form of Michael Nikolaievitch the Innocent!

In the morning a note from the Marshal of the Court.

Monsieur le Marechal had no particular good news, evidently, for in terms quite without enthusiasm he invited the young man to luncheon for that same day, rather early, at midday, as he wished to see him once more before he left for France. "I see," said Rouletabille to himself; "Monsieur le Marechal pronounces my expulsion from the country"—and he forgot once more the Gounsovski luncheon. The meeting-place named was the great restaurant called the Bear. Rouletabille entered it promptly at noon. He asked the schwitzar if the Grand Marshal of the Court had arrived, and was told no one had seen him yet. They conducted him to the huge main hall, where, however, there was only one person. This man, standing before the table spread with zakouskis, was stuffing himself. At the sound of Rouletabille's step on the floor this sole famished patron turned and lifted his hands to heaven as he recognized the reporter. The latter would have given all the roubles in his pocket to have avoided the recognition. But he was already face to face with the advocate so celebrated for his table-feats, the amiable Athanase Georgevitch, his head swathed in bandages and dressings from the midst of which one could perceive distinctly only the eyes and, above all, the mouth.

"How goes it, little friend?"

"How are you?"

"Oh, I! There is nothing the matter. In a week we shall have forgotten it."

"What a terrible affair," said the reporter, "I certainly believed we were all dead men."

"No, no. It was nothing. Nitchevo!"

"And poor Thaddeus Tchitchnikoff with his two poor legs broken!"

"Eh! Nitchevo! He has plenty of good solid splints that will make him two good legs again. Nitchevo! Don't you think anything more about that! It is nothing. You have come here to dine? A very celebrated house this. Caracho!" He busied himself to do the honors. One would have said the restaurant belonged to him. He boasted of its architecture and the cuisine "a la Francaise."

"Do you know," he inquired confidently, "a finer restaurant room anywhere in the world?"

In fact, it seemed to Rouletabille as he looked up into the high glass arch that he was in a railway station decorated for some illustrious traveler, for there were flowers and plants everywhere. But the visitor whom the ball awaited was the Russian eater, the ogre who never failed to come to eat at The Bear. Pointing out the lines of tables shining with their white cloths and bright silver,

Athanase Georgevitch, with his mouth full, said:

"Ah, my dear little French monsieur, you should see it at suppertime, with the women, and the jewels, and the music. There is nothing in France that can give you any idea of it, nothing! The gayety—the champagne— and the jewels, monsieur, worth millions and millions of roubles! Our women wear them all—everything they have. They are decked like sacred shrines! All the family jewels— from the very bottom of the caskets! it is magnificent, thoroughly Russian—Muscovite! What am I saying? It is Asiatic. Monsieur, in the evening, at a fete, we are Asiatic. Let me tell you something on the quiet. You notice that this enormous dining hall is surrounded by those windowed balconies. Each of those windows belongs to a separate private room. Well, you see that window there?—yes, there—that is the room of a grand duke—yes, he's the one I mean—a very gay grand duke.

Do you know, one evening when there was a great crowd here—families, monsieur, family parties, high-born families—the window of that particular balcony was thrown open, and a woman stark naked, as naked as my hand, monsieur, was dropped into the dining-hall and ran across it full-speed. It was a wager, monsieur, a wager of the jolly grand duke's, and the demoiselle won it. But what a scandal! Ah, don't speak of it; that would be very bad form. But—sufficiently Asiatic, eh? Truly Asiatic. And—something much more unfortunate—you see that table? It happened the Russian New Year Eve, at supper. All the beauty, the whole capital, was here. Just at midnight the orchestra struck up the Bodje tsara krani (note 1) to inaugurate the joyful Russian New Year, and everybody stood up, according to custom, and listened in silence, as loyal subjects should. Well, at

_____

1. The Russian national anthem.

that table, accompanying his family, there was a young student, a fine fellow, very correct, and in uniform. This unhappy young student, who had risen like everybody else, to listen to the Bodje tsara krani, inadvertently placed his knee on a chair. Truly that is not a correct attitude, monsieur, but really it was no reason for killing him, was it now? Certainly not. Well, a brute in uniform, an officer quite immaculately gotten-up, drew a revolver from his pocket and discharged it at the student point-blank. You can imagine the scandal, for the student was dead! There were Paris journalists there, besides, who had never been there before, you see! Monsieur Gaston Leroux was at that very table. What a scandal! They had a regular battle. They broke carafes over the head of the assassin—for he was neither more nor less than an assassin, a drinker of blood—an Asiatic. They picked up the assassin, who was bleeding all over, and carried him off to look after him. As to the dead man, he lay stretched out there under a table-cloth, waiting for the police—and those at the tables went on with their drinking. Isn't that Asiatic enough for you? Here, a naked woman; there, a corpse! And the jewels—and the champagne! What do you say to that?"

"His Excellency the Grand Marshal of the Court is waiting for you, Monsieur."

Rouletabille shook hands with Athanase Georgevitch, who returned to his zakouskis, and followed the interpreter to the door of one of the private rooms. The high dignitary was there. With a charm in his politeness of which the high-born Russian possesses the secret over almost everybody else in the world, the Marshal intimated to Rouletabille that he had incurred imperial displeasure.

"You have been denounced by Koupriane, who holds you responsible for the checks he has suffered in this affair."

"Monsieur Koupriane is right," replied Rouletabille, "and His Majesty should believe him, since it is the truth. But don't fear anything from me, Monsieur le Grand Marechal, for I shall not inconvenience Monsieur Koupriane any further, nor anybody else. I shall disappear."

"I believe Koupriane is already directed to vise your passport."

"He is very good, and he does himself much harm."

"All that is a little your fault, Monsieur Rouletabille. We believed we could consider you as a friend, and you have never failed, it appears, on each occasion to give your help to our enemies.

"Who says that?"

"Koupriane. Oh, it is necessary to be one with us. And you are not one with us. And if you are not for us you are against us. You understand that, I think. That is the way it has to be. The Terrorists have returned to the methods of the Nihilists, who succeeded altogether too well against Alexander II. When I tell you that they succeeded in placing their messages even in the imperial palace. . ."

"Yes, yes," said Rouletabille, vaguely, as though he were already far removed from the contingencies of this world. "I know that Czar Alexander II sometimes found under his napkin a letter announcing his condemnation to death."

"Monsieur, at the Chateau yesterday morning something happened that is perhaps more alarming than the letter found by Alexander II under his napkin."

"What can it be? Have bombs been discovered?"

"No. It is a bizarre occurrence and almost unbelievable. The eider downs, all the eider down coverings belonging to the imperial family disappeared yesterday morning." (note 1)

"Surely not!"

"It is just as I say. And it was impossible to learn what had become of them—until yesterday evening, when they were found again in their proper places in the chambers. That is the new mystery!"

---

1. Historically authentic.

"Certainly. But how were they taken out?"

"Shall we ever know? All we found was two feathers, this morning, in the boudoir of the Empress, which leads us to think that the eider downs were taken out that way. I am taking the two feathers to Koupriane."

"Let me see them," asked the reporter.

Rouletabille looked them over and handed them back.

"And what do you think the whole affair means?"

"We are inclined to regard it as a threat by the revolutionaries. If they can carry away the eider downs, it would be quite as easy for them to carry away..."

"The Imperial family? No, I don't think it is that."

"What do you mean, then?"

"I? Nothing any more. Not only do I not think any more, but I don't wish to. Tell me, Monsieur le Grand Marechal, it is useless, I suppose, to try to see His Majesty before I go?"

"What good would it do, monsieur? We know everything now. This Natacha that you defended against Koupriane is proved the culprit. The last affair does not leave that in any reasonable doubt. And she is taken care of from this time on. His Majesty wishes never to hear Natacha spoken of again under any pretext."

"And what are you going to do with that young girl?"

"The Tsar has decided that there shall not be any trial and that the daughter of General Trebassof shall be sent, by administrative order, to Siberia. The Tsar, monsieur, is very good, for he might have had her hanged. She deserved it."

"Yes, yes, the Tsar is very good."

"You are very absorbed, Monsieur Rouletabille, and you are not eating."

"I have no appetite, Monsieur le Marechal. Tell me,—the Emperor must be rather bored at Tsarskoie-Coelo?"

"Oh, he has plenty of work. He rises at seven o'clock and has a light English luncheon— tea and toast. At eight o'clock he starts and works till ten. From ten to eleven he promenades."

"In the jail-yard?" asked Rouletabille innocently.

"What's that you say? Ah, you are an enfant terrible! Certainly we do well to send you away. Until eleven he promenades in a pathway of the park. From eleven to one he holds audience; luncheon at one; then he spends the time until half-past two with his family."

"What does he eat?"

"Soup. His Majesty is wonderfully fond of soup. He takes it at every meal. After luncheon he smokes, but never a cigar—always cigarettes, gifts of the Sultan; and he only drinks one liqueur, Maraschino. At half-past two he goes out again for a little air—always in his park; then he sets himself to work until eight o'clock. It is simply frightful work, with heaps of useless papers and numberless signatures. No secretary can spare him that ungrateful bureaucratic duty. He must sign, sign, sign, and read, read, read the reports. And it is work without any beginning or end; as soon as some reports go, others arrive. At eight o'clock, dinner, and then more signatures, working right up to eleven o'clock. At eleven o'clock he goes to bed."

"And he sleeps to the rhythmical tramp of the guards on patrol," added Rouletabille, bluntly.

"O young man, young man!"

"Pardon me, Monsieur le Grand Marechal," said the reporter, rising; "I am, indeed, a disturbing spirit and I know that I have nothing more to do in this country. You will not see me any more, Monsieur le Grand Marechal; but before leaving I ought to tell you how much I have been touched by the hospitality of your great nation. That hospitality is sometimes a little dangerous, but it is always magnificent. No other nation in the world knows like the Russians how to receive a man, Your Excellency. I speak as I feel; and that isn't affected by my manner of quitting you, for you know also how to put a man to the door. Adieu, then; without any rancor. My most respectful homage to His Majesty. Ah, just one word more! You will recall that Natacha Feodorovna was engaged to poor Boris Mourazoff, still another young man who has disappeared and who, before disappearing, charged me to deliver to General Trebassof's daughter this last token— these two little ikons. I entrust you with this mission, Monsieur le Grand Marechal. Your servant, Excellency."

Rouletabille re-descended the great Kaniouche. "Now," said he to himself, "it is my turn to buy farewell presents." And he made his way slowly across la Place des Grandes-Ecuries and the bridge of the Katharine canal. He entered Aptiekarski-Pereoulok and pushed open Pere

Alexis's door, under the arch, at the back of the obscure court.

"Health and prosperity, Alexis Hutch!"

"Ah, you again, little man! Well? Koupriane has let you know the result of my analyses?"

"Yes, yes. Tell me, Alexis Hutch, you are sure you are not mistaken? You don't think you might be mistaken? Think carefully before you answer. It is a question of life or death."

"For whom?"

"For me."

"For you, good little friend! You want to make your old Pere Alexis laugh—or weep!"

"Answer me."

"No, I couldn't be mistaken. The thing is as certain as that we two are here—arsenate of soda in the stains on the two napkins and traces of arsenate of soda in two of the four glasses; none in the carafe, none in the little bottle, none in the two glasses. I say it before you and before God."

"So it is really true. Thank you, Alexis Hutch. Koupriane has not tried to deceive me. There has been nothing of that sort. Well, do you know, Alexis Hutch, who has poured the poison? It is she or I. And as it is not I, it is she. And since it is she, well, I am going to die!"

"You love her, then?" inquired Pere Alexis.

"No," replied Rouletabille, with a self-mocking smile. "No, I don't love her. But if it is she who poured the poison, then it was not Michael Nikolaievitch, and it is I who had Michael Nikolaievitch killed. You can see now that therefore I must die. Show me your finest images.

"Ah, my little one, if you will permit your old Alexis to make you a gift, I would offer you these two poor ikons that are certainly from the convent of Troitza at its best period. See how beautiful they are, and old. Have you ever seen so beautiful a Mother of God? And this St. Luke, would you believe that the hand had been mended, eh? Two little masterpieces, little friend! If the old masters of Salonika returned to the world they would be satisfied with their pupils at Troitza. But you mustn't kill yourself at your age!"

"Come, bat ouclzka (little father), I accept your gift, and, if I meet the old Salonican masters on the road I am going to travel, I shan't fail to tell them there is no person here below who appreciates them like a certain pere of Aptiekarski-Pereoulok, Alexis Hutch."

So saying Rouletabille wrapped up the two little ikons and put them in his pocket. The Saint Luke would be sure to appeal to his friend Sainclair. As to the Mother of God, that would be his dying gift to the Dame en noir.

"Ah, you are sad, little son; and your voice, as it sounds now, hurts me."

Rouletabille turned his head at the sound of two moujiks who entered, carrying a long basket.

"What do you want?" demanded Pere Alexis in Russian, "and what is that you are bringing in? Do you intend to fill that huge basket with my goods? In that case you are very welcome and I am your humble servant."

But the two chuckled.

"Yes, yes, we have come to rid your shop of a wretched piece of goods that litters it."

"What is this you say?" inquired the old man, anxiously, and drawing near Rouletabille. "Little friend, watch these men; I don't recognize their faces and I can't understand why they have come here."

Rouletabille looked at the new-comers, who drew near the counter, after depositing their long basket close to the door. There was a sarcastic and malicious mocking way about them that struck him from the first. But while they kept up their jabbering with Pere Alexis he filled his pipe and proceeded to light it. Just then the door was pushed open again and three men entered, simply dressed, like respectable small merchants. They also acted curiously and looked all around the shop. Pere Alexis grew more and more alarmed and the others pulled rudely at his beard.

"I believe these men here have come to rob me," he cried in French. "What do you say, my son?—Shall I call the police?"

"Hold on," replied Rouletabille impassively. "They are all armed; they have revolvers in their pockets."

Pere Alexis's teeth commenced to chatter. As he tried to get near the door he was roughly pushed back and a final personage entered, apparently a gentleman, and dressed as such, save that he wore a visored leather cap.

"Ah," said he at once in French, "why, it is the young French journalist of the Grand-Morskaia Hotel. Salutations and your good health! I see with pleasure that you also appreciate the counsels of our dear Pere Alexis."

"Don't listen to him, little friend; I don't know him," cried Alexis Hutch.

But the gentleman of the Neva went on:

"He is a man close to the first principles of science, and therefore not far from divine; he is a holy man, whom it is good to consult at moments when the future appears difficult. He knows how to read as no one else can—Father John of Cronstadt excepted, to be strictly accurate—on the sheets of bull-hide where the dark angels have traced mysterious signs of destiny."

Here the gentleman picked up an old pair of boots, which he threw on the counter in the midst of the ikons.

"Pere Alexis, perhaps these are not bull-hide, but good enough cow-hide. Don't you want to read on this cow-hide the future of this young man?"

But here Rouletabille advanced to the gentleman, and blew an enormous cloud of smoke full in his face.

"It is useless, monsieur," said Rouletabille, "to waste your time and your breath. I have been waiting for you."

XVI

BEFORE THE REVOLUTIONARY TRIBUNAL

Only, Rouletabille refused to be put into the basket. He would not let them disarm him until they promised to call a carriage. The Vehicle rolled into the court, and while Pere Alexis was kept back in his shop at the point of a revolver, Rouletabille quietly got in, smoking his pipe. The man who appeared to be the chief of the band (the gentleman of the Neva) got in too and sat down beside him. The carriage windows were shuttered, preventing all communication with the outside, and only a tiny lantern lighted the interior. They started. The carriage was driven by two men in brown coats trimmed with false astrakhan. The dvornicks saluted, believing it a police affair. The concierge made the sign of the cross.

The journey lasted several hours without other incidents than those brought about by the tremendous jolts, which threw the two passengers inside one on top of the other. This might have made an opening for conversation; and the "gentleman of the Neva" tried it; but in vain. Rouletabille would not respond. At one moment, indeed, the gentleman, who was growing bored, became so pressing that the reporter finally said in the curt tone he always used when he was irritated:

"I pray you, monsieur, let me smoke my pipe in peace."

Upon which the gentleman prudently occupied himself in lowering one of the windows, for it grew stifling.

Finally, after much jolting, there was a stop while the horses were changed and the gentleman asked Rouletabille to let himself be blindfolded. "The moment has come; they are going to hang me without any form of trial," thought the reporter, and when, blinded with the bandage, he felt himself lifted under the arms, there was revolt of his whole being, that being which, now that it was on the point of dying, did not wish to cease. Rouletabille would have believed himself stronger, more courageous, more stoical at least. But blind instinct swept all of this away, that instinct of conservation which had no concern with the minor bravadoes of the reporter, no concern with the fine heroic manner, of the determined pose to die finely, because the instinct of conservation, which is, as its rigid name indicates, essentially materialistic, demands only, thinks of nothing but, to live. And it was that instinct which made Rouletabille's last pipe die out unpuffed.

The young man was furious with himself, and he grew pale with the fear that he might not succeed in mastering this emotion, he took fierce hold of himself and his members, which had stiffened at the contact of seizure by rough hands, relaxed, and he allowed himself to be led. Truly, he was disgusted with his faintness and weakness. He had seen men die who knew they were going to die. His task as reporter had led him more than once to the foot of the guillotine. And the wretches he had seen there had died bravely. Extraordinarily enough, the most criminal had ordinarily met death most bravely. Of course, they had had leisure to prepare themselves, thinking a long time in advance of that supreme moment. But they affronted death, came to it almost negligently, found strength even to say banal or taunting things to those around them. He recalled above all a boy of eighteen years old who had cowardly murdered an old woman and two children in a back-country farm, and had walked to his death without a tremor, talking reassuringly to the priest and the police official, who walked almost sick with horror on either side of him. Could he, then, not be as brave as that child?

They made him mount some steps and he felt that he had entered the stuffy atmosphere of a closed room. Then someone removed the bandage. He was in a room of sinister aspect and in the midst of a rather large company.

Within these naked, neglected walls there were about thirty young men, some of them apparently quite as young as Rouletabille, with candid blue eyes and pale complexions. The others, older men, were of the physical type of Christs, not the animated Christs of Occidental painters, but those that are seen on the panels of the Byzantine school or fastened on the ikons, sculptures of silver or gold. Their long hair, deeply parted in the middle, fell upon their shoulders in curl-tipped golden masses. Some leant against the wall, erect, and motionless. Others were seated on the floor, their legs crossed. Most of them were in winter coats, bought in the bazaars. But there were also men from the country, with their skins of beasts, their sayons, their touloupes. One of them had his legs laced about with cords and was shod with twined willow twigs. The contrast afforded by various ones of these grave and attentive figures showed that representatives from the entire revolutionary party were present. At the back of the room, behind a table, three young men were seated, and the oldest of them was not more than twenty-five and had the benign beauty of Jesus on feast-days, canopied by consecrated palms.

In the center of the room a small table stood, quite bare and without any apparent purpose.

On the right was another table with paper, pens and ink-stands. It was there that Rouletabille was conducted and asked to be seated. Then he saw that another man was at his side, who was required to keep standing. His face was pale and desperate, very drawn. His eyes burned somberly, in spite of the panic that deformed his features Rouletabille recognized one of the unintroduced friends whom Gounsovski had brought with him to the supper at Krestowsky. Evidently since then the always-threatening misfortune had fallen upon him. They were proceeding with his trial. The one who seemed to preside over these strange sessions pronounced a name:

"Annouchka!"

A door opened, and Annouchka appeared.

Rouletabille hardly recognized her, she was so strangely dressed, like the Russian poor, with her under-jacket of red-flannel and the handkerchief which, knotted under her chin, covered all her beautiful hair.

She immediately testified in Russian against the man, who protested until they compelled him to be silent. She drew from her pocket papers which were read aloud, and which appeared to crush the accused. He fell back onto his seat. He shivered. He hid his head in his hands, and Rouletabille saw the hands tremble. The man kept that position while the other witnesses were heard, their testimony arousing murmurs of indignation that were quickly checked. Annouchka had gone to take her place with the others against the wall, in the shadows which more and more invaded the room, at this ending of a lugubrious day. Two windows reaching to the floor let a wan light creep with difficulty through their dirty panes, making a vague twilight in the room. Soon nothing could be seen of the motionless figures against the wall, much as the faces fade in the frescoes from which the centuries have effaced the colors in the depths of orthodox convents.

Now someone from the depths of the shadow and the appalling silence read something; the verdict, doubtless.

The voice ceased.

Then some of the figures detached themselves from the wall and advanced.

The man who crouched near Rouletabille rose in a savage bound and cried out rapidly, wild words, supplicating words, menacing words.

And then—nothing more but strangling gasps. The figures that had moved out from the wall had clutched his throat.

The reporter said, "It is cowardly."

Annouchka's voice, low, from the depths of shadow, replied, "It is just."

But Rouletabille was satisfied with having said that, for he had proved to himself that he could still speak. His emotion had been such, since they had pushed him into the center of this sinister and expeditious revolutionary assembly of justice, that he thought of nothing but the terror of not being able to speak to them, to say something to them, no matter what, which would prove to them that he had no fear. Well, that was over. He had not failed to say, "That is cowardly."

And he crossed his arms. But he soon had to turn away his head in order not to see the use the table was put to that stood in the center of the room, where it had seemed to serve no purpose.

They had lifted the man, still struggling, up onto the little table. They placed a rope about his neck. Then one of the " judges," one of the blond young men, who seemed no older than Rouletabille, climbed on the table and slipped the other end of the rope through a great ring-bolt that projected from a beam of the ceiling. During this time the man struggled futilely, and his death-rattle rose at last though the continued noise of his resistance and its overcoming. But his last breath came with so violent a shake of the body that the whole death-apparatus, rope and ring-bolt, separated from the ceiling, and rolled to the ground with the dead man.

Rouletabille uttered a cry of horror. "You are assassins!" he cried. But was the man surely dead? It was this that the pale figures with the yellow hair set themselves to make sure of. He was. Then they brought two sacks and the dead man was slipped into one of them.

Rouletabille said to them:

"You are braver when you kill by an explosion, you know."

He regretted bitterly that he had not died the night before in the explosion. He did not feel very brave. He talked to them bravely enough, but he trembled as his time approached. That death horrified him. He tried to keep from looking at the other sack. He took the two ikons, of Saint Luke and of the Virgin, from his pocket and prayed to them. He thought of the Lady in Black and wept.

A voice in the shadows said:

"He is crying, the poor little fellow."

It was Annouchka's voice.

Rouletabille dried his tears and said:

"Messieurs, one of you must have a mother."

But all the voices cried:

"No, no, we have mothers no more!"

"They have killed them," cried some. "They have sent them to Siberia," cried others.

"Well, I have a mother still," said the poor lad. "I will not have the opportunity to embrace her. It is a mother that I lost the day of my birth and that I have found again, but—I suppose it is to be said—on the day of my death. I shall not see her again. I have a friend; I shall not see him again either. I have two little ikons here for them, and I am going to write a letter to each of them, if you will permit it. Swear to me that you will see these reach them."

"I swear it," said, in French, the voice of Annouchka.

"Thanks, madame, you are kind. And now, messieurs, that is all I ask of you. I know I am here to reply to very grave accusations. Permit me to say to you at once that I admit them all to be well founded. Consequently, there need be no discussion between us. I have deserved death and I accept it. So permit me not to concern myself with what will be going on here. I ask of you simply, as a last favor, not to hasten your preparations too much, so that I may be able to finish my letters."

Upon which, satisfied with himself this time, he sat down again and commenced to write rapidly. They left him in peace, as he desired. He did not raise his head once, even at the moment when a murmur louder than usual showed that the hearers regarded Rouletabille's crimes with especial detestation. He had the happiness of having entirely completed his correspondence when they asked him to rise to hear judgment pronounced upon him. The supreme communion that he had just had with his friend Sainclair and with the dear Lady in Black restored all his spirit to him. He listened respectfully to the sentence which condemned him to death, though he was busy sliding his tongue along the gummed edge of his envelope.

These were the counts on which he was to be hanged:

1. Because he had come to Russia and mixed in affairs that did not concern his nationality, and had done this in spite of warning to remain in France.

2. Because he had not kept the promises of neutrality he freely made to a representative of the Central Revolutionary Committee.

3. For trying to penetrate the mystery of the Trebassof datcha.

4. For having Comrade Matiew whipped and imprisoned by Koupriane.

5. For having denounced to Koupriane the identity of the two "doctors" who had been assigned to kill General Trebassof.

6. For having caused the arrest of Natacha Feodorovna.

It was a list longer than was needed for his doom. Rouletabille kissed his ikons and handed them to Annouchka along with the letters. Then he declared, with his lips trembling slightly, and a cold sweat on his forehead, that he was ready to submit to his fate.

XVII

The Last Cravat

The gentleman of the Neva said to him:
"If you have nothing further to say, we will
go into the courtyard."

Rouletabille understood at last that hanging
him in the room where judgment had been
pronounced was rendered impossible by
the violence of the prisoner just executed.
Not only the rope and the ring-bolt had
been torn away, but part of the beam had
splintered.

"There is nothing more," replied Rouletabille.

He was mistaken. Something occurred to
him, an idea flashed so suddenly that he
became white as his shirt, and had to lean

on the arm of the gentleman of the Neva in order to accompany him.

The door was open. All the men who had voted his death filed out in gloomy silence. The gentleman of the Neva, who seemed charged with the last offices for the prisoner, pushed him gently out into the court.

It was vast, and surrounded by a high board wall; some small buildings, with closed doors, stood to right and left. A high chimney, partially demolished, rose from one corner. Rouletabille decided the whole place was part of some old abandoned mill. Above his head the sky was pale as a winding sheet. A thunderous, intermittent, rhythmical noise appraised him that he could not be far from the sea.

He had plenty of time to note all these things, for they had stopped the march to execution a moment and had made him sit

down in the open courtyard on an old box.
A few steps away from him under the shed
where he certainly was going to be hanged,
a man got upon a stool (the stool that would
serve Rouletabille a few moments later) with
his arm raised, and drove with a few blows of
a mallet a great ring-bolt into a beam above
his head.

The reporter's eyes, which had not lost their
habit of taking everything in, rested again on
a coarse canvas sack that lay on the ground.
The young man felt a slight tremor, for he
saw quickly that the sack swathed a human
form. He turned his head away, but only
to confront another empty sack that was
intended for him. Then he closed his eyes.
The sound of music came from somewhere
outside, notes of the balalaika. He said to
himself, "Well, we certainly are in Finland";
for he knew that, if the guzla is Russian the
balalaika certainly is Finnish. It is a kind of
ccordion that the peasants pick plaintively in

the doorways of their toubas. He had seen and heard them the afternoon that he went to Pergalovo, and also a little further away, on the Viborg line. He pictured to himself the ruined structure where he now found himself shut in with the revolutionary tribunal, as it must appear from the outside to passers-by; unsinister, like many others near it, sheltering under its decaying roof a few homes of humble workers, resting now as they played the balalaika at their thresholds, with the day's labor over.

And suddenly from the ineffable peace of his last evening, while the balalaika mourned and the man overhead tested the solidity of his ring-bolt, a voice outside, the grave, deep voice of Annouchka, sang for the little Frenchman:

> "For whom weave we now the crown
>   Of lilac, rose and thyme?
> When my hand falls lingering down

Who then will bring your crown
Of lilac, rose and thyme?

O that someone among you would hear,
And come, and my lonely hand
Would press, and shed the friendly tear—
For alone at the end I stand.

Who now will bring the crown
Of lilac, rose and thyme?"

Rouletabille listened to the voice dying away with the last sob of the balalaika. "It is too sad," he said, rising. "Let us go," and he wavered a little.

They came to search him. All was ready above. They pushed him gently towards the shed. When he was under the ring-bolt, near the stool, they made him turn round and they read him something in Russian, doubtless less for him than for those there who did not understand French. Rouletabille had hard work to hold himself erect.

The gentleman of the Neva said to him further:

"Monsieur, we now read you the final formula. It asks you to say whether, before you die, you have anything you wish to add to what we know concerning the sentence which has been passed upon you."

Rouletabille thought that his saliva, which at that moment he had the greatest difficulty in swallowing, would not permit him to utter a word. But disdain of such a weakness, when he recalled the coolness of so many illustrious condemned people in their last moments, brought him the last strength needed to maintain his reputation.

"Why," said he, "this sentence is not wrongly drawn up. I blame it only for being too short.

Why has there been no mention of the crime I committed in contriving the tragic death of poor Michael Korsakoff?"

"Michael Korsakoff was a wretch," pronounced the vindictive voice of the young man who had presided at the trial and who, at this supreme moment, happened to be face to face with Rouletabille. "Koupriane's police, by killing that man, ridded us of a traitor."

Rouletabille uttered a cry, a cry of joy, and while he had some reason for believing that at the point he had reached now of his too-short career only misfortune could befall him, yet here Providence, in his infinite grace, sent him before he died this ineffable consolation: the certainty that he had not been mistaken.

"Pardon, pardon," he murmured, in an excess of joy which stifled him almost as much as the wretched rope would shortly do that they were getting ready behind him. "Pardon. One second yet, one little second. Then, messieurs, then, we are agreed in that, are we? This Michael, Michael Nikolaievitch was the the last of traitors."

"The first," said the heavy voice.

"It is the same thing, my dear monsieur. A traitor, a wretched traitor," continued Rouletabille.

"A poisoner," replied the voice.

"A vulgar poisoner! Is that not so? But, tell me how—a vulgar poisoner who, under cover of Nihilism, worked for his own petty ends, worked for himself and betrayed you all!"

Now Rouletabille's voice rose like a fanfare. Someone said:

"He did not deceive us long; our enemies themselves undertook his punishment."

"It was I," cried Rouletabille, radiant again. "It was I who wound up that career. I tell you that was managed right. It was I who rid you of him. Ah, I knew well enough, messieurs, in the bottom of my heart I knew that I could not be mistaken. Two and two make four always, don't they? And Rouletabille is always Rouletabille. Messieurs, it is all right, after all."

But it was probable that it was also all wrong, for the gentleman of the Neva came up to him hat in hand and said:

"Monsieur, you know now why the witnesses at your trial did not raise a fact against you that, on the contrary, was entirely in your favor. Now it only remains for us to execute the sentence which is entirely justified on other grounds."

"Ah, but—wait a little. What the devil! Now that I am sure I have not been mistaken and that I have been myself, Rouletabille, all the time I cling to life a little—oh, very much!"

A hostile murmur showed the condemned man that the patience of his judges was getting near its limit.

"Monsieur," interposed the president, "we know that you do not belong to the orthodox religion; nevertheless, we will bring a priest if you wish it."

"Yes, yes, that is it, go for the priest," cried Rouletabille.

And he said to himself, "It is so much time gained."

One of the revolutionaries started over to a little cabin that had been transformed into a chapel, while the rest of them looked at the reporter with a good deal less sympathy than they had been showing. If his bravado had impressed them agreeably in the trial room, they were beginning to be rather disgusted by his cries, his protestations and all the maneuvers by which he so apparently was trying to hold off the hour of his death.

But all at once Rouletabille jumped up onto the fatal stool. They believed he had decided finally to make an end of the comedy and die with dignity; but he had mounted there only to give them a discourse.

"Messieurs, understand me now. If it is true that you are not suppressing me in order to avenge Michael Nikolaievitch, then why do you hang me? Why do you inflict this odious punishment on me? Because you accuse me of causing Natacha Feodorovna's arrest? Truly I have been awkward. Of that, and that alone, I accuse myself."

"It was you, with your revolver, who gave the signal to Koupriane's agents! You have done the dirty work for the police."

Rouletabille tried vainly to protest, to explain, to say that his revolver shot, on the contrary, had saved the revolutionaries. But no one cared to listen and no one believed him.

"Here is the priest, monsieur," said the gentleman of the Neva.

"One second! These are my last words, and I swear to you that after this I will pass the rope about my neck myself! But listen to me! Listen to me closely! Natacha Feodorovna was the most precious recruit you had, was she not?"

"A veritable treasure," declared the president, his voice more and more impatient.

"It was a terrible blow, then," continued the reporter, "a terrible blow for you, this arrest?"

"Terrible," some of them exclaimed.

"Do not interrupt me! Very well, then, I am going to say this to you: 'If I ward off this blow—if, after having been the unintentional cause of Natacha's arrest, I have the daughter of General Trebassof set at liberty, and that within twenty-four hours,—what do you say? Would you still hang me?'"

The president, he who had the Christ-like countenance, said:

"Messieurs, Natacha Feodorovna has fallen the victim of terrible machinations whose mystery we so far have not been able to penetrate. She is accused of trying to poison her father and her step-mother, and under such conditions that it seems impossible for human reason to demonstrate the contrary. Natacha Feodorovna herself, crushed by the tragic occurrence, was not able to answer her accusers at all, and her silence has been taken for a confession of guilt. Messieurs, Natacha Feodorovna will be started for Siberia tomorrow. We can do nothing for her. Natacha Feodorovna is lost to us."

Then, with a gesture to those who surrounded Rouletabille:

"Do your duty, messieurs."

"Pardon, pardon. But if I do prove the innocence of Natacha? Just wait, messieurs. There is only I who can prove that innocence! You lose Natacha by killing me!"

"If you had been able to prove that innocence, monsieur, the thing would already be done. You would not have waited."

"Pardon, pardon. It is only at this moment that I have become able to do it."

"How is that?"

"It is because I was sick, you see—very seriously sick. That affair of Michael Nikolaievitch and the poison that still continued after he was dead simply robbed me of all my powers. Now that I am sure I have not been the means of killing an innocent man—I am Rouletabille again! It is not possible that I shall not find the way, that I shall not see through this mystery."

The terrible voice of the Christ-like figure said monotonously:

"Do your duty, messieurs."

"Pardon, pardon. This is of great importance to you—and the proof is that you have not yet hanged me. You were not so procrastinating with my predecessor, were you? You have listened to me because you have hoped! Very well, let me think, let me consider. Oh, the devil! I was there myself at the fatal luncheon, and I know better than anyone else all that happened there. Five minutes! I demand five minutes of you; it is not much. Five little minutes!"

These last words of the condemned man seemed to singularly influence the revolutionaries. They looked at one another in silence.

Then the president took out his watch and said:

"Five minutes. We grant them to you."

"Put your watch here. Here on this nail. It is five minutes to seven, eh? You will give me until the hour?"

"Yes, until the hour. The watch itself will strike when the hour has come."

"Ah, it strikes! Like the general's watch, then. Very well, here we are."

Then there was the curious spectacle of Rouletabille standing on the hangman's stool, the fatal rope hanging above his head, his legs crossed, his elbow on his knees in that eternal attitude which Art has always given to human thought, his fists under his jaws, his eyes fixed—all around him, all those young men intent on his silence, not moving a muscle, turned into statues themselves that they might not disturb the statue which thought and thought.

XVIII

A Singular Experience

The five minutes ticked away and the watch commenced to strike the hour's seven strokes. Did it sound the death of Rouletabille? Perhaps not! For at the first silver tinkle they saw Rouletabille shake himself, and raise his head, with his face alight and his eyes shining. They saw him stand up, spread out his arms and cry:

"I have found it!"

Such joy shone in his countenance that there seemed to be an aureole around him, and none of those there doubted that he had the solution of the impossible problem.

"I have found it! I have found it!"

They gathered around him. He waved them away as in a waking dream.

"Give me room. I have found it, if my experiment works out. One, two, three, four, five. . ."

What was he doing? He counted his steps now, in long paces, as in dueling preliminaries. And the others, all of them, followed him in silence, puzzled, but without protest, as if they, too, were caught in the same strange day-dream. Steadily counting his steps he crossed thus the court, which was vast. "Forty, forty-one, forty-two," he cried excitedly. "This is certainly strange, and very promising."

The others, although they did not understand, refrained from questioning him, for they saw there was nothing to do but let him go ahead without interruption, just as care is taken not to wake a somnambulist abruptly. They had no mistrust of his motives, for the idea was simply untenable that Rouletabille was fool enough to hope to save himself from them by an imbecile subterfuge. No, they yielded to the impression his inspired countenance gave them, and several were so affected that they unconsciously repeated his gestures. Thus Rouletabille reached the edge of the court where judgment had been pronounced against him. There he had to mount a rickety flight of stairs, whose steps he counted. He reached a corridor, but moving away from the side where the door was opening to the exterior he turned toward a staircase leading to the upper floor, and still counted the steps as he climbed them. Some of the company followed him, others hurried ahead of him. But he did not seem aware of either the one or the other, as he walked along living only in his thoughts. He reached the landing-place, hesitated, pushed open a door, and found himself in a room furnished with a table, two chairs, a mattress and a huge cupboard. He went to the cupboard, turned the key and opened it. The cupboard was empty. He closed it again and put the key in his pocket. Then he went out onto the landing-place again. There he asked for the key of the chamber-door he had just left. They gave it to him and he locked that door and put that key also in his pocket. Now he returned into the court. He asked for a chair. It was brought him. Immediately he placed his head in his hands, thinking hard, took the chair and carried it over a little behind the shed. The Nihilists watched everything he did and they did not smile, because men do not smile when death waits at the end of things, however foolish.

Finally, Rouletabille spoke:

"Messieurs," said he, his voice low and shaken, because he knew that now he touched the decisive minute, after which there could only be an irrevocable fate.

"Messieurs, in order to continue my experiment I am obliged to go through movements that might suggest to you the idea of an attempt at escape, or evasion. I hope you don't regard me as fool enough to have any such thought."

"Oh, monsieur," said the chief, "you are free to go through all the maneuvers you wish. No one escapes us. Outside we should have you within arm's reach quite as well as here. And, besides, it is entirely impossible to escape from here."

"Very well. Then that is understood. In such a case, I ask you now to remain just where you are and not to budge, whatever I do, if you don't wish to inconvenience me. Only please send someone now up to the next floor, where I am going to go again, and let him watch what happens from there, but without interfering. And don't speak a word to me during the experiment."

Two of the revolutionaries went to the upper floor, and opened a window in order to keep track of what went on in the court. All now showed their intense interest in the acts and gestures of Rouletabille.

The reporter placed himself in the shed, between his death-stool and his hanging-rope.

"Ready," said he; "I am going to begin"

And suddenly he jumped like a wild man, crossed the court in a straight line like a flash, disappeared in the touba, bounded up the staircase, felt in his pocket and drew out the keys, opened the door of the chamber he had locked, closed it and locked it again, turned right-about-face, came down again in the same haste, reached the court, and this time swerved to the chair, went round it, still running, and returned at the same speed to the shed. He no sooner reached there than he uttered a cry of triumph as he glanced at the watch banging from a post. "I have won," he said, and threw himself with a happy thrill upon the fatal scaffold. They surrounded him, and he read the liveliest curiosity in all their faces. Panting still from his mad rush, he asked for two words apart with the chief of the Secret committee.

The man who had pronounced judgment and who had the bearing of Jesus advanced, and there was a brief exchange of words between the two young men. The others drew back and waited at a distance, in impressive silence, the outcome of this mysterious colloquy, which certainly would settle Rouletabille's fate.

"Messieurs," said the chief, "the young Frenchman is going to be allowed to leave. We give him twenty-four hours to set Natacha Feodorovna free. In twenty-four hours, if he has not succeeded, he will return here to give himself up."

A happy murmur greeted these words. The moment their chief spoke thus, they felt sure of Natacha's fate.

The chief added:

"As the liberation of Natacha Feodorovna will be followed, the young Frenchman says, by that of our companion Matiew, we decide that, if these two conditions are fulfilled, M. Joseph Rouletabille is allowed to return in entire security to France, which he ought never to have left."

Two or three only of the group said, "That lad is playing with us; it is not possible."

But the chief declared:

"Let the lad try. He accomplishes miracles."

XIX

THE TSAR

I have escaped by remarkable luck," cried Rouletabille, as he found himself, in the middle of the night, at the corner of the Katharine and the Aptiekarski Pereoulok Canals, while the mysterious carriage which had brought him there returned rapidly toward the Grande Ecurie. "What a country! What a country!"

He ran a little way to the Grand Morskaia, which was near, entered the hotel like a bomb, dragged the interpreter from his bed, demanded that his bill be made out and that he be told the time of the next train for Tsarskoie-Coelo. The interpreter told him that he could not have his bill at such an hour, that he could not leave town without his passport and that there was no train for Tsarskoie-Coelo, and Rouletabille made an outcry that woke the whole hotel. The guests, fearing always "une scandale," kept close to their rooms. But Monsieur le directeur came down, trembling. When he found all that it was about he was inclined to be peremptory, but Rouletabille, who had seen "Michael Strogoff " played, cried, "Service of the Tsar!" which turned him submissive as a sheep. He made out the young man's bill and gave him his passport, which had been brought back by the police during the afternoon. Rouletabille rapidly wrote a message to Koupriane's address, which the messenger was directed to have delivered without a moment's delay, under the pain of death! The manager humbly promised and the reporter did not explain that by "pain of death" he referred to his own. Then, having ascertained that as a matter of fact the last train had left for Tsarskoie-Coelo, he ordered a carriage and hurried to his room to pack.

And he, ordinarily so detailed, so particular in his affairs, threw things every which way, linen, garments, with kicks and shoves. It was a relief after the emotions he had gone through. "What a country!" he never ceased to exclaim. "What a country!"

Then the carriage was ready, with two little Finnish horses, whose gait he knew well, an evil-looking driver, who none the less would get him there; the trunk; roubles to the domestics. "Spacibo, barine. Spacibo." (Thank you, monsieur. Thank you.)

The interpreter asked what address he should give the driver.

"The home of the Tsar."

The interpreter hesitated, believing it to be an unbecoming pleasantry, then waved vaguely to the driver, and the horses started.

"What a curious trot! We have no idea of that in France," thought Rouletabille. "France! France! Paris! Is it possible that soon I shall be back! And that dear Lady in Black! Ah, at the first opportunity I must send her a dispatch of my return—before she receives those ikons, and the letters announcing my death. Scan! Scan! Scan! (Hurry!)"

The isvotchick pounded his horses, crowding past the dvornicks who watched at the corners of the houses during the St. Petersburg night. "Dirigi! dirigi! dirigi! (Look out!)"

The country, somber in the somber night. The vast open country. What monotonous desolation! Rapidly, through the vast silent spaces, the little car glided over the lonely route into the black arms of the pines.

Rouletabille, holding on to his seat, looked about him.

"God! this is as sad as a funeral display."

Little frozen huts, no larger than tombs, occasionally indicated the road, but there was no mark of life in that country except the noise of the journey and the two beasts with steaming coats.

Crack! One of the shafts broken. "What a country!" To hear Rouletabille one would suppose that only in Russia could the shaft of a carriage break.

The repair was difficult and crude, with bits of rope. And from then on the journey was slow and cautious after the frenzied speed. In vain Rouletabille reasoned with himself. "You will arrive anyway before morning. You cannot wake the Emperor in the dead of night." His impatience knew no reason. "What a country! What a country!"

After some other petty adventures (they ran into a ravine and had tremendous difficulty rescuing the trunk) they arrived at Tsarskoie-Coelo at a quarter of seven.

Even here the country was not pleasant. Rouletabille recalled the bright awakening of French country. Here it seemed there was something more dead than death: it was this little city with its streets where no one passed, not a soul, not a phantom, with its houses so impenetrable, the windows even of glazed glass and further blinded by the morning hoar-frost shutting out light more thoroughly than closed eyelids. Behind them he pictured to himself a world unknown, a world which neither spoke nor wept, nor laughed, a world in which no living chord resounded. "What a country! 'Where is the chateau? I do not know; I have been here only once, in the marshal's carriage. I do not know the way. Not the great palace! The idiot of a driver has brought me to this great palace in order to see it, I haven't a doubt. Does Rouletabille look like a tourist? Dourak! The home of the Tsar, I tell you. The Tsar's residence. The place where the Little Father lives. Chez Batouchka!"

The driver lashed his ponies. He drove past all the streets. "Stoi! (Stop!)" cried Rouletabille. A gate, a soldier, musket at shoulder, bayonet in play; another gate, another soldier, another bayonet; a park with walls around it, and around the walls more soldiers.

"No mistake; here is the place," thought Rouletabille. There was only one prisoner for whom such pains would be taken. He advanced towards the gate. Ah! They crossed bayonets under his nose. Halt! No fooling, Joseph Rouletabille, of "L'Epoque." A subaltern came from a guard-house and advanced toward him. Explanation evidently was going to be difficult. The young man saw that if he demanded to see the Tsar, they would think him crazed and that would further complicate matters. He asked for the Grand-Marshal of the Court. They replied that he could get the Marshal's address in Tsarskoie. But the subaltern turned his head. He saw someone advancing. It was the Grand-Marshal himself. Some exceptional service called him, without doubt, very early to the Court.

"Why, what are you doing here? You are not yet gone then, Monsieur Rouletabille?"

"Politeness before everything, Monsieur le Grand-Marechal! I would not go before saying 'Au revoir' to the Emperor. Be so good, since you are going to him and he has risen (you yourself have told me he rises at seven), be so good as to say to him that I wish to pay my respects before leaving."

"Your scheme, doubtless, is to speak to him once more regarding Natacha Feodorovna?"

"Not at all. Tell him, Excellency, that I am come to explain the mystery of the eider downs."

"Ah, ah, the eider downs! You know something?"

"I know all."

The Grand Marshal saw that the young man did not pretend. He asked him to wait a few minutes, and vanished into the park.

A quarter of an hour later, Joseph Rouletabille, of the journal "L'Epoque," was admitted into the cabinet that he knew well from the first interview he had had there with His Majesty. The simple workroom of a country-house: a few pictures on the walls, portraits of the Tsarina and the imperial children on the table; Oriental cigarettes in the tiny gold cups. Rouletabille was far from feeling any assurance, for the Grand-Marshal had said to him:

"Be cautious. The Emperor is in a terrible humor about you."

A door opened and closed. The Tsar made a sign to the Marshal, who disappeared. Rouletabille bowed low, then watched the Emperor closely.

Quite apparently His Majesty was displeased. The face of the Tsar, ordinarily so calm, so pleasant, and smiling, was severe, and his eyes had an angry light. He seated himself and lighted a cigarette.

"Monsieur," he commenced, "I am not otherwise sorry to see you before your departure in order to say to you myself that I am not at all pleased with you. If you were one of my subjects I would have already started you on the road to the Ural Mountains."

"I remove myself farther, Sire."

"Monsieur, I pray you not to interrupt me and not to speak unless I ask you a question."

"Oh, pardon, Sire, pardon."

"I am not duped by the pretext you have offered Monsieur le Grand-Marechal in order to penetrate here."

"It is not a pretext, Sire."

"Again!"

"Oh, pardon, Sire, pardon."

"I say to you that, called here to aid me against my enemies, they themselves have not found a stronger or more criminal support than in you."

"Of what am I accused, Sire?"

"Koupriane—"

"Ah! Ah! . . . Pardon!"

"My Chief of Police justly complains that you have traversed all his designs and that you have taken it upon yourself to ruin them. First, you removed his agents, who inconvenienced you, it seems; then, the moment that he had the proof in hand of the abominable alliance of Natacha Feodorovna with the Nihilists who attempt the assassination of her father your intervention has permitted that proof to escape him. And you have boasted of the feat, monsieur, so that we can only consider you responsible for the attempts that followed.

"Without you, Natacha would not have attempted to poison her father. Without you, they would not have sent to find physicians who could blow up the datcha des Iles. Finally, no later than yesterday, when this faithful servant of mine had set a trap they could not have escaped from, you have had the audacity, you, to warn them of it. They owe their escape to you. Monsieur, those are attempts against the security of the State which deserves the heaviest punishment. Why, you went out one day from here promising me to save General Trebassof from all the plotting assassins who lurked about him. And then you play the game of the assassins! Your conduct is as miserable as that of Natacha Feodorovna is monstrous!"

The Emperor ceased, and looked at Rouletabille, who had not lowered his eyes.

"What can you say for yourself? Speak—now."

"I can only say to Your Majesty that I come to take leave of you because my task here is finished. I have promised you the life of General Trebassof, and I bring it to you. He runs no danger any more! I say further to Your Majesty that there exists nowhere in the world a daughter more devoted to her father, even to the death, a daughter more sublime than Natacha Feodorovna, nor more innocent."

"Be careful, monsieur. I inform you that I have studied this affair personally and very closely. You have the proofs of these statements you advance?"

"Yes, Sire."

"And I, I have the proofs that Natacha Feodorovna is a renegade."

At this contradiction, uttered in a firm voice, the Emperor stirred, a flush of anger and of outraged majesty in his face. But, after this first movement, he succeeded in controlling himself, opened a drawer brusquely, took out some papers and threw them on the table.

"Here they are."

Rouletabille reached for the papers.

"You do not read Russian, monsieur. I will translate their purport for you. Know, then, that there has been a mysterious exchange of letters between Natacha Feodorovna and the Central Revolutionary Committee, and that these letters show the daughter of General Trebassof to be in perfect accord with the assassins of her father for the execution of their abominable project."

"The death of the general?"

"Exactly."

"I declare to Your Majesty that that is not possible."

"Obstinate man! I will read—"

"Useless, Sire. It is impossible. There may be in them the question of a project, but I am greatly surprised if these conspirators have been sufficiently imprudent to write in those letters that they count on Natacha to poison her father."

"That, as a matter of fact, is not written, and you yourself are responsible for it not being there. It does not follow any the less that Natacha Feodorovna had an understanding with the Nihilists."

"That is correct, Sire."

"Ah, you confess that?"

"I do not confess; I simply affirm that Natacha had an understanding with the Nihilists."

"Who plotted their abominable attacks against the ex-Governor of Moscow."

"Sire, since Natacha had an understanding with the Nihilists, it was not to kill her father, but to save him. And the project of which you hold here the proofs, but of whose character you are unaware, is to end the attacks of which you speak, instantly."

"You say that."

"I speak the truth, Sire."

"Where are the proofs? Show me your papers."

"I have none. I have only my word."

"That is not sufficient."

"It will be sufficient, once you have heard me."

"I listen."

"Sire, before revealing to you a secret on which depends the life of General Trebassof, you must permit me some questions. Your Majesty holds the life of the general very dear?"

"What has that to do with it?"

"Pardon. I desire that Your Majesty assure me on that point."

"The general has protected my throne. He has saved the Empire from one of the greatest dangers that it has ever run. If the servant who has done such a service should be rewarded by death, by the punishment that the enemies of my people prepare for him in the darkness, I should never forgive myself. There have been too many martyrs already!"

"You have replied to me, Sire, in such a way that you make me understand there is no sacrifice—even to the sacrifice of your amour-propre the greatest a ruler can suffer—no sacrifice too dear to ransom from death one of these martyrs."

"Ah, ah! These gentlemen lay down conditions to me! Money. Money. They need money. And at how much do they rate the head of the general?"

"Sire, that does not touch Your Majesty, and I never will come to offer you such a bargain. That matter concerns only Natacha Feodorovna, who has offered her fortune!"

"Her fortune! But she has nothing."

"She will have one at the death of the general. Now she engages to give it all to the Revolutionary Committee the day the general dies—if he dies a natural death!"

The Emperor rose, greatly agitated.

"To the Revolutionary Party! What do you tell me! The fortune of the general! Eh, but these are great riches."

"Sire, I have told you the secret. You alone should know it and guard it forever, and I have your sacred word that, when the hour comes, you will let the prize go where it is promised. If the general ever learns of such a thing, such a treaty, he would easily arrange that nothing should remain, and he would denounce his daughter who has saved him, and then he would promptly be the prey of his enemies and yours, from whom you wish to save him. I have told the secret not to the Emperor, but to the representative of God on the Russian earth. I have confessed it to the priest, who is bound to forget the words uttered only before God. Allow Natacha Feodorovna her own way, Sire! And her father, your servant, whose life is so dear to you, is saved. At the natural death of the general his fortune will go to his daughter, who has disposed of it."

Rouletabille stopped a moment to judge of the effect produced. It was not good. The face of his august listener was more and more in a frown.

The silence continued, and now the reporter did not dare to break it. He waited.

Finally, the Emperor rose and walked forward and backward across the room, deep in thought. For a moment he stopped at the window and waved paternally to the little

Tsarevitch, who played in the park with the grand-duchesses.

Then he returned to Rouletabille and pinched his ear.

"But, tell me, how have you learned all this? And who then has poisoned the general and his wife, in the kiosk, if not Natacha?"

"Natacha is a saint. It is nothing, Sire, that she has been raised in luxury, and vows herself to misery; but it is sublime that she guards in her heart the secret of her sacrifice from everyone, and, in spite of all, because secrecy is necessary and has been required of her. See her guarding it before her father, who has been brought to believe in the dishonor of his daughter, and still to be silent when a word would have proved her innocent; guarding it face to face with her fiance, whom she loves, and repulses because marriage is forbidden to the girl who is supposed to be rich and who will be poor; guarding it, above all—and guarding it still— in the depths of the dungeon, and ready to take the road to Siberia under the accusation of assassination, because that ignominy is necessary for the safety of her father. That, Sire—oh, Sire, do you see!"

"But you, how have you been able to penetrate into this guarded secret?"

"By watching her eyes. By observing, when she believed herself alone, the look of terror and the gleams of love. And, beyond all, by looking at her when she was looking at her father. Ah, Sire, there were moments when on her mystic face one could read the wild joy and devotion of the martyr. Then, by listening and by piecing together scraps of phrases inconsistent with the idea of treachery, but which immediately acquired meaning if one thought of the opposite, of sacrifice. Ah, that is it, Sire!

Consider always the alternative motive. What I finally could see myself, the others, who had a fixed opinion about Natacha, could not see. And why had they their fixed opinion? Simply because the idea of compromise with the Nihilists aroused at once the idea of complicity! For such people it is always the same thing—they never can see but the one side of the situation. But, nevertheless, the situation had two sides, as all situations have. The question was simple. The compromise was certain. But why had Natacha compromised herself with the Nihilists? Was it necessarily in order to lose her father? Might it not be, on the contrary, in order to save him? When one has rendezvous with an enemy it is not necessarily to enter into his game, sometimes it is to disarm him with an offer. Between these two hypotheses, which I alone took the trouble to examine, I did not hesitate long, because Natacha's every attitude proclaimed her innocence: and her eyes, Sire, in which one read purity and love, prevailed always with me against all the passing appearances of disgrace and crime.

"I saw that Natacha negotiated with them. But what had she to place in the scales against the life of her father? Nothing— except the fortune that she would have one day.

"Some words she spoke about the impossibility of immediate marriage, about poverty which could always knock at the door of any mansion, remarks that I was able to overhear between Natacha and Boris Mourazoff, which to him meant nothing, put me definitely on the right road. And I was not long in ascertaining that the negotiations in this formidable affair were taking place in the very house of Trebassof! Pursued without by the incessant spying of Koupriane, who sought to surprise her in company with the Nihilists, watched closely, too, by the jealous supervision of Boris, who was jealous of Michael Nikolaievitch, she had to seize the only opportunities possible for such negotiations, at night, in her own home, the sole place where, by the very audacity of it, she was able to play her part in any security.

"Michael Nikolaievitch knew Annouchka. There was certainly the point of departure for the negotiations which that felon-officer, traitor to all sides, worked at will toward the realization of his own infamous project. I do not think that Michael ever confided to Natacha that he was, from the very first, the instrument of the revolutionaries. Natacha, who sought to get in touch with the revolutionary party, had to entrust him with a correspondence for Annouchka, following which he assumed direction of the affair, deceiving the Nihilists, who, in their absolute penury, following the revolt, had been seduced by the proposition of General Trebassof's daughter, and deceiving Natacha, whom he pretended to love and by whom he believed himself loved. At this point in the affair Natacha came to understand that it was necessary to propitiate Michael Nikolaievitch, her indispensable intermediary, and she managed to do it so well that Boris Mourazoff felt the blackest jealousy. On his side, Michael came to believe that Natacha would have no other husband than himself, but he did not propose to marry a penniless girl! And, fatally, it followed that Natacha, in that infernal intrigue, negotiated for the life of her father through the agency of a man who, underhandedly, sought to strike at the general himself, because the immediate death of her father before the negotiation was completed would enrich Natacha, who had given Michael so much to hope. That frightful tragedy, Sire, in which we have lived our most painful hours, appeared to me, confident of Natacha's innocence, as absolutely simple as for the others it seemed complicated. Natacha believed she had in Michael Nikolaievitch a man who worked for her, but he worked only for himself. The day that I was convinced of it, Sire, by my examination of the approach to the balcony, I had a mind to warn Natacha, to go to her and say, 'Get rid of that man. He will betray you. If you need an agent, I am at your service.' But that day, at Krestowsky, destiny prevented my rejoining Natacha; and I must attribute it to destiny, which would not permit the loss of that man. Michael Nikolaievitch, who was a traitor, was too much in the 'combination,' and if he had been rejected he would have ruined everything. I caused him to disappear! The great misfortune then was that Natacha, holding me responsible for the death of a man she believed innocent, never wished to see me again, and, when she did see me, refused to have any conversation with me because I proposed that I take Michael's place for her with the revolutionaries. She would have nothing to do with me in order to protect her secret. Meantime, the Nihilists believed they were betrayed by Natacha when they learned of the death of Michael, and they undertook to avenge him. They seized Natacha, and bore her off by force. The unhappy girl learned then, that same evening, of the attack which destroyed the datcha and, happily, still spared her father. This time she reached a definite understanding with the revolutionary party. Her bargain was made. I offer you for proof of it only her attitude when she was arrested, and, even in that moment, her sublime silence."

While Rouletabille urged his view, the Emperor let him talk on and on, and now his eyes were dim.

"Is it possible that Natacha has not been the accomplice, in all, of Michael Nikolaievitch?"

he demanded. "It was she who opened her father's house to him that night. If she was not his accomplice she would have mistrusted him, she would have watched him."

"Sire, Michael Nikolaievitch was a very clever man. He knew so well how to play upon Natacha, and Annouchka, in whom she placed all her hope. It was from Annouchka that she wished to hold the life of her father. It was the word, the signature of Annouchka that she demanded before giving her own. The evening Michael Nikolaievitch died, he was charged to bring her that signature. I know it, myself, because, pretending drunkenness, I was able to overhear enough of a conversation between Annouchka and a man whose name I must conceal. Yes, that last evening, Michael Nikolaievitch, when he entered the datcha, had the signature in his pocket, but also he carried the weapon or the poison with which he already had attempted and was resolved to reach the father of her whom he believed was assuredly to be his wife."

"You speak now of a paper, very precious, that I regret not to possess, monsieur," said the Tsar coldly, "because that paper alone would have proved to me the innocence of your protegee."

"If you have not it, Sire, you know well that it is because I have wished you to have it. The corpse had been searched by Katharina, the little Bohemian, and I, Sire, prevented Koupriane from finding that signature in Katharina's possession. In saving the secret I have saved General Trebassof's life, who would have preferred to die rather than accept such an arrangement."

The Tsar stopped Rouletabille in his enthusiastic outburst.

"All that would be very beautiful and perhaps admirable," said he, more and more coldly, because he had entirely recovered himself, "if Natacha had not, herself, with her own hand, poisoned her father and her step-mother!— always with arsenate of soda."

"Oh, some of that had been left in the house," replied Rouletabille. "They had not given me all of it for the analysis after the first attempt. But Natacha is innocent of that, Sire. I swear it to you. As true as that I have certainly escaped being hanged."

"How, hanged?"

"Oh, it has not amounted to much now, Your Majesty."

And Rouletabille recounted his sinister adventure, up to the moment of his death, or, rather, up to the moment when he had believed he was going to die.

The Emperor listened to the young reporter with complete stupefaction. He murmured, "Poor lad!" then, suddenly:

"But how have you managed to escape them?"

"Sire they have given me twenty-four hours for you to set Natacha at liberty, that is to say, that you restore her to her rights, all her rights, and she be always the recognized heiress of Trebassof. Do you understand me, Sire?

"I will understand you, perhaps, when you have explained to me how Natacha has not poisoned her father and step-mother."

"There are some things so simple, Sire, that one is able to think of them only with a rope around one's neck. But let us reason it out. We have here four persons, two of whom have been poisoned and the other two with them have not been. Now, it is certain that, of the four persons, the general has not wished to poison himself, that his wife has not wished to poison the general, and that, as for me, I have not wished to poison anybody. That, if we are absolutely sure of it, leaves as the poisoner only Natacha. That is so certain, so inevitable, that there is only one case, one alone, where, in such conditions, Natacha would not be regarded as the poisoner."

"I confess that, logically, I do not see," said the Tsar, "anything beyond that but more and more of a tangle. What is it?"

"Logically, the only case would be that where no one had been poisoned, that is to say, where no one had taken any poison."

"But the presence of the poison has been established!" cried the Emperor.

"Still, the presence of the poison proves only its presence, not the crime. Both poison and ipecac were found in the stomach expulsions. From which a crime has been concluded. What state of affairs was necessary for there to have been no crime? Simply that the poison should have appeared in the expulsions after the ipecac. Then there would have been no poisoning, but everyone would believe there had been. And, for that, someone would have poured the poison into the expulsions."

The Tsar never quitted Rouletabille's eyes.

"That is extraordinary," said he. "But of course it is possible. In any case, it is still only an hypothesis.

"And so long as it could be an hypothesis that no one thought of, it could be just that, Sire. But if I am here, it is because I have the proof that that hypothesis corresponds to the reality. That necessary proof of Natacha's innocence, Your Majesty, I have found with the rope around my neck. Ah, I tell you it was time! What has hindered us hitherto, I do not say to realize, but even to think, of that hypothesis? Simply that we thought the illness of the general had commenced before the absorption of the ipecac, since Matrena Petrovna had been obliged to go for it to her medicine-closet after his illness commenced, in order to counteract the poison of which she also appeared to be the victim.

"But, if I acquire proof that Matrena Petrovna had the ipecac at hand before the sickness, my hypothesis of pretense at poisoning has irresistible force. Because, if it was not to use it before, why did she have it with her before? And if it was not that she wished to hide the fact that she had used it before, why did she wish to make believe that she went to find it afterwards?

"Then, in order to show Natacha's innocence, here is what must be proved: that Matrena Petrovna had the ipecac on her, even when she went to look for it."

"Young Rouletabille, I hardly breathe," said the Tsar.

"Breathe, Sire. The proof is here. Matrena Petrovna necessarily had the ipecac on her, because after the sickness she had not the time for going to find it. Do you understand, Sire? Between the moment when she fled from the kiosk and when she returned there, she had not the actual time to go to her medicine-closet to find the ipecac."

"How have you been able to compute the time?" asked the Emperor.

"Sire, the Lord God directed, Who made me admire Feodor Feodorovitch's watch just when we went to read, and to read on the dial of that watch two minutes to the hour, and the Lord God directed yet, Who, after the scene of the poison, at the time Matrena returned carrying the ipecac publicly, made the hour strike from that watch in the general's pocket.

"Two minutes. It was impossible for Matrena to have covered that distance in two minutes. She could only have entered the deserted datcha and left it again instantly. She had not taken the trouble to mount to the floor above, where, she told us and repeated when she returned, the ipecac was in the medicine-closet. She lied! And if she lied, all is explained.

"It was the striking of a watch, Sire, with a striking apparatus and a sound like the general's, there in the quarters of the revolutionaries, that roused my memory and indicated to me in a second this argument of the time.

"I got down from my gallows-scaffold, Your Majesty, to experiment on that time-limit. Oh, nothing and nobody could have prevented my making that experiment before I died, to prove to myself that Rouletabille had all along been right. I had studied the grounds around the datcha enough to be perfectly exact about the distances. I found in the court where I was to be hanged the same number of steps that there were from the kiosk to the steps of the veranda, and, as the staircase of the revolutionaries had fewer steps, I lengthened my journey a few steps by walking around a chair. Finally, I attended to the opening and closing of the doors that Matrena would have had to do. I had looked at a watch when I started. When I returned, Sire, and looked at the watch again, I had taken three minutes to cover the distance—and it is not for me to boast, but I am a little livelier than the excellent Matrena.

"Matrena had lied. Matrena had simulated the poisoning of the general. Matrena had coolly poured ipecac in the general's glass while we were illustrating with matches a curious-enough theory of the nature of the constitution of the empire."

"But this is abominable!" cried the Emperor, this time definitely convinced by the intricate argument of Rouletabille. "And what end could this imitation serve?'"

"The end of preventing the real crime! The end that she believed herself to have attained, Sire, to have Natacha removed forever—Natacha whom she believed capable of any crime."

"Oh, it is monstrous! Feodor Feodorovitch has often told me that Matrena loved Natacha sincerely."

"She loved her sincerely up to the day that she believed her guilty. Matrena Petrovna was sure of Natacha's complicity in Michael Nikolaievitch's attempt to poison the general. I shared her stupor, her despair, when Feodor Feodorovitch took his daughter in his arms after that tragic night, and embraced her. He seemed to absolve her. It was then that Matrena resolved within herself to save the general in spite of himself, but I remain persuaded that, if she had dared such a plan against Natacha, it would only be because of what she believed definite proof of her step-daughter's infamy. These papers, Sire, that you have shown me, and which show, if nothing more, an understanding between Natacha and the revolutionaries, could only have been in the possession of Michael or of Natacha. Nothing was found in Michael's quarters. Tell me, then, that Matrena found them in Natacha's apartment. Then, she did not hesitate!"

"If one outlined her crime to her, do you believe she would confess it?" asked the Emperor.

"I am so sure of it that I have had her brought here. By now Koupriane should be here at the chateau, with Matrena Petrovna."

"You think of everything, monsieur."

The Tsar moved to ring a bell. Rouletabille raised his hand.

"Not yet, Sire. I ask that you permit me not to be present at the confusion of that brave, heroic, good woman who has loved me much. But before I go, Sire—do you promise me?"

The Emperor believed he had not heard correctly or did not grasp the meaning. He repeated what Rouletabille had said. The young reporter repeated it once more:

"Do you promise? No, Sire, I am not mad. I dare to ask you that. I have confided my honor to Your Majesty. I have told you Natacha's secret. Well, now, before Matrena's confession, I dare to ask you: Promise me to forget that secret. It will not suffice merely to give Natacha back again to her father. It is necessary to leave her course open to her—if you really wish to save General Trebassof. What do you decide, Sire?"

"It is the first time anyone has questioned me, monsieur."

"Ah, well, it will be the last. But I humbly beg Your Majesty to reply."

"That would be many millions given to the Revolution."

"Oh, Sire, they are not given yet. The general is sixty-five, but he has many years ahead of him, if you wish it. By the time he dies—a natural death, if you wish it—your enemies will have disarmed."

"My enemies!" murmured the Tsar in a low voice. "No, no; my enemies never will disarm. Who, then, will be able to disarm them?" added he, melancholily, shaking his head.

"Progress, Sire! If you wish it."

The Tsar turned red and looked at the audacious young man, who met the gaze of His Majesty frankly.

"It is kind of you to say that, my young friend. But you speak as a child."

"As a child of France to the Father of the Russian people."

It was said in a voice so solemn and, at the same time, so naively touching, that the Tsar started. He gazed again for some time in silence at this boy who, this time, turned away his brimming eyes.

"Progress and pity, Sire."

"Well," said the Emperor, "it is promised."

Rouletabille was not able to restrain a joyous movement hardly in keeping.

"You can ring now, Sire."

And the Tsar rang.

The reporter passed into a little salon, where he found the Marshal, Koupriane and Matrena Petrovna, who was "in a state."

She threw a suspicious glance at Rouletabille, who was not treated this morning as the dear little domovoi-doukh. She permitted herself to be conducted, already trembling, before the Emperor.

"What happened?" asked Koupriane agitatedly.

"It so happened, my dear Monsieur Koupriane, that I have the pardon of the Emperor for all the crimes you have charged against me, and that I wish to shake hands before I go, without any rancor. Monsieur Koupriane, the Emperor will tell you himself that General Trebassof is saved, and that his life will never be in danger any more. Do you know what follows? It follows that you must at once set Matiew free, whom I have taken, if you remember, under my protection. Tell him that he is going to make his way in France. I will find him a place on condition that he forgets certain lashes."

"Such a promise! Such an attitude toward me!" cried Koupriane. "But I will wait for the Emperor to tell me all these fine things. And your Natacha, what do you do with her?"

"We release her also, monsieur. Natacha never has been the monster that you think."

"How can you say that? Someone at least is guilty."

"There are two guilty. The first, Monsieur le Marechal."

"What!" cried the Marshal.

"Monsieur le Marechal, who had the imprudence to bring such dangerous grapes to the datcha des Iles, and—and—"

"And the other?" asked Koupriane, more and more anxiously.

"Listen there," said Rouletabille, pointing toward the Emperor's cabinet.

The sound of tears and sobs reached them. The grief and the remorse of Matrena Petrovna passed the walls of the cabinet. Koupriane was completely disconcerted.

Suddenly the Emperor appeared. He was in a state of exaltation such as had never been known in him. Koupriane, dismayed, drew back.

"Monsieur," said the Tsar to him, "I require that Natacha Feodorovna be here within the next two hours, and that she be conducted with the honors due to her rank. Natacha is innocent, and we must make reparation to her."

Then, turning toward Rouletabille:

"I have learned what she knows and what she owes to you—we owe to you, my young friend."

The Tsar said "my young friend." Rouletabille, at this last moment before his departure, spoke Russian?

"Then she knows nothing, Sire. That is better, Sire, because Your Majesty and me, we must forget right from today that we know anything."

"You are right," said the Tsar thoughtfully. "But, my friend, what am I to do for you?"

"Sire, one favor. Do not let me miss the train at 10:55."

And he threw himself on his knees.

"Remain on your knees, my friend. You are ready, thus. Monsieur le Marechal will prepare at once a brevet, which I will immediately sign. Meantime, Monsieur le Marechal, find me, in my own closet, one of my St. Anne's collars."

And it was thus that Joseph Rouletabille, of "L'Epoque," was created officer of St. Anne of Russia by the Emperor himself, who gave him the accolade.

"They combine the whole course of time in this country," thought Rouletabille, pressing his hand to his eyes to hold back the tears.

For the train at 10:55 everybody had crowded at Tsarskoie-Coelo station. Among those who had come from St. Petersburg to press the young reporter's hand when they learned of his impending departure were Ivan Petrovitch, the jolly Councilor of the Emperor, and Athanase Georgevitch, the lively advocate so well known for his famous exploits with knife and fork. They had come naturally with all their bandages and dressings, which made them look like glorious ruins. They brought the greetings of Feodor Feodorovitch, who still had a little fever, and of Thaddeus Tchitchnikoff, the Lithuanian, who had both legs broken.

Even after he was in his compartment Rouletabille had to drink his last drink of champagne. When nothing remained in the bottle and everyone had embraced and re-embraced him, as the train did not start quite yet, Athanase Georgevitch opened a second "last" bottle. It was then that Monsieur le Grand Marechal arrived, out of breath. They invited him to drink, and he accepted. But he had need to speak to Rouletabille in private, and he drew the reporter, after excuses, out into the corridor.

"It is the Emperor himself who has sent me," said the high dignitary with emotion. "He has sent me about the eider downs. You forgot to explain the eider downs to him."

"Niet!" replied Rouletabille, laughing. "That is nothing. Nitchevo! His Majesty's eider downs are of the finest eider, as one of the feathers that you have shown me demonstrates. Well, open them now. They are a cheap imitation, as the second feather proves. The return of the false eider downs, before evening, proves then that they hoped the substitution would pass undetected. That is all. Caracho! Collapse of the hoax. Your health! Vive le Tsar!"

"Caracho! Caracho!"

The locomotive was puffing when a couple were seen running, a man and a woman. It was Monsieur and Madame Gounsovski.

Gounsovski stood on the running-board.

"Madame Gounsovski has insisted upon shaking hands. You are very congenial."

"Compliments, madame."

"Tell me, young man, you did wrong to fail for dinner at my house yesterday."

"I would have certainly escaped a disagreeable little journey into Finland. I do not regret it, monsieur."

The train trembled and moved. They cried, "Vive la France! Vive la Russe!" Athanase Georgevitch wept. Matrena Petrovna, at a window of the station, whither she had timidly retired, waved a handkerchief to the little domovoi-doukh, who had made her see everything in the right light, and whom she did not dare to embrace after the terrible affair of the false poison and the Tsar's anger.

The reporter threw her a respectful kiss.

As he said to Gounsovski, there was nothing to be regretted.

All the same, as the train took its way toward the frontier, Rouletabille threw himself back on the cushions, and said:

"Ouf!"

A Note About the Author

Gaston Leroux (1868–1927) was a French journalist and writer of detective fiction. Born in Paris, Leroux attended school in Normandy before returning to his home city to complete a degree in law. After squandering his inheritance, he began working as a court reporter and theater critic to avoid bankruptcy. As a journalist, Leroux earned a reputation as a leading international correspondent, particularly for his reporting on the 1905 Russian Revolution. In 1907, Leroux switched careers in order to become a professional fiction writer, focusing predominately on novels that could be turned into film scripts. With such novels as The Mystery of the Yellow Room (1908), Leroux established himself as a leading figure in detective fiction, eventually earning himself the title of Chevalier in the Legion of Honor, France's highest award for merit.

The Phantom of the Opera (1910), his most famous work, has been adapted countless times for theater, television, and film, most notably by Andrew Lloyd Webber in his 1986 musical of the same name.

A NOTE FROM THE PUBLISHER

Spanning many genres, from non-fiction essays to literature classics to children's books and lyric poetry, Mint Edition books showcase the master works of our time in a modern new package. The text is freshly typeset, is clean and easy to read, and features a new note about the author in each volume. Many books also include exclusive new introductory material. Every book boasts a striking new cover, which makes it

CPSIA information can be obtained
at www.ICGtesting.com
Printed in the USA
JSHW052229261222
35376JS00006B/92